DREAM WAFER

A Novel

Han Soo Lee MD

Copyright © 2015 Han Soo Lee, MD
All rights reserved.

ISBN: 1507648960
ISBN 13: 9781507648964
Library of Congress Control Number: 2015903460
CreateSpace Independent Publishing Platform
North Charleston, South Carolina

PREFACE

DEAR READER,

If you tend to think like an amateur Sherlock Holmes and have an inquisitive, analytical mind,
And want to learn some known facts or futuristic ideas about dreams,
Yet, complicated gory plots don't appeal to you,
this story is waiting for you.

People ordered dreams of their choice in this story.
Far in the future, you might be able to order dreams of your choice, too.
You may say it is only the author's fantasy and wishful thinking.
Yes, it is.
By the time you finish reading this story, you may find yourself having similar wishful fantasies and say,
"I've learned something. The story makes me feel good."

CHAPTER 1
DREAM WAFER

Steve thought he heard loud rapid honking from the car behind his. It took a few seconds of awakening before he realized that his car was straddling on the wrong side of the double solid line and was about to run head on to an oncoming truck. Trying to get out of the truck's impending ruin, Steve made a frantic right spin on his wheel. With the truck's and his car's hellish braking noises, his car skidded past the right side lane, skipped the highway shoulder, and scraped the guard rails with horrific metal rattling. His car finally came to a jolting halt after thirty more feet of dusty dragging. In his rear view mirror, Steve saw the truck wiggling its monster body briefly, and then picking up speed to go on its way.

On board an ambulance to the nearest ER, Steve felt a sting in his head. He had a big bump on his forehead. The ER doctor listened to Steve about what really happened and checked him thoroughly. The doctor said, based on the x-rays and CT scans, there were no broken bones or signs of internal injury. Steve realized that the passenger side front tire of his car gave him a lifesaving buffer while it was shredded to many pieces.

Soon after his discharge from the ER, Steve called his family doctor.

"Doctor Prensky, yesterday I almost got killed as I dozed off on my wheel..." Steve described what happened to him and his car on his way home from work and added, "Just like the first sleeping pills you prescribed for me, the new ones did not help me, either. I'm really having bad sleep problems with terrible dreams. Lately, I have been making bad mistakes on my job. I'm afraid it's going to get worse."

"Sorry to hear that. If I remember it correctly, your sleep problems started a few months ago, and around that time, you said you were having some unusual job-related stress. How is it going with your job now?"

"The job situation has not changed much. I believe my poor sleep and nightmare made it harder for me to handle the same stress. Is there any different medicine for me?"

"Perhaps…rather than prescribing another sleeping pill, I have a better idea. Considering how long you had the sleep problems, you might want to consult Dr. Julian Jupitren. He would be the right person who could help you better than anyone else at this time."

"Who is Dr. Jupitren?"

"He is a well-known and highly respected professor in psychiatry. I have known him since my medical student years."

"Do you really think I need to see a psychiatrist?"

"Well, I think it would be the best choice at this time. Unlike the first sleeping pills that I gave you, the pills you tried this time had two chemical elements, one for sleep induction and the other for maintaining sleep. Yet they didn't work.

Dr. Jupitren is not an ordinary psychiatrist. He is a dream and sleep specialist. The *Cyber Tribune*'s science section reported a detailed account on his *dream shop* a few years ago. Are you sure you haven't heard of him or read about him?"

"I vaguely remember that he had been mentioned in the *Cyber Tribune* for his invention. Wasn't it about something to do with changing people's dreams?"

"Yes, you're right."

"But, I don't remember the details. At that time, I didn't have any sleep or dream problems, and I paid very little attention to it."

"Just a minute, Steve. In my file here, I've found the Cyber Tribune's editorial clip about him and his invention. Why don't I send it to your Thumputer right now?

My office nurse says I have my next patient waiting. Please try to see Dr. Jupitren soon. If there's anything else I could do for you, please call me again."

"All right, Dr. Prensky, thank you very much."

A short while later, Dr. Prensky's office sent the News clip to Steve's Thumputer. Steve then projected it in a readable font onto his living room wall.

The News article started with the following heading:

"You Can Buy Dreams of Your Choice from Acmeon Lab, the Dream Shop."

"*Acmeon Lab, the Dream Shop*?" Steve went on to read the article.

In the Acmeon Lab of Long Island, New York, Dr. Julian Jupitren, after years of research, finally succeeded in inventing the epoch-making method of dream modification, by which you could order dreams of your choice. The method was devised on the basis of intricate scientific principles of sleep chemistry and genetic physiology, utilizing the person's genome.

To order your dreams, you would go to the Acmeon Lab in person and take certain tests first. If you live far away from Acmeon Lab, you may take the tests by mail.

At the lab, you would take a test called a Polygene Analysis as well as other tests and will have a clinical interview with Dr. Jupitren. After the interview, you would request your dreams by answering a computerized questionnaire. Answering it means that you are ordering your dream scenes and stories, some of which might just be your wish fulfillment in disguise.

It would shorten your interview time if you brought your Thumputer, the new 16G microcomputer that became available this year. Usually people wear it on their thumbs.

By now, most of you know that the Thumputer is a bit larger than the ring that you wear on your ring finger. As of this year, the Department of Commerce announced that the Thumputer would gradually replace most ID cards that you carry in your wallet. If you are not using the Thumputer yet, do not worry. You just bring yourself to the Lab.

There have been several major media's positive reviews on Dr. Jupitren's dream-modification method and his Dream Shop. However, one of the reviewers made rhetorical remarks: "Will there be any religious theorists who may take Dr. Jupitren's dream-modifying idea to be a blasphemous move of modern mankind? If men's dreams were rendered and molded into a genetic, neurochemical artifice, would it block or interfere with the divine revelation that was meant to reach the dreamer otherwise?..."

As you read this article, some of you may still wonder, "Wow, how would it be possible to order my dreams? Is it real? Is it some kind of a trick? Who is running the Acmeon Lab? A magician?"

However, as aforementioned, the founder of the dream shop is a well-known, respected research psychiatrist who worked on the idea for many years, all based, on scientific principles of human genetics and sleep physiology. When you order your dreams, you will receive a "Dream Wafer," a skin patch, which is the very product of Dr. Jupitren's invention.
With dreams of their choice, Dream Wafer users usually had peaceful sleep as well.

Steve read the *Cyber Tribune* article again. Then he browsed other related websites and found a good number of links under the search word "Dream Wafer."

He read every Dream Wafer website he could find. Then he opened the web pages about Dr. Julian Jupitren. Most Dream Wafer users gave five stars to the doctor.

Finally, Steve made an appointment to see Dr. Jupitren.

The Acmeon Lab building was located a short distance away from the city's North Mall of Long Island, New York.

On his way to Acmeon Lab, Steve strolled through the mall and thought, "What will happen to the mind-restoring function of dreams when people artificially change their dreams? Will there be a long, lingering, weird effect from the changed dreams? Will I develop psychological or physical dependence on Dream Wafer? If dreams are implicated in man's creativity, will the packaged dreams stifle my creative sparks? How would the psychologists or psychiatrists do their dream interpretations on the modified dreams? Does the inventor of the packaged dreams have answers to those questions?"

Steve came to an interesting part of the huge, effulgent mall as the time display on his Thumputer showed it was ten thirty in the morning. Till his appointment time, he had another hour. He decided to spend a little more time browsing his surroundings.

There was a newly built multistory building for air-scooter parking with open aerial views facing the Long Island Sound. From any level of the parking floors, heavyweight elevators would lug up the air-scooters to the top of the building. Then they would take off by ascending at ninety degrees straight up from the scooters' departure pad on the building's roof, just like the helicopters do. And, the arriving air-scooters likewise descended straight down vertically to the scooters' arrival pad. Those arrivals would then be dispatched down to the lower-level parking spaces.

Along the wide aisles of the mall, he saw a series of stores specializing in electronic dolls, robots, and air-scooters. Out of curiosity, he browsed a new model of air-scooter. It had two built-in seats. The driver could fly it at an altitude of half a mile in the air, with up to 250 pounds extra load in the rear trunk of the scooter. On the ground highways, it could run just like any conventional cars. Its advantage was that it could glide in the air as fast as two hundred miles per hour on a Depot Solar energy pack, backed up with high-power lithium-silicon polymer batteries.

The air-scooter idea was very interesting to Steve, but its price tag quickly chilled his interest. He said to himself, "Maybe, someday I would rent one of them if I really need it." Then he thought of his older sister, Jenny, who commutes in her air-scooter every day.

Another store in the mall displayed pill-sized food capsules. Taking three of them would be as good as eating three meals for a day. The insert said, "You must drink sufficient water along with the capsules. By taking one pill three times a day and drinking six to eight glasses of water daily, you could go on living without eating for ten days and would not have any medical problems."

There was a store called Espio-Nano Company. It sold robots of various kinds. They had many flying objects. Most of them looked like various species of flying insects. The storeowner told Steve that those insects were spy gadgets packed with multiple nano-electronic capabilities, about which Steve was quite familiar, since his company had produced similar spy gadgets called *Dronettes*.

Then, he headed for the Acmeon building. The whole entrance area of Acmeon Lab was crowded and bustling. That day, there was a scientific symposium in session, held in the Acmeon Lab's two-hundred-seat auditorium.

Outside the auditorium, curious crowds were at the information booths, asking various questions about the idea of buying one's dreams. The man at the booth handed out brochures to many inquirers and answered their questions. One of them asked about the benefits of Dream Wafers. Steve carefully listened to the man's answer.

"The main purpose of Dream Wafer is to correct disturbing dreams so that you can have quality sleep, and function better in the daytime rather than letting it be abused for entertainment or recreational purposes. That's why Dr. Jupitren made it a rule that a physician should interview each candidate individually in order to determine if the Wafer is the right solution for that person's dream and sleep problems. Besides, one of the Dream Wafer's special functions is to let people go back to certain past time periods so that they would retrieve forgotten thoughts or imageries from their unconscious long-term memories."

Out of curiosity, Steve picked up a copy of the symposium's brochure from the information booth's display rack. It listed lecture titles, which he quickly glanced through:

"Gene Sequencing Refined via New Biochemical Technique; REM Sleep Modulator Reanalyzed and Enhanced; Computerized-Analysis on Relationship of Foot Temperature and Dream Contents; Chemico-genetic retrieval of long-term memories; Negative Effects of Sleeping Pills and Alcohol on Dream Wafer Composition…"

Steve thought those topics were way over his head. He was not there to attend the specialists' symposium anyway. He came there to see Dr. Jupitren and find out if ordering new dreams would be the answer to his sleep problems. He left the information-booth area and headed for Dr. Jupitren's office.

CHAPTER 2
STEVE'S FIRST VISIT TO ACMEON LAB

It was easy to find Dr. Jupitren's office, which was on the third floor of the main Acmeon building. On his way to the doctor's office, Steve passed several rooms with big windows, through which he could see that the walls were packed with computers and shelves loaded with ultramodern devices and many bottles of chemicals.

As Steve entered the office, one of Dr. Jupitren's front-office staff greeted him. "Hi, may I help you? I'm Helen, office manager and assistant to Dr. Jupitren."

Steve was quite taken aback by her radiant beauty and charming smile. Steve's voice could not hide his excitement as he answered her. "Hi, I'm Steve Spencer. I came early for my eleven-thirty appointment with Dr. Jupitren."

Checking his name on the appointment book, she asked him to take a seat and said, "Mr. Spencer, thank you for returning your completed health-history form on time. We received it yesterday."

"Oh, that form. It was quite detailed and very long. It took me a while to fill it out."

"Many clients say the same thing about the form. But it helps the doctor get to know you better. Dr. Jupitren has reviewed your health-history form already."

"That's nice. Is he at the symposium?"

"Yes, he's been tied up since early this morning. After seeing a few clients, he went to the Symposium Hall to give a lecture. He'll be back here by eleven thirty."

Helen was dressed neatly and spoke in a clear voice. She seemed alert and astute in her manners. She continued, "While waiting for the doctor, we can start the three preliminary routine tests. For the first one, while wearing this cap snugly on your head, please hold this computer probe with your hand until it beeps at the end of five minutes. Then you can remove the cap. And please put the probe back on this stand.

Next, you will breathe into this tube two times and then place the cover back on it. The third test is a gene sampling. To do that, please keep this pea-sized sponge ball against either side of your mouth and roll it a few times with your tongue. Then place it in this cup. That's all."

Within ten minutes, Steve completed the three requested tests.

Then she said, "We still have some extra time for another required step before Dr. Jupitren returns. I'll need to download your biometric data."

With Steve's permission, she transferred his biometric data from his Thumputer to Dr. Jupitren's computer wirelessly. It took only a minute.

Steve asked her, "What were the cap and the computer probe for?"

"Oh, you just had a very detailed EEG—that is electroencephalography, the brain-wave test. It would have taken us nearly two hours to do the same test years ago. With the cap and probe, we've collected very detailed and sophisticated brain-wave information in an incredibly short time. It took us just five minutes!"

"It's amazing! How about the breathing-tube test?"

"It's to assess various chemicals in your exhaled breaths. It will produce more than a hundred volatile metabolites' nano-concentration information, which we need for Dream Wafer composition in case you receive the Wafer prescription today."

At that point, Dr. Jupitren returned to the office. Helen told him, "Your eleven-thirty appointment, Mr. Steve Spencer, is here."

The doctor greeted Steve with a friendly handshake and said, "Hi, Mr. Spencer. I'm Dr. Jupitren. I'll be with you shortly."

Helen said to the doctor, "I've completed his three pre-Wafer tests. The genome-data collection is in progress, but the other test results and his biometric data should be in your computer under the new-patients file. And you've already reviewed his health-history form, which is in your office."

"Thank you, Helen."

Inside his office, Dr. Jupitren offered a seat to Steve and started to review highlights of Steve's biometric information. Meanwhile, feeling somewhat anxious, Steve quietly settled in his seat.

A very short while later, Dr. Jupitren asked in a resonant voice, "Was it easy to find my office?"

"Yes, it was. I arrived about an hour before my appointment. So I strolled through the North Mall and saw stores selling various electronic devices. It was very interesting to see some of the newer inventions. And at the Acmeon information booth near the Symposium Hall, I listened to one of your assistants, who explained about the Dream Wafer."

"I'm glad you have already heard of our main tool, the Dream Wafer."

Then, having reviewed Steve's biometric data, the doctor picked up Steve's health-history form and read certain parts of it aloud. "You're twenty-eight years old, single, electronic engineer. Graduated from the New York Polytech Academy six years ago. After more experience, now you're a PD at Perihelion Energy Company. So, what do you do as the program director?"

"Well, I oversee a number of concurrent projects to transfer solar energy to various robots' power-storage systems. Some of the robots that our company produced, known as 'Dronette-6' have already been used this year by the secret services of the Euro-American Coalition. I've been involved in robotics since the Dronette-4 version was launched three years ago. My responsibility in the Dronettes' work was mainly computer programming."

"I see. Then you must have extensive computer-programming knowledge."

"It's true to a certain extent. But I'm still learning computer-related matters practically every day."

Steve thought Dr. Jupitren seemed to be in his late-fifties. He spoke cautiously with a learned person's dignity, often looking straight into Steve's eyes.

Dr. Jupitren asked many basic interview questions while recording Steve's answers in his file.

"You wrote here in the form that you're six feet tall and weigh one hundred and fifty pounds. Were there any weight changes during the past six months?"

"Maybe, I've lost a couple of pounds."

"How's your general health?"

"Other than having poor sleep and bad dreams, I'm in pretty good health."

"You described in the form that you've been having those problems for several weeks."

"Probably for a little longer than several weeks, on and off."

"On the average, how many hours of sleep did you manage to get at night?"

"Four or five hours, maybe less some nights."

"Any significant mood changes? Or mood shifts, from low to high?"

"No. I don't believe so."

"Have you been under any chemical influence?"

"No, but I had tried the sleeping pills my primary care physician, Dr. Prensky, prescribed. They didn't work well. So, he referred me to you, and I discontinued the pills last week."

"Dr. Henry Prensky called me last week, telling me about your sleep problem."

"It's nice of him to have informed you about me."

"He is a real gentleman and a very good doctor. I've known him for a long time."

Dr. Jupitren continued his questions. "Do you have problems initiating sleep? Or do you wake up in the middle of the night or early in the morning and then cannot go back to sleep?"

"I often wake up in the middle of the night mostly with bad dreams and have trouble falling asleep again."

Steve reported to the doctor how bad his daytime drowsiness was. He recounted how he fell asleep behind the wheel while driving and almost had a fatal head on collision with a truck, only a week previously.

"Actually, Dr. Prensky told me about your insomnia and the near miss head-on collision episode. You were lucky." Saying so, the doctor scanned Steve's EEG, which was normal.

"Did you have any headache or visual problems since the accident?"

"No, but the bad dreams and insomnia got worse."

Dr. Jupitren nodded his head and asked, "What's the general nature of your bad dreams?"

"Mostly, I get very anxious about my whereabouts, because I get lost in the dream, searching for a direction or a way out. In addition, very often, I worry about making the deadlines on my projects at work. In dreams, I misplace important items, such as my Thumputer. A few times, I dreamt that I misplaced my job-related electronic data. At other times I dreamt of walking into important meetings with the expected report materials half missing."

After a brief thoughtful pausing, the doctor asked, "Have you been under any stress lately?"

"One thing I'm certain of is that about two months ago, I had to replace the main engineer in the middle of a very important project at my company. He had to take a sudden long medical leave. He still is on the leave. The project's technical complexity and increased workload became a heavy challenge for me. I think my sleep problem and bad dreams might have started around that time…I mean when the engineer took his medical leave."

"I understand. Are you managing the work any better by now?"

"Yes, only just a little better. But the main burden is still on my shoulders, and my poor sleep is creating additional stress."

Steve answered many more questions about his family history, childhood memories, any notable traumatic events, his relationships with others, his work history in more detail, and his personal goals or aspirations.

Steve asked, "I wonder if the Dream Wafer would help me."

"I think it would. Then you will dream of less anxious themes, and your sleep might improve to a normal level in a week or so. But I think the lasting solution will come when you manage your job-related stresses better with the help of Dream Wafer."

"I see. So, I need a mental crutch until I solve my job-related problems."

"That's an apt analogy. The Dream Wafer should be considered as a special kind of palliative tool."

Dr. Jupitren instructed, "After this interview, which is about to end, please go to the Annex Library on this floor for a computerized questionnaire session that might take an hour or longer. The answers to the questionnaire have to be very accurate because all the answers will be matched subsequently to your entire genome."

Steve had several more questions to ask Dr. Jupitren but had to limit to a few urgent ones only, because there were other candidates waiting to see the doctor.

Steve thought Dr. Jupitren had inquisitive but gentle, caring manners and his presence made him feel at ease. He felt Dr. Jupitren understood him very well in the first interview.

While walking to the Annex Library for the questionnaire session, Steve passed an area where Dr. Jupitren's several assistants were busy working on their projects. Two of them conversed to each other in a language, of which nationality he could not discern.

Steve wondered, "Was it a technical jargon or a foreign language that I've never heard of before?"

One of the two, whom people called Zenon, threw an uncanny furtive glance at Steve. Zenon was working with another man, named Yaru, who did not seem to pay much attention to people around him. Steve responded with a hesitant smile to Zenon but received only a bland head nod from him. Steve felt a little uneasy.

In the Annex Library, there were three other clients. Everyone was busy answering the 135-point questionnaire.

Steve keyed in his answers to several abstruse questions and their sub questions on the computer. However, other questions were straightforward. While going through the questionnaire, he felt each question demanded quite a bit of self-searching before he clicked the Select-buttons and then the Enter-key.

The other three candidates seemed to be working on different pages of the same questionnaire. They were silent and seemed quite serious about what they were doing. Occasionally they consulted the brochure that was on the desk, looking up for the questionnaire items' meaning.

In the middle of their questionnaire session, Helen came in and announced that their Dream Wafers would be ready in an hour or two after the completion of the questionnaire. If they wanted to receive the Wafers at that time, they may wait in the adjacent waiting room. Otherwise they may return on another day.

All four of the candidates decided to wait for their Dream Wafers. After completing the questionnaire, they had a brief chance to be acquainted with each other, still sitting in the computer area of the Annex library.

One of them, Alex who worked in a sleep laboratory somewhere else was quite knowledgeable about dream mechanisms. He said his problems were frequent night terror, sleepwalking, and daytime drowsiness. In one of his sleepwalking episodes, he'd ended up finding himself in his pajamas outside his house on a cold, rainy night.

Another candidate, Brandon Sweza, was a lawyer specializing in *international arms and weapons limitations treaties*. He said he had tons of time-sensitive work piled up on him and his work caused tension and anxiety. His problems were eerie dreams and severe insomnia.

The third candidate was a medical student, Jane. She learned about the Dream Wafer from her professor, Dr. Sobien Molton, who referred her to Dr. Jupitren because of her anxiety dreams and interrupted sleep.

While they were still talking there in the Annex Library, Zenon walked in. He was the one Steve had seen earlier on his way to the library. Zenon placed a few more brochures on the wall's bookrack. His face was pale and emotionless, and he had a little drag on his left foot as he walked by. He had an uncanny gaze, and Steve could not tell in what direction or what depth he was focusing while he was working on the bookrack.

Steve saw that Zenon spent a good several minutes standing in front of the rack placing the brochures. Zenon then made some adjustment to the CCTV camera using a handheld remote control. Steve did not make much of it then. Steve felt like saying something to him, but before Steve could get his attention, Zenon left the room. Steve felt a bit uneasy about him again.

Steve took a closer look at the setup of the library. Shelves with books and e-books covered the walls. There were five desks with computers, Thumputer battery chargers, and pens with writing pads. On the wall, there were PA system speakers and an abstract oil painting in frame. Above the brochure rack, Steve saw the inconspicuously placed CCTV camera that Zenon had just adjusted.

By that time, a few other candidates came in to work on their questionnaires and Steve's group went into the adjacent waiting room. Later in the midafternoon, Dr. Jupitren and Helen came in to give the four candidates their Dream Wafers.

Giving an envelope and a package to everyone, Helen said, "This package has a two-week supply of your Dream Wafers, and in the envelope you will find a manual on how to use the Wafer. As you will see soon, the Dream Wafer is a quarter-sized, thin skin patch. You will wear it, one per night on your temple area to get the dreams you have ordered. During the two-week period, you are allowed to skip the Wafers for two or three nights if you wish."

After Helen left the library, Dr. Jupitren asked them, "Do you have any questions?"

Alex asked, "Since a part of the Wafer's composition has to do with antianxiety chemicals, will there be any withdrawal effect or dependency, causing worse tension or nightmares when we skip or discontinue the Wafer?"

Dr. Jupitren shook his head. "Not really. The Dream Wafer's mechanism of action is quite different from most ordinary antianxiety medicines, such as all the Benzodiazepines. Besides, the Wafers are not used on a long-term basis. Whereas, in psychiatry, the antianxiety medicines are often used for longer periods, especially for people with recurrent panic disorders.

On rare occasions, some clients' Wafer usage lasted a year, but none of them actually used their Wafers continuously for that length of time. They used Wafers only episodically, on an as-needed basis, for a few weeks or a couple of months at the most, because the desired Wafer effect was achieved within that period."

Alex asked another question. "At the sleep lab where I work, we routinely do polysomnography, but here I just went through a five-minute EEG. Do you ever need to do other tests beside the EEG?"

"Yes, but not everyone needs polysomnography. What the five-minute EEG yields is quite sufficient. Certain sleep-disorder patients with complex physical disorders such as sleep apnea and any doubtful seizure disorders, at times may need polysomnography before their Dream Wafers can be prescribed."

"Thank you."

Then, Steve asked a question. "Is there any medication or food we should avoid while using the Dream Wafers?"

"Generally, Dream Wafer has no serious interaction with any foods or general medicines except certain psychiatric medications. Actually, during the first interview, I ruled out any contraindicated medicines you might be on. The only exception is alcohol, which you should limit. Better yet, avoid it because alcohol cancels certain functions of Dream Wafer."

Both Alex and Steve thanked the doctor for his reassuring answers. Then Brandon asked a question. "Does the Dream Wafer cure a person's sleep disorder? Or only give supportive care through symptom relief?"

"That's a very good question. Dream Wafer is on the caring side, like a crutch, rather than curing, although in reality the Wafer works in both caring and curing ways. To explain it better, let me pick an analogous situation. When treating a broken bone, a properly applied cast does not cure the fracture by itself but helps by holding the broken bones aligned together so that healing, that is curing, can take place. So, what the Wafer does is similar to the function of the cast."

"Thank you, Doctor. I understand."

Then Jane asked, "About the Dream Wafer use, I wonder whether it is safe for pregnant women, not necessarily for the women but for the unborn babies."

"I'm glad you asked that question. I've been running a laboratory-animal experiment for a few years, using fifty Cavia porcellus, which people call guinea pigs. So far, the experiment revealed no teratogenic effect of Dream Wafer on the guinea pigs' fetal samples. I will observe the experiment results for another year. For now, however, I would recommend that pregnant women stay away from Dream Wafer use."

The candidates had asked Dr. Jupitren additional questions about the Dream Wafer and what to expect from it. With his answers, they all felt reassured that Dream Wafer would be quite safe to use.

CHAPTER 3
STEVE'S DREAMS

At bedtime that evening, following the instructions closely, Steve applied the Wafer patch on his right temple skin. Unlike other nights, he fell asleep within a few minutes.

In his dream, Steve was at a beach, relaxing in a recliner under a palm tree, feeling a pleasant breeze over his face, and he gazed at the calm ocean where sailboats passed by peacefully.

Then, still in the same night, he dreamt he was in a tropical garden, sitting comfortably in a cool hut, which happened to be his office. There, the office workers, who had transformed into tropical birds, reported to him in cheerful melodies that all his projects and paper work were completed on time.

He heard distant singing and the chirping of tropical birds. When their singing turned into pearly piano sounds, he woke up fully to his six-thirty alarm clock music, which was Chopin's piano piece *Raindrop Prelude*.

They were incredibly peaceful dreams in contrast to those nightmarish ones he had before. The themes and the scenery in those new dreams were close to what he'd ordered by answering the questionnaire at the Annex Library. "It's incredible!" He thought.

On subsequent nights, Steve had dreams of similar themes as the first night's dreams, which were all about peace, serenity, and being free from job stress. Each time, there were variations within the given theme. The dreamt places were a mixture of where he'd actually visited and various images or pictures he'd seen in real life. Likewise, the dream stories were a mixture of real experiences and imaginary plots, all within the same requested themes.

During the first two weeks, Steve did not need the Wafer on certain days. He skipped it a few times, as he was permitted to, and had no rebound effect or return of the bad dreams. Throughout the Wafer trial period, his newly earned peaceful dreams virtually guided and protected his sleep, and he was more alert and ready to meet the following days' challenges.

During one of his follow-up visits, he thanked Dr. Jupitren for the peaceful dreams that had improved his sleep a great deal. He also reported that his job performance rose and he felt much less stressed while working. He felt like he had almost recovered his old self.

In the subsequent months, he revisited Dr. Jupitren a few more times and received Dream Wafers of different themes of his choice. Every time, the Wafer application was quite successful, as it induced dreams that he requested to have.

As time went on, Steve found himself feeling more than willing and happy to revisit Acmeon Lab. He wondered why. As Helen's charming image loomed up in his mind and overlapped with the Acmeon Lab ambience, Steve realized that Helen was the reason and caught himself with self-conscious smiles.

In the meantime, Steve heard and read about Acmeon Lab's popularity soaring. Augmenting Dr. Jupitren's reputation further, people from certain public and academic circles upheld the Dream Wafer concept highly and gave full credit to Dr. Jupitren.

On the other hand, curiosity, skepticism, and denunciation by various sectors of psychosocial and theological fields triggered open criticisms on the very idea of artificially modifying dreams. Steve thought he might someday ask Dr. Jupitren how the doctor would respond to those criticisms, especially to those remarks that came from orthodox psychologists.

Some critics remarked, "Acmeon Lab's new concept goes against the long-standing psychological wisdom, which maintains that uninterpreted dreams are like unread letters or untranslated poems. But Acmeon is disturbing such sacrosanct principles by artificially changing dream contents."

Those critics' remarks reminded Steve of what a psychologist once said, "Uninterpreted dreams are like uncashed checks. That's why you should try to have your dreams interpreted to get the best value out of them."

A few times, Steve attempted to find the meaning of his dreams. However, he often could not recall details of his dreams, let alone finding their meanings. He heard that other people also did not remember their dreams well.

During one of his later visits with Dr. Jupitren, Steve asked, "I wonder how much of our dreams we do remember."

"Well, we only remember roughly five percent of our nightly dreams. But, of course, there are some individual variations. I mean, some people tend to remember their dreams better than others."

"What makes that variation or the difference?"

"Statistics say that generally women remember dreams better than men. Actually, pregnant women remember dreams even better because of their hormonal changes and longer hours of pregnancy-induced sleep."

"That's interesting."

"There is another well-known finding about dream recollection. From what part of your sleep you wake up makes a big difference. Have you heard of REM sleep?"

"Yes, I understand that we dream mostly during the REM sleep."

"Correct. Therefore, let's say you woke up at the buzz of your alarm clock. Suppose it so happened that the alarm went off in the middle of your REM sleep; then you would certainly remember your dreams better than waking from the middle of a non-REM sleep."

"I see. Then, if I woke up during a non-REM sleep, how much of a dream would I remember?"

"The recall would be very poor, because there was much less dream in progress anyway."

"How can I time it so that I would wake up in the middle of a REM sleep?"

"We cannot plan such timing intentionally, but with the Dream Wafer, we can program it to a certain limited degree."

"I see. But I still wonder why generally we cannot remember dreams well."

"As you can imagine, within our brains, there is intricate memory-chemistry in progress. To put it in easy terms, there are brain chemicals needed for recallable memory formation. During the non-REM sleep, very little dreaming occurs and the functions of those chemicals are practically undetectable, resulting in very little memory formation. But in REM sleep, there is some detectable chemical activity. That's why we do remember our dreams from the REM sleep. Of course, during our wakeful state, those chemical functions are at their best."

"Can the Dream Wafer do something about the brain chemicals to enhance our recollection of dreams?"

"Yes. However, with due respect for the law of nature, we have to be very modest about our request for remembering our dreams better. If our request goes beyond certain limits, we are calling for serious consequences, such as a manic state or psychosis. Therefore, to safeguard every Dream Wafer user, the Wafer program has built-in mechanisms to maintain gene-mandated safety limits in everyone's requested items."

"That's reassuring. I have another elementary question. What is the real benefit of dream interpretation?"

"To answer that question, I have to refer to many volumes of books. But, if I dare to condense my answer into one sentence, dream interpretation enables us to learn more about our hidden inner selves and to gain wisdom to solve difficult life problems we might have."

"Then it will be a long haul for me. It will take lifelong effort to benefit from my dreams."

"You're right. It's not a one-time deal. We learn from our dreams as we go on living."

"I see." Steve checked his Thumputer time display and said, "I just thought of another question about remembering dreams. May I ask that question now?"

"Yes, we still have a good deal of time left."

"Thank you. I heard that some people can train themselves to recall their dreams better. Is it possible?"

"To some extent, yes. With conscious effort, I believe one can improve dream recall."

"Really? How do they do it?"

"You may keep a memo pad and a pen on your night table and jot down your dream contents immediately after waking up, either in the middle of the night or in the morning. Many people, while going through certain forms of psychotherapies, want to recall dreams better for their later treatment sessions, and they resort to note-taking at the night table. Even if you write down one or two short entries every time you wake up from your dream, your dream diary eventually would yield a cohesive gestalt, and you can derive meanings from them per individual night or several nights strung together.

In reality, you can get away with jotting down one or two key words to capture the main themes of your dream. Also, if you wrote down how you felt during your dreams in a single word, such as 'scared,' 'relieved,' or 'happy,' it would help you to recall your dreams better. Generally, we tend to remember dreams that were charged with strong emotion, such as high degree of fear, anger, anxiety, or happiness.

Another approach to recalling dreams a little better is using the well-known five *W*s and *how*. Right after you wake up in the morning, review your dream by asking who, when, where, what, why, and how. By doing so, you may commit the dream contents to your memory much better, and later you will be able to recall them more readily.

Another fact about dream recall is that we cannot willfully plan to have certain dreams, although some lucid dreamers claim that through training, they can control their dreams' plots and remember the dreams better. Whereas, the Dream Wafer, without training, lets us have the dreams of our choice, making it easier to remember them also."

Steve thanked Dr. Jupitren for taking time to answer his questions.

A number of weeks later, Steve revisited Dr. Jupitren. He reported, "For the past several weeks, I have slept much better without bad dreams, and I did not need Dream Wafers. On top of it, to my great relief, my company told me yesterday that the key engineer I have been replacing for many months is returning to work full time starting next week. I know I'll have much less stress on my job when he returns. So, I thought maybe it's about time for me to wean off from the Wafers. I would like to see if I could do well without the Wafers for another couple of months, with a goal to discontinue them completely."

"I'm very glad that you have done well." Dr. Jupitren responded. "I think your plan sounds good." During the remaining time of the session, Dr. Jupitren reviewed Steve's overall progress since he came to Acmeon Lab and explained in plain terms about his personality strength and how to reinforce such strength in the future. Dr. Jupitren remarked, "Should there be any recurrent or new problems in the future, please feel free to call me. I wish you good luck."

After expressing his appreciation again, Steve came out of his last session with the doctor. As he came to the waiting area, Steve saw Helen helping a couple of candidates fill out their health-history forms. Suddenly, he realized he couldn't find the right words to say good-bye to her.

Seeing Steve was somewhat hesitant in her office area, Helen excused herself from those candidates and asked Steve, "Do you want me to make another appointment with Dr. Jupitren?"

"No, thank you. It won't be necessary this time. I had the last session with him today. He said that I might do all right without Dream Wafers from now on."

"That's nice. Congratulations!"

"Well, thank you very much for all your help. I was very fortunate to have met you, Helen. I only hope this is not the last time I see you. I hate to say good-bye."

"Please be in touch." Helen's tone sounded like she was sorry to see him go.

"I may come back. Who knows?"

"Anyway, please come by and say hello to us when you have time. Good luck to you."

"Thank you, again. Good-bye."

As he left the Acmeon Lab area, Steve thought to himself, "Will I ever be back here to see her again?" Suddenly, an unfamiliar, rueful feeling seized him, and he shook his head, silently saying, "Where is this disconsolate feeling coming from? It's not like me!"

He reminisced over the events that happened to him at Acmeon Lab during the past year. Each time he came to Acmeon Lab for supportive psychotherapy and for his Dream Wafer renewal, he had found himself paying extra attention to Helen. Her charming smile and caring words did not fail to entrap his heart. She was a bundle of intelligence, beauty, and contagious calmness.

Often sensing that she addressed him with thoughtfulness and extra care, Steve wished she had expressed her special feelings for him. Yet, having seen her being kind and caring to everyone else she encountered, Steve was not sure about her feelings for him, and he held himself back.

Later on, however, he felt puzzled about why he had let his emotional momentum slide by and lost the opportune moments to tell her how attracted he was to her. He blamed himself for his indecisiveness and hesitation.

From various sources, Steve continued to learn about Acmeon Lab's steady progress and expansion since his last visit with Dr. Jupitren. News about Dr. Jupitren's work on the Dream Wafer spread widely to Canada, Europe, and other parts of the world.

Responding to the increasing number of clientele, in order to accommodate the increased demand for Dream Wafers, Acmeon Lab had to expand its operational setup.

The large number of newly hired employees reflected Acmeon's rapid growth. Mailing out huge numbers of sampling kits for polygene analyses, breath tests, and other related tests to remote users meant extra work hours for Acmeon Lab staff. In addition, upon receiving those dry ice-packed samples, to analyze and process them according to the remotely completed questionnaire requests required many devoted, skillful hands. To produce flawless Dream Wafers and then finally send them out to various parts of the world proved to be quite labor intensive.

CHAPTER 4
DREAM WAFERS OF JOHN Q AND JOAN Q

In an afternoon session, Dr. Jupitren saw John Q, a client who had started his Dream Wafer recently. He needed to come in several days sooner than his scheduled follow-up appointment.

John reported, "Since I applied my Dream Wafer, I've been feeling generally much better, and my nightmares went away. I'm very happy about it. But the dreams I had were not what I requested. That's why I wanted to see you today rather than later."

"I see. Here I have my notes on your last visit. Let's review them together. And, please let me know if any part is incorrect…Before you started the Wafers, in your repeated dreams, you said that you were put in jail in a strange town for things you didn't do. Moreover, no one understood you, because everyone there spoke only in foreign languages. Somehow, the scary thing you realized was that you would never get out of there alive."

"Yes, that's what I told you then. So, at the last visit, I requested a dream that I would travel freely around the world as a multi-linguist. But most of all, I wanted to dream that I become a gold medalist in speed skating in the next winter Olympic Games, for which I am in training."

"So, what kind of dream did your current Wafer let you have instead?"

"Four days in a row, I dreamt that I was a rich man giving big amounts of charity money to orphans and displaced families in the world. But no scenes of Olympic Games or speed skating."

"I'm surprised to hear that. I have not seen anyone yet who had a similar experience as yours. I mean, having dreams that they did not request. I will look into what happened with your Wafers as well as your initial requests, and will let you know what I would find."

"Thank you. Can I continue to use the same Wafers?"

"Well, although they helped you to some extent, since we are not sure what really happened, I think the right thing to do is to discontinue those Wafers at this point. By the way, did you leave your unused Wafers at home?"

"No, I have brought them all here to show you."

"Good! I'm glad you brought them with you. Please let me keep them here at the lab. I will thoroughly check them out and let you know as soon as possible about what caused such unexpected results and what we should do about it next. Thank you for coming in today to let me know about it. You did the right thing."

After a careful follow-up on John's Wafer, Dr. Jupitren discovered that despite all the precautions Acmeon Lab had taken, at the nadir of mail-service efficiency, the Wafer labels of John Q and Joan Q were mistakenly switched. As a result, they received each other's Dream Wafers. He alerted his assistants about the error immediately.

Dr. Jupitren went one step further by closely scrutinizing the anatomical brain to pinpoint which specific brain sites were affected by the Wafers that John used. Dr. Jupitren also followed up on what happened with Joan Q's case.

A few weeks later, he called his assistants to his office and gave them a detailed review about those two Wafer candidates. He used the anatomical brain model to explain his points.

"Fortuitously, John and Joan both had two similar presenting problems, namely, nightmares and sociopathic traits. As I told you last week, due to our labeling mistake, they received each other's Wafers.

On a closer tracing, I found that Joan's Dream Wafer worked on two separate areas of John's central nervous system. The first area of concern was this nightmare-related brain sites. Joan's Wafer helped John to sleep without nightmares. Additionally, Joan's Wafer affected John's fear-mediating neural complex within the limbic system, the mood center. When Joan's Wafer activated John's brain function in this area, John became more aware of the consequences of his antisocial behavior. Subsequently, his heightened awareness, which is a special form of anxiety, made him curb his sociopathic behaviors more readily than before.

In a nutshell, although John ended up having someone else's dream scenes, they were far better than his old nightmares, and he kept on using the wrong person's Wafers for five nights.

One of the remaining questions is what would have happened to John if he'd received his own original Wafer. Well, after reviewing John's answers to his 135 point-questionnaire, I discovered that he gave appropriate answers about his nightmares. However, to the questions about his sociopathic tendency, he gave inappropriate answers by falsifying personal facts because of the very sociopathic tendency he had. Joan Q, on the other hand, despite her sociopathic traits, gave reasonably truthful answers when she responded to the questionnaire. Therefore, if he had applied his own Wafer, he would have dreamt his requested scenes of Winter Olympic games, speed skating et cetera. And it would have worked on his nightmares, but not on his sociopathy.

Subsequently, I explained it to John and advised him to correct his answers to his questionnaire. With the corrected version of his Wafers, he has remained symptom-free from nightmares. This time, he dreamt the themes he requested, which were about the next winter Olympics' speed-skating competitions. There he became the polyglot gold medalist and he was very happy about it. When I saw him in subsequent sessions, maybe my biased expectation might have influenced me—I felt there were the faint early signs of improvement in his sociopathic traits. However, to be sure, I need to follow up on this sociopathy issue much further.

Meanwhile, the other question was what happened to Joan, who received John's Dream Wafer by the same labeling error. Fortunately, she had to postpone the use of her wrong Dream Wafer without realizing it was a wrong one. What happened was that her surgeon was going to perform the previously scheduled elective surgery on her foot under general anesthesia. The surgeon was unsure how her Dream Wafer and the general anesthesia would interact and advised her to postpone her Dream Wafer application.

Postoperatively, Joan was about to try her new Dream Wafer, which was actually John Q's wafer. However, by then, we had discovered the labeling error and contacted her just in time, preventing her from using John's Wafers.

Of course, her own Wafer version was mailed to her soon afterward. As of today, she reported that her Wafers helped her with her two main problems and she was able to sleep normally, dreaming what she ordered on the questionnaire."

Dr. Jupitren continued his explanation. "Prompted by those two error cases, the mailing service suddenly became a sensitive issue. One of the potential problems is that if a Wafer fell in a wrong recipient's hands due to delivery mistakes or any other reason, theoretically it would result in either no effect at all or, worse yet, severe untoward reactions. Depending on the case, those reactions could range from auditory, visual, tactile, or kinesthetic hallucinations to somnambulism or brief psychosis, with consequential accidents and confusions.

John Q's case had a really fortunate ending. Nevertheless, such labeling errors should never be repeated." With this remark, Dr. Jupitren ended his long explanation.

Later, he reported John Q's case to his Academy. However, he did not foresee what John Q's case had in store for his future clinical decision-making.

As time went on, Dr. Jupitren strongly felt the need to find a competent professional assistant with a serious interest in dreamology. The assistant should be willing to work side by side with him in clinical patient care and research projects.

Around that time, hearing about Acmeon Lab's expansion, a number of researchers with genetics and chemistry backgrounds sent in their résumés, inquiring about any possible work position at Acmeon Lab.

After reviewing those résumés, Dr. Jupitren picked one of them. The candidate was Dr. Sobien Molton, who had an impressive résumé and happened to be one of Dr. Jupitren's junior alumni of the same medical school.

Later, during the personal interview with Dr. Molton, Dr. Jupitren reviewed his résumé again. "Biochemistry major, PhD, then studied medicine at SUNY. Later, continued with molecular biology and genetics research for seven years. Hmm…great. Sobien, how did you first get interested in genetics?"

"As soon as I entered my first genetics research several years ago, I knew that's the road I wanted to tread along because I saw limitless interesting research possibilities in genetics. Other fields did not even come close to the genetics as my choice."

"I remember your first research was on a new DNA alteration method. Am I right?"

"Yes, it was on a rodents' DNA-modifying method known as Chemical Razor. It is a variant of DNA methylation technique. And the DNA came from the pancreatic Langerhans cells' modulating genes."

"What was the ultimate application of your DNA modification?"

"Well, it was mainly for genetic treatment of diabetes. A similar DNA-alteration technique might lead to new treatment for Parkinson's disease also."

"I see. I'd like to read your research papers that you listed here in your résumé and hear more about them from you at another time. Now let me ask you a few other things. Have you been following up on my Dream Wafer theories?"

"Of course, I have read most of your publications on the subject in the major journals for the past ten-plus years."

"I'm glad to hear that. So, when will you be able to start to work at Acmeon Lab?"

"After I complete my current project in two to three months."

"What's the nature of the project, if you don't mind?"

"It's about anti-angiogenesis factors against rodent cancer-cell growth."

After they exchanged more technical information, Dr. Jupitren asked the young doctor some personal questions.

At the end of the interview, Dr. Jupitren asked him to come back for another meeting soon after completing his project. At that time Dr. Jupitren would discuss with him about his future work at Acmeon Lab. Sobien thanked him and left. Dr. Jupitren was glad to find that Sobien was quite knowledgeable about the Dream Wafer's mode of action.

After his patient-care hours, Dr. Jupitren went to the restricted West Room of the Plant as usual. There, he engrossed himself working on the *virtual brain model* almost every day. Using the model, he followed up on the labeling-error incident and reexamined the related Dream Wafer's mechanisms. He has been pouring his time, energy, and considerable financial assets into upgrading the *virtual brain* model, which in turn produced significant and useful research results one after another.

For him, the *virtual brain* model became the most valued and cherished possession among all his research tools.

A couple of uneventful months went by, but something worrisome was brewing.

CHAPTER 5
COMPUTER CONSULTANT STEVE

One day, Steve received a call from Dr. Jupitren's office. It was Helen on the phone. Steve was very happy to hear from her. After exchanging pleasant greetings, Helen said, "Dr. Jupitren wants to see you. It is not about your Dream Wafers but about a quite different matter."

"Well, whatever it's about, I'm very happy just to hear from you. I'm ready to listen. Please go ahead."

"Our Acmeon computer program malfunctioned today. We've never had such problem before. And Dr. Jupitren thought that you, with your expert knowledge and experience in computers, might be able to help us tackle the problem. So, he is inviting you as a computer consultant, not as Acmeon Lab's client."

"I see. I'm surprised and delighted that Dr. Jupitren considered me for the job. But why not Acmeon Lab's own computer department people?"

"Our computer department's chief engineer, Mr. Morris is on a medical leave. He is the one whom Dr. Jupitren trusted the most. That might be the main reason, but Dr. Jupitren said he had some other reasons why he wanted to consult someone from outside. He said he will explain it to you when he sees you later."

"I see. From what I hear, it sounds like a quite urgent problem. Isn't it?"

"Yes, it is. Dr. Jupitren will personally tell you the details when you come over here. Would you be able to help us?"

"I wish I could say 'yes' right away. But, considering my job at Perihelion Energy and the computer problems you're having at Acmeon, first I have to find out if I can handle both responsibilities at the same time. So, before I give Dr. Jupitren my final answer, I'll soon come over there and discuss with him about the extent of the work I need to do."

"I understand. I like your cautious approach. When would you be able to come over?"

"Well, by six this evening. Is that a good time for him?"

"Yes, it will be. I'll let him know. Thank you very much."

By the time Steve arrived at Acmeon Lab, Dr. Jupitren was waiting for him. He thanked Steve for coming so readily and willingly. Without any delay, Dr. Jupitren said, "Our Dream Wafer production stopped as of today. Something serious happened to our Wafer program during the weekend. This morning, the program stopped abruptly. I checked the system and found the last part of Wafer program, the twelfth module, was malfunctioning."

"Do you mean the Wafer manufacturing process stopped by itself?"

"Yes."

"Any clue as to what might have caused it?"

"I suspect someone hacked it and copied the main program during the weekend. The twelfth module is the last part of the program that deals with dream-duration control. If any unauthorized copy is made, as a built-in safety measure, certain parts of the twelfth module get auto-deleted, and it gives false assurance to the hacker that the copying was completed."

"I see. The error was at the twelfth module, where the program was partly auto-deleted due to probable hacking. Is that right?"

"Yes, that's correct. So, about the current situation, I announced today to Acmeon Lab staff that we are holding off the Dream Wafer composition temporarily due to some computer problems. Unfortunately, our CCTV-camera monitoring system did not record any images because it stopped working periodically during the nights. I don't know why it behaved like that. Considering the CCTV camera's strange behavior, I suspected that the hacking could be an inside job. That's why I decided to consult someone independent from outside, like you, while my trustworthy computer department director, Mr. Morris, is away on medical leave. His main function was to maintain tight security over the Dream Wafer programs. If he was here, the hacking would not have happened."

"I can understand how you feel about his absence. So, as it is now, what needs to be done first? And, where is the Dream Wafer program?"

"Well, the most urgent job is to repair the damaged module so that we continue producing Dream Wafers with minimal interruption. We have to start at the Plant where the main program is. We will go there shortly."

Getting ready to go to the Plant, Dr. Jupitren collected the program manuals, original-program discs, and technical references in a tote bag.

"What will the hackers do with the partially altered program that they copied?" Steve asked.

"By manually overriding the error messages, they can still run the program and force it through without the last module that deals with final genetic trans-matching. At the end, the program would produce defective, counterfeit Wafers."

"I see. So, what will happen to anyone who tries the counterfeit Wafers?"

"They will be unable to wake up on time!"

"For how long?"

"It may take a few extra hours to wake up or sometimes even longer to become fully alert and functional. Even if the user happens to wake up from any stage of sleep, the serious thing is that the user may not realize subjectively that he or she is still half-asleep and will start the day as usual in a somnambulistic state, making serious mistakes. Therefore, if the impairment is subtle, not only the person himself but also others around the person may not notice that the counterfeit Wafer user is under an altered level of consciousness. That's why there would be no one to warn such users that they are not fully awake and are imminently accident-prone.

In addition, if any greedy criminals duplicate the counterfeit Wafers and sell them to ill-informed people with parasomnia, that is, sleep-related disorders or bad dreams, there will be catastrophic consequences. We don't know if during the past weekend the hackers already sold the defective Wafer formulas to any underground manufacturers, who sooner or later would mass-produce the counterfeit Wafers."

"Now I understand that the problems are potentially very serious…Are we ready to go to the Plant now?" Steve asked.

"Yes, but before we go, let me just give you a brief overview of Acmeon Lab's layout so that you can find your way around here easily."

"Thank you. That certainly will help me."

Dr. Jupitren opened a detailed map of Acmeon Lab and pointed to a number of spots in the map, saying, "As you see, we are here in my office, which is on the east side of the third floor in this main building. On the other side of this floor, the chemical labs with computers and the Annex Library, as you can see in the map, are here. Of course, you have been to the Annex Library a number of times before."

"Yes. I also remember the quite long hallway, too."

After reviewing the area map in detail, Dr. Jupitren said, "Please keep this extra copy of the map with you. Now, let's walk downstairs…On this second floor, we have offices for the engineers, chemists, and most of the other departments, including personnel, payroll, medical labs, and so on… On this ground floor, we have the main auditorium, a few conference rooms, and a dining hall. Usually the dining hall is open during lunch hours only and is closed by midafternoon."

As they were about to pass by the dining hall, Dr. Jupitren said, "Let's make a brief stop here. Helen told me that she would come down here ahead of us and get something to eat for three of us."

"That's very considerate of her. To get here on time, I didn't have a chance to eat yet."

"That makes three of us. We are ready for an extra energy supply."

Inside the empty dining hall, they saw Helen setting three trays on a table. Each tray had a hero sandwich, an orange, and a cup of coffee.

Steve greeted her. "Hi, Helen. I thought you went home for the day. Very nice to see you again. How have you been?"

"Very well. Thank you. You seem to be in good spirits."

"Yes, I am. Dr. Jupitren and I are quite ready for the extra energy. Thanks for the meal."

"You're very welcome. Please help yourself. Here are some cucumber pickles."

The three of them had a lively conversation while having their sandwiches. After putting the empty trays back on a counter, they left the dining hall. Soon they stepped out of the main building and headed toward the Plant.

Pointing to a separate building, Dr. Jupitren said, "Our Plant is located westerly over there, about thirty yards away. As you see it, the Plant is a one-story building. That's where the composition of Dream Wafer is finalized. Within that building, we have a conveyor system that transfers the finished Wafers to the adjacent mail department. Also, in the Plant, I have my second office."

They entered the Plant building. Electronic security within the Plant was rather tight. They passed through a few noisy gateway security devices before stepping into the farthest end compartment. There on the wall, behind the computer, Steve saw unfamiliar recording panels and gauges in motion.

"What does that panel do?" Steve asked.

"It's to identify and make recordings of whoever stood in front of the computer." Helen answered. "It also recognizes the person's weight for identification purposes."

"What if a person carries an extra weight," Steve asked, "such as an extra load of tools or other heavy equipment while walking around the area?"

Helen looked at Dr. Jupitren and said, "Uncle Jules, would you explain it to Mr. Spencer?"

Surprised at how she addressed Dr. Jupitren, Steve asked before Dr. Jupitren could answer, "Helen, did you say 'Uncle'? So, he is your…"

"Yes, he is my Uncle."

Looking at both of them, Steve said, "Please call me Steve. It is wonderful to know that you're related. And I feel honored being invited to partake in your problem solving."

Dr. Jupitren said, "Well, again, I thank you, Steve, for availing yourself so readily. As you will learn, this Plant has many delicate contraptions. The weight-based recording on the wall is actually an infrared detector of the person's true weight. Besides, the CCTV camera is a part of the surveillance system, of course. Therefore, any extra weight the person may carry would not matter. The infrared weight detector, supplemented with the CCTV camera's computation, will measure the person's weight accurately. But if the camera stops working, the surveillance information may not be complete."

Steve said, "I see. Could you tell me what the other recording panel measures?"

"Well, it is a special hygrometer, which is a part of the humidity-controlling HVAC system. We have to keep the humidity below certain levels, or else undesirable ionizers might cause electrical discharges, disturbing certain electrochemical process.

As you may learn more about it later, the Wafer is partly processed through nanogram particles. If a speck of dust as tiny as ten nanograms in size is mixed up in the manufacturing process, the Wafer will malfunction. For that reason, this room is air-cleansed all the time, using constant positive pressure, which brings triple-filtered outside air through HEPA (High Efficiency Particulate Arrestance) filters into this sealed room where we are standing. So, in effect, while the filtered air is brought in, the room air steadily leaves the room with any dust or airborne pollutants.

You may wonder what happened to the dirt on the bottom of your shoes. You can take a quick look at them now. See? As you walked in, passing those three noisy thresholds, the cleansing mechanisms thoroughly removed all the unwanted dirt or particles from your shoes and from your garments. In addition, the floor has a dust-repellent coating. It keeps the floor dust-free. You may not be able to see your shoe prints on the floor now, but when I turn on this switch and get the infrared scan, you'll see the prints on the floor."

As he was saying it, Dr. Jupitren went to the wall near the door, flipped a switch, and continued his explanation. "You can see our footprints, or, more accurately, shoe prints, that we made when we came in. This scanning will serve multiple functions, which we may use later."

There were many more gauges and panels within the immediate area, about which Steve thought he would ask Dr. Jupitren or Helen sometime later. At that point, he wondered, "What made Dr. Jupitren trust me so much that he would reveal all this to me?"

Surprisingly, at that very moment, Dr. Jupitren said, as if he'd read Steve's mind, "You may wonder, Steve, how and why I feel free to tell you all this. You see, we were impressed by the way you presented yourself to us during the past year or so. And your extensive computer knowledge was very reassuring. Besides, we checked your computer-related credentials and general background profile from a number of sources. Of course, Helen did most of the checking."

"I see." Saying so, Steve smiled at Helen while listening to Dr. Jupitren, who said, "I hope you don't mind that we checked your background. We needed to convince ourselves that you were a trustworthy man."

"I certainly understand what you went through under the circumstances. I have no problem with what you did." Steve said, smiling. "Besides, I don't mind it, because I have nothing to hide."

Returning Steve's smile with his own broad smile, Dr. Jupitren said, "Yes, your record was impeccably clean. Thank you, Steve, for your understanding."

With the help of Helen and Dr. Jupitren, Steve spent good half an hour checking the main computers at the Plant. He used his own electronic tools that he'd brought with him and analyzed the Dream Wafer software. It consisted of twelve modules with complex parallel programs, which processed multiple chemicals and genes. As Dr. Jupitren said, the twelfth module had a number of missing program lines with traces of subtle cyber-intrusion fingerprints.

Steve discussed with Dr. Jupitren about the extent of restoration work involved. He listed a three point-plan for his work and explained it to Dr. Jupitren and Helen:

1. Restore the working copy of the program.
2. Shield the current programs against future hackers. Consider installing the latest anti-hacking software version available.
3. Make an inventory of the existing surveillance system within the Acmeon buildings and outside CCTV cameras. Replace any outdated models or parts. If indicated, upgrade the overall surveillance system.

Steve said, "I understand your urgent situation. I'll start with the work item number one tonight but I may need your help as I go through certain steps."

With all the original program copies and the technical data of the Dream Wafer program that Dr. Jupitren brought from his main office, Steve worked concentratedly without any interruption. It kept all three of them quite busy. To their surprise, they restored the twelfth module within a few hours.

To test the restoration results, Dr. Jupitren ran an abridged version of the Wafer program, starting from the first module all the way to the end of the twelfth module. He exclaimed, "It is fixed!"

Dr. Jupitren and Helen thanked Steve for his skillful work and willing attitude. Steve was happy to have completed the repair job. He did not forget to thank them for their immediate help through number of steps he had taken for the repair work.

It was getting late. Steve looked at his Thumputer time. It was ten thirty. Steve said, "About the listed number two work, tomorrow I'll try to install the latest version of an anti-hacking device." He said he would come to the lab in the evening hours and would finish the remaining projects on the list as fast as he could.

Dr. Jupitren said he liked Steve's work plan and promised to recompense him generously for his work. He asked Steve if he would be available in the future for any other computer-related work after completing the listed work. Dr. Jupitren said he was thinking about redesigning the Wafers' outer appearance, especially the serial numbers from the current six-digit to eight-digit system for easy visual identification so that they can readily separate them from any counterfeits.

After a brief estimate, Steve replied, "I'll try my best to do those projects as well, but I'll be able to work here only after the usual work hours at my company."

"Of course. I understand that." Dr. Jupitren was glad to have Steve's promise and thanked him again.

Then Helen asked Dr. Jupitren if he was going to report the hacking incident to the police.

Dr. Jupitren answered, "We never had this kind of problem before and I'm not sure if it calls for just a police report. It would be more likely that we need to inform the local FBI office or Internet Crime Complaint Center. If it is of a larger scale crime involving national security, of course the US Secret Service will handle it."

"I see." Helen asked Dr. Jupitren, "Can you ask Sergeant Billy about this?"

"Yes, I'll think about it. At least we can run the Wafer program as of tomorrow and the hackers would not know about our cautious counter-maneuvering."

"Who is Sergeant Billy?" Steve asked.

"He, William Warren is a police sergeant at our local police precinct. He is a good friend of ours. I know I can rely on him. I'll have a personal talk with him about Acmeon problem without making an official report yet. I'm sure he will tell me to whom and when to make the official report."

"That's wonderful." Steve said.

Helen added, "Billy is a very reliable person. I'm glad, Uncle Jules, you have such a dependable loyal friend."

"Well, we have accomplished a lot tonight. Thank you so much, Steve and Helen. I'm glad I invited you for our computer problems, Steve. This evening, I saw you working very hard, as if you were the owner of this lab."

"I agree, Uncle Jules. He was the perfect person for the job. Thank you, Steve."

Packing his tools, Steve responded, "It has been my pleasure. Thank you both for trusting me."

"Now, let's go home," Dr. Jupitren said.

As they left Acmeon Lab, Steve's Thumputer time display showed ten forty-five.

Since then, every minute of the day when Steve was not involved in his daily robotics work at Perihelion Energy Company, he thought about Acmeon's situation.

"What are the hackers' motives?" Steve kept on questioning, "Could it really be an inside job? If so, who is the likely one? Who wants to steal the program? The hackers themselves? Or someone who hired the hackers?"

Dr. Jupitren's assistants Zenon and Yaru came to Steve's mind. He recalled the strange language they'd conversed in around the lab on his first day at Acmeon Lab.

Steve decided to come to the Acmeon building only after every Acmeon worker had left for the day so that he would avoid bumping into any of them, especially Dr. Jupitren's assistants. He did not want to let anyone know that he was working on Acmeon Lab's security.

However, Steve still needed Dr. Jupitren's guidance or Helen's presence in order to get around Acmeon Lab's machinery and computers. Helen volunteered to extend her work hours so that she would be around when Steve came there. Steve was happy about it.

On many occasions, whenever Steve needed Helen's help, she was right there with the correct answers or proper materials he asked for. Steve did not find any pretentious streak in her manners. She was smart and modest. He felt Helen's presence made his work all the more pleasant, despite the late hours and tediousness of some parts of the project. Many a time he thanked her for her help, and she would reply with polite "You're-welcome" smiles.

Ever since Steve came to Acmeon Lab for the computer work, he'd noticed an unidentified locked room in the Plant next to Dr. Jupitren's second office. Steve saw concealed heavy bundles of cables from the Plant's computers linking into that room. Steve asked Helen one day, "What's in that room?"

She cautiously answered, "Oh, that room! Only Uncle Jules goes in there. It is called the West Room, which is restricted to everybody else. I have not been in that room myself, either. Uncle Jules usually spends hours in that room. I heard there is a virtual human-brain model in the center of the room."

"Virtual human-brain model! I can't imagine how it would operate."

"Uncle Jules said almost all of his Dream Wafer-related experiments had gone through the *virtual brain*. He said that because it was so delicate and brittle, he had to keep everyone off except the ULPA engineers."

"You mean the ultralow-particulate-air engineers?"

"Yes. I know they often check the humidity and the air quality inside the West Room. Just to do that, they wear *clean-room suit* with masks, headgears, and special gowns."

"Will I need to wear the clean-room suit, too?"

"No, the computer software that you will be working on is not in the West Room. Uncle Julian at times wears a clean-room suit with headgear under yellow lighting when he deals with photosensitive chemicals in the West Room. He said he will continue to work on the *virtual brain*, perfecting it to be as close as possible to a natural human brain."

"I hope the *virtual brain* did not get disturbed during the recent hacking incidents."

"It didn't. Whenever Uncle Jules locks the West Room door, it automatically separates itself completely from the rest of the Acmeon computers and Dream Wafer programs."

"That's ingenious."

Steve continued his work in the evenings exactly according to his schedule.

Weeks later, on one Saturday evening, Steve went to the City Library to get some new information on robotics and solar energy for his project at Perihelion Energy Company. Accidentally, he found that there was an interesting meeting under way in one of the lecture halls in the library.

The meeting was about astrology. He thought he might get inside the lecture hall to have a ten-minute sampling on the topic, as it aroused his curiosity. He was not sure if they would allow him to sit in.

The gatekeeper of the meeting seemed to disallow nonmembers' admission to the meeting. However, when Steve chanced himself, the gatekeeper was in the middle of distributing flyers to the group of about sixty attendees and somehow did not stop him from passing through the lecture-hall door. They all had mini-computers with recently downloaded palm-reading program and everyone was quite busy trying it.

Within a few minutes in there, what Steve happened to hear made him extra alert as a woman speaker said the words "Acmeon Lab"!

She said, "In the past year, we the members of AAPA (Astrologers & Palmists Assembly) defenselessly witnessed the wicked group of Acmeon Lab diverting our clients by giving them dream-maker patches. We are losing our business, because our clients no longer seem to have bad dreams, which we used to deal with for them. We have to come up with the next plan of action so that the Acmeon group will run out of steam. That is the first item of today's agenda."

"The second item is for everyone to learn how to use the new palm-reading software that you just received. The software, I remind you, is a restricted version unavailable to nonmembers. When you do the palm reading, you should let your computers process the verbal information you get from your clients. Actually, you don't need to do much with your clients' palms per se, because your computer program will do all the reading anyway. Make sure you put their information onto your new program. At the end, you all will get one set of uniform readout from your computer.

If your clients visit our other AAPA members for a second or even third opinion, they would get the answer that is same as the one they got in the first place, provided you all used the same palm-reading program. Then, our clients will trust our palm-reading skills, and to that extent, our business will do better. Everyone understand?"

At that point, some of them looked at Steve curiously and whispered to each other. Their faces had searching expressions and seemed to question, "Who is he? Is he a new member? If not, what is he doing here?"

Steve got up and hurriedly left the hall, feeling that at any moment they might pelt challenging questions at him. He was most curious about what plans against Acmeon Lab they had come up in the remainder of the evening.

The next morning, Steve called Acmeon Lab hoping to speak to Dr. Jupitren, who was busy seeing a new Dream Wafer candidate. Instead, Steve told Helen everything he had seen at the City Library the previous evening.

"Don't you think Dr. Jupitren should inform the police about the AAPA?" Steve asked.

"I believe he is already aware of them. Not too long ago, he had received some unpleasant anonymous calls, and he discussed with Bill about them. Soon, Bill found that those calls came from the AAPA people."

"Is that right? So, what kind of people are they?"

"Bill said that AAPA is a heretical group not approved by the main body of orthodox ULAP (United League of Astrologers and Palmists). AAPA is just profit oriented and is not strapped with ideas of helping the public. In fact, the main orthodox ULAP is after them to disperse their selfish practice because they are misrepresenting what the mainstream palmists and astrologers do for the needy public."

"I see. After being in their meeting only briefly, I couldn't figure out what kind of people they were. Did Bill do anything about them?"

"As far as I know, he increased the police surveillance. Now Bill and his men are keeping close watch on the AAPA's next move."

"That sounds good. At any rate, please tell Dr. Jupitren about what I have told you."

"Yes, I will. Thank you, Steve."

In the following week, with Helen's help, Steve reviewed the monitors and CCTV cameras throughout Acmeon Lab. He checked the recorded images, especially from the cameras in the Annex Library and the chemical Plant. The Plant's camera skipped monitoring for four and half hours between 10:00 pm - 2:30 am during the preceding several weeks. The Annex Library's camera also skipped for four and half hours but during the mid-day, 10:00 am - 3:30 pm. However, the CCTV cameras in the other parts of Acmeon Lab worked normally.

For no apparent reason, a few days later, the Plant's camera began skipping during the mid-day rather than at mid-night.

Puzzled, Steve asked Helen, "Who is allowed to go in there at the Plant?"

"Besides me, Uncle Julian, Mark and some other technical staff."

"I see. We should let Dr. Jupitren know about this unusual CCTV black-out period."

The next morning, Steve spoke to Dr. Jupitren about the CCTV camera and suggested that the local police could watch or scan Acmeon Lab without displaying their presence for number of weeks or months, especially during the hours between 10:00 pm and 2:30 am. Steve suspected some Acmeon workers might have tampered the cameras.

Steve suggested that they check the background information of some of Acmeon's employees. With Dr. Jupitren's permission, Helen reviewed personnel files on suspicious Acmeon employees, including Dr. Jupitren's assistants.

According to the Acmeon Lab files, everyone had worked there for longer than seven to nine years except Zenon Zelinski and Yaru Yanovsky, who had been working there for three years. They both graduated from the Gentronics Academy of Warsaw several years previously and reportedly had shown substantial knowledge in electronics and genetics.

From the Federal Information Bureau's public files, Helen collected additional information on several workers of Acmeon Lab but no suspicious entries turned up.

Even after Helen and Dr. Jupitren left Acmeon Lab for the day, Steve often remained alone at Acmeon's Annex Library a little longer, wrapping up his evening's work. Steve frequently glanced over Acmeon's premises, especially the Plant area, either visually or via CCTV camera, to see if any intruders might be detected. Nothing happened for days, and he gave up his own surveillance for the time being.

During that week, Dr. Jupitren received an updated report from Acmeon's personnel department about Mark Morris, who was still in and out of hospitals, and his medical leave had been extended to a long-term disability category.

Dr. Jupitren called Steve to tell him about Mr. Morris. "Mark is now on a long-term medical leave status, but I may not hire anyone to replace him at this juncture. So, I want to ask you, if you would help us whenever there are any cybersecurity issues on Acmeon Lab computers. However, I will delegate all the routine computer matters to our IT engineers. As before, I'll compensate you well for your work."

Steve answered that he would avail himself when needed at Acmeon Lab in the evening as he did before. Dr. Jupitren thanked him and asked him to maintain the same working relationship with Acmeon Lab. Then, he gave Steve detailed instructions about the necessary steps regarding how to get inside the Plant by himself, if needed, since in the future he might need to work there alone.

Meanwhile, in anticipation of the possible surfacing of counterfeit Dream Wafers, Dr. Jupitren thought of developing an antidote against the somnambulistic complication. He spent many days working late in the lab. He felt he was racing against time.

Weeks went by, and one evening, during one of Steve's working visits at Acmeon Lab, Dr. Jupitren said excitedly, "Steve, look at this! For many years, no, rather for many decades, the world's neuroscientists wanted to treat somnambulism medicinally but the conventional treatment result was usually equivocal. And yet, the secret for the effective treatment of somnambulism was hiding all this time right here in the genetic modification methods of the chemicals that is part of our Dream Wafer program.

With this gene-based antidote that I have just succeeded in synthesizing, I'll be able to reverse the somnambulism that is caused by counterfeit Wafers. I'm going to name the pill *Antisom*."

"That's wonderful!" Steve said. "Do you need its synthesizing process computerized?"

"Certainly. I will pinpoint in a diagram the parts that would need your programming."

"I'll be ready for it anytime. Is the antidote going to look like the Dream Wafers in appearance?"

"No, it will be an oral tablet. If it proves to be very effective, its use eventually would be extended to the treatment of somnambulism caused by other causes such as temporal-lobe seizures, neuro-developmental immaturity, stress, and certain drugs' side effects."

In anticipation of the need to use Antisom anytime soon, Dr. Jupitren initiated his application to FDA, requesting an approval to use the medicine under the 'Compassionate Use of not-yet-approved Medicine On emergency' clause.

A few months elapsed since the hacking incident. The *Cyber Tribune* had awful news, which Dr. Jupitren had been afraid might pop up any day.

The news headline read:

Trans-Alpha Jet Air and Acmeon Lab to be Investigated by Aviation Commission and Federal Chemical Administration.

According to the Aviation Commission's preliminary report, a pilot of Trans-Alpha Jet Air manifested symptoms of a disorder, which the neuroscientists called somnambulism. Due to the stated condition, the pilot lost control of the aircraft for nearly twenty minutes at 3:30 this morning. The airliner started from JFK Airport, New York, and was on its way to Narita International Airport, Tokyo, Japan.

Two heroic New York City police officers in civilian clothes, who happened to be on board subdued the confused and wildly agitated pilot. Their timely intervention enabled the copilot, Mr. Frank Fairmont to take charge of the cockpit. The flight with 250 passengers aboard had to make an emergency landing on the Pacific Islands, fortunately without any reported life-threatening casualties.

The copilot completed the originally planned flight to Tokyo. However, the pilot, Sam Dayer, was brought back from the Pacific Islands to LA, California, for further questioning.

The Aviation Commission in conjunction with the team of the Federal Chemical Administration will investigate to find any causal connection between Acmeon Lab's Dream Wafer and the pilot's behavior.

Beside the airliner news, there were several reported auto accidents under investigation. The drivers involved in those auto accidents were wearing Wafers on their temples when seen in the emergency rooms. Reportedly, those auto accidents occurred throughout New York and adjacent tri-state highways.

Later, Helen asked Dr. Jupitren, "The news said those drivers still had the Wafers on their temples when checked in the ERs. Why didn't the drivers remove their Wafers?"

"I think they most likely used the counterfeit Wafers, which did not wake them up normally, and they ended in somnambulistic states. Of course, in that condition, they would be unable to think of removing the Wafers. The same thing must have happened with the pilot, too. He was still wearing the Wafer when he was brought to LA General Hospital."

Within a few days, inspectors from the Federal Chemical Administration came to Acmeon Lab and audited Acmeon Lab's entire client registry. They did not find the names of the confused pilot or the drivers who caused those recent auto accidents.

The investigation continued for several days. Their inspections on Dream Wafer's composition process and the Plant's procedures yielded no deficiencies in Acmeon Lab's operation.

Dr. Jupitren entreated the investigators to follow up on the pilot and those auto-accident cases and find out from where they obtained the counterfeit Wafers. His sole objective was to make the counterfeit Wafer manufacturers to stop producing those counterfeits by the injunction of police or government authorities.

The pilot was directly admitted to LA General Hospital's maximum-security unit right after the incident. Dr. Jupitren requested the hospital's administrator and the local police chief of Boyle Heights, LA to secure the Dream Wafer from the pilot's skin. With ample explanation, he asked them to Express Mail the Wafer to him at Acmeon Lab for chemical analysis.

Subsequently, Dr. Jupitren received the very Wafer, which he was able to analyze. He found that the Wafer was a counterfeit, bearing a seven-digit serial number rather than the six digits of genuine Acmeon's Dream Wafers. Likewise, he confirmed that counterfeit Dream Wafers caused the preceding week's suspicious auto accidents as well.

All the counterfeit Wafers that were analyzed showed deficient twelfth modules, causing faulty wake-up mechanisms.

Through the National Public Radio's emergency broadcasting system, Dr. Jupitren made nationwide warning announcements to the public asking them to stay away from any Dream Wafer that was not manufactured by Acmeon Lab.

Dr. Jupitren thought that in order to stop the proliferation of counterfeit Wafers, he needed to trace their sources first. Therefore, he requested that the LA Police Department find out where Sam Dayer bought the counterfeits. However, the psychiatrist in charge of Sam Dayer's treatment informed the police that they would not get accurate information about the source of the counterfeits because the pilot's mental status was not normal yet.

CHAPTER 6
STEVE'S PURSUIT OF INTRUDERS

One evening, Steve came to Acmeon as usual and said to Dr. Jupitren and Helen, "I'm wondering if Zenon had anything to do with the counterfeits."

"Why him?" Helen asked.

"I remember seeing him adjust the CCTV camera angles at the Annex Library on my first day at Acmeon. Somehow, I can't help but think about him."

"You could be right, Steve," Dr. Jupitren said. "But whether it is Zenon or anyone else, we don't have any objective evidence yet. We have to be very careful on matters like this."

"Uncle Jules, do you think that four and a half hours are long enough for anyone to break in and copy the program?"

"Well, it's long enough to copy at least one of the twelve modules. After that, they could come back for more. But I could be wrong."

"Then, how about checking the suspicious employees' files?" Steve suggested. "I mean, this time, you could get the level III personal information on very suspicious ones."

Helen asked, "But, don't we need permission from some federal authority?"

"I think so." Steve said. "Helen, do you know what that level III information is?"

"Not the whole details but I heard it includes information like bank accounts, health records, electronic messages, any police records, and also the person's GPS trace for some defined time periods."

Dr. Jupitren said, "By the way, the level III information rule has exceptions, if the situation is a life-threatening emergency. Suppose you know that there is an impending treason or someone is planning a homicide or suicide, you have to break the privacy rules to notify the proper person or body of authority. Especially in psychiatry, duty to warn about impending homicide is an exception known as the *Tarasoff law*. The law mandates that if there is an imminent homicide case and you happen to know who the intended victim is, you should notify the endangered person as soon as possible, despite the confidentiality rule. However, you should be able to give sufficient proof for such imminent dangers if you are breaking the level III information rule."

Steve said quickly, "Then, I think we sure have an exceptional situation here. It is potentially life-threatening to the public. What if the NYC cops weren't there on board the Trans-Alpha Jet Air flight? On top of it, what about those car accidents throughout the neighboring states caused by the counterfeit Wafer users? I myself want to check the level III info on some suspicious Acmeon employees to begin with. Would there be any legal problems for our probing?"

"Well, I will document what we have discussed this evening," Dr. Jupitren said. "Someday, if the FBI questions us about our level III information probing, I'll show our dated discussion record to them, and I'll take the blame. So, for the record, you are doing the level III probing because I asked both of you to do it since it is a matter of public emergency. And, thank you, Steve for your concern. You didn't need to trouble yourself with this problem." Saying this, Dr. Jupitren was resolute but looked tired from all the recent stressful events.

"Uncle Jules, why don't you go home now and get some rest? You had a long day. We will do a little more check on the computer and will continue it tomorrow. Earlier, you told me that Aunt Jamie has your car this evening. Shall I call her now?"

"Yes, please. Thank you, Helen."

A short while later, Helen told Dr. Jupitren, "I spoke to Aunt Jamie. She is coming to pick you up soon."

"Thanks. How late will you be up here? It's getting late."

"My Mom will pick me up on her way home from the art studio."

"Then, she will probably get here around nine. It's another half hour to go. How about you, Steve? How late will you stay?"

"Tomorrow, my work at Perihelion Energy starts much later than usual because my division will be moving to another office building in the morning. I have already packed all my office stuff in several boxes for the movers. So, tonight I can stay here a bit longer, maybe till ten thirtyish?"

"I see. Don't work too hard. Just in case you need to call me, please keep my contact numbers handy."

"Yes, I will. Thank you."

While waiting for his wife's arrival, Dr. Jupitren continued to read the letters that piled up on his desk from the day's mail in his office.

Helen and Steve went to her front office to continue their cyber search using two separate computers. Helen asked, "How much hacking experience did you have?"

"When I was at New York Polytech Academy several years ago, I had one semester of a computer course called 'E-FPAR', the 'Electronic Forced Probe and Retrieval,' a fancy title for hacking, and I did pretty well."

"I took that course, too. By any chance, was the course called E-FPAR 101 Plus?"

"Yes, it was. Do you remember much of what you learned, Helen?"

"I do, but how about you? Did you do any more hands-on practice since leaving the Academy?"

"Yeah. After graduating from the Academy, I worked for the Scientific Archives in Washington, DC. Hacking, in fact, was a required part of the job, and of course I had a federal permit, which I still have."

Mrs. Jupitren arrived at the Acmeon office. Helen got up from her seat to greet her.

"Hi, Aunt Jamie, was the traffic all right?"

"It wasn't bad. How are you?"

"I'm doing fine. Thank you." Helen turned to Steve, who stood up politely next to his desk. "Steve, this is my aunt, Mrs. Jupitren."

"How do you do? I'm Steve Spencer. I'm helping Dr. Jupitren to iron out some of Acmeon's computer problems."

"I've heard plenty of good things about you from Jules. I thank you for helping him. But aren't you all working too long hours?"

Helen answered, "I'm sure we will go back to the routine schedule pretty soon."

"Considering how hard Dr. Jupitren works," Steve added, "our extra work seems rather slight."

"Please come with me, Uncle Jules is in his office." Arm in arm with Jamie, Helen led her to his office.

As they were walking into his office, Dr. Jupitren received a call from Bill Warren, who said, "I was at one of the North Mall stores next to your Acmeon building to buy something for my wife. And I saw your office was still brightly lit. So I just called you to say Hi. You're working late today."

"Thanks, Bill. I see Jamie just came up to go home with me. She is the driver this evening. Helen and Steve are still here, too."

"Well, let me come up there and say hello to you all."

Hearing about Bill's surprise visit, Mrs. Jupitren said, "Bill is such a friendly man!"

Very soon Bill was at the door with his greeting, "Hi, everybody!"

Hearing Bill's voice, Dr. and Mrs. Jupitren came out of his office to welcome him.

"So, Jamie, you're the chauffer this evening, I hear."

"Yes, I am. It's nice to see you in good spirit as usual."

Dr. Jupitren introduced Steve to Bill. "This is Steve Spencer. I told you about him the other day. You know what he is doing for Acmeon Lab."

"Certainly, I do."

Bill said to Steve. "Nice to meet you. I'm Bill Warren. Jules told me you've done a lot for Acmeon Lab."

"Thank you, Mr. Warren. Glad to meet you." Steve and Bill shook hands. Bill gave his business card to Steve, saying, "Please keep it handy. It has my contact numbers."

After brief friendly chatting, Dr. and Mrs. Jupitren left the office with Bill.

Steve asked Helen, "Is Bill Warren a longtime friend of Dr. Jupitren?"

"Yes, for more than ten years; ever since he came to our local precinct. He is a very dependable person. Acmeon Lab's people like him and his team of officers."

"Is he a family man?"

"Yes, he and his wife have two sons. The older one is a freshman at the NYC Police Academy, and the younger one is a high school senior. Bill's wife and Aunt Jamie are good friends, too."

"I see. He seems to be a nice person. Besides, he is built like a tank."

"You said it right. He is a Tae Kwon Do third-dan black belt."

"No wonder. He looks strong and very fit."

"His youngest brother, Dominick, is just like Bill. He is a black belt, too."

"Is that right?"

"I heard Bill is going to Singapore for Dominick's wedding in a few weeks."

"Singapore? That far away?"

"The bride's family lives there."

"I see. Now, let's get back to our e-FPAR business. We don't have much time left for our stuff here."

Steve and Helen quickly probed the level III files of several employees. When they checked on Zenon's file, the following information came up:

Name: Zenon Zelinski
Nationality: Polish-American, US citizen by naturalization at 17 years of age
Age: 35
Language: English, Lechitic Polish and Grypsera dialect of Polish
Education: Master's in electronics (Graduated from Gentronics Academy of Warsaw at age 27)
Marital status: Single
Family: Father, deceased during the insurgence of Southern Poland cities. Lives with mother, a seamstress, and an older sister, Stellona, 37-year-old with a 9-year-old daughter.
Bank accounts: Savings 120,000 Euro with Polowealth Bank; 225,000 Euro with Morgan-Slovak Securities, Inc.
Recent transactions:
3/21: Credit/electronic transfer 30,000 US dollars from Brandon Cumlen's account of International Trading House, Singapore
4/23: Credit/transfer from Brandon Cumlen: 22,000 US dollars from the same Trading House, Singapore
Debits: On the first day of every month for past reporting period of one year, 1,000 US dollars per month to the Games and Rifles Company
Health: Status post-polio, left-leg paresis; mild eye-muscle weakness (strabismus)
Religion: Unspecified
Special remarks:
Arrested for illegal possession of a firearm and misdemeanor at age 29. Make of weapons: Walther PPK. Fined $2,000; completed community service 150 hours, one year after the arrest
Bullied in adolescence by schoolmates; ostracized by fellow students; was ridiculed for handicap due to polio sequelae, mostly for limping; eye-muscle weakness.

Helen frowned at her monitor and exclaimed, "This whole report on Zenon is fishy!"

"Yeah, the file makes him look suspicious. Helen, I see this Brandon Cumlen is giving him lots of money. Have you heard of him? Is that name familiar to you?"

Helen combed through the registry of Acmeon employees and Dream Wafer clients, looking for Brandon Cumlen. She showed Steve a list of several Acmeon clients with the first name Brandon and two other Brandons among the Acmeon employees but no one with the last name Cumlen. Helen and Steve broke into all Brandons' files but came up with no one suspicious, except Brandon Sweza, one of the Acmeon clients. For some technical reason, neither Brandon Cumlen's nor Brandon Sweza's files could be probed.

Steve thought to himself, "Brandon Sweza was the candidate I met on the very first day at Acmeon's Annex Library. Sweza said he was a lawyer working on international treaties over weapons and arms limitation. His files must be using a different computer language. That's probably why I cannot get through to his data. Is it possible that Brandon Sweza is in fact Brandon Cumlen whose files I cannot break into, either? Could it be that Cumlen used an alias when he registered with Acmeon Lab?"

Helen asked Steve, "What are you thinking?"

"This guy, Brandon Sweza, he is Acmeon's client. Isn't he?"

"Yes, I remember him. He used to get the Wafers for himself lot more than average clients did. A while ago, he asked me out, and I casually went out with him a few times. A funny man. He was very curious about many things."

"Are you still going out with him?"

"No, nothing happened between us. Whenever we were together, he would ask me all kinds of questions."

"Questions about you?"

"No, not about me so much but about Acmeon Lab; how the Wafers were invented, where Acmeon Lab's machine parts came from, how long it takes to make the Wafers from scratch, things like that. I felt he was not much interested in me. So I did not call him back, and we just left it that way."

"I see…" Steve seemed absorbed in some thoughts.

Helen wanted to get his attention back and asked, "Steve, do you want to say anything?"

"I don't know what to say." Saying so, Steve smiled with inexplicably pursed lips and a mild ripple of a shoulder shrug.

Short minutes later, Steve tried to ask her some question while reading the texts on his computer monitor, but Helen was deep in her own thoughts and seemed preoccupied. Steve tapped his desk lightly with his fingers, trying to get her attention and called her, "Helen!"

She snapped out of her brief reverie and answered, "Yes, Steve?"

"What were you thinking about so seriously? Anything on your monitor?"

"No, nothing." Helen caught herself realizing that she just came out of her brief fantasy, in which she savored that Steve had some special feelings for her. She had a fleeting thought, "Is he perhaps jealous of Sweza?"

Steve asked, "Did Brandon Sweza ever call you again since your last date?"

"No! I haven't talked to him since I saw him several months ago, and it was not even a date."

"I see…" That was all Steve said, and he kept on working on his computer.

Steve and Helen did not like the special remarks on Zenon's file: Arrested for possession of weapons! He went to the rifle shop only three weeks ago and spent $1,000.

Steve thought to himself, "Zenon could have purchased a rifle or a pistol. Besides, what is the Grypsera dialect of Polish? Was he talking in that language with the other guy, Yaru, at the lab?"

"Helen, do you know what the Grypsera dialect of Polish is?"

"As far as I know, it's a dialect spoken among the descendants of criminals and recidivist convicts and prison inmates in the southeast part of Poland. Those who spoke Grypsera dialect, in truth, were originally regional patriots and nationalists. The dialect started long before the 1800s, in the era of the three Russian partitions of Poland. The dialect has multiple ancient language sources, such as Yiddish, German, Russian, and Ukrainian."

"That's some elegant speech, Helen. How did you know all that? You talk like a history professor!"

"Zenon told me about it once. He said in his blood, the spirit of Grypsera's tenacity was flowing, and I did not understand what he was talking about. But I did not ask him at that time what he meant by that. We are probably dealing with a very daring character here."

Helen's office phone buzzed. It was from her mother.

"Helen, it's me. As usual, I'm parked next to your office building, in front of the chocolate store, the Parking Lot 4."

"Yes, Mom, I'll be down in a few minutes."

Helen turned her computer off. She said, "My Mom's here. We have accomplished a lot today. I'll say good night now. Are you going to stay longer?"

"Yes, maybe another couple of hours?"

"Don't work too hard, Steve. Good night."

"Just one moment, Helen. I'll come along with you." Steve got up from his seat and walked with her to the elevator. For some reason, the elevator was very slow in coming up.

Helen said, "Well, I can walk down the stairs. Why don't you return to the office?"

"Let me go with you. I'd love to meet your Mom, too."

"Thank you. She will be happy to meet you."

"Come to think of it, I don't know your mom's full name."

"She is Mrs. Elva Humayor."

"Thank you, Helen. I'm glad I'll be meeting her."

While descending the first few steps on the stairs, Steve took her heavy bag from her, lightening her load.

"Thank you."

"No problem. Helen, 'tis quite heavy."

"Yeah, all the extra papers. And today, I brought a few computer manuals in the bag. That's why."

As they reached the middle of the last staircase, Steve switched his grip on the heavy bag to his other hand. At that moment, he misjudged a step and staggered badly. Helen quickly held him with her arms, stopping him from falling down.

Steve steadied himself and said, "Wow! It was close. Thank you, Helen."

"That's all right."

Impressed by her quick and strong grip, Steve almost blurted out that she had strong arms, but he thought it would be a somehow mixed compliment and said instead, "You are my guardian angel and you're very quick!"

Steve took several more cautious steps down to the main floor. As they were going through the exit door, he said, "Here we are, Helen. Without your quick move, I might have taken a bad fall on the stairs. Thank you again."

"Not at all."

Helen's mother stepped out of her car, waving her hand at them. Helen waved back and walked with Steve toward her mother.

"Hi, Mom, this is Steve Spencer."

"Hi, I'm Elva. Nice to meet you."

"How do you do, Mrs. Humayor? Helen told me much about you and your artwork."

"Helen told me a lot about you, likewise, and I was looking forward to meeting you. I'm glad we've met today."

"Now I can see where Helen got her beauty." Steve remarked heartily.

After they exchanged cordial words with each other, Helen left with her mother. Steve returned to the third-floor office.

On their way home in the car, Mrs. Humayor said, "He certainly is a likeable, handsome young man, as you said. I can see why you like him so much."

"I'm glad you like him, too, Mom."

Having finished some more work, Steve decided to check the Plant before he would return to his apartment. He activated his LXG (laser-X ray-Gauged) stun gun that he'd brought with him.

While he was in his final year at New York Polytech Academy, he had a chance to use the LXG during a class assignment. With a few of his classmates, he went to a field survey in the Adirondack trails to check electronic-echo differential along specified trails. It was a part of the graduation credit requirements.

During the assignment, they carried LXG stun guns to protect themselves from unexpected wildlife attacks. The LXG came with a permit. It would stun animals or humans within 150 feet.

The LXG had three level intensities assigned to three different triggers: the weakest degree would give a 150- to 200-pound living entity a severe daze or fall; the second degree would make it fall down, causing to lose consciousness for couple of minutes; and the third degree would cause unconscious state for ten to thirty minutes.

At the Adirondack trails, Steve used it a couple of times quite effectively on the second-degree trigger, against hungry bears. Starting that year, highway police troopers also began using LXGs.

Lately, after renewing his permit, Steve started carrying the stun gun with him again. It was easy to carry around, as it was a half-palm size, flat, and lightweight.

It was close to 11:00 pm. Steve thought, "It would be an opportune time to check the Plant tonight. In the near future, I may not have another night I can stay this late. I want to check the infrared footprint scan tonight, too."

He double-checked the LXG in his holster before leaving the main building.

CHAPTER 7
TWO INTRUDERS

Coming out of the main building, Steve faced westerly, walking toward the Plant. Despite the light from nearby South Street lamps, the plush shrubs cast thick shade around the Plant area.

Much to his surprise, Steve saw two dark, moving silhouettes on the east side of the Plant. There was no time for him to call Bill or anyone else at the security service. If he made any noise or a wrong move, they would spot him. They attempted to open the Plant's east-side entrance door but quickly gave it up and crept, squatting, to the northern part of the Plant. There, at the northern-entrance area, they faded into the shadow cast by the building and the taller shrubs.

Steve lied in wait motionlessly to see what they were about to do. He could not see their faces because they wore what appeared to be night-vision goggles. Steve was unsure if they had seen him already. He reached for his LXG.

The two intruders must have gotten inside the Plant through the north-side window. Steve waited for a while, but the Plant's inside remained unlit. The alarm did not go off, either. They must have disabled it quickly. Steve could see their heads' silhouettes moving faintly within the building, but he could not see what they were doing there in the dark. Several minutes went by.

Steve crept to get close to the north-side window. However, having the advantage of night-vision goggles, they spotted Steve, decided to give up their planned action, and dashed out of the Plant through the south-side door of the building. Steve ran after them with his LXG ready and shouted, "Hey, you! Stop! Or I'll shoot you!" But they jumped into their car. Steve threw two shots of degree-I rays at them. The rays only made big sparks on the rear bumper as they sped away.

As they fled, Steve heard their panic-stricken, breathless exchange of words but could not make out what they were saying. Most likely, they did not get what they were looking for, because the time they took in there was not long enough to do anything, even if they had night-vision goggles on. Steve checked the time. It was 11:15 pm.

Right afterward, Steve went inside the Plant and turned on the infrared floor scan. He saw two pairs of shoe prints: one with ordinary walking prints and the other with incomplete C-shaped drags on the left foot. Steve thought, "Was Zenon one of them? Could those C-shaped drags be his shoe prints?" He checked the CCTV camera, but again it did not have any recorded images at all.

After his adrenaline surge simmered down, Steve thought of calling Dr. Jupitren or Helen, but it was near midnight, and he decided to put it off until the next morning. But he managed to get in touch with Bill and told him about what had just happened. Bill sent one of his assistants Michael, who rushed in and confirmed that there was no apparent property damage. After communicating with Bill about his survey, Michael told Steve that Bill would see Dr. Jupitren in the morning. Steve thanked Michael and left Acmeon Lab.

Steve thought of the incident while driving to his apartment. "Everything I know about Zenon points to the possibility that one of the two silhouettes could be his. The only thing that did not fit well in the whole picture was that those two felons seemed much taller than Zenon. Why did the CCTV camera not work? Did they turn it off? Did someone from Acmeon manipulate it beforehand for them?"

The next morning, Steve called Dr. Jupitren and explained in detail what happened the night before. Dr. Jupitren said he had already heard about it from Bill. Dr. Jupitren asked Steve if he could see him and Helen at his office in the evening around six o'clock.

By midafternoon, Steve's division had completed moving. As soon as he unpacked his boxes, he went through the technical information on the spy Dronettes and reviewed their night-vision capabilities. He thought of installing one of the new Dronettes in Acmeon's Plant area to monitor nighttime intruders. "If I use the latest Dronette-6.12, it would take pictures of any intruders, even in the dark. It would not matter if the Acmeon building's cameras worked or not."

Reading the Dronette's technical manual, Steve realized that he needed a few small but critical parts in order to assemble the new Dronette-6.12 unit. The Espio-Nano Company had listed those parts in their e-catalog. He planned to visit the Espio-Nano Company rather than digging for the parts from his own company's warehouse.

Later, Steve called Helen at Acmeon Lab.

"Hi, Helen, have you heard from Dr. Jupitren about what happened last night after you went home?"

"Yes, most of it. How awful. Are you all right?"

"Yes, I'm fine now. Thank you. But it shook me up last night."

"Did you get to see who they were?"

"Not at all. Even inside the Plant, they did not turn the lights on and tried to do something in the dark, wearing their night-vision goggles."

"Didn't the alarms work?"

"No. How in the world they defused the alarms so quickly in the dark, I have no idea. It takes me much longer to defuse the north entrance alarms. It must be an inside job."

"Did you say both of them had night-vision goggles on?"

"Yes, both of them. And I couldn't see their faces. But, they seemed taller than Zenon. Anyway, it was too dark in the northern part of the Plant."

"When you went inside the Plant afterward, was there anything out of place or suspicious?"

"Yes, there were some unusual footprints. I will tell you about them later this evening. Dr. Jupitren asked me to see him there at six. Will you be there, too?"

"Of course."

"How was Dr. Jupitren today?"

"Oh, he was busy seeing a number of Dream Wafer candidates. He also had two visitors from the FDA and another from Trans-Alpha Jet Air. They were here to finalize their investigation. He had very little time for anything else."

"Is he in any trouble?"

"I don't think so. From what I heard all day, the FDA didn't say anything about stopping him from prescribing the Dream Wafers. The only thing I heard was the FDA's warning that our lab and the Plant should be guarded more tightly against any intruders. If we fail to protect our main programs again, they will issue a conditional suspension of Acmeon's operation."

"Well, unbeknownst to the FDA, Acmeon had a break-in again just last night. Of course, Acmeon should reinforce security on the Dream Wafer program more tightly, especially at the Plant."

"I agree."

CHAPTER 8
BEHIND THE PICTURE FRAME

As Steve arrived at Acmeon Lab, he saw Dr. Jupitren and Helen waiting for him.

While they were walking toward the Plant, Steve asked Dr. Jupitren, "Did you keep an eye on Zenon today after I spoke to you in the morning? Did he seem as usual?"

"Yes, he did. Is there anything special about him?"

"Well, I always felt uneasy when I looked at him in his eyes. I couldn't tell whether he was looking at me or at something behind me. His eyes used to make me feel that he was hiding something from me. Didn't you feel that way about him sometimes?"

"You're not alone about that. It's because he has an eye-muscle weakness called 'strabismus' or 'squint.' His condition is of a very mild degree. That's why he may give uneasy feelings to people who are unaware of his subtle eye problems. If the condition is not treated very actively before six years of age, the symptoms tend to persist. Known as 'non-paralytic strabismus,' it is often hereditary."

"I see. Now I understand it. In fact, in his file, Helen and I saw yesterday that he had weak eye muscles. All this time, I misunderstood him unfairly. At least, I should have given him the benefit of the doubt. Thank you for clearing it up for me."

As they stepped inside the Plant, Steve said, "When I checked the floor with the infrared screen last night, right after the incident, I saw shoe prints that showed left-foot drag. Don't you suspect it could be his…I mean Zenon's? I'll show you what part of the floor had the drag, which I called an incomplete C-shape shoe print."

"Today a few people came in here," Dr. Jupitren said, "and they must have stepped over the shoe prints you saw last night." However, the three of them looked for the shoe prints on the entire Plant floor under the infrared screen.

"Look at them! The shoe prints are still there." Steve said. "And they show left-foot drag."

After carefully observing the shoe prints, Dr. Jupitren said, "Those shoe prints certainly show that the person who was here last night had a left-foot drag. You both seem to think they are Zenon's shoe prints. But I don't think so. The weight sensor indicates the two intruders were much heavier than Zenon to begin with. Additionally, Zenon's foot drag is from the polio that he had as a child. Polio causes a lower motor-neuron weakness or paralysis, which means the affected limbs are usually flaccid. Therefore, the affected foot is weak with flabby muscle tone, causing foot drop, which is a common polio sequela. The knee-joint muscles usually retain some strength, enough to bend the knee. So, the condition would produce footprints with more or less of a straight-line drag rather than a C-shape.

However, when a person has an upper motor-neuron disorder, such as the gait impairment seen in a later phase of mild to moderate stroke, there would be a C-shaped drag that is called circumduction gait. That's what we see here. It is because the involved leg muscles are partially paralyzed but are in a spastic state. Being unable to bend the spastic knee joint normally, the person has to swing the leg and foot outwardly when walking in order to avoid stumbling on the weak hanging toes, making C-shaped drag marks. At the lab, every day I see how Zenon walks and I don't think those C-shaped drags we see here are his shoe prints."

Steve and Helen thanked him for his explanation.

Dr. Jupitren asked, "Do you suspect anyone else?"

Helen answered, "Maybe, I'd like to show you this." Helen handed a few pages of printouts to Dr. Jupitren. "Last night, Steve and I checked the level III info on a dozen of Acmeon's people. Here, please look at this printout on Zenon."

Reading it, Dr. Jupitren said, "I knew about his past weapons-possession charges. But these strange moneys going to his Polowealth Bank here in New York from the foreign bank in Singapore are begging for more explanation. Besides, he has been transferring money to the Games and Rifles Company. He might have bought a gun, maybe a rifle. We can't be sure. As far as I know, he is not into hunting."

Steve added, "Money went to Zenon a few times from a questionable man, Brandon Cumlen. We have no information on Cumlen except that he has Singapore bank accounts. He is not among the Acmeon clients. But we found Brandon Sweza among Acmeon's clients. It was odd to find that Brandon Sweza also has Singapore bank accounts. We tried to probe into their files, but we could not get through either of theirs because Singapore banks seem to use a different computer language of their own on certain special accounts.

First we need to find if Brandon Cumlen and Brandon Sweza are one person with two different surnames. Then, we need to find why Zenon is receiving money from Cumlen. We also need to find out whether Zenon buys weapons from the rifle store. If so, why? Are they involved in counterfeit Wafers? If they are, we could trace the manufacturers."

Having listened to Steve's long report, Dr. Jupitren slowly remarked, "Unfortunately, we don't have any hard evidence. However, one thing is clear. Internally, we have to follow security rules strictly to safeguard Acmeon Lab's operation. Also, as you suggested before, I'll ask Bill to increase the police surveillance for Acmeon after the usual work hours."

Helen said, "For now, I wish we knew who the last night's intruders were and how to stop them. I suspect the intruders were trying to sabotage our operation or steal the Wafer formulas."

Steve, looking at Dr. Jupitren, cautiously said, "I think Helen is right. And I have some new ideas about Acmeon's security issue. May I mention them now?"

"Certainly," Dr. Jupitren answered. "I need everyone's ideas and suggestions. But, first let's go to my office and talk some more. We were standing up all this time."

The three of them walked to his office within the Plant and sat down on chairs.

Steve said, "You mentioned that you will ask Bill to increase the police surveillance, but I think they should patrol in unmarked cars or in civilian clothes to confuse the felons. And, in the event they dare to break in again, wouldn't you like to prepare yourself with newer, more effective countermeasures?"

"What kind of countermeasures?" Dr. Jupitren asked.

"I have been thinking that the Dronettes could be one of the countermeasures."

"How?"

"The Dronettes are remotely-controlled spy machinery, as you know. They come in extremely small sizes and yet are capable of emitting powerful LXG beams within a few hundred feet of trajectory. So I have been thinking about our company's latest Dronettes, which are night-vision equipped and will take pictures in the dark. Using the image transmissions from the Dronettes, you will be able to identify the intruders wherever you are, since the images will be transmitted to your Thumputer."

Helen asked, "What will you do when you receive the intruders' images to your Thumputer?"

"It depends on what you want to do." Steve answered. "The Dronettes under your command can remotely shoot LXG stunning rays and temporarily disable the intruders. And the same command will automatically alert Bill's team, who then would stop or catch them right then and there."

"It sounds pretty good." Dr. Jupitren said. "But, I'm afraid there might be certain practical problems with the remote LXG use."

Helen, looking at Dr. Jupitren, asked, "Do you mean we need some kind of permit from the police or the state?"

"Yes, probably from the state. There must be some limitation on the remote use of it. I'll check with Bill about the latest rules."

While Steve was making more suggestions about the security issues, Dr. Jupitren looked at the Po Kim's oil painting on the wall as he used to do whenever he came in the office. For a split second, he had a feeling that the picture frame seemed a little tilted. Without saying anything, he walked toward the picture frame, thinking that he would adjust it. Touching the frame, he took a closer look at it from different angles. Abruptly he turned around, beckoning Steve and Helen to pay attention to him. Putting the right hand's forefinger on his pouted lips, he quietly asked for their silence, and at the same time, he pointed at the back of the picture frame with his left hand. He hand gestured to them to come forward, close to the picture.

Steve and Helen, in total silence, walked toward the picture and directed their attention to where Dr. Jupitren was pointing. Out of his pocket, Dr. Jupitren took a penlight and turned it on. Their eyes anxiously followed the light, peeking behind the picture frame. To their astonishment, there was an electronic bug, live and active with electric wiring and micro-antennas!

All three of them silently thought, "Those two intruders must have put it in there last night!" It must have already sent the three Acmeonites' conversation to the sinister eavesdroppers! The three of them looked at each other speechlessly with "Now what?" and "What do we do next?" expressions.

Without much delay, Dr. Jupitren grabbed a pen and a sheet of blank paper and quickly jotted down some words, which Helen and Steve read silently:

"Hush! When I ask you what you think about my idea, just say you agree with me."

Helen and Steve nodded yes to Dr. Jupitren.

Dr. Jupitren moved close to the picture frame, hoping the remote eavesdroppers would hear him better and said, "Well, Steve, your plan sounds reasonable and well thought out. I agree with you, especially about the idea of having the security guards around Acmeon's premises without police uniform. I will ask Bill to have his officers cover Acmeon Lab during the weekday nights, starting at 5:00 pm and continue until 8:00 am the following morning, and for twenty-four hours during the weekends. All officers on duty will carry LXG stun guns and counter-ray(CR) devices in addition to their usual firearms. What do you think?"

Steve and Helen said at the same time, "I agree with you."

Dr. Jupitren continued. "I will also ask the police to show up within a couple of minutes when we send them our distress calls. Well, it will cost Acmeon extra funds to have such increased police coverage, but it will be a very worthwhile service for us. Don't you think so?"

"I agree with your plan. I will feel secure when I'm alone in the office."

Steve, likewise, said loudly, "Certainly I think it will be well worth the expense."

Dr. Jupitren said, "Steve, I suggest that you carry your LXG and CR device with you whenever you come around here. And, of course, I will let Bill's officers know who you are and tell them how they can identify you from distance. I don't want their friendly fire landing on your back!"

"Thank you. I will carry my LXG and CR device with me."

Dr. Jupitren said clearly, turning in the picture's direction, "Good. I will ask Bill to start the police coverage right now, starting this evening. Well, it's getting late. Let's continue tomorrow and discuss more about improving the security of Acmeon. Thank you very much, Steve, for your suggestions."

"You're welcome. I have some more ideas about Acmeon's security, but I'll save them till the next time we get together."

"Are we leaving now?" Helen asked.

"Yes." Both men concurred.

They did not touch the bug and left the Plant's office room. When they were outside, Dr. Jupitren said, "You can easily imagine that they will not dare to break in again for a while if they heard what we said about hiding the increased police force and arming ourselves with LXG guns and CR devices. In reality, I have the feeling that we won't need the extra service of Bill's security unit for a while."

Steve said, "I think you may be right. But just in case the eavesdropping bug did not work properly and they heard only some parts of our conversation or misunderstood us, they may still try to break in. For that possibility, I'll have my Dronettes ready. If those intruders dare to break in, this time my Dronettes can blitz them, even if they are hiding in the dark."

Dr. Jupitren said, "Steve, thank you for your thorough foresight and concern for Acmeon's security. But I'm afraid you are overextending yourself and your work at Perihelion Energy might suffer."

Steve responded, "I'm thinking of keeping my extra vigil here at Acmeon possibly for two or three more nights only. If they don't show up within that time, I'll assume they eavesdropped our conversation and decided to chill out. Meantime, by using my Dronettes, I will monitor Acmeon Plant remotely from my office or from my apartment."

"Thank you, Steve, for minding Acmeon Lab so seriously. But please have Bill and his men do their professional job, and you should be very careful not to get in any harm's way."

Helen agreed with Dr. Jupitren and asked Steve to take it easy.

The next day Dr. Jupitren took the eavesdropping device from behind the picture frame, disabled it by disconnecting the wires, and brought it over to Bill Warren. By just looking at the device, Bill knew right away which manufacturer made it and which groups of criminals in the area were using it. He said, "This will help us to find the crooks. It will be a matter of time."

Then Bill said, "Jules, as you asked me a few days ago, I spoke to Richard Hunt, who, as we all know, is an expert in e-FPAR (electronic-Forced Probing and Retrieval). He works for the FBI. In fact, my youngest brother, Dominick, and Rich's niece Pam are getting married in a few weeks. Pam is from Singapore. So Rich's family and some of my family will be going to Singapore to attend their wedding. At any rate, I explained to Rich that we needed to get level III information on two Brandons' files. I told him that we got most of their general level III information but not their Singapore bank-accounts records, which are the very ones we are interested in."

"So, what did Richard say?"

"Well, after a good couple of hours of research, Richard called me back and said that according to the Singapore banking system, for the kind of information we want to have we will have to show up at the Singapore bank in person."

"Really? Why? Can't he get the information here through the computers?"

"The answer is no. Richard said when he tried to get the information by talking to the bank directly, they turned down his request. But, Jules, don't worry about it. Since he and I are going to be in Singapore soon for the wedding anyway, we will find some time there to get the information. Rich told me that the bank said no to his request because, first of all, we don't have the account owners' written consent or request. Secondly, the International Trading House in Singapore and Singapore's banking system have a special security clause to mandate our personal appearance in order for them to confirm our identity. Actually, Cybermax Asteroid, the bank's cloud computing company, is asking us to register through a high level of bio-identification, including retinal recording, before we can review anyone else's banking record."

"Really, that strict? I suppose if we had Singapore accounts, they would protect our accounts in the same strict way."

"I think so."

"At any rate, soon you and Rich will become in-laws."

"That's right. Lucky me! By the way, Jules, about the bank account matter… let's keep it only between you and me until I return to New York."

"Yes, I'll remember that."

Later in the evening, Dr. Jupitren met with Steve, who came to Acmeon just to measure the dimensions of the building structures where the Dronette surveillance system would be installed. Helen was still in Dr. Jupitren's office, where the three of them had another unscheduled meeting.

While discussing Acmeon's security issues, to confirm some information on LXG and CR devices, Helen said to Steve, "I know that the original inventors who designed the LXG stun gun also invented the CR device. As far as I know, the CR device, just like a shield, is capable of bouncing the LXG ray and will echo it back to the LXG ray's originator. That's all I know about them."

"Then what would happen, Helen, if you shot the LXG first?"

"If the enemy is armed with a CR device, I'll be stunned or knocked out as soon as I shoot my LXG at the enemy target, because my ray will boomerang back to me. But the enemy will not get affected by my LXG ray. Isn't that right?"

"Yes, you're right. But if you and your enemy both had CR devices on, then neither you nor the enemy would suffer from the bouncing rays."

"That's good to know."

Steve continued. "Likewise, if we shoot the degree-III trigger, without CR devices on us, we are risking serious self-injury. That's why, to be on the safe side, we should use only the degree-I or II trigger when we are unsure about whether the enemy has activated CR device or not. By the way, US federal law banned the use of the degree-III trigger anyway because it's lethal when fired repeatedly. One needs a special permit to carry the third-degree trigger. Without the permit, you would get felony charges just for carrying it, let alone using it."

Helen responded, "So, we all should be armed with CR devices, anyway."

"You both are right." Dr. Jupitren said. "Very recently, Bill told me that every officer in his precinct soon would have CR devices, too. As of now, no one has both LXG and CR devices except Bill and you. Steve, please order the LXGs and CRs from Espio-Nano Company for Helen and me. We've got the permits last week."

"Sure. I will."

CHAPTER 9
STEVE AT ESPIO-NANO COMPANY

Days went by. As expected, no intruders approached Acmeon Lab's premises again. The Acmeonites' staged conversation must have thrown cold water on the intruders' scheme. Dr. Jupitren's love for the Po Kim's oil painting led him to spot the hidden bug behind the picture frame. Because of the incident, he earned a stretch of quiet time and could devote himself to do more work in his office.

Steve did not need to come to the Acmeon area often, and yet he spent a good deal of time in front of his computers for Acmeon-related work in the evenings. Collaborating closely with Dr. Jupitren, Steve completed programming the eight-digit serial number system of the Dream Wafers replacing the old six-digit system.

In the meantime, Steve did not slacken in his vigilance. While awaiting Bill's answer to the question on whether remote LXG shooting was legally permissible or not, Steve continued his work on the new Dronette. First, he upgraded the Dronette to perform night-vision functions. Then he attached the remotely controlled LXG stun gun and micro-CR to the Dronette.

Steve had been to the Espio-Nano Company a few times to purchase parts for the Dronettes. There he also ordered LXGs and CR devices for Dr. Jupitren and Helen. During his subsequent visit to the same company, Steve discovered something unexpectedly.

At Espio-Nano Company, the salesclerk Jim said to Steve apologetically, "Here, I have these two LXGs that you ordered. But I'm sorry, Mr. Spencer, we just sold the last CR device to someone else, the kind of CR you were looking for."

"Didn't you tell me, Jim, that you had one CR in stock when I spoke to you yesterday?"

"Yes, I did, but I'm terribly sorry. I didn't realize you needed it so soon. I'll order two CRs for you today. It will take a week or so before we will get the next shipment. We will call you as soon as we receive them."

At that moment, a female worker's voice rang out from an adjacent office behind Jim's counter. The voice asked him, "Excuse me, Jim, do you remember the customer who bought the CR device this morning?"

"Yeah, why, Joyce?"

She asked him loudly, "I know he bought one set today. And didn't he order just one more?"

"Yes, only one more. Any problem?"

"You wrote two, not one. I will correct his invoice entry."

"Sorry, it's my mistake."

Joyce, still in a loud voice, said, "One more question."

Jim looked at Steve and said, "I'm sorry. Just one moment, please." Then Jim turned his face toward her office direction and said loudly, "Joyce, please hold it. I need to attend to a customer now. I'll answer you later."

However, Steve gestured to Jim and said, "It's all right. Please go ahead and answer her. Take your time." Steve became curious and wished to find out more about the CR-device deal and pretended he was not in any rush, turning pages of a catalog on the counter, listening to their conversation.

Jim said to Steve, "Thank you." Then he turned around and asked, "Joyce, what's your next question?"

"Oh, Jim, I'm having trouble with your squiggly handwriting. The last name of the same customer, does it start with *J* or *Y*?"

"It should be *Y*, Yanovsky."

"Thank you, that's all."

Jim processed the sale of two LXGs for Steve and continued with the CR orders. Jim read the invoice to Steve, verifying the order items. But because Steve was busy thinking about Yanovsky's CR purchase, he could not hear Jim well.

Jim asked Steve, "Sir, would that be all? Can I show you anything else from our catalog?"

Straightening up, Steve answered, "No, thanks. I'll take those two LXGs with me. Please call me when you get my two CR orders."

Steve continued to wonder, "Why is Yanovsky buying another CR device after he already bought one? Besides, it didn't take much for me to find who bought what and how many from this store. So, anyone else can easily find what I'm buying here, too."

Then Steve said, "I have a special request, Jim. Would you please keep my purchase information in strict confidence and let no one else know about it, because my job is very sensitive. OK?"

Jim nodded and said, "Certainly. I'll keep it that way as you wish."

Steve thanked him and was turning around to leave the Espio-Nano Company's counter area when Joyce came out of the back office and walked toward Jim's front counter. Steve was able to see her face from the corner of his eyes. He could not believe who came into his visual range. She was the baleful palmist speaker, a board member of the AAPA meeting that he'd stumbled into months ago.

"What is this? Is there any connection of this Espio-Nano company with AAPA?" Steve felt puzzled.

When Steve returned to his office in Perihelion, he received a call from Dr. Jupitren. "Hi, Steve, are you very busy?"

"Yes, a little, as usual. May I help you with something?"

"Yes. First, I wanted to let you know what Sergeant Bill said about the remote LXG shooting."

"Are we permitted to shoot remotely?"

"Yes, but only in a life-and-death situation or in self-defense. And you can use only the first degree of LXG-ray."

"I see. Then, it's unlikely that we can shoot the intruders remotely. We were thinking about Acmeon Lab after working hours, when there would be no one else but the hypothetical intruders. So we can't call that a life-and-death situation or self-defense."

"I agree with you, Steve. Now, I have another matter to ask of you. Bill took off for a week or so to attend his younger brother's wedding. Before Bill left, he told me that while he is away, John Collins, who is Bill's first assistant, would be in charge of routine operations at the precinct. And Bill and I thought it would be proper for me to introduce you to John. So I would like to ask you if you could come over to Acmeon today after your work, and you and I would go over to meet with John and his security team."

Steve answered thoughtfully, "Yes, I will come by. But I'm wondering if I am being recruited for something other than computer-related work."

"Oh, no, I just want you to keep an open communication with them. In case you need to speak to Bill directly for anything about Acmeon's cybersecurity, and if he is away or unavailable, you would get in touch with John Collins instead. I don't want you to assume any dangerous tasks. Bill or John will not let you be in any harm's way. Steve, you are still our trusted extramural consultant, and I know you're eager to help me. I want to be sure you're protected in any situation. That's why I want you to meet John Collins and his crew. Please continue your relationship with us as before."

"Thank you, I appreciate it. I'll be there around six o'clock."

After talking with Dr. Jupitren on the phone, Steve couldn't stop thinking. "When are they going to break in again? What if they break in while Bill is away? Bill's men don't even have their CRs yet. Will Helen and Dr. Jupitren be safe from their attack? I should let them arm themselves as soon as possible with the LXG and CR I'm getting. However, how could Helen or Dr. Jupitren actually handle the LXGs? Shooting the LXGs shouldn't be any part of their jobs!"

In the middle of thinking about this, suddenly Steve felt uneasy. "What am I getting into? Why am I doing this for Acmeon? I should not assume the role of Acmeon Lab's security guard. Yet, something compels me to go on fighting the unseen saboteurs."

As he kept on pondering, Helen's sweet face and her whole person loomed up in his mind. A new sentience and realization dawned on him that he was eager to do the work for Acmeon because, more than anything, Helen was there. Suddenly, he realized he missed her very much. At the same moment,

Dr. Jupitren's austere, pensive face and his hardworking stance flashed in his mind, too.

On his way to Acmeon Lab, he stopped at the City Library. The librarian, Jimena Munez, greeted him. Steve asked her for the library's monthly public-meeting schedule.

Jimena was friendly and asked him, "Is there anything in particular you're looking for?"

"Just want to know what kind of lectures or meetings you are having here lately."

Jimena handed him the monthly meeting schedule. He started to read it carefully but tried to make his visit appear to be a casual one and said, "Ms. Munez, you have all those books there. Nowadays, do people really read them?"

"Not as much as they used to years ago, as you know. Everyone is into e-books, tablets, and super-smartphones these days. We have been freely lending Kindle Fires, Newtons, or Nooks to our patrons, too."

While he let her talk, Steve spotted the familiar AAPA meeting in the schedule, which would be at 8:30 on Friday evening. That's two days later. He thought of something as he looked at the location of the meeting room. Then he pointed to the opposite-end bookshelves, marked "Section *M*," which was farthest from the meeting room.

"Ms. Munez, what kind of books do you have over there at the Section *M*?"

"*M* is the music section. History of music, tons of operatic-music interpretations, special effects, like the four-dimensional music collections, pop music, and so on."

"I see, thank you. By the way, do you have individual reading rooms for average patrons?"

"Yes, upstairs. We have a dozen of those reading rooms."

"Would I be able to use one of the reading rooms on any weekday evening?"

"Surely, at any time while the library is open. The individual reading rooms are free and not much in use in these summer months."

"Do I need to check in here with you first?"

"No, it's not necessary during the summer. You can walk straight upstairs and just turn the 'occupied' dial-sign on the door. And the reading room will be all yours. If you need any help, I'll be here all this week during the evening shift."

"Thank you very much, Ms. Munez."

Steve went to Acmeon Lab, where he gave the two new units of LXG to Dr. Jupitren. "I was able to secure these two, but the CRs will be available by sometime next week."

"Thank you very much, Steve. I'm wondering how Helen is going to handle this awful thing."

"I believe she will be able to manage it pretty well if she really has to do it. By the way, while I was getting those LXG's at Espio-Nano company, I found something puzzling and I wanted to tell you. Accidentally, I discovered Yanovsky bought a CR there and placed another order for a CR set, most likely for Zenon Zelinski. I didn't know what to make of it. When I went to my office, I checked level III information on Yanovsky but didn't find anything suspicious."

"That's certainly puzzling and disturbing information. Since we don't have any hard evidence against them, let's keep it quiet until we discuss the matter with Bill."

Then, Steve and Dr. Jupitren went to the police precinct and met with John Collins. They discussed Acmeon's security matters. They exchanged information on their contact methods and communication codes. Later, John introduced Steve to his team of officers.

As Dr. Jupitren had reassured him earlier, Steve felt at ease and glad that he was acquainted with John and his crew. The only thing they all felt uncomfortable about was that none of them had been armed with CR devices yet, except Steve and Bill.

CHAPTER 10
LXG SHOOTING EPISODE

The next evening, after work hours, no one was at Acmeon Lab, but all the building lights were on as usual. Practically all the lights in every room of the lab, streetlamps, floodlights, and movement sensors were in working order. It made the area look rather pleasant and calm. It emanated a deterrent air against any subversive ruse.

On his phone, Steve communicated and confirmed the whereabouts of John's team. They monitored the Acmeon buildings, using remote surveillance devices and patrolled the nearby streets.

Later, Steve called Helen. "Are you on your way to Acmeon?"

"Yes, I'm about to pass the K Street diner, Allegory. Did you arrive at Acmeon already?"

"No, not yet. I just thought of a different plan. Helen, why don't we meet at Allegory first? We will have something to eat there and then go to Acmeon Lab. I have a lot to tell you. Now, the Acmeon area is well covered. I've just communicated with John's team. Three of them are around Acmeon, patrolling in civilian clothes. Shall we meet at Allegory in five minutes?"

"OK, Steve. I'll take a table in the mezzanine."

Soon, Steve arrived at Allegory and met with Helen. He seemed a little tense. He looked around, gave a sweeping glance at the crowds downstairs, and sat down facing Helen. He quietly pointed to his belt, where his LXG stun gun and CR device were holstered. Helen gave him an I-see-them nod and said, "Uncle Jules gave me a new LXG this morning and he said you got them for us from the Espio-Nano. Thank you, Steve."

"You're very welcome. It's my pleasure."

"I'm going to learn how to handle it. I may need your help."

"Sure, I'll do my best. You will do all right." Steve whispered to Helen, "Is this place safe for us to talk?"

"Yes. Allegory is no place for scheming rogues. I'm sure there are no eavesdropping bugs around here. The woman owner of this diner, whom I trust, is a close friend of my Mom's."

"That's reassuring."

"There are only a couple of diners like this in the whole city. Many diners are turning into huge kiostrants nowadays, the hybrid of kiosk and restaurant."

"Yeah, I myself often go to the kiostrant near my company," Steve said while browsing the menu. "And I usually grab a lunch pack from the vending machine. While eating, I charge my laptop, Thumputer, and wrist-phone batteries."

Steve put down the menu, saying he would order a curried rice plate. He continued. "At lunchtime in the kiostrant, I see busy young people hurry in just to pick up the hot food that they preordered through their wrist-phones. Very often, they munch their sandwiches, simultaneously talking on their Thumputers or wrist-phones. Often they drink coffee while standing, just like at the highway rest-stop restaurants in Europe. When done with the coffee, they rush back to their offices."

Helen said she would order the same curried rice.

Steve said, "It dawned on me that it has been a long time since we sat at any dining table together like this."

"True. We were always busy with our work. You have been working practically on two jobs lately. Uncle Jules is very grateful for what you have done for Acmeon. I thank you, too."

"You're very welcome. I enjoy working for Acmeon."

"Uncle Jules and I feel we're lucky to have you for our cybersecurity."

"Well, Helen, I want you to know your presence at Acmeon makes all the difference for me."

"Thank you for saying that." Helen quietly realized that whenever he was around, she, too felt extra happy to be with him.

A waiter came to their table and took their orders.

Steve told her about his recent visit to the Espio-Nano Company, where he learned that Yaru bought a CR device and placed an order for another CR set. Steve said, "I wonder if Yaru is getting the extra CR for Zenon."

"I never imagined Yanovsky would be involved with stun guns." Shaking her head, Helen said, "Maybe Billy can have one of his officers, Louis or Jack, frisk Yanovsky under a pretense and then check on the fed permit for his stun gun and the CR. At the same time, Louis or Jack can question what Yanovsky is up to."

"Not a bad idea." Steve nodded and said, "If he is frisked, he will think he is having a bad day and might divulge some clue. We will ask Dr. Jupitren about this idea later. By the way, Dr. Jupitren said Bill went out of the States to attend a family wedding. And, I went to the precinct with Dr. Jupitren yesterday to meet John, who is to cover Bill during his absence. I also met John's crew."

The waiter returned to the table with their two orders. Helping himself to the curried rice, Steve said, "I have heard about the report by Dr. Martin Prince of King's College, London that India is one of the few countries with lower incidence of Alzheimer's disease for a couple of reasons."

"What reasons?"

"He said that the people in India meditate and pray more than others do, and they also eat more curry, which contains turmeric. It's known that the curcumin in turmeric preserves memory function by inhibiting beta-amyloid accumulation in the brain."

"Interesting! But about the prayer, I wonder if people in India really pray more than we do."

"I suppose all people pray more or less to similar extent."

"I think so, too."

"Sorry, Helen, I've gotten distracted. Going back to what I was telling you, I saw someone at the Espio-Nano spy-gear store. I couldn't believe it. A female worker at the store happened to be the board member I saw at the AAPA!"

"Really? What do you make of it?"

"The woman was unfamiliar with Yanovsky's name and asked Jim, the salesclerk there, how to spell his name. So, I think it's unlikely that Yanovsky is involved with the AAPA. Anyway, I ordered CR devices for you and Dr. Jupitren while I was there."

Unexpectedly, Steve's wrist-phone buzzed, stopping his conversation with Helen. The call came from John Collins, who was patrolling the Acmeon area.

"Steve, I want to tell you about an incident we just had." John sounded excited, talking rapidly. "There were two men wearing night-vision goggles sneaking around Acmeon Plant's north entrance. We approached them and asked if we could help them, as they seemed lost. They were quite startled when they saw us. Suddenly, they dashed toward their car, a brown SUV. They ran fast, and we could not catch up to them. So, I had to use my stun gun. I pulled the second-degree trigger, and one of the two slumped down, but the other one got away. We will watch the stunned one on the ground until he wakes himself up. Please let Dr. Jupitren know what's happening here. Are you far away from Acmeon Lab?"

"No, I'm at Allegory. I can get there in five minutes. John, you guys don't have any CR devices on you yet. Do you?"

"Nope. Not yet. Only Bill has one, but he is not here today, as you know."

"I have one CR device on me," Steve said. "You need protection just in case the escaped one returns and starts shooting his LXG. I'd better hurry and come over there now."

"Great. Thank you. Guess what? Actually, we just took one CR device off the stunned guy's belt. He did not have enough time to use it against us. If he had activated his CR, I would be the one lying down here. You know that."

"Of course! You were lucky. John, can you activate that set right now?"

"Yeah, I'll try. But—Oh my God! Steve, the guy who got away…Ouch! I got hit…in…"

"John! Are you all right? John, what's happening? John!…Good grief! Something happened. The line went dead."

Steve quickly told Helen about what he'd just heard from John and asked her not to come to Acmeon with him but to stay behind and notify Dr. Jupitren about what had happened. He tore out of K Street and headed to Acmeon Lab, checking his LXG and CR device on his holster.

As it had happened many times before, things did not go the way Steve anticipated.

He pulled his car all the way up near the north entrance of the Plant and saw three bodies lying on the ground. What a dreadful scene! All three of Bill's men, including John Collins, were lying there on the ground.

Cautiously Steve stepped out of his car. Checking for any hidden dangers around him, Steve approached them and saw John and two other patrols, Jack and Louis, were in obvious distress. Clutching their heads with clawed hands, they groaned in a daze.

"Thank Heavens! They are not dead. They are just stunned and dazed. What happened in the last five minutes?" Steve thought to himself.

He shook each of them, calling them by their names. He tried to jar them out of their daze. He got ice packs out of his car and placed them over their foreheads to hasten their recovery.

By then, having heard Helen's report, Dr. Jupitren rushed in and immediately checked the LXG-stricken officers' vital signs and examined them for any obvious injuries. "Fortunately, none of them got seriously hurt. Steve, did you see anyone leaving when you arrived here?"

"No, I didn't. When I came in, I was very surprised to see them lying on the ground. A short while ago, John must have been standing right here as he was telling me on the phone about the two intruders. John said he knocked one of them down with his LXG. But the other one got away. John was going to keep an eye on the stunned one on the ground until I arrived here. But as you see, both of the intruders are gone!"

"As my car was turning around the North Road corner," Dr. Jupitren said, "a car passed fast in my opposite direction, making a long screech, and I couldn't help but watch the driver. He had heavy goggles on. In the passenger seat, another figure was slumped, leaning on the window of the car, which was a brown SUV."

"That's them! John told me about the brown SUV just before he was hit! The one that ran away must have returned and shot his stun gun at John and then Jack and Louis, too. Seeing all three of them fall down, he must have crept over here and dragged his accomplice into their car. They must have barely cleared the incoming North Road corner when you passed them. I came by the South Road. Maybe, that's why I didn't see them."

"Well, Steve, I'm glad you are OK. I think John and the other two will recover soon. It seems they were hit with the second-degree LXG trigger."

Remembering what John had told him on the phone seconds before he stopped talking, Steve checked John's holster. It was empty. The forfeited CR was gone.

Steve explained to Dr. Jupitren how one CR device was supposed to be on John's holster. "But the intruder who returned to fetch his stunned accomplice, in that hurried moment, must have taken the CR device back out of John's holster."

"The intruder must have a shrewd mind." Dr. Jupitren said.

Hoping to see any image of the intruders, Steve and Dr. Jupitren checked the Plant's outside CCTV camera. However, they found the camera charred and mangled by the intruders. They could not retrieve any recorded image of the incident. Those intruders must have destroyed the camera with their LXGs as soon as they came in the area. Feeling disheartened and angry, they stood there for a while speechlessly.

Breaking the silence, Steve said, "As we replace the damaged camera, why don't we install CR device on the new camera?"

"A great idea." Dr. Jupitren responded. "Starting at the north entrance first, we may install the CRs on the cameras over the Plant's other entrance doors as well…But if they use a handgun instead, the CR would be powerless. Yet, I think the sneaking intruders are likely to use LXG because it makes much less noise than the guns."

In a while, John and the other two regained consciousness. They drank some cold soda that Dr. Jupitren brought to them. They still seemed dazed.

Trying to get his senses back fully, John shook his head from side to side. He then said to Steve and Dr. Jupitren, "Thank God, we are all alive. Steve, while I was talking to you, the escaped one returned and shot me with his stun gun. The ray hit me in my belly, and I doubled over, falling down instantly. But I faintly knew what was happening around me and saw Jack and Louis fall down right there next to me. But I couldn't do anything for them. My body was paralyzed."

Steve asked, "What happened then?"

"I must have passed out completely. That's all in a flash."

"John, look at your holster!" Steve said. "The returned guy must have taken the CR device back out of your holster. See here? It's empty."

Only then did John realize that his short-lived booty was gone, but his own LXG was still tightly fastened to his holster on the other side.

Eventually all three of them regained consciousness fully.

A while later, Dr. Jupitren called Bill in Singapore and told him what had happened at Acmeon.

Bill anxiously asked, "Are my guys really all right now?"

"Yes, they are. We called their families and explained what happened to them. They understood the situation well and remained calm. All three of them just went home, picked up by their families."

"I'm glad none of my guys needed to go to the hospital. Did you get any clue who those intruders were?"

"No. Unfortunately, they destroyed the surveillance cameras with their stun guns, and they got away after shooting LXG at three of your guys!"

"What a shame! Everyone in my squad should have had CRs. What about a CR for you and Helen?"

"Steve is getting our CRs by next week but meantime he got LXGs for us."

"I see. Well, it certainly looks like we've got another challenge there. Whoever they are, we should catch them sooner or later."

"Bill, where will you be staying?"

"We've already checked in at Park Royal Hotel on Kitchener Road. It's quite warm, and people are all shut in the air-conditioned buildings."

"How is Rich doing?"

"He and his wife also checked in at this hotel. Four of us had the dinner together. But what happened there at Acmeon is bothering me, since I'm so far away."

"Don't worry, Bill. We'll manage. I'm sure John and his team will do all right."

"Thank you, Jules. In a short while, I'll call John at home and ask him how he is doing. Also, I'll give him some suggestions about how to follow up on the incident. If it's not too late, I'm going to call Jack and Louis as well to see how they are doing and will cheer them up."

"I'm sure they will appreciate your call. From a medical point of view, they all will feel fine after a good night's sleep."

"That sounds good…And here, Rich and I will go to the Singapore bank tomorrow to get the information on Brandon Cumlen and Brandon Sweza. Also, we will find out where and why they are sending their money."

"Thanks a lot, Bill. Enjoy your visit there, and have a wonderful time at the wedding."

CHAPTER 11
STEVE PREPARING TO GO TO AN AAPA MEETING

The following morning, Steve called Dr. Jupitren to ask about how John and the other two officers faired. Dr. Jupitren said that he had just finished speaking with John Collins, who reported feeling OK by the morning and the other two also sounded all right.

At that point, unexpectedly Steve said to Dr. Jupitren, "I'm sure you remember what I told you about how I stumbled into the AAPA meeting at the City Library a few months ago. This time, I'm thinking about sitting in on their next meeting, which will be at 8:30 this evening, at the City Library."

"Really? But didn't you tell me they don't allow nonmembers admission?"

"Yes, I did. They don't, but I would get in by asking to become a member, disguised as an older person, just like most of them."

"Are you sure you want to do that?"

"Yes. And once I'm in there, I might find new clues about their schemes against Acmeon Lab."

"Well, I can't force you not to. I appreciate what you're trying to do for Acmeon. But please be extra careful. I'll alert John Collins."

"Thank you. I'll be very careful."

Later, Steve called Helen. "Hi, Helen. I didn't call you last night. It was too late. We were all tied up till midnight. You must have heard about it from Dr. Jupitren already."

"Yes, he told me. It's fortunate that none of them got hurt. Did you rest up well?"

"Not really. I had a jolting dream, and I woke up early in the morning."

"Did you think of using Dream Wafers again by any chance?"

"After only one bad-dream night? No, I did not. Now, I'd like to ask you to do something for me this afternoon."

"Really? What is it?"

"Actually, I meant to ask you for it yesterday at the Allegory but John's call took away my chance to speak to you. You once casually said that at the art studio, you had special cosmetic lessons on disguising techniques. Didn't you?"

"Yes, I did. Why?"

"It may sound odd and silly, but I need your disguising artwork on me for this evening. I'm going to sneak into the AAPA meeting incognito to find what kind of schemes they are making against Acmeon. Would you do the disguise work on me?"

"Sure, but isn't it dangerous to be at that meeting uninvited?"

"Not really. Maybe there is a small risk, but I'll take it. At worst, I'll tell them all off and then bolt out or call John Collins."

"You sound like you're really determined. It will be very interesting to see how you appear under a disguise. What time do you need to be there?"

"No later than eight this evening. How much time will you need to disguise me into an older person?"

"About a good half hour. But how old do you like to appear to be?"

"Most of those AAPA attendees seemed like they were in their late fifties or mid-sixties. So I want to be about that age. Can you do it?"

"Of course. I have everything I need to do the disguise work except one item."

"What's that?"

"The voice imitator."

"The voice imitator? I've heard about such a thing existed but never seen it and never thought of it as part of your disguise makeup."

"The idea is that if your face looks much older, your voice should go with the age."

"I see. Where do I get the voice imitator, and how does it work?"

"I know where we can get one. It is a mouthpiece. But usually it's a good idea to try it out a few times on yourself, because it comes in different sizes. Usually, if you still have all thirty-two teeth intact, you need size A, and if you have lost your four wisdom teeth and have only twenty-eight, then the imitator's size is B, etc."

"That's interesting!"

"In the center of the mouthpiece, it has an electronic voice box that mimics the older person's voice as you speak. You can produce a man or boy's voice of different ages, even a woman's voice. You can actually fine-tune it manually."

"Really! Where should I go to get it?"

"To save your time, I'll go with you. It's a bit hard to find that place. If you come to my Acmeon office by four thirty, I'll do the disguise makeup and then we will go to the voice-imitator place together."

"Thank you very much, Helen. That sounds great."

Later, Helen's disguise work was easily finished. Steve appeared old, with gray hair, wax-wrinkled facial skin, fake age spots, and a gray beard. Then, they went to a place to get the voice imitator.

He picked the size *B* voice imitator, which was a perfect fit for him. With the voice imitator on, it was impossible for anyone to detect his identity, as his voice was so fitting to his appearance. Helen suggested that he should practice an age-appropriate gait and posture as well. As they walked outside, people thought Helen was walking with her father.

Helen said, "Steve, this evening, you are not Steve Spencer from now on. Here…"

Out of her bag, she took out an outdated driver's license and said, "This is an old driver's license of my Uncle Hank Oswin, my Mom's cousin. From now on, your name is Hank Oswin. I know your birthday is in December, but now you're going to remember Hank's birthday, which is August first. It happens to be the same birthday as mine. But Uncle Hank is thirty years older than me. Now, look at Hank's picture in the license and yourself in the mirror."

Steve couldn't believe his eyes. As he looked at himself in the mirror, his disguised face appeared like an exact replica of Hank's face in the license! Steve thought, "How skillful she is! And how thorough she is to think of all the details in advance despite such short notice."

He exclaimed, "I'm really impressed. What can I say? What a skill!"

Helen responded with her usual modest manner. "Come on, Steve…I mean Mr. Hank Oswin."

"Thanks a lot. When did you find the time to prepare all the materials and tools?"

"I told Uncle Jules about what we were up to, and he gladly let me have some free time today. He said you spoke to him this morning about your evening plan."

"Yes, I did. Thanks to you and him. So, Uncle Hank is your Mom's cousin. Then, how is Uncle Jules related to your parents?"

"He is my Mom's older brother. He is three years older than Mom."

"I see. Does your Mom have any other siblings?"

"No, just Uncle Jules."

"Thank you. I've got it all. Now, your Mom's cousin Hank Oswin has the same birthday as yours, August first. And you said he is thirty years older than you. Since he is now almost fifty-six, you must be almost twenty-six. Right?"

"Yes, you figured it out all right. I'll be twenty-six in a few months. Steve, we still have one more thing to settle."

"What's that?"

"As you see in the license, its expiration date lapsed three months ago."

"I was thinking about it, too. What do you suggest I do?"

"If you don't want to take any chances, we will drive another fifteen minutes to get to John Collins's office and see him there. Do you want to see John?"

"John? Why?"

"At the Industrial Espionage Unit, John is in charge of ID cards of all sorts, either detecting the fake ones or making tactically fake IDs. In your case, he will help us to get a tactically fake one with Hank's photo and an active expiration date on it. John will make the whole thing a legitimate document."

"Of course, I'd gladly take the extra fifteen-minute ride."

Steve called John, "Do you feel all right after the last evening's LXG incident? No headache or sick feelings?"

"I feel all right. Thank you, Steve for what you did for three of us last evening."

"Don't mention it. I'm glad you're all right." Then, Steve explained what he and Helen were coming to see him about. John said that Dr. Jupitren already spoke to him about Steve's evening plan.

At John's office, in order to get Hank's license modified, John took Steve's fingerprints along with a photocopy of Steve's own driver's license, and he wrote Steve's Thumputer serial number in a ledger. Then John sent an e-notice to the DMV's special-service. John told Steve that the Hank's new license would expire in seven days.

It took only a few minutes for John to change Steve's ID. Now Hank's name and date of birth were registered in Steve's mind as well as in John's official ledger.

John said, "I heard you'll be at the City Library tonight around eight. We'll keep an extra eye around the Library. Good luck with it, Steve…I mean, Mr. Oswin."

"Thank you very much, John. Now I feel I'm a real detective with a new name!"

On the way out of John's office, Steve said, "Helen, earlier you told me that Uncle Hank OK'd your idea to let me use his old license. Since we now actually have the new license with his photo in it, shouldn't we let him know about it and thank him?"

"You're right, Steve. You are so proper. I'll call him right now."

Helen called Uncle Hank to explain how the remaking of his license went and thanked him for trusting her judgment. She also told him that the new license was good for seven days and handed the phone to Steve. He likewise thanked Hank for allowing him such a special privilege and said, "I will be very careful not to get into any mischief for your name's sake!"

As they were driving back to Helen's Acmeon office, Steve said, "Helen, would you do one more thing for me?"

"Sure."

"Will you call the City library at eight tonight? In the library, there is an *M* section with music books. When you call in, the librarian might be at her desk, very close to the AAPA meeting hall, which is near the library's entrance door. The opposite end of the meeting hall area is the *M* section. I want you to distract her attention by asking any questions about music. She said there are books on operas. You may inquire about *The Magic Flute* or *La Bohème* and their libretto authors, composers, names of the prima donna, and premiere years, etc., and make the librarian stay far away from the AAPA meeting hall for several minutes. The longer the librarian stays in the *M* section the better it will be for me."

"What if the librarian uses a computer search to answer my questions and remains at her desk?"

"Well, if I were to handle such a situation, uh…I would tell the librarian that I was looking for the anthology with green covers on so and so subject, or something like that. Since she cannot find the 'green covers' readily from her computer search, she would leave her seat to walk toward the *M* section. At any rate, please use your imagination to keep her away from the meeting-hall entrance for several minutes, starting at eight sharp."

"OK. I understand. I'll remember to call the librarian at eight."

Helen and Steve returned to Acmeon Lab, where Steve had left his car before they went to the voice-imitator dealer's place. Standing next to his car, Steve clasped his own hands together and assumed an old man's stance, saying in jest through his voice imitator, "Being a fifty-six-year-old, now I must be under Hank's spell, because I feel suddenly much older already. Helen, do you still like me and love me?"

With a playful smile, Helen answered, "My heart has not changed an iota over the years. You may be much older now, but you are still the lovely Steve Spencer I know!"

Still in an old man's stance, Steve slowly bent forward, kissing her on her hand and said through the imitated oldish voice, "Thank you, my dear!"

"You're welcome, my sweetheart." Helen said with a smile.

For a split moment, Steve felt their comic dialog struck something deep in his heart, carrying them in a flash far into the imaginary future.

Then, Helen drove to her mother's art studio for some of her own projects. Steve went to his Perihelion Energy Company office to fetch his Dronette-6.12, which he planned to bring to the AAPA meeting.

CHAPTER 12
CHROMEGA WATCH

Steve packed the Dronette-6.12's remote control and the foldable infrared keyboard for typing. He double-checked the dronette's camera, night-vision sensor, acoustic reception, and LXG as well as its counter-ray capability. Then he made sure his new driver's license was with him.

The AAPA's meeting time 8:30 pm was approaching.

Near 8:00 pm, the summer's daylight finally began to give way to twilight. Steve, now Hank Oswin, drove his car slowly into the City Library's parking lot. He could see the AAPA attendees showing up one by one. It was getting a bit dusky, but Steve recognized the woman who was getting out of her car. Having seen her twice already, Steve knew she was Joyce from Espio-Nano.

It was 8:02 pm. Steve entered the City Library. He saw the librarian, Ms. Munez, talking into her wrist-phone, walking toward the *M* section, far away from the AAPA meeting-hall area. While Ms. Munez was at the *M* section, Steve walked upstairs to one of the reading rooms with his odd-looking equipment bag, unnoticed by anyone.

From the second floor, Steve could look down at the AAPA meeting-hall entrance. The double door was half-open. He quickly sent the Dronette-6.12 into the air. Quietly passing through the open double door, it flew inside the hall and perched on the ceiling in a dark spot of shadow thrown by the ceiling ornaments. Remotely, he adjusted its camera angles.

He then locked up all the Dronette appurtenances in the wall cabinet. As he left the reading room, he made sure to turn the "occupied" dial-sign on the door.

Steve called Helen. "Thank you for keeping the librarian away from her desk. Good job! You called the librarian at the right time, and I was able to set up the Dronette inside the hall, where they're about to start their meeting. With the remote control in my pocket, I can record the whole meeting while sitting in the meeting hall. The librarian did not see me with my funny bulky bag. Thanks to you again. Now, I'm downstairs, and this time, I'll try to get inside the meeting hall myself as Hank Oswin."

"Do you want me to come over there now and help you with anything?"

"No, not now. If I need your help, I'll call you right away. Thank you, Helen."

At the meeting-hall entrance, Steve greeted the door monitor, "Good evening. I'd like to register for the meeting."

The door monitor peered at him, "Sir, are you a new AAPA member? I don't think we've met before."

"No, we have not. How do you do? I'm Hank Oswin."

"Hi, I'm Anna."

"I'm not a member yet but would like to become one, starting this evening."

"I need some information from you and the membership-application fee."

"Ah, the fee. That I'm not prepared for. I did not bring my credit chips. But may I start the application by giving you all the necessary information except the fee? And, sit in as an auditor?"

The door monitor reluctantly said, "All right. You may sit in, but voting or voicing your opinion is not allowed till you become a member."

"I understand. Thank you."

"Before you go in, I need some information about you. You are Hank. How do you spell your last name?"

"*O-s-w-i-n.*"

"May I see your driver's license?"

"Yes, here it is."

Checking the license closely, Anna said, "So, you are almost fifty-six years old. Oh, your license is about to expire in seven days. Did you know that?"

"Yes, I did. Thank you for reminding me about it anyway. I should go to the DMV soon."

"How long have you been a psychic?"

Steve got a bit hesitant but said, "Only…for several years."

Anna asked him other routine questions. Her last question was "Any other skills or interests?"

"I've done some reading in astrology and *I Ching*, the book of changes. I subscribe to the monthly *Palmistry* magazine, and I'm about to get the palm-reading software."

Without further fuss, Steve was given a seat in the back row. He looked up at the ceiling and made sure the Dronette was still there with the appropriate camera angle.

As the meeting started, Steve pushed buttons on the remote control in his pocket to let the Dronette transmit AV recordings of the meeting to his console in the individual reading-room upstairs.

Joyce, the meeting coordinator, said to the assembly, "At the last meeting, we decided to slow down Acmeon's Dream Wafer production because it was hurting our business. To achieve the stated goal, during that meeting, you commissioned me to make contact with someone at Acmeon Lab. I have made some progress. The person who is affiliated with Acmeon Lab is scheduled to come here today to discuss his plan with the board during the intermission of this meeting."

Just like at the last AAPA meeting, the whole assembly spent a good deal of time discussing the new palm-reading software. Then they elected a few writers among them to publish advertising articles in various news media, promoting and bolstering several members' fortune-telling feats and reputations. One clever speaker suggested that those writers should incite the public to become more aware of their anxieties and seek consultation with psychics.

After a while, the general meeting went into an intermission. Joyce and four board members were about to walk into an adjacent boardroom through a door.

Steve quickly ran upstairs to maneuver the Dronette-control console so that he could remotely move the Dronette to the boardroom. When the last board member was entering the boardroom, Steve was able to slip the Dronette into the room just before the door was closed. The Dronette wasp perched on the ceiling of the boardroom with its open-camera views.

Sitting in the individual reading room upstairs, Steve monitored the whole board meeting remotely. Near the end of the board meeting, someone walked into the boardroom. The upper half of his face was hidden under a low-set tiger-striped beret and a pair of dark eyeglasses. Most of the lower half of his face was hidden behind a curled-up, wide shirt collar. Throughout the meeting, he revealed neither his full face nor his full name. They just called him "Mr. O."

Steve thought to himself, "If he is affiliated with Acmeon Lab, in which department is he supposed to be working? Well, I can't see his full face, anyway. Maybe he's a disgruntled former employee of Acmeon?"

The beret man said, "You hired me to destroy Acmeon's Dream Wafer program by sabotaging their software and the computers. But I'm obligated by another agent to do something to the contrary. I cannot talk to you freely about my deal with the other agent now. So what I'm saying is that my men cannot do the two conflicting jobs at the same time. If my men succeed in what you asked me to do, my other contract will be lost. My greater interest is hanging on that contract.

Therefore, I'm asking you, AAPA board members, to give me a little more time to work it out before I get the results you want to see. In two months, if I can't produce the result, I will refund you the entire prepayment amount."

Steve's plan was to let the Dronette shoot LXG at the man, knocking him out soon after he steps out of the building and check his identity. Or pin him down and call John to arrest him.

Steve noticed the tiger-striped beret man was about to leave the boardroom unexpectedly by a backdoor that would open directly to the parking lot. Steve had anticipated that the beret man would leave by the main door that he came in through and kept the Dronette near the door. The backdoor was at some distance from the main door. By maneuvering the console, he tried to have the Dronette follow the beret man by the backdoor. However, Joyce closed the boardroom door quickly right after the man left the room, and Steve could not get the Dronette out of the room in time.

Despite all the smarts the Dronette had, it would not fire its stunning ray against anyone outside the room, because its vision was blocked. Steve helplessly watched the beret man fading away from the building. There was no time to call for John's help.

Steve decided to run after him. By the time Steve ran downstairs and rushed out of the building, the beret man took off his dark glasses and ambled, haughtily swaying his torso sideways, getting closer to his parked car. About fifty feet away from his car, he remotely started the car, which was parked with its front facing the parking-lot exit.

Steve sprinted toward him. But only a couple of steps ahead of Steve, the man just got inside his car, unaware of Steve's fast approach, and was about to close the car door. Steve swiftly grabbed his left wrist forcefully and shouted, "Stop the engine!"

Frightened by Steve's sudden grip and shouting, the man took one quick, scared look at Steve. In that short moment, Steve could see the man's whole face clearly.

Sensing the imminent reality, the man hurriedly hit the gas pedal, making the car jolt forward out of the parking space, and sped away toward the exit sign. It was utterly impossible for Steve to hold on to the escapee's wrist. In the dark, Steve heard the car door slam noisily from the accelerating car's reverse momentum. He could not read the license plate as the rear lights weren't turned on.

Stopping his reflex-like chasing motion, Steve stood there, only to find in his hand a wristwatch that he'd just pulled off the beret man's left wrist.

Inside the library, Steve scrutinized his loot. It was an expensive Chromega watch with an expandable gold-plated wristband. Steve said to himself, "After all, I've got this wristwatch! Well, I also have recorded the information about what the beret man was going to do against Acmeon Lab as enticed by the abominable AAPA."

All that time, officers Louis and Jack were right outside the meeting hall entrance watching the crowd but did not recognize Steve because he acted the perfect Hank Oswin. Besides, he ran downstairs from the second floor reading room and rushed out of the library's main door. Louis and Jack concentrated on the general meeting hall area and missed the whole action that went on outside in the parking lot.

The following day was Saturday. Being off from his Perihelion Energy job, Steve went to Acmeon Lab as he'd planned to attend part of the symposium there and listen to Dr. Jupitren's presentation. He also brought the Dronette's AV records on the AAPA's meeting and the Chromega watch to Dr. Jupitren and Helen. He told them in detail what happened at the City Library the previous evening.

At Steve's suggestion, Helen quickly checked the previous night's GPS data on Yanovsky and Zelinski. Neither Zelinski nor Yanovsky was at the City Library on the previous night. Yanovsky stayed in his home, and Zelinski was in the north shore of New Jersey all evening.

Steve handed the Chromega watch to Dr. Jupitren and said, "When Bill returns from his trip, please ask him if he could get any information or clues from the watch or its owners."

"Yes, I will. Thank you, Steve. That's a very good idea."

Helen irately said, "Shouldn't we file an official report to the police now? And stop the AAPA's plot and punish them for attempted libel, mayhem, or something?"

Dr. Jupitren said, "Helen, I appreciate your concern, but about the beret man, should he find out what police are doing with AAPA, he may hide away, and we may lose him for good. When the police is ready to get him, we will make the AAPA contact him and Bill or John will arrest him. And about the AAPA, Steve's monitored records on the AAPA meeting will be sufficient evidence to lodge severe charges against them. Meantime, we should reinforce our security measures and continue our vigil while Bill is away."

"I think you're right, Uncle Jules. Now I see we need to be careful about how to approach the whole thing and when to report to the police."

Steve added, "The tiger-striped beret man said he was affiliated with Acmeon. Who could he be?"

Helen asked, "Can we review the Dronette's AV recording on him one more time? Maybe we can identify him."

The three of them carefully checked the Dronette's recorded images but could not identify who he was.

"What do you think, Steve?" Dr. Jupitren asked.

"The beret man could be deceiving the AAPA. He may not be affiliated with Acmeon at all. Let's wait and see what Bill and John might suggest we do on our part."

As the morning symposium hour was approaching, Dr. Jupitren went to the Symposium Hall. Helen went to the Plant, where she would collate and set up Dr. Jupitren's lecture materials that he would be using later for the second part of his presentation. Steve took an audience seat at the Symposium Hall to hear Dr. Jupitren's lecture.

CHAPTER 13
QUESTIONS AT THE SYMPOSIUM

The Acmeon Lab's two-hundred-seat Symposium Hall was full with eager audience. Most of them were neuroscientists and physiologists with special interests in the science of dreams. A renowned scholar from the Dream Research department, Bio-medical division of Munio Veritas University, Rome introduced Dr. Jupitren to the audience. After long, respectful applause, the audience slipped into expectant silence.

Dr. Jupitren stood tall at the podium, quietly reminding everyone about his nickname, 'the humble giant.'

"Distinguished international visiting scholars, colleagues, ladies, and gentlemen, I am standing here today with my gratitude and much indebtedness to you all for your personal support and your special interest shown in my work on the Dream Wafer concept.

The United States' nationwide Human Genome Project, as you all know well, went through the completion of human-genome mapping several decades ago. Its impetus is still widely felt in many frontiers of medical specialties.

Gene-based prediction of certain diseases' susceptibilities, genetic engineering of new drug development, chemico-genetic cancer treatment, and other gene-based therapies are only a small part of the larger picture of gene-oriented research and development… Genetic modification on multitudes of brain chemistry has made it possible to modify the contents of dreams, albeit the related technology is still in its infancy…"

After giving in-depth explanations on the whole topic of modifying dreams with Dream Wafers, Dr. Jupitren said he was ready to answer any questions from the floor.

A hand went up in the audience. "Dr. Jupitren, do you believe in dream interpretation? If you do, how do you think your Dream Wafers might affect the dream interpretation, since the dream contents per se are now changed artificially with the Dream Wafers?"

Dr. Jupitren replied, "I certainly do believe in dream interpretation. If a person is actively utilizing the Dream Wafers, interpretation of the dream may produce an approximate portrait of the person's psyche. However, once the person is free from the effect of the Wafer, that is, after one to two weeks of Wafer-free period, the reported dreams will reflect the natural state of the person's mind. This will allow resumption of the conventional dream interpretation in psychotherapeutic settings.

However, please allow me to make a counterpoint here. Even though Dream Wafers modify the person's dream, I believe the modified dream is still replete with many significant meanings worthy of interpretation. It is because the very process, by which the Dream Wafer candidate answers the questionnaire items, is influenced by his *unconscious determinants*. Therefore, dreams induced by Dream Wafers could be a reflection of the unconscious domain of the dreamer and are appropriate targets for meaningful interpretation.

Thus, we could maintain a hypothesis that the Dream Wafer candidates are already starting their *dream-work* when they intentionally respond to the questionnaire items while awake!

I know this hypothesis is not in full alignment with the classical psychoanalytic view, which says the *dream-work* proper has been largely the function of the unconscious."

"Thank you, Dr. Jupitren for your answer," responded the audience member. "And, if I may, I have another question. Was there any psychological or physical dependence on the Dream Wafers among your clients?"

Dr. Jupitren shook his head gently as he began his reply:

"As far as I have observed since the inception of Dream Wafer, there was no true dependence in terms of withdrawal-related recurrent or rebound anxiety dreams. It is because the Dream Wafer is not a conduit through which external chemicals are infused into one's system.

Dream Wafer's function is to *modulate selected genes' expression,* which will lead to certain activity levels of selected endogenous chemicals. Those chemicals eventually will help to achieve desired brain function, thereby inducing requested themes of dreams. In other words, Dream Wafers let the person use his inner chemical resources rather than delivering extraneous chemicals that would induce dependence.

Most conventional psychotropics on a long-term use may induce the involved cells' receptor sensitivity-changes and resultant dependence. Unlike most psychiatric medications, the Dream Wafers were seldom used on a long-term or continuous basis anyway. Another factor for dependence proneness lies in specific chemicals' unique metabolic pathways, which vary widely according to the substances in question. Dream Wafer's mechanism of action did not trigger such receptor sensitivity-changes or dependence-prone metabolic processes.

On the psychological side, some clients reported that in the middle of their sleepless nights, they were apprehensive about having recurrent "bad" dreams and felt tempted to use their Wafers right then and there. However, adhering to the instruction that they received from my office, so far, every one of them refrained from using it at a wrong time of the night. They were emphatically informed that the Wafer was programmed to run for seven to eight hours, and, therefore, it must be applied the same number of hours before their scheduled wake-up time.

My team is currently working on how to address this very issue so that someday people might use a Dream Wafer version with a shorter duration of action. However, because the sleep architecture is built on everyone's unique non-REM stages and REM sleep structure, we have to negotiate with the Nature very cautiously so as not to cause complications such as night terror or nightmare or somnambulism."

"Thank you again, Dr. Jupitren."

Dr. B from the floor asked, "Would you briefly summarize the dream theories, from either psychological or biological viewpoints, that existed before you embarked on your dream-changing work?"

Dr. Jupitren nodded and began his explanation:

"During the first part of this presentation, we have already given a lengthy tribute to the earlier scholars' psychological thoughts on dreams such as Freud's instinct and unconscious theories along with Carl Jung's archetypes, symbolisms, and creative function of dreaming. We also reviewed Adlerian view of dreams' problem solving functions. Then we touched upon some of the biological theories. Therefore, please allow me to review briefly a few highlights of biological dreamology findings that I did not cover yet.

Toward the end of Neo-Freudian era, two Harvard scholars in 1977, proposed the *activation-synthesis model of dream mechanism* when the pendulum of dreamology research began to swing from psychology to the side of biology.

Those two scholars were John Allan Hobson and Robert McCarley from Harvard. On EEG, they saw brain wave bursts during REM sleep, which were traced to be due to the neural activities from the pons, geniculate body, and occipital lobe of the brain. Then those activities propagated to the prefrontal cortices, where dreams were synthesized. Therefore, they put the dreams as epiphenomena secondary to the intrinsic pons area's physiological activities.

However, other researchers reported PET scan results that proved the putative dream activities actually took place in the limbic area, the brain's emotion centers, rather than in the global frontal cortices. Another researcher described his patients who reported complex dreams while they had damaged pons. Those reports minimized the importance of pons in dream formation. As a result, such observation questioned the exactitude of the activation-synthesis model.

On the other hand, some theorists, such as Francis Crick and Graeme Mitchison in 1983, thought dreams had no meaning to be interpreted. They said the dreams were a mere physiological neural process by which the brain ridded itself of clutters of memories so as to let the brain clean and be ready for other important tasks. Their theory was known as "*reverse-learning hypothesis*" on the function of REM sleep or as "*unlearning theory*" of dreams. Their theory later was challenged by other researchers' conflicting data.

Some researchers discovered new physiological functions of REM sleep apart from its role in dreaming. One such new discovery came years ago from a New York ophthalmologist who stated that rapid eye movement stirs the intraocular fluid, which lets the needed oxygen to reach the cornea while eyes are closed during sleep. Without the REM-stirred oxygen, the cornea would lose its viability.

Furthermore, branches of biological science such as cytogenetics research, gene-expression theories, functional genomics, epigenetic findings, and gene-informatics sprouted with great vigor.

Not surprisingly, some new biological dream theories provoked skepticism about the validity of psychoanalytic views of dreams. However, those new biological discoveries on dreams could not prove that a psychoanalytic view of dreams was invalid. If it were invalid, it would not have helped so many people for so many years through dream interpretations.

I found myself placed in the middle of the great whirl of new genetic-research movements of many varieties and innumerable new discoveries in genetics of dreams. The impetus to my Dream Wafer concept came from the findings that REM sleep architecture could be modified by a number of special chemicals. Furthermore, those chemicals were under the expression of various identified genes and epigenomic elements.

Therefore, I started probing the possibility of dream modification through ways of modifying the expression of those genes. As a result, such changed genes induced changes in selective chemicals. Finally those chemicals produced changed contents of dreams, namely the *requestable dreams*."

"Thank you very much, Dr. Jupitren."

The next question came from a genetics historian. "Dr. Jupitren, I'm curious if anyone else ever had a Dream Wafer-like idea. I mean, was there any earlier published work or hypothesis proposed by any pioneers in dream modification?"

Dr. Jupitren responded:

"I, too, was curious about that. So far, I have not found any published theories or thoughts on dream modification. However, when I was a third grader in primary school, my classmate's father wrote a story for the children in the school magazine. The title was 'Dream Store'. In that story, children bought dreams of their choice from a colorful vending machine that was run by an old wise man, who acted like the Wizard of Oz. Afterward, recalling the 'Dream Store' story from time to time, I imagined, since my medical school years, the possibility of modifying dreams through biological means.

Another dream-modifying idea came remotely from a legend of Native Americans of the Great Plains. They believed that there were good and bad dreams in the air. They made dream nets, which looked like circular butterfly nets, called "dream catchers" that they hung inside the tepee or lodge, often on a baby's cradleboard. They would decorate the dream catchers with feathers, beads, and wind chimes around their net hoops, hoping that they would beautify the good dreams.

Their legend says that the good dreams pass through the center openings of the dream catcher to reach the sleeping person but the bad dreams are trapped in the web of the net. Then, at the dawn's light, the trapped bad dreams would perish.

Primitive was the legend, it nevertheless conveys unremitting human desire to control dreams.

Then, just a few years ago, I found a visionary who had a related idea, not from a scientific angle but from a poet's viewpoint. He lived circa two hundred some years ago, who was an English poet, dramatist, and physician, Dr. Thomas Lovell Beddoes. He had written a poem on dreams, among other writings of his. The title of it is 'Dream-Pedlary,' and I must have a partial copy of the poem here with me."

Dr. Jupitren leafed through his lecture notes and said, "Aha, here it is. If you allow me, I shall read it to you. I happen to have only the first half of the poem here with me." With that remark, he cleared his throat and began reading:

'Dream-Pedlary'
If there were dreams to sell,
What would you buy?
Some cost a passing bell;
Some a light sigh,
That shakes from Life's fresh crown
Only a rose-leaf down.
If there were dreams to sell,
Merry and sad to tell,
And the crier rung the bell,
What would you buy?

A cottage lone and still,
With bowers nigh,
Shadowy, my woes to still,
Until I die.
Such pearl from Life's fresh crown
Fain would I shake me down.
Were dreams to have at will,
This would best heal my ill,
This would I buy.

Dr. Jupitren added, "The legend about Dr. Beddoes says that he was a deeply troubled young man. Born in Bristol, England, he wandered through many places in Europe. In Göttingen, he studied medicine, motivated by his hope of discovering physical evidence of a human spirit that survives the death of the body.

Since he was looking for a dream that would best heal his ill, I have imagined from time to time that he would have bought the Dream Wafers for himself, if he was our contemporary."

The genetics historian thanked Dr. Jupitren for the interesting answer.

Another audience member, Dr. D posed a question. "I'm a life member of the Rabbinical Seminary of Mount Sinai. I would like to hear your experience with any of your clients who might have reported any religious conflicts regarding the use of the Dream Wafers."

Dr. Jupitren cautiously answered, "I had a small number of clients with some religious concerns. Most of them wanted to know whether the Dream Wafers would result in permanent dream-modifying effects. Some questioned if dream modification would constitute an act against God, and they were hesitant to use their Dream Wafers. Presumably, they did not want to have any prolonged, persistent brain effects from Dream Wafers, fearing they would lose their communication with their Deity or be discredited of their rabbinical ability.

My answers to them have been that Dream Wafers would not cause any permanent ill effects on their basic brain functions. And if they were concerned that dream modification might be an act against God, then they should refrain from using Dream Wafers. It should be a personal choice.

Most of my religious clients felt relieved to learn that the Wafer effect was safe and time limited. And they were happy that their anxiety dreams improved with Dream Wafer application and their sleep likewise improved while having their dreams of choice."

Dr. D thanked Dr. Jupitren for his brief and clear answer.

Next, Dr. E raised a question, "I wonder if you could tell us about any other motivating forces that prompted your Dream Wafer invention."

Dr. Jupitren gave a brief, thoughtful pause before replying:

"Well, I can think of two parts of my answer to your question. The first was the pressing need we had decades ago to develop extra treatment methods for veterans with PTSD.

I myself had served in the US military operations in Afghanistan as an army psychiatrist. Many times, I experienced extremely stressful life-threatening events. The stress levels I coped with were very similar to what the military servicemen I treated had to endure. I suffered from insomnia and nightmares as much as they did. In addition, I had to cope with other physical symptoms secondary to visceral form of leishmaniasis, which only aggravated the PTSD symptoms.

After I was discharged from the services, a number of veterans with PTSD came to my office asking for help. Searching for effective ways of helping them and helping me in the equal measure, I reviewed then-prevailing methods of PTSD treatment. Soon I realized that although supportive psychosocial therapy was an essential part of treating PTSD, many of my patients needed more than what the psychosocial treatment could offer. Some anxiolytics and antiadrenergic medicines were in the PTSD treatment regimen but they, too, had side effects or dependency problems. In order to overcome those treatment methods' limitations, I decided to work on Dream Wafers, hoping they would ease the anguish of veterans with PTSD.

Of course, not only the wartime combat casualties but also many other horrific events in our civilian life, including natural disasters and various life-threatening circumstances, would precipitate PTSD. Thus, developing additional treatment methods for PTSD became all the more important and urgently needed."

"The second part came from many discerning people's growing awareness about what the meritocracy-centered modern culture was doing to people. Such cultural mores were prone to put emphasis on outer appearances, instant visible merits, or apparent strength rather than encouraging people to look for the inner counterparts of them.

As a result, we were gradually losing our old knack of introspective reflection in our daily life. Gradually, we grew unfamiliar with our inner selves. In a way, we were straying from ourselves. I believed this had eventually led us to experience an anxiety, just like the kind of anxiety a stray child would feel. This particular anxiety seemed to be the basis of modern man's dread and a cause for the discontentment of our time. Probably, that's why more people were reporting anxiety dreams.

Therefore, I wanted to help people by relieving their anxiety dreams with Dream Wafers.

Additionally, I hoped Dream Wafers would help people reclaim their inner-directedness, because in the process of ordering dreams, while answering the long questionnaire, candidates are urged to pay quite a bit of attention to what and who they are. Similarly, when they review their Dream Wafer-induced dreams, they repeat the self-searching introspection all over again. Eventually, as a result of the repeated self-searching, they would become more aware of their inner authentic selves.

I was afraid that without sustained self-view or introspection, our inner real authentic selves would fade out of our grip and retreat to the dungeons of psychological exile. I hoped people's interest in dreams, making choices of their dreams through Dream Wafer in particular, would let them become more introspective. However, I am not saying that Dream Wafer experience is the only way to reclaim our knack of introspection. There are other ways, as you are well aware of, such as various forms of psychotherapies, meditations, prayers, and multitude of individual-specific ontological experiences."

Dr. E who had asked the question expressed his concurring sentiment and thanked Dr. Jupitren.

The moderator of the symposium announced that he would accommodate only one more question from the floor in view of the time constraint.

Dr. F asked, "So far, we have heard of only proper use of Dream Wafers. However, wasn't there any abuse or misuse of Dream Wafers?"

"Yes. Unfortunately, some abuses and abuse potentials have loomed up, which were rather similar to the worldwide history of narcotics. Misuse due to lack of information on Dream Wafers has been a much less serious problem than the outright malicious alteration of the Wafers to produce counterfeits.

Reportedly, various new versions of counterfeit Dream Wafers were abused for mind-controlling or brainwashing purposes by certain cults. In some countries the dictator regimes altered Dream Wafer derived chemicals to keep their people in the dark. Some other regimes used Wafer derived chemicals in spray form to control riots. There, the Wafer turned into weaponry. Ostensively, some sectors of underground profiteers had altered Wafers only to promote and sell grotesque dream scenes with wild escapades of violent or pornographic nature targeting naïve thrill seekers.

I am afraid, without stricter governmental prohibition, those greedy reprobates will continue to mass-produce counterfeit Wafers for illegal profits. As far as the current countermeasures are concerned, the US government is establishing international agreements with neighboring countries to prohibit any trafficking of counterfeit Dream Wafers across the international borders. In a similar vein, Acmeon's genuine Dream Wafers have been categorized as a Class-V(five) controlled substance by the Federal Drug Administration, leaving very little room for abuse within the States."

There were more hands up for further questions. However, the moderator announced that the scheduled Q & A session was over and the main part of the symposium should be adjourned.

Having listened to Dr. Jupitren's whole presentation to the end, most of the attendees left the symposium feeling that the purported claim on the Dream Wafers' therapeutic potential was not overstated.

Steve sat through Dr. Jupitren's presentation, including the Q & A session. He felt he learned a number of new things about dreams and Dream Wafers, although some of it was too technical for him. For the rest of the day, he went to the Annex Library to read more on electronics subjects in relation to Dream Wafer programs.

Following the main lectures at the Symposium Hall, five renowned dreamology researchers with a prior invitation from Dr. Jupitren accompanied him to his Plant office for the second part of the day's presentation.

As requested by Dr. Jupitren, Helen brought out six sets of *clean-room suits with headgear* for the five guests and Dr. Jupitren. One of the five visitors said that he had never worn such a suit before and made everyone laugh. Dr. Jupitren briefly described the need for strict air-quality control. He explained the nature of the various technical support he was receiving from the engineers of ANSI (American National Standards Institute) in order to maintain the West Room and the whole Plant in good order.

Finally, he opened the West Room to them. Everyone appeared a little funny in the one-size-fits-all clean-room suits with headgear, but they cautiously approached the *virtual brain*, making keen observations.

Dr. Jupitren explained the notable research value of the *virtual brain* model, which was sitting in the center of the room. He explained and demonstrated what the *virtual brain* was capable of doing. On his commanding inputs, the model brain displayed many neurophysiological feats.

One of them asked Dr. Jupitren, "Apart from the *virtual brain* per se, I see over there, on the west-side wall of this room, a large window, which does not appear to be any ordinary brand of window we know of. Besides, I have noticed that the curtains consist of a few layers of gray sheaths that are moving by themselves. Those curtains were opening or closing with no apparent rhythm or reason. What's the significance of them?"

"I have carried out number of solar-energy related experiments on the *virtual brain*. I discovered that there were subtle differences in the quantitative test results when the same experiments were carried out under artificial lights versus direct sunlight.

Likewise, depending on whether it is solar energy or an incandescent light, genes differentially processed the light-energy-related neurotransmitters.

Therefore, in order to have a standardized test basis, I conducted light energy-related experiments only when the direct sunlight of specific luminosity was available. In order to maintain the constant luminosity of the room, this light sensor mobilizes the necessary number of curtain layers. That's why you see their constant movements.

So, on a day like today when it is partly cloudy and a bit windy, in order to maintain the constancy of this room's luminosity, we will see the curtains busy opening or closing, namely, subtracting or adding layers of sheaths. On a clear day, the curtains would move relatively slowly, depending on the passage and strength of the sunlight. As a result, the room will maintain a selected degree of brightness.

In reality, I had to work often under artificial lights because I usually came to this West Room after my usual daytime work. Furthermore, for certain projects, I had to use yellow lighting to minimize light-energy-related errors whenever I made some patterned coating that involved micro-photolithography. Therefore, wishing to have the ideal experimental setting under solar energy, number of projects had to be postponed according to my schedule as well as the weather."

One of the visiting researchers asked another question. "May I ask you, Dr. Jupitren, how long it took you to build this *virtual brain*?"

"Well, I have not measured the exact time, but I may say, longer than two hours a day for seventeen years, almost without skipping a day, except for personal days off or family vacations here and there."

"I see. Is this *virtual brain* model secure in this room?"

"Yes, I think so. This room is fireproof and its original design documents and technical manuals are kept in a separate fireproof safe as well.

Regarding its safety— as a model, the virtual brain has a lot of neuronal circuits, although they are only a fraction of a real brain's circuits. Its circuits are extremely brittle. Therefore, I kept a rule not to open this room to anyone else. However, today we broke the Lex non scripta."

Another visitor commented with a question. "Your *virtual brain* model has an outer encasing structure that looks like a real person's head and neck. What's the function of this white baseball cap-like structure on the model's head? That makes it appear all the more like a real person wearing a white baseball cap."

"I'm glad that you pointed it out. The cap-like structure is a detachable EEG electrode lattice, and the front visor is a handle that conceals the wireless brain-wave microtransmitter units. I hold it by the handle when I align the electrodes on the model brain or remove the whole EEG lattice."

"Is this *virtual brain* capable of its own thinking?"

"No, not at all. However, it can perform many complex tasks instantly only if a human hand presses the Enter key. Its mathematical IQ, once the Enter key initiates it, is way above genius level, for which there are no known test batteries yet. From its memory and cyber-consultation function, it will answer a whole gamut of questions ranging from daily life facts to quantum physics."

"Does it have any clinical application programs?"

"Yes. A number of them especially on medical diagnoses and treatment issues."

"Would you give us one such example that can be used in psychiatry?"

"Well, CASD (computer aided speech differentiation) is one of them. It's an adjunct diagnostic tool. Usually, psychiatrists are well versed about making differential diagnosis on incoherent speech. However, at times, certain abnormal speech can be a diagnostic challenge. In such cases, CASD will tease out, for instance, fragmented speech due to brain syndrome caused by alcohol or other CNS (central nervous system) depressants apart from semantic condensation of schizophrenic speech or bipolar disorder's speech reflecting flight of ideas, etc."

"Does the incoherent patient need to be brought in here since the CASD is a part of the *virtual brain*?"

"No, not the patient himself. I just bring the recorded speech samples and gene information of the patient for the *virtual brain* to process them. However, its drawback is that it is without the nonverbal, visual diagnostic cues of the patient."

"I see. But I wonder how it works."

"It first analyzes the speech by utilizing the grammatical or semantic data files, acoustic tonality profiles, word count per unit of time, and multilingual dictionaries, etc. And then, the final answer comes from the individualized gene vulnerability-screening for various major psychiatric disorders."

"Thank you, that's very interesting."

Among the *virtual brain*'s multiple functions, the gene-mandated chemical processing on dream formation was the main topic during the long stretch of Q & A's and Dr. Jupitren explained the model brain's electro-chemical and genetic physiology.

Near the end of the session, one of the guests asked, "We have just seen your demonstration that the model brain is capable of the basic sensory functions, such as visual, acoustic, or olfactory perception once the Enter key initiates them. So, my question is how this brain model would respond differently to two conflicting sensory inputs. For example, would it respond to euphonic sound differently from cacophony?"

"So far I have seen that they invoke quite different responses in these two separate locations of the temporal lobes and their association fibers. Incidentally,

I recently discovered a very interesting phenomenon that occurs in those two areas when you give two opposing stimuli at the same time: while one area actively responds to euphonic sound, the other area that is for the cacophony gets suppressed below normal level when measured by their action potential amplitudes. This finding could be extended to explain why we are unable to focus fully on two different subjects simultaneously." Dr. Jupitren pointed out those two locations using a needle-sharp laser-beam pointer. "I have confirmed it by cross-checking them with f-MRI findings of real persons' brains."

The guest asked another question. "If it is so, I wonder how the two sites will respond to power-saw noise versus religious music."

"I don't have any specific answer to that question. I've never compared such unique situations.

Perhaps, you were thinking of the earlier groups of experimenters who tried to focalize the spiritual brain regions. They reported their findings about the so-called 'God spot', and religiosity and the like in certain areas of temporal lobes and right inferior parietal lobe of human brains. Were you thinking of such research?"

"Yes, precisely. I was thinking about those groups of researchers. Are you not running any similar research with this *virtual brain*? I mean trying to define religion, God, spiritual experience, and so on with certain brain sites?"

"No. Not at all. However, I have come across some reporters, who misrepresented such human-subject experimental results and derived far-fetched anti-religious conclusions. Later, with those conclusions, some of them tried to incite atheism by artificially confining the deity within the human brain. They tried to bolster atheism by claiming that God was a neuronal phenomenon in a specific spot in the brain. Atheists feasted on that kind of claims. I believe the original experimenters must have had pure scientific goal to study brain's regional functions but some people, as I've already said, had distorted the results to bolster their anti-religious claims.

I eschew such line of sensitive research. Those reporters or the interpreters of such experiments remind me of what the former Russian Premiere Khrushchev said in his antireligious propaganda speech. He gave the speech to the Soviet Communist Party's Central Committee. His speech was about one of Russia's astronauts. You may remember the Russian cosmonaut Yuri Gagarin, the first human who traveled into space aboard *Vostok 1* in 1961. Reportedly, Nikita Khrushchev said, 'Gagarin flew in space, and he said he saw no God up there.' But it is hard to believe Gagarin really said it. I remember reading Gagarin's colleague and friend Colonel Valentin Petrov, who publicly clarified that Gagarin did not make such a statement."

The doctor who listened to Dr. Jupitren's explanation responded, "I concur with you. Thank you very much for sharing your thoughts on that particular subject."

After some more of Q & A's and demonstration on the *virtual brain*'s gentronic structures and theories, the second part of the presentation session was adjourned.

CHAPTER 14
BILL'S REPORT

Soon after returning to New York from his trip to Singapore, Bill came to Acmeon Lab one evening and met with Dr. Jupitren. Helen and Steve were there, too.

Dr. Jupitren said, "Bill, before you give us your report, I want to tell you something unusual that happened while you were away. Actually it is how Steve secured this Chromega watch." Dr. Jupitren handed the watch to Bill and gave him an account of what happened at the AAPA meeting in the City Library. Steve supplemented it with additional details of the incident.

Carefully tucking away the Chromega Watch, Bill praised Steve and said, "I admire your courage and ingenuity. You've practically done our job! I will take this watch to our forensic unit and check it out."

Then, Bill said. "In Singapore, as we expected, the church wedding ceremony was beautiful, and the reception at the One Paradise on Admiralti Street was tremendous. I'll tell you all about it some other time. But now, let me concentrate on what Richard and I found about the accounts of some individuals of whom you had questions.

We were easily cleared for accessing level III information on Cumlen and Sweza as we presented ourselves there in person. Of course, we went through the bio-identification including retinal registry among other identity verifications. However, we did not need to do much of the information search because the bank staff did all the data search for us. They said there were no illegal transactions by Cumlen or Sweza. Also, the bank verified that Sweza and Cumlen are definitely two different individuals.

Based on the bank records and what Zelinski told me about his personal information, I learned the following: Cumlen hired Zelinski as one of the computer-programmer teams to write the programs that will run the New Jersey Computer-Theme Park, known as NJ Com-T Park, which has been under construction already for some time. Zelinski has been writing the computer programs mostly during weekends when he was off from Acmeon Lab. The money Zelinski received from Cumlen was nothing but his wage for the computer work he did for Cumlen."

Dr. Jupitren, Helen, and Steve were surprised at what Bill just told them. Expecting more news, they listened to Bill's next report.

"As far as Brandon Sweza was concerned, he had nothing to do with Zelinski's money. Brandon Sweza just had invested his fund to a Canadian perfume company. And I secured a complete list of that company's products. This is it. Please take a look, Jules."

In that list, Dr. Jupitren found no Dream Wafer-related chemicals at all.

Bill continued, "Well, the next information was not from the Singapore bank. Actually, after I returned to Long Island, I went to Polowealth Bank of New York, where Zenon Zelinski has his accounts. It's a bit unusual story. Zenon had been sending money to the gun store 'Games and Rifles' for reasons other than buying firearms.

When Zenon was arrested six years ago, he was initially accused of involuntary manslaughter. Although it was clearly an accident, the deceased man's family sued him for large sums of money. So, Zenon needed to hire a very good lawyer to defend himself. At that time, Zenon's sister Stellona got the 'lawyer fee money' from her husband and helped Zenon. Subsequently, his charges were dropped to a misdemeanor level.

Later, his sister got divorced. She requested alimony and child-support money for their then-three-year-old daughter from her divorced husband. Naturally, the man turned to Zenon and asked him to pay the 'lawyer-fee money' back. Since then, Zenon started paying his ex-brother-in-law, initially five hundred dollars and later thousand dollars in monthly installments."

Bill paused a moment, looking at the three of them, and said, "You may wonder why I'm telling you all this. Stellona's ex-husband has been the owner of Games and Rifles all those years."

Dr. Jupitren said, "Ah, that's what it was. Thank you very much, Bill, for all the work you've done to collect those facts. Now, one of the few things that still remains unclear is why Zenon and Yanovsky bought the CR devices lately. Do you have any idea?"

Bill, scratching the side of his head, said to Dr. Jupitren, "After you handed me the bug device a while ago, I checked it out right away. As I've told you before, that device has been used by known criminal groups in certain areas in Long Island.

After some sleuthing around those groups, I came to a tentative conclusion that both Zelinski and Yanovsky were under some kind of threat from those criminal groups and being forced to do unwanted deeds, and that's why they are arming themselves with the CR devices. But I don't have specific information yet to answer your question now."

The urgent question through the remainder of the evening meeting fell on the unidentified character, the tiger-striped-beret man. Bill said his next investigation would start with AAPA to trace the identity of the beret man.

Despite all the concerted effort, Dr. Jupitren felt unsettled because the source of counterfeit Dream Wafer manufacturer was still in the dark.

After Bill left for his precinct, Helen said she often felt unprotected in her office when she was by herself in the office.

Steve suggested that they might consider installing a floating surveillance system Dronette-6.12s in the main building and the Plant area. He explained that it meant dispatching several wasp-sized Dronettes throughout the designated Acmeon areas and keeping the main monitor and remote-control console in Helen's office. Steve said he was sure Helen could quickly learn how to maneuver the Dronette wasps, surveilling the entire Acmeon area, monitoring people's conversations if necessary.

Subsequently, with Dr. Jupitren's consent, Steve installed the Dronette surveillance system, feeling very glad he could do it, especially for Helen.

For days, Acmeon Lab's operation was uneventful. Helen's surveillance with the Dronettes reported nothing out of ordinary. She was getting better in handling the new surveillance system.

Meanwhile, whenever Helen had some free time, using her own LXG set, she practiced fast aiming and sharpshooting, despite others' apprehension about her involvement with the stun gun.

CHAPTER 15
ZENON ZELINSKI AND THE CCTV CAMERA TIMER

One day, on the Dronette-6.12 monitor in her office, Helen saw Zenon manipulating the Annex Library's CCTV camera timer. He was the only one in the library at that time. She got up from her seat, moved closer to the monitor and stared at it anxiously. Zenon was definitely adjusting the timer. He kept looking at the wall and then the window that was facing the wall. He referred to a note that he pulled out of his pocket while readjusting the CCTV camera timer.

Then Yaru Yanovsky walked in the library. Helen's gaze was glued to the monitor. A telephone call came into her office, but she let it be diverted to the message-recording mode and continued to watch them on her monitor. She could clearly hear what they were saying.

Helen thought of calling Dr. Jupitren and Steve to let them know what was happening at the Annex Library, but she could not turn away from watching her monitor. She did not want to miss anything.

Zenon, still handling the CCTV camera's timer, asked, "Yaru, did your team finish the updating assignments already?"

"Yeah, I had my entire team of twelve tech's on the project, and we could finish it on time. How about your team, Zenon? It's already lunchtime."

"My team has to finish the same assignments after lunch. By the way, about the CR device that you got for me…maybe I'll unpack it after the end of today's schedule. Was it hard to set it up?"

"No. It's a piece of cake! It took me just about five minutes. But what are you doing now?"

"Nothing big," Zenon casually answered. "I'm adjusting the timer on the CCTV camera. I'll go back to my work soon after I finish this."

Yaru questioningly looked at Zenon and said, "Why bother with the timer now? Don't you remember, Zenon, the doctor told us not to touch the CCTV cameras?"

"I know that," Zenon said, smiling, "but I believe what I'm doing now is a kind of applied science. I'll explain it to you later, but now, let me concentrate on it."

Zenon looked at Po Kim's big oil painting on the library wall. He briefly looked at the window that was facing the painting. He did this a few more times. He took out an engineer's protractor and tried to measure certain angles between the painting and the window.

Yaru was about to walk out of the library when Zenon called him back. "Yaru, come back here and help me. Can you hold this protractor for me, while I take a look at the angle from a distance?"

"OK, Professor Zelinski, you owe me a good explanation about this. I can't figure out what you're doing."

At that point, a few Dream Wafer candidates walked into the library to have their questionnaire sessions and took their seats in front of the computers. Zenon said something to Yaru in a muted voice, wishing not to disturb the candidates.

Helen increased the Dronette monitor's volume, but their conversation trailed off into inaudible muttering. How frustrating! Helen kept the monitor on and called Dr. Jupitren, who was in the middle of interviewing someone. On her insistence, he came out to the front office, where Helen was poring over the Dronette monitor.

After listening to Helen's explanation, Dr. Jupitren said, "I have to question them about it later. Please ask Bill if he can come to Acmeon's library by five thirty this afternoon, and have Yanovsky and Zelinski see us at the same time in the Annex Library." Clenching his jaws, Dr. Jupitren hurried back to his interview room, where a candidate was waiting to continue the interview with him.

There were a few more new candidates and some revisiting clients who came to see Dr. Jupitren. He felt his attention drifting at times during the treatment sessions with his patients, as he was still preoccupied with what Helen had reported to him earlier.

By five thirty, Dr. Jupitren was still in the treatment session with his last patient.

About that time, Steve arrived with his electronics toolbox, not knowing about the special meeting that Dr. Jupitren was going to have with Bill in the Annex Library.

At the front office, Steve said, "Hi, Helen, I just came by today to repair one of your Dronettes in the Plant area, because it needs new parts to function fully."

"It's good that you are here. Uncle Jules is going to have a special meeting with Zenon and Yaru about what they were doing with the Annex library's CCTV camera at lunchtime today. Actually, he asked Bill to be at the meeting, too."

"Really? What happened? Did they do anything wrong?"

"We don't know yet. But my Dronette recording caught Zenon doing something strange with the CCTV camera, and Uncle Jules knows about it. He will question Zenon at the meeting."

"Is that right? I wonder if I could sit in at the meeting, too."

"I'll ask Uncle Jules about it now."

Helen spoke to Dr. Jupitren on the phone and then told Steve, "Uncle Jules says he is glad that you are here. Earlier, he could not ask you to attend the meeting because he felt he was imposing on you, but since you are here, he'd like to have you at the meeting."

"Good. Then soon we'll see what's what. You know that I wanted to ask them about their dealings with the CCTV cameras all this time anyway."

"I feel bad for them. Uncle Jules is quite upset. Do you think they are really hiding something?"

"We will see. I only have a nagging suspicion about them, but we don't have any hard evidence."

Yaru and Zenon finished their work early and came to the Annex Library on time. Zenon asked, "Yaru, do you have any idea what this meeting with Dr. Jupitren is all about?"

"Helen said there were some important matters involving you and me."

Zenon shrugged his shoulders and resignedly said, "She said nothing to me. I felt somewhat intimidated, because she was rather unfriendly. She practically ordered me to be here at five thirty. It was unlike her. I have no idea what this meeting is about." Zenon looked worried and kept his head down, waiting for the meeting to start.

Yaru turned to him and said casually, "Zenon, guess what I think."

"What?"

"Maybe we will get a raise. Think positive!"

"You're out of your mind, Yaru. Did you forget you got the last big raise only six months ago? Today, Helen said it could be a serious matter. Maybe they are letting us go!"

Yaru, in a subdued tone, said, "Do you know something? I overheard Dr. Jupitren talking to someone seriously on the phone a few times. Something had happened at the Plant, and he seemed upset, but he did not say anything to us about it. All we were told was not to touch the CCTV cameras, not to go near the Plant unless it is work hours, watch out for any strangers around the Plant or the mail-service area, and things like that. I don't think they know we are being threatened by this gypsy guy Akandro Oladre."

"Don't you ever utter his name again!" Zenon said hurriedly. "He is a bad news. If we keep saying no to him, someday he will come back with weapons and do something stupid."

"I think so, too. He scares me. These days, I often check my rearview mirror when I drive home. Did he ever follow you?"

"No, I don't think so. But who knows?"

CHAPTER 16
ZENON ZELINSKI ON MONO-RAY

Dr. Jupitren, Steve, Helen, and Bill came into the Annex Library. Zenon and Yaru got up from their seats to meet them.

Dr. Jupitren said, "Please take a seat, everybody." He tried to hold his excitement down as he imagined a scene in which Zenon was unexpectedly incriminated and handcuffed in front of them. In a somber tone of voice, trying to soothe his ruffled feelings, Dr. Jupitren continued, "Helen reported to me that Mr. Zelinski and Mr. Yanovsky were in this library during lunch hour today and they showed some strange activities."

At that point, Zenon and Yaru picked up their heads with anxious frowns and looked at Dr. Jupitren, who looked back at them and said, "Helen happened to be nearby this library at lunchtime today. She overheard your conversation that alluded to some strange plan or science matter that neither she nor I could understand. So, I would like to hear from both of you about what you were doing in this room at that time. Helen, do you have anything to add?"

"Yes. I overheard Mr. Yanovsky ask Mr. Zelinski about what he was doing with the CCTV camera timer. Then Mr. Zelinski answered that it was some kind of science matter. Soon after that, Mr. Zelinski took out a protractor and asked Mr. Yanovsky to hold it for him, saying that he was going to measure something."

Helen had her Dronette monitor's AV record ready to replay it, just in case they denied or omitted any crucial facts.

Everyone looked at Zelinski and then at Yanovsky. Yaru said, with tongue in cheek, "I don't know why it is such a serious matter. Besides, I didn't even know myself what Zenon was doing with the CCTV camera."

Not convinced, Bill stared at Yaru and said, "Interesting! You didn't know what Mr. Zelinski was doing."

"That's right. When he was about to explain it to me, we were interrupted, because a few Dream Wafer candidates came in and we did not want to disturb them. So we stopped talking."

Steve, Dr. Jupitren, and Bill looked at Helen. She nodded to indicate that he was telling them the truth.

"Then, Mr. Zelinski, why don't you explain yourself now?" Dr. Jupitren asked him.

To everyone's surprise, Zenon seemed as calm as he had always been. He stood up from his seat to begin his explanation:

"What I'm going to tell you is a plain truth, but it may bore some of you because there is a bit of technical information in it. First of all, I admit that I went against what Dr. Jupitren asked all of us—that is, not to touch the CCTV camera timer. But after you hear my explanation, I hope you will forgive me.

When we installed the new CCTV camera about a year and half ago, I read its technical information carefully and discovered that while the camera is on, its sensor will emit a nontoxic electromagnetic radiation called Mono-ray. Because its radiation is soft and of short wavelength, it gets blocked easily.

When there is no direct sunlight, we have no problem with this Mono-ray radiation. However, under bright sunlight, it's a different matter. As you all know it well, the ultraviolet spectrum of sunlight—more specifically, UV lights *A*, *B*, and *C*—has different wavelengths, *A* being the longest and *C* the shortest, and each of them has different physical or chemico-thermal properties.

There is another UV, which has a shorter wavelength than UVC, called extreme UV, or abbreviated as EUV. Incidentally, the next one with a much shorter wavelength than EUV is X ray.

Please bear with me. It may seem irrelevant to you, but shortly you will understand what I was doing with the picture and CCTV camera timer.

When the sun's elevation angle, termed 'altitudinal azimuth,' is less than 50 degrees, the UVB rays usually do not reach us. Because UVB's wavelength is relatively short, it gets blocked by the stratosphere's ozone layer before it can reach the earth. Only the UVA, with the longest wavelength, will pass through the ozone layer and reach us.

Acmeon Lab's GPS address is latitude 40° north at longitude 073°west. Therefore, according to the established solar altitudinal azimuth calculation, in the month of July, at 10:00 in the morning, the sun's elevation angle reaches greater than 50 degrees and remains higher than that angle till 2:30 in the afternoon. After 2:30 pm the sun's azimuth drops below 50 degrees. Thus, the time between 10 am and 2:30 pm is the sun's zenith hours during most of July.

When the sun's elevation angle is greater than 50 degrees, the UVB rays can finally penetrate the ozone layer and reach the earth's surface. The real problem here is that much of the UVB rays come through that window, during the sun's zenith hours. When UVB rays collide with the Mono-rays, UVB rays change into EUV rays.

The EUV rays have worse destructive properties than UVB rays on the painting. As such, the EUV rays destroy the chemical bonds between the oil paint and the canvas material of the picture. The end result is the separation of the paint material from the canvas and deterioration of the artwork."

Zenon pointed to the picture on the wall that was facing the window. Everyone looked at the picture and then turned back to him to hear what else he was going to say.

"I have observed the sunlight that comes through that big window hits the picture right in its center, deteriorating the painting during the sun's zenith hours, as I have just explained, because the CCTV camera's Mono-ray changes UVB rays to EUV rays. Therefore, to protect the picture, I measured the approximate elevation angle of the sun and readjusted periodically the CCTV camera's daily Mono-ray emission time. I mean I reprogrammed the camera so that it would skip monitoring during the zenith, which is the middle of the day. I thought that stopping the camera's operation during that period would not jeopardize Acmeon's security surveillance per se, because during that zenith period, we are all here, literally in the middle of broad daylight. However, as far as the picture was concerned, it was the danger period. So, periodically, a few times per season, I reprogrammed the CCTV camera's scanning schedule so as to avoid the picture's danger time period according to a given time of the year. I did something similar at the Plant's office, where another Po Kim's oil painting faces a huge window."

"However, there in the Plant, I made senseless mistakes, not just once but two times, by putting the turn-off time as PM instead of AM on the CCTV camera's timer. That caused some blank time on the camera around midnight instead of midday. But I corrected it right after I realized my mistakes each time."

"In conclusion, my suggestion is either we move the pictures to other safer spots or replace the CCTV cameras with a safer model that does not emit Monorays. Or we may consider reframing those pictures with special glass covers that have a high sun-protection factor."

At that point, Dr. Jupitren rose from his seat and walked toward Zenon. He gave him a hearty handshake, saying, "Thank you so very much, my friend. You have to forgive me, for I anticipated a totally different account of your dealings with my pictures and the camera."

"Wonderful!" Helen said with relief.

Steve stepped forward, shook hands with Zelinski, and said emphatically, "You're a real scientist with a heart in the right place. I owe you an apology for having groundless doubts over your good intentions."

Yaru said to Zenon with a relieved smile, "Why didn't you tell me about it earlier?"

Zenon sheepishly shrugged his shoulders. "I didn't think it was such a big deal. Readjusting the timer, every five to six weeks, took me each time only four or five minutes during the lunch hour."

Bill got up from his seat and said, "I'm very impressed by your devoted and caring attitude toward the people and your workplace. For me, it was a good science lesson, too. Thank you, Mr. Zelinski." Bill left the room, saying to Dr. Jupitren for everyone to hear, "Jules, you used to say 'Appearance is not necessarily the whole truth.' How true!"

Zenon and Yaru came out to the parking lot. Zenon said, "Getting a raise, huh?"

"Well, well, no raise, of course, and nobody raised hell, either. You have done well, Professor Zelinski! See you tomorrow."

Still tarrying at the library, Dr. Jupitren said to Helen and Steve, "We were so wrong about Zenon. He is a good man after all."

Steve concurred, "I feel the same way. This afternoon, I just came to fix one of the Dronettes in the Plant, but instead I came to this meeting. I'm glad I did."

Helen chimed in. "We weren't fair to Zenon all this time. We should have spoken to him sooner."

Steve said, "But I'm still thinking about the episode when two night-vision-goggled felons snuck in and Planted the bug behind the picture at the Plant. Then, few days later, two thugs LXG-rayed three of Bill's men outside the building. Yet we have no lead or clue for those two incidents. By the way, we still don't know why Yaru and Zenon have LXGs and CR devices."

Helen asked Dr. Jupitren, "Would it be a good idea for one of Bill's men to stop them one day and find the reason why they carry those weapons?"

"I don't think it would be a desirable choice." Dr. Jupitren answered. "Instead, I should have a personal talk with Zenon or Yaru one of these days. They will tell me why."

He thought for a moment and said to Steve, "I wonder if you, on your own, might approach Ms. Munez at the City Library without alarming her. She might lead you to the board member of the AAPA who should know about the beret man."

"OK. I will try to talk to her."

CHAPTER 17
IN SEARCH FOR THE TIGER-STRIPED-BERET MAN

One evening Steve went to the City Library.

At the counter, he found Ms. Munez, who was helping a high-school student to find a book on astronomy. Waiting for his turn, Steve checked the scheduled meetings and spotted the AAPA meeting listed for 8:30 pm Friday the following week.

After downloading the e-book quickly to the student's tablet, Ms. Munez said, "Here it is, *Astronomy 101*. Happy Reading!"

The student thanked her and left.

Steve greeted, "Hi, Ms. Munez."

"May I help you?" Facing Steve, Ms. Munez asked, "Uh, didn't I see you the other day? Mr...?"

"I'm Steve Spencer. Unlike the student who just left with his astronomy material, I'm looking for a good book on astrology."

Bemused, she peered at Steve curiously and said, "We have some books on that subject and they are getting popular these days."

Sparing Steve's response, she continued, "Well, beside the books, there is a software on palm reading with introduction to astrology. Many people, in fact, have borrowed the software lately."

Acting surprised, Steve asked, "Did you say many people?"

"Yes, the other day a group of palmists rented our lecture hall for their meeting. And dozens of them wanted to borrow the same palm-reading software."

Seeing no one else on the checkout line behind him, Steve and Jimena Munez kept on talking. "Wow," Steve said, "I'm not the only one digging for what my future has in store for me. I'd like to borrow books on palm reading and one of the astrology history books."

"No problem. You will have them in just a few minutes."

"Great. Thank you. Here is my ID chip and my Thumputer."

While waiting for the e-book being downloaded, Steve said, "Excuse me, Ms. Munez, do you know of anyone who attended the last lecture on astrology?"

"No, I have not spoken to any of them. The subject is totally out of my field...But, yes, wait a minute. I remember the woman who usually schedules their meeting. Actually, the city charges a nominal fee for private use of the meeting halls here in the City Library, and she paid the fee with her check."

Steve asked, "Do people still write checks?"

"I had the same question, too. So I asked her if she would like to use her Thumputer credit keys instead."

"What was her answer?"

"She said it would be easier for her to display the payment records if she wrote her check. She said she can show the single canceled check copy to the assembly members, should she be asked for the receipt. She did not care to let all the assembly members see the printed list of her credit card charges."

"She must be a careful person. I'd like to meet her and get some help on my questions as I read the astrology book."

"You must be an eager learner. Or are you looking for a special friend?"

"Oh, I'm just into learning the subject."

"All right. I can ask her to give you a call if she cares to. Her name is Joyce Pehna. What is your wrist-phone number?"

Recognizing the name Joyce from Espio-Nano Company and seeing her later at the AAPA meeting, Steve thought it must be the same person. He said, "Thank you. Here is my number."

Ms. Munez wrote down his phone number. Then she handed the requested reading materials to Steve.

Showing his satisfaction, Steve said, "Thank you. Reading this astrology and palm reading stuff will be fun…When Joyce calls me, I'll ask her if I can attend the lecture during their assembly."

"Of course you can ask her for that, but I thought they admitted their members only."

"Is that so? Thank you for that information."

"You're welcome."

As he left the City Library, he thought of his sister, Jenny, who still often writes checks rather than charging to her Thumputer-linked credit system.

The next morning Steve got a call from Joyce.

"Hello, I'm Joyce Pehna. Ms. Munez at the City Library told me to give you a call. Is this Mr. Spencer?"

"Yes. Thank you for your call, Ms. Pehna. I borrowed a couple of books on astrology and palm reading from the library. I thought if I became a member of your assembly, I would possibly find my mentors on the subject."

"I see. You want to apply for AAPA membership first. Am I right?"

"Yes. That's what I would like to do. Where do I start?"

"Now we have the screening committee for new members. They have to see you in person first to ask some personal questions. If they OK you, then you will pay the application fee."

"Thank you for the information. Is it possible for me to sit in as an auditor to your meetings, couple of times before I start the application?"

"Well, I will ask the committee and let you know if it's doable."

Steve was puzzled. Not too long ago, he, as Hank Oswin, easily got an auditor's seat in the back row. But why not now? He had to dredge up a plausible question quickly.

"Well, a friend of mine, Hank, told me that you allowed him to take a sample of the meeting some time ago, that is, before he became a full member of the AAPA. Would it have made a difference if I, without any prior inquiry, just showed up at the meeting as Hank did?"

Joyce paused a moment and said, "Oh, you're talking about Mr. Hank Oswin. I was told that we let him sit in at the last meeting as an auditor even though he was not a member yet. But since then, because of some new issues within the assembly, the procedure to admit any new member has been changed. I think the screening committee is still waiting for Mr. Oswin's call for his interview."

"Some new issues!" Steve thought that maybe she was talking about their scheme against Acmeon and some complication of it. He decided to try his last ploy and asked, "Can I pay the fee now and then be allowed to sit in as an auditor at the assembly before the interview?"

"No, sir. Sorry."

"No exceptions?"

"No, it's really not up to me. It is up to the committee."

Pretending disappointed, Steve told her he might call her again for the interview.

After ending the conversation with Joyce Pehna, Steve thought, "To follow the tiger-striped beret's trace to his den, I must break through the AAPA barrier one way or another. She and the beret man are in the same evil camp! And I'm almost there."

Meanwhile, Bill called Dr. Jupitren and said he had some leads on the Chromega watch owner. Bill said the following.

The Chromega watchmaker is one of the top-brand vintage wristwatch manufacturer in New York state. They have been assigning a serial number to every watch they produced. At the forensic unit, John Collins' team retrieved the serial number of the watch. Then John contacted the regional Chromega watch distributor, and with the serial number, they quickly tracked down the original owner's information.

The watch belonged to Alfonso Ramos of 4033 Swan Road, Brooklyn, New York. Date of purchase was six years ago on his birthday. Bill Warren's team checked Alfonso's ten-year police record, which had only a couple of minor misdemeanors. Information on his relatives was unavailable. He was reported missing during the hurricane that hit the eastern New Jersey and Staten Island shores a year ago. According to his home-mortgage company's record, he worked as a longshoreman near Laurence Harbor, New Jersey.

Since the hurricane, the 4033 Swan Road house was in foreclosure for several months. Strangely, someone else was living there, according to the bank that dealt with the foreclosure sale. Maybe the person made a deal with the new owner to stay on as a renter but it was unknown who that person was.

Dr. Jupitren quietly listened to Bill's explanation and said, "Whoever lives in that house might know something about the missing man."

Bill said, "I think so, too. Soon, I'll go out personally to that house to find any clue."

"Bill, please be extra careful. I'll tell Steve what you've found about the watch."

A few days later, Bill said to Steve. "Soon, John Collins and I are going to drive out to 4033 Swan Road in Brooklyn...Of course, we don't know who lives there. When we come face-to-face with the individual in that house, and if he happens to be the tiger-striped-beret man, you may be able to identify him better than we can, since you saw him at the AAPA meeting. Would you be able to come along with us?"

After brief thoughtful moments, Steve answered yes.

In time, on Steve's day off, he accompanied Bill and John Collins to the Swan Road house. Bill had a house search warrant.

The house was at the end of Swan Road. Strangely, the front door was left unlocked and there was no one in the house. The three of them cautiously walked inside. The whole house was in shambles and was desolate. They inspected every room carefully. On the kitchen table, Steve saw the unmistakable tiger-striped beret.

"Bill, look at that hat on the kitchen table over there!"

All three of them recognized it. They instantly went into an alert state.

Right after that, John pointed to other familiar objects and said, "Look over there!"

They saw a holster with an LXG stun gun and a CR device on the kitchen shelf.

Bill said, "We don't know how many people live in this house, but one of them must be the tiger-striped-beret man we are looking for."

Steve and John nodded. "Yes."

Bill said quickly, "Whoever lives here, he went out leaving the front door unlocked and without carrying his weapons. It's likely that he didn't go out too far. He may return at any time. When he sees our police van in his driveway, he may try to run away. He may not be armed with an LXG, but it's still possible that he might carry a handgun. We have to watch out. John, go out quickly and remove our van from this area."

John drove the van a few blocks away and radioed to Bill. "I'm parked three blocks north of the house, and from here I can see the traffic moving in and out of the end of Swan Road. I'll radio you when I see any suspicious car approaching the 4033 house."

"OK, John, we'll wait for your signal."

Then Steve and Bill quickly took down the holster from the kitchen shelf. Steve deftly reversed the polarity of the LXG's and CR device's batteries and then placed the holster back on the shelf.

After a while, John's radio message came in. "Bill, I see a US postal letter-carrier truck heading to the end of Swan Road. It's a white postal truck with loaded parcels."

"Is there anyone else beside the driver?"

"No. Only the driver."

"Good, John. We'll be ready for anything. Hang on!"

From the kitchen, Steve and Bill could see the mail truck coming in their direction. The truck stopped in front of the house. A uniformed mail carrier stepped out of the truck with a package and headed to the front door. Peeking out the kitchen window, Steve recognized that the mail carrier was not the man they were looking for.

Bill, in his police uniform, did not want to alarm the mail carrier and stayed in a room away from the front door. Steve answered the doorbell.

"This package is for Mr. Oladre. Is he not home?"

"Oh, he just stepped out to get something to eat. He'll be back any minute."

"I see. He must have gone out to buy lottery tickets as usual. I'll leave the package here for him, but I need your signature. How are you related to him?"

"I'm his friend, Steve. Let me sign it."

Before he signed the parcel receipt, Steve carefully read the receiver's name, which was Akandro Oladre. Steve remembered the AAPA board members calling the beret man Mr. O. Steve felt tense, thinking the parcel recipient must be the same man. The parcel's sender was the Espio-Nano Company. Steve imagined the man must be buying weapons from that Company. Steve signed the receipt in intentionally distorted scribbles, thinking that the Espio-Nano clerks might recognize his usual signature otherwise. The mail carrier drove away.

Bill radioed John, "The unsuspecting mail carrier just left the area. John, continue to look out."

Steve told Bill about the parcel recipient and the sender. They discussed how to entrap Akandro when he would return.

Soon, John radioed Bill. "Hello, hello, Bill, this is John. I see a black passenger car going to your direction…"

Bill responded to John. "Follow that car. If the car pulls into 4033, block its exit with your van. If the driver runs into the house to get his weapons, I will pounce on him. But if he tries to run away from the house, use your LXG. As you saw, his CR device and LXG are here in the kitchen. Steve disabled them anyway. But just to be sure, keep your CR open. Be careful. He might be armed with another LXG or a gun."

Bill and Steve saw the black car pulling into the driveway. Following the car, John's police van came in, blocking it. A stocky, curly haired driver came out of the car. Seeing the police van behind his parked car, he ran toward the house.

As the man approached the house, Steve looked out a window and recognized that the man was the one he saw at the AAPA meeting and in the City Library parking lot. Steve told Bill that the man was the very one they were looking for. The man did not see Steve or Bill inside the house, as they hid themselves in the adjacent room away from the kitchen.

As Bill and Steve anticipated, the man ran to the kitchen, grabbed the LXG and CR device off the shelf, dashed back to the front door, and tried to shoot the LXG at John, who was just stepping out of the van. The LXG did not work, to his dismay. He ran back toward the kitchen.

Steve quickly whispered to Bill, "His name is Akandro Oladre."

Bill charged into the kitchen pointing his handgun at Akandro. Steve followed one step behind Bill and aimed his LXG at the bewildered Akandro.

Bill loudly called out, "Hold your hands up! Akandro Oladre, you are under arrest!"

John rushed in, aiming his LXG at Akandro.

When Akandro saw Bill's and John's police uniforms with their epaulet and handguns, he offered no resistance. Bill's hands moved very quickly and did not allow any countermotion from Akandro Oladre. Bill handcuffed him.

Bill checked Akandro's left wrist and saw healed scratch marks stretching from the wrist to the back of his hand.

Receiving many thanks from Bill and John, Steve went back to his apartment. Bill and John took Akandro to the precinct.

In the precinct's watch-house, Bill questioned Akandro. "Who approached you first, asking you to do something against Acmeon Lab?"

"I think it was the AAPA."

"What do you mean you think? Then there must be others who approached you. Who were they?"

Akandro, blinking his eyes in search for an answer, said hesitantly, "Before the AAPA, there were some more." Akandro then remained silent, trying to recall the fuzzy facts.

Bill prompted him again. "Come on, who were they? And when?"

"A cosmetic company in Islet Republic, about a year ago."

"What's the name of the company?"

"I don't know. I never spoke to them directly. I only dealt with their middleman."

"How did they end up making a deal with you?"

"I told the middleman I was a software broker and gave him my phony account-ledger copies."

"All right then. I'll come back to the Islet Republic Company later. But now, tell me about the AAPA first. How much did they give you, and what did they ask you to do?"

"They gave me twenty thousand dollars and asked me to mess up Acmeon's computer."

"Who from the AAPA contacted you?"

"It was Joyce Pehna."

"What exactly did she ask you to do?"

"She asked me to destroy Acmeon's main computer and the software."

"Did you ask her why you were supposed to do such a thing?"

"No."

"The easy money they gave you blinded you. Huh?"

Akandro did not answer Bill.

"So, what did you actually do for them?"

"I knew two guys who now work at Acmeon Lab. So, I tried to get them to do the job for me."

"What're their names?"

"Zenon Zelinski and Yaru Yanovsky."

"When and how did you meet them for the first time?"

"About two years ago at the North Mall Arcade where I used to work as a game room clerk…"

"What were they doing there at the arcade?"

"They used to come in for e-games and I got to know them."

"So?"

"I contacted Zenon and Yaru a few months ago and told them I would give them five thousand dollars apiece if they mess up or burn Acmeon's main computer and the software."

"What kind of answer did they give you?"

"They said I was crazy. They didn't care about the money. Even after I said I would give them seventy-five hundred each, they refused to do it. They said they would call the police if I bothered them again. I got frustrated and threatened them."

"What did you say when you threatened them?"

"I said if they ratted on me, I would kill them…Please don't write it down. I didn't mean it but I just wanted to scare them."

"You are carrying an LXG stun gun and a counter-ray device. Do you have the state permits to carry them?"

"No."

"Then, the state will confiscate your devices."

With sharp disbelieving stare, Bill continued his questioning. "Now, about the cosmetic company in Islet Republic. You said you only spoke with the company's middleman. What's his name?"

"Marcel T."

"Marcel who?"

"He never gave me his full name."

"Where in the Islet Republic is that company?"

"Marcel said it's near the capital city of the Islet Republic. But I don't know what city."

"How much did they pay you?"

"Five thousand dollars."

"That's all?"

"They said when the deal goes through, they would pay me fifteen thousand dollars."

"What did they ask you to do?"

"To get a copy of the Dream Wafer program."

"So, what did you do? I have the police report anyway. Don't try to hide anything."

"First time, I tried to hack Acmeon's Dream Wafer program remotely. But I couldn't get it. So, the same night…that was a Saturday, I sent two boys to Acmeon. They broke into the Acmeon Plant and made a copy of the Dream Wafer program."

"What did you do with the copy?"

"I gave the copy to the middleman, Marcel T. I thought it was a good copy, but soon they found out it was a chopped-up one."

"How did they find that out?"

"Marcel T told me the company's engineers sent him a message saying the copy was no good and I should get a good one. But, even later, I could not get the good copy because by then Acmeon had put in new anti-hacking program. And the company canceled the contract. I ended up with no extra money from them."

"Are you still in contact with Marcel T?"

"No."

"When did you speak to him last?"

Dream Wafer

"A year ago."

"Can you call him again?"

"No, I can't get him. His telephone number was discontinued."

"You said at the AAPA meeting that you could not destroy Acmeon's program because first you needed to make the program copy for another agent. Who was it?"

"It was an agent from a Eurasian country."

"What was the deal?"

"They wanted to buy the Dream Wafer program, and I said that I could make a deal with Acmeon and buy the program for them. I said, again, I was a software broker. They said after the deal goes through, I would get a fifteen percent commission."

"How much prepayment did you get from the agent?"

"Twenty-five thousand dollars."

Bill kept on with his questioning. "Then I suppose they didn't ask you to break in or steal the program. Did they?"

"No, they didn't."

"You got the money. And what did you do actually?"

"I sent the same two boys who were supposed to copy the Wafer program. They tried, but one of them got LXG-shot by a cop, and the whole thing didn't go through."

"What are the boys' names?"

"I called them 'Tick' and 'Tack.'"

"What are their full names?"

"Tihko Piroiz and Takis Tantalos."

"What're their cell phone numbers?"

Akandro recited two numbers, which Bill jotted down in his e-memo pad. Bill dialed one of the numbers and let Akandro talk on the speakerphone mode, as he was still in handcuffs. Bill ordered him, "When Tick or Tack answers you, don't tell him you are on a speakerphone."

Tick answered, "Hey, Akandro, wassup?"

"Nothing much. Where are you at?"

"Club Esperanza. I have been trying to talk to you. How come you don't answer my calls?"

"I had trouble with my phone." Akandro fudged his answer.

"Why don't you fix it? Man, I called you many times."

Akandro asked, "What are you up to these days?"

"Tack and I ran out of all the cash you gave us. So, we were going to ask you for some more."

"How could you run out of it so fast?"

"We blew it in Atlantic City."

"Gambling?"

"Yeah."

"You're impossible. Is Tack with you now?"

"No, he just went to his sister's family in New Jersey."

"What are you doing at the Esperanza?"

"We just hang out here. Tack and I couldn't break in that Acmeon place. I almost got killed there. We told you about it."

"I know. Too bad! Tick, I'm tied up. I can't help you."

Tick asked peevishly, "When can I see you?"

"Not for a while."

"What do you mean? You said the same thing last time when you were locked up. Were you busted?"

"Not really."

Tick said grumpily, "I don't like it, man. Someone is twisting your arm. You don't talk like you. Before your GPS catches me, I'm gonna hang up. I'm not really at Club Esperanza now. I lied."

Click. The call ended there.

Bill had already traced Tick's GPS location and his telephone number: it was not Club Esperanza but a lumberyard, Giovanni & Sons Lumber in Smithtown, Long Island. Bill made a GPS notation in his e-note next to Tick's name. Bill continued his questioning. "What other things did you ask Tick and Tack to do?"

"To get the LXG stun gun and CR device for me."

"So, what did they do?"

"They stole the LXG and CR for me."

"When and where did they steal them?"

"About six months ago, from the Espio-Nano Company at the North Mall."

"What else did they do?"

"Tick and Tack put an eavesdropping bug behind a picture in the Acmeon Plant."

"What did you hear from the bug?"

"Acmeon was going to have tighter security but would hide police patrols from the public to fool us."

"And?"

"We stopped bothering Acmeon."

"Who else did you work for? Tell me the truth!"

Akandro tried hard to recall. "There were others who asked me to get the copy of the Dream Wafer program from Acmeon Lab, but I can't remember all their names. Some gave me just a few hundred bucks and asked me to get the copy first, and then they would pay me if I brought the copy to them. Honestly, I don't remember their names now."

Bill's questioning continued for another hour until Akandro was transferred to the detention center. Bill questioned him in particular about the Chromega watch that he took from Alfonso.

The next day, Bill went to Acmeon Lab, telling Dr. Jupitren details of what he gleaned from Akandro Oladre, who was behind all the incidents that happened to Acmeon during the preceding twelve months or so.

Dr. Jupitren said pensively, "So, it seems that some company in Islet Republic got the incomplete Dream Wafer copy and produced the counterfeits. But we don't know exactly where or who is making the counterfeits! I have to contact the pilot Sam Dayer soon. He seems to be the only one who should know about the manufacturer."

"You're right, Jules. We will trace them one way or another. Now, about the tiger-striped beret…Steve was a big help at the Swan Road house. He knew exactly how to handle each situation. He was a very good team player.

According to Akandro's confession, the watch certainly came from Alfonso Ramos, the original owner. During the hurricane, Alfonso was on board a ship somewhere between Keyport and Laurence Harbor, New Jersey, attending to some cargo on deck."

Dr. Jupitren listened quietly, and Bill continued his report. "Akandro jumped aboard to extort money from Alfonso, threatening he would whistle-blow on Alfonso for having his hands in smuggling illegal immigrants. That day, Alfonso refused to give him the money. Enraged with Alfonso, Akandro overpowered him, yanked the Chromega watch off his wrist, and debarked. That was the last time Akandro saw Alfonso, so he claimed. But we are going to find out if there was any foul play, maybe a fatal push or blow. Or, even a shootout.

What made me more suspicious was that he said he went to Alfonso's house to live there as soon as he found out that Alfonso did not return to his house. Besides, Akandro had prior police records…a bad recidivist's record with felony, some with mayhem charges, most of them by illegal contracts."

"I wonder," Dr. Jupitren said, "what really happened to Alfonso."

"If he was alive," Bill answered, "he should have already returned to his house in Brooklyn. But he has been missing for a year. If he was mortally wounded, either by the hurricane or by Akandro's foul play, he must have turned up as a dead body."

"Bill, why don't you check with the harbor masters of Keyport or Laurence Harbor? Or the police there? That's where he was last seen, according to Akandro, anyway."

"I was about to tell you that's what I was going to do next, Jules. In fact, I have the harbor masters' telephone numbers here with me. We will see what they can tell us. At least, they may tell us that they found one or many unidentified bodies after the hurricane swept those harbors."

"Bill, you're going to be quite busy for a while with Alfonso's case. Is there anything else you wanted to tell me today?"

"Oh, yes. Another thing. I'm sorry to relay this blunt news to you, Jules. Akandro confessed that he was going to burn down part of Acmeon Plant. It was one of the deals with AAPA! He will be locked up in the cell for a good while."

Dr. Jupitren said, "Wow, come to think of it, had Steve not seized the Chromega watch, Acmeon could have faced awful damage." Dr. Jupitren felt chills in his back as he imagined his cherished *virtual brain* model on fire.

Bill said, "To say the least, we owe it to Steve's quick, brave move. As I said already, he was very helpful at the Swan Road house."

"I agree. He's one of a kind. Smart and quick. Well, Bill, what next? I wonder how else I should do to safeguard my Wafer program."

"Oh, you just continue as usual, keeping Acmeon Lab's security as tight as before. Meanwhile, we will continue to beef up Acmeon's security by increasing our surveillance hours. Besides, we will monitor Akandro's cell phone to see if any other planned criminal activities are brewing. As long as Akandro is detained, you shouldn't worry much, Jules. I'll sweep up the AAPA as well. I think I'll start with Joyce Pehna. Steve told me she works at Espio-Nano in the North Mall. I can arrest her there."

Bill continued, "About Yanovsky, who lately bought CR devices from Espio-Nano... As I suspected all along, Akandro admitted that he enticed Yanovsky and Zelinski to copy your Wafer program, but they would not give in. So, Akandro threatened them. Naturally, they armed themselves with CR devices because they knew he had an LXG."

"I see. That explains it."

Later in the evening, Steve came to Acmeon Lab. Dr. Jupitren told Steve what he heard from Bill and said, "After I heard Bill's report, I spoke with Zenon and

Yaru about their CR devices. I confirmed what Bill told me about them. When I told Zenon and Yaru about Akandro's arrest, they were very relieved. By the way, both of them had a proper license for the CR device. I'm glad that Zenon and Yaru are good people.

I also want to say many thanks to you. If you didn't scrape that watch off Akandro's wrist, we would still be in a big quandary. On top of it, Steve, you risked yourself by going out to the Swan Road house with Bill. I can't thank you enough."

"You're very welcome. I'm glad I was some help to you and Acmeon Lab."

Feeling huge relief, Steve came out of Dr. Jupitren's office. Helen was finishing up for the day.

"Hi, Steve, you must have heard all about it from Uncle Jules."

"Yeah, what a relief! Now I don't need to play with my Dronette, and I don't have to bother you to dispense your art skill, disguising me into Hank Oswin. I don't have to finagle the poor librarian, Jimena, with my lies and all the pretentions."

"You seem to feel bad that you lied to her."

"In a way, yes, I do."

"But you had to do it for the just cause."

"But I wouldn't go around bragging about what I did at the City Library."

"Steve, that's you all right." Helen thought his compunction was adorable.

"Helen, a few days ago, you told me about your special artwork and hinted I should give you some feedback on it."

"Ah, that! Thank you for remembering it. It's not a big thing but just a new idea." Helen looked at her desk clock and said, "I'll tell you about it next time when you're here. Now I have to go to the studio with my Mom. She must be waiting for me outside."

Steve went outside with her to say hello to her mother. "Good evening, Mrs. Humayor. I hear you are on your way to the studio."

"Yes, we are, as usual. Jules told me about how you have been helping him out with the lab's problems. I thank you for him."

"Not at all, Mrs. Humayor. In fact, Helen has been a keen detective herself and was very helpful in problem solving."

"That's nice of you to say so. Thank you. Someday you should visit us. I'll show you our art room at home and the paintings Helen and I worked on."

"Thank you. I'll be looking forward to it."

"We will be happy to see you at our home. Good night."

Helen waved her hand through the rolled-down window as they left for their studio.

CHAPTER 18
TO MOM ON MY BIRTHDAY

The next afternoon, right after finishing the day's work at Acmeon Lab, Helen took several greeting cards out of her art portfolio and spread them on her desk.

Arriving at her office, Steve unloaded a small brown paper bag and his camera. "Hi, are you done for the day?"

"Yes, just now."

"Good. I brought two turkey sandwiches and Moca-Mola."

"Thank you. You must be coming straight from Perihelion."

"Yeah, I had a busy day as usual. I wanted to see your artwork and came from my job as soon as I was done." Pointing at the colorful cards on her desk, Steve asked, "Are they the artwork you told me about?"

"Yes."

"Did you draw them all?"

"Yeah, I made them at the studio. It took me a few weeks to finish them."

"They look like greeting cards to me. What kinds are they?"

"Birthday cards."

"The colors are beautifully blended, and the floral designs look quite professional. This splendid bouquet of flowers are outstanding. Did you make them with certain people in mind?"

"Yes. They are all for mothers."

"For mothers? So, they are Mother's Day cards."

"No, they are birthday cards."

Not quite understanding her, Steve picked up one of the cards and looked at it closely.

"Please read the cover of the cards." Helen said.

Steve read it aloud, "To Mom on my birthday…Do you mean you give this card to your Mom on your birthday?"

"Yes. If you wish, you can give one of them to your Mom on your birthday, too."

"It is an amazing idea. I've never thought of giving a card to my mother on my birthday." Steve opened the card and read the message inside.

Dear Mom,
All through the years and whenever my birthday came by, I have received so much love and affection from everyone, especially from you, Mom.
   Now on my birthday, I want to say thank you for bringing me into this world and having loved me so dearly.
With love, Helen, on my birthday

"Helen, it's wonderful! It's so sweet. You must be proud of yourself for having come up with such a beautiful idea and then making the lovely cards by yourself."

"Thank you, Steve."

"When did you first have the idea to make these cards?"

"Well, while I was on Dream Wafers years ago."

"You were on Dream Wafers! Why?"

"My college boyfriend, Jonathan, died from cancer. Right after that, I had bad dreams for weeks and was very sad and lonely. Many nights, Mom would go up to her room to pray for me and then come to my room to comfort me."

"I can imagine."

"Then, sometime before my birthday, Mom spoke to Uncle Jules, and he suggested that I try the Dream Wafers. So, I did. The Wafers really helped me out of my misery, and my nightmares went away. By the time my birthday came up, I was feeling much better and not sad or lonely. Then I realized how much I was loved and cared for by my parents, especially by Mom, who was there for me all the while when I was miserable. That day, I thought of giving Mom a card on my birthday."

"I see. A wonderful idea! But have you thought of giving a similar card to your father, too?"

"Yes, I'm thinking about a card with 'To My Parents on My Birthday' as the title. But for now, I think a card for Mom will do."

"I see. I'm sure a lot of people must feel just like you do. People will love your card's idea. It will be a new genre in the greeting-card world. Maybe someday you could make them in three-dimensional e-cards."

Reaching for the paper bag, Steve said, "Oh, boy! We forgot about the sandwiches. Let's eat them now and drink the Moca-Mola."

"Thank you for the sandwich. I'm pretty hungry."

"Do you know how old the Moca-Mola is?" Steve was rather jocular.

Helen replied without searching for an answer. "No idea. Do you?"

"Yes, I know it very well because my parents told me that it first came out in the year I was born."

"Then, Moca-Mola is twenty-eight years old, just like you."

"Right. Moca-Mola, I heard, is made from mocha-coffee extract but is much milder than a mocha, and I like Moca-Mola better. It's less sugary, too. People dropped the *h* from its name and just called it Moca-Mola. Anyway, I'm glad you like it, too. Moca-Mola has a nice sounding ring to it."

"Yeah, it rhymes with Coca-Cola."

"By the way, did you show your latest cards to your Mom?"

"Yes, I did. She liked them. Actually, I gave her one on my last birthday, too. She loved it."

Unpacking his camera and tripod, Steve said, "Helen, you wouldn't mind if I took pictures of your cards."

"Not at all. Go ahead."

"I will turn some of them into e-cards. For the flowers, I'll try 3-D printing, and I'll bring them all to you. I'll create basic templates so that you may use them for the new cards you would make. Actually, you could make some of them 4-Ds."

"4-Ds?"

"Yes, you will have three dimensions visually; the fourth dimension is the sound part, the spoken messages or songs that you'll hear when you open the card."

Helen thanked him for his thoughts on her cards and casually asked, "How often do you get to see your parents?"

Packing his camera and tripod back into his tote bag, he answered, "Once in a couple of months and on most holidays."

"I heard they live in Fort Lee, New Jersey. Are they doing well?"

"Yes, but they are getting on in years. And they asked my sister, Jenny, to live with them. But she practically lives in her New York *officetel* because she is extremely busy."

"Is Jenny still working at Luxen Tech?"

"Yes and no."

"What do you mean, 'yes and no'?"

"Sometimes she works for them, but some other times I believe Luxen Tech is working for her."

"How is it possible? What does she do there?"

"Well, her dissertation was on optical instruments' industrial application. One night three years ago, she called me at midnight in her eureka moment and woke me up. She shouted for joy on the phone, saying, 'I found it, Steve! I found it! The wall, the optical magic wall!' Actually I had some idea about what she had been up to. So I knew right away why she was so excited. I, too, jumped out of bed and congratulated her."

Helen asked curiously, "The magic wall? What is that?"

"Think of a huge convention hall. Her invention creates any number of smaller rooms ad lib out of the one big hall more or less instantly, all optically."

"Optically?"

"Precisely. Luxen Tech initially hired her for solar-energy generators. They asked her to develop new ways of harnessing solar energy beyond the usual photovoltaic methods. After her daily Luxen Tech work, whenever she found free time, she ran her own research on the Optical Wall. She wrestled with the idea for years. Then, one day, voilà! She got it. It's a formidable magical barrier made mostly of electronic plasma-like material. According to her, it is safe and soundproof, yet can be folded away instantly."

"Wow, what a great invention!"

"The Luxen Tech technicians are installing the Optical Walls in so many buildings throughout the country. Its utilitarian potential is beyond my imagination. Now they are building schools with the Optical Wall concept in mind, in many cities in New York State. As I said already, with the Optical Walls, you can turn an auditorium instantly into any number of classrooms, as many as you need it to be. In school setting, each new room has a door, which connects to an exit to the hallways and finally to outdoors. It's amazing."

"So what does she do now at her company?"

"She hires and trains Optical Wall-installation technicians. She oversees their work within the company. According to her contract, certain portions of the revenue go to Luxen Tech's treasury and the rest gets credited to her own account. And, her company's managerial officers report to her about the Optical Wall-related business. That's why I said Luxen Tech is working for her as well."

"Now I see. She must have made lots of money."

"Without a doubt. When I asked her how she was doing with her money the other day, guess how she answered me in jest…She said when she pays for her bread and milk at grocery stores, she does not have to worry about getting the exact change from the store clerks!"

Helen said, laughing, "What a lucky hyperbole! Is Jenny married?"

"Not quite. She is almost married…to the Optical Walls, which sometimes we call the magic walls. The walls are wrapping her so tightly that she cannot look at anything else. The magic walls are her idol and her husband."

"Then, Steve, you should find *a prince charming on a white horse* and let him break through the Optical Walls to rescue her with a magical kiss!"

"Are you thinking of Snow White? Or, *Siegfried* from Wagner's *Das Rheingold*?"

"Well, I was thinking about *Siegfried* going through the fire walls to sleeping *Brünnhilde* and his magical kiss awakening her from the sleeping spell."

Steve somewhat excitedly said, "Swell! We are in synch; we are thinking of the same scenes in the third ring cycle of Wagner's opera. But it's a pity. Nowadays we, just like many others, find no time to sit through the old classical forms of art. We practically collapse and lock up those gems that we call classical art into evanescent strokes in the cage of CDs' megabytes. And we find very little time to revisit them. It's rare if we catch them with our eyes or ears in the ways those artists originally meant us to appreciate them. We have to admit it's like that because we live in this ultrafast, rushed generation!"

"Steve, on that eloquent note, we need to *rush* to wrap up and go home before it gets too late."

"You're right, Helen. Let's get ready to go home. We have another full day tomorrow."

CHAPTER 19
OVERFLOW EFFECT OF DREAM WAFERS

On Monday morning, Helen took out several e-letter copies from her desk drawers as she said good morning to Dr. Jupitren. "I have been getting these e-letters from our clients. Would you take a look at them?"

After reviewing all of them, Dr. Jupitren said, "They are reporting positive 'overflow effect' from the Dream Wafers even after they wake up in the morning.

Helen, when you tried yourself the earlier version of Dream Wafer years ago, didn't you have a similar overflow effect as those people?"

Nodding slowly, Helen said, "Come to think of it, yes, I did. Somehow, I did not make the connection until now."

"So what do you say? Do you recall anything in particular?"

"Yes. Do you remember how miserable I was after Jonathan died?"

"Yes, I do remember. You were quite depressed for weeks."

"I was having morbid, scary dreams practically every night then. But within a week after you prescribed the Dream Wafers for me, not just my bad dreams quieted down, but by daytime, my sad mood started to lift. I did not realize it then, but now it seems that it was most likely the Wafers' overflow effect."

"I do remember that, too. I never told you this—but about a month after Jonathan's funeral, his parents came to this office to thank me for the extra medical help I offered them during his last months. You were here with me when they came to see me."

"I remember that day rather well."

"You probably were getting the overflow effect of the Wafers. That day you were somehow too cheery when you saw the heartbroken folks. So I tried to stifle your upbeat feelings by sidetracking your conversation with his parents, hoping to spare them from unintended additional hurt feelings. They were still grief stricken then. Don't take me wrong. I felt relieved for your sake but not quite so for them that day."

Helen demurely said with a light sigh, "You're right. I was not appropriate in my manners that day. Looking back, I vaguely remember that I tried to ease them of their morose grief, but I overdid it. Probably my Wafers' overflow effect made me act like that."

"I think so, too. Do you still miss Jonathan?"

Helen answered yes with a quiet nod.

"Well, I didn't mean to bring your sad memory back. I only wanted to confirm that the overflow effect happened to you, too. In fact, last week, several patients on Dream Wafers reported their experiences, which were all similar overflow effects."

Dr. Jupitren thought, "If one can have the overflow effect by choice or as an option within the Dream Wafer program, it would be far more desirable." He decided to check some references and his earlier observation notes on it.

After lengthy record review over several days, he found the clue that all the patients with such positive overflow effects had one thing in common: every one of them requested on the Dream Wafer questionnaire for the highest intensity of selected sub-items that would induce strong expression of the genes that control mood-related chemicals.

Confirming the Dream Wafers' therapeutic potential to lift depressive moods, eventually the Dream Wafer program was modified so that it would produce the desirable overflow effects by choice.

The next day Steve came to see Dr. Jupitren and said, "Today, I have read the news that some groups of foreign chemists altered the Wafer-related chemicals, using them in a massive spray form. Reportedly, such chemicals were used to control the riots in some of the Eurasian countries' borders."

Dr. Jupitren pensively said, "I wonder how our Wafers got so mutilated that they practically turned into a criminal weapon in those far-out places of the world."

Steve asked, "How do they use the Wafer in riot control?"

"Well, as you've probably read it already, it was not the Wafer itself they used. They used only certain parts of the counterfeit Dream Wafer program to extract a few chemical concoctions of their own, turning them into spray forms. The spray's net result will be as if every rioter was on multiple Wafers without the program-ending module. As a result, some will lose their urge to fight, and others, on the contrary, will become unusually aggressive and violent. They will not know why or against whom they are fighting. Only lots of chaos will prevail.

Once sprayed, the rioters will be unable to have any convergent forces as a group and will fail in achieving their primary goal of the riot. Only mass confusion will prevail. That's what the despot regime wants to achieve. While in the riot, if some of them had their own lethal weapons to begin with, in their confused state, the toxic chemicals would let them wield those weapons against other rioters. Literally, the rioters will kill each other. Chemical spraying is utterly criminal."

"Is there anything you or anyone else could do to help the situation?"

"Actually, I was thinking about it, too. For instance, spraying the antidote to wake them all up. But that's only in theory. I don't think it will ever be possible because the antidotes need to be genetically matched individually for each person. The only thing I can do at this point is urging the UN's ad hoc committee to persuade the riot controllers to stop using the chemical sprays made from counterfeit Wafers. I should write to the UN right away.

Reportedly, the UN's chemical weapons inspection teams already confirmed the evidence that massive use of chemical spraying took place in the region, sacrificing many human lives. Nevertheless, for weeks, the UN Security Council, due to one or two veto votes, has been unable to build global public opinion strong enough to pit against the despot regime. I, as an individual denizen of the world, should beseech Washington to file a petition to The Hague International Criminal Court and Amnesty International to impose an immediate injunction against the abuse of counterfeit Wafer-related chemical sprays in that region."

"Do you want me to do anything now to ease your work?"

"No, thank you, Steve. Please go on with your planned projects. I'll be all right."

Steve quietly left Dr. Jupitren's office and went to the Plant's entrance area to do some more work for CR-device on the CCTV cameras.

Dr. Jupitren started to draft those petitions.

Later in the evening, Dr. Jupitren called the copilot of the Trans-Alpha Jet Air flight, Mr. Frank Fairmont. "Hi, I have been trying to reach Mr. Sam Dayer, the pilot. But so far, somehow, I could not get hold of him. Could you help me to reach him?"

"Yes, I can. Is there anything in particular that you are concerned with?"

"Well, I wanted to speak to him about the Dream Wafer that he used at the time of the Trans-Alpha Jet Air incident."

"I see."

"Would you ask him to get in touch with me? Please tell him I'm anxious to speak with him."

"Certainly. I will."

The next day, Dr. Jupitren received Sam Dayer's call.

"Yes, I'm Julian Jupitren. How are you? Your copilot, Mr. Fairmont, must have asked you to call me."

"Yes, Frank said you were anxious to speak to me."

"Yes, I am. Thank you for your call. So, how have you been since you returned to New York from LA?"

"I have been doing fairly well. Is there anything I can answer you on the phone now?"

"Well, if it is all right with you, since you are not too far from my Acmeon Lab, I would like to meet with you in my office. I want to get some information about the Wafer you used. And, if you want, I will be able to explain the basics of Dream Wafers to you when we meet. But, if you prefer, I can come to your house instead."

"Well, I'll meet you there at your Acmeon Lab. But on one condition."

"One condition?"

"Yes, Doctor, I would feel more comfortable if I could have my lawyer sit in with us."

"Oh, yes, you can. If his presence would make you feel comfortable, it's fine with me. Please come with him."

"Thank you. My lawyer is Debbie Ascher."

"Ah, a lady lawyer. She is welcome. How about at one thirty, Thursday, this week? It's the day after tomorrow."

"It's a deal. Thank you. We'll see you then."

CHAPTER 20
DR. JUPITREN WITH STUDENTS

On Wednesday morning, a group of second-year SUNY(State University of NY) med students arrived at one of Acmeon Lab's conference rooms. "Good morning, sir." One of them greeted Dr. Jupitren. "On behalf of our class, I thank you for accepting our request to have a special lecture session with you in Acmeon Lab. Our professor, Dr. Sobien Molton, must have already spoken to you about our visit today."

"Yes, he did, and your school sent me a notice, too. Everybody, please take a seat."

All eleven of them sat down.

"I heard from Dr. Molton that most of you are now taking courses in behavioral sciences. Is that right?"

"Yes, sir."

"Well, before I give you my talk on the Dream Wafer program, I'm open to any questions you might have about sleep and dreams."

One of the students raised her hand. "Hi, I'm Jane. Not too long ago, I was here for my anxiety dreams, and you prescribed me the Dream Wafers."

"Hello, Jane. I do remember you. It's nice to see you again. I recall that you did very well with your Dream Wafers. Didn't you?"

"Yes. They were quite effective. Within about a week of Dream Wafer application, I became free from my disturbing dreams. I have been fine since then."

"I'm very glad to hear that. So, Jane, did you have any questions?"

"Yes. Could you explain the process of dream formation and dream interpretation?"

"Certainly. That's a good, basic question. There have been many written theses on the subject. Apart from the biological theories on dream formation, can any of you explain what the psychological term *dream-work* means? How about you, Jane?"

"I have read that the *dream-work* concept originated from the early psychoanalytic thoughts of the 1900s. *Dream-work* is an unconscious psychological process by which the raw dream material turns into dreams."

"Very good. What specific psychological processes are usually involved in *dream-work*?"

"Condensation, symbolization, displacement, dramatization and the like, I believe."

"Excellent. Have you heard the term 'wish fulfillment of dreams'?"

"Yes."

"Then, of those main processes you mentioned, which ones are involved in wish fulfillment of dreams?"

"All of them, sir."

"Correct. Now, I will ask the next questions to some other students. How about you, over there. Your name?"

"Tom Moresby."

"Tom, can you explain how any of those processes Jane mentioned operate in *dream-work*?"

Tom answered without hesitation. "Suppose a young man, whom we will call George, was very angry with his father for some reason. Soon, George thought it was not right to hold anger of that degree against his father. So, he felt a certain guilt. Later in his sleep, that is, in his dream, George aggressively pushed a ballplayer, causing him to fall down on a basketball court. George saw in the dream that the basketball player was left-handed.

When he woke up, he thought the ballplayer reminded him of his father, who was also left-handed. Here, the identity of the ball player and his father were merged or *condensed* through their left-handedness. Thus, George was angry with the ballplayer but not with his father. Namely, his original guilt-producing angry feelings were *displaced* to someone else. The net psychological gain is that he got protected from the original guilt feeling.

"Excellent, Tom. Then how would you apply what you just said, if you were to do the dream interpretation?"

This time, Tom hesitated and said, "Well, I'm not sure. That's where I would like to hear your expert explanation. I have never done any formal dream interpretation."

"Actually, Tom you just went through the reverse process of the *dream-work*, which involved two out of the four mechanisms Jane mentioned. Namely, you traced displacement and condensation. So, you just did a very good dream interpretation without calling it as such. If I may add another point— George's anger is an *abstract feeling* but through the dream work, it was *dramatized* as a visible aggressive pushing action."

Dr. Jupitren continued his explanation. "In an actual dream-interpretation session, you ask your patients or clients to think over the dreams that they reported to you. Let them think repeatedly about their dreams until some associated thoughts emerge in their minds. You only encourage them to review their dreams within a given context that is specific to them.

You are not to hint at any universal meaning of symbols or common dream themes in response to their dream contents. What I'm saying is that you do not give your own reactive thoughts to the reported dream contents. The dreamers would tell you what they just thought of in association with the original dream material. The dreamers will discover the meaning of their own dreams as you give them neutral encouragement to go on with their own associative thinking. This process was introduced as *free-association technique* by Sigmund Freud in 1900, as you may know.

Maybe at some other time, I will go over Jungian approach known as *amplification or active imagination*, which has similar elements as Freud's' free association technique."

"In a nutshell, the reverse tracing of the *dream-work* process is the essence of dream interpretation. Now, I have another question for Jane. You used the term '*raw dream material*.' What does the raw material consist of?"

"Oh, things like what happened to me or what I was thinking or feeling… practically everything about my experiences that I had before the dream."

"True. That's right. But let me clarify it a little further. Generally, psychologists and psychiatrists think of three kinds of raw dream materials: *day residue, nocturnal sensory impression,* and *id impulses*, those three. Of course, the term *id* is from Freud's *structural theory of mind, in which he explained his very well-known Id, Ego,* and *Superego.*"

Dr. Jupitren continued:

"*Day residue* is what you saw or experienced recently, say, within the past few days or hours before you went to sleep. I believe most of you might have dreamt about something that happened to you hours or days before you went to sleep.

A likely example would be seeing a white horse in a parade yesterday and then dreaming a white elephant tonight. Here, the color white and the four-legged animal are the day residues that were carried over into your dream. Although we call it *day residue*, events taken place several days prior to your sleep could still be considered under the same term.

The *nocturnal sensory impression* is the physical condition of the dreamer and the dreamer's physical environment. Even if we are asleep, most of our sensory functions are still maintained at certain levels. Therefore, if the room temperature is quite low, you may dream of glacial scenery rather than a hot summer beach. If your arm was pressed with a weight, such as a book or a misplaced laptop, you would dream someone was pressing or tightly holding your arm. If your bladder is getting full, your dream will come up with scenes in which you keep looking for an appropriate place to relieve yourself until you wake up. The auditory functions also give rise to sound-related dreams. For instance, raging thunderstorm noises may let you dream of battle scenes.

The third element, *id impulses*, is far more important than the other two I have just mentioned. The unconscious id impulses being the major latent source of dream material, they are the main object of dream interpretation. Id impulses, through *dream-work*, namely 'unconscious mechanisms,' provide most of the dream material to the dreamer. In other words, dreamers weave manifest dreams out of their id impulses, which are the latent dreams.

When dreams are constructed from the *id*, the primary dream contents are uncensored, illogical, and without chronology. However, in the later part of dream formation, those crude dream contents go through an editing by the ego. Freud termed it as *ego's secondary revision of the dream.* Namely, the secondary revision being under the ego's rational processing, the dream gets a little more coherent and understandable, although it is still not perfect. That's why when we wake up, thanks to the ego's revision of the dreams, some aspects of the dreams seem to have a certain plot or logic, albeit still crude, that we can recognize and talk about. Although this secondary revision is closer to conscious work than unconscious work of the mind, it is still considered a part of the dream mechanism."

Then, Dr. Jupitren explained about various neurophysiological and genetic theories of dream formation including those of Dream Wafer. The students combed through the 135 questions and sub-questions of Wafer questionnaire, raising more questions.

Some students brought up ethical issues regarding the Dream Wafer concept. A few of them said that initially they were skeptical about the possibility of modifying dreams neurochemically and genetically.

Dr. Jupitren responded, "During the Middle Ages and even till the late 1800s, many scholars and visionary thinkers with innovative ideas or discoveries were accused of being heretics and were persecuted and even executed. This was so in the domains of science, religion, politics, and many other fields. Among many, you may recall the heliocentricism propounded by Nicolaus Copernicus and Galileo Galilei. Their observation-based conviction made them to become the target of severe persecution, which came from the un-informed, rigid-minded mass who were instigated by the religious power then prevailed. We all should feel a special indebtedness to our predecessors for the enlightenment they achieved through their painstaking efforts and self-sacrifices.

Unlike our forefathers' time, we live in an era of better sensibility and of higher tolerance regarding different opinions. We can now announce publicly, without feeling threatened for our lives, that what we have discovered is true to our best knowledge, even though the majority of people might not believe us yet."

Robert, another student raised a different question, "When people use the 'I have a dream…' expression, we understand that they have an aspiration or fervent wish. Obviously, they don't mean their usual nightly dreams. However, would you say there is any overlapping meaning between the two?"

"A very good question. Semantically they are supposed to be taken as two different meanings. However, I believe when a person uses that 'I have a dream' expression, actually he is making a statement, which is tantamount to the gestalt meaning of his recurrent dreams that he had forged for lifetime. It is a long drawn unconscious process that finally reached the person's conscious awareness, prompting to be expressed in those expressive words."

Another student asked, "As I'm trying to understand how the Dream Wafers work, I cannot help but think of the conceptual similarity of *lucid dreaming*. Would you comment on the difference between Dream Wafer-induced dreams and lucid dreams?"

"Yes, it's an important question. The term '*lucid dream*,' which was coined by Dutch physician Van Eeden in the early 1900s means that the dreamers are aware that they are dreaming while asleep. Later, some people claimed that in lucid dreams, they willfully or by training could control their dreams' plots.

The claimed ability to control one's dream plot might be plausible as long as there is an active volition supported by a functioning level of consciousness. However, the physiological truth is that people's volitional levels do not remain in a steady state but fluctuate through sleep hours with a tendency to drop to zero. If their volitional level is not zero, then they are not sound asleep. Therefore, as people's sleep deepens, along with their decreasing level of consciousness, their volition or willful controlling ability descends to lower levels. During the deep sleep, just like their skeletal muscles remain in a nearly paralyzed state, they cannot think normally, either, let alone controlling the dream plot to significant degrees.

To complicate the issue, some of the lucid dreamers claim that they can derive certain therapeutic benefits from such lucid dream experiences. It all sounds theoretically plausible. However, despite volumes of testimonials on various benefits of lucid dreams might be there, substantial systematic research results have not been forthcoming, because the subject matter is very difficult to standardize for research. One such difficulty in evaluating those claims comes from the very fact that there is no clear consensus as to how to define the therapeutic benefits of lucid dreams.

It is reasonable to say that for average persons, the lucid dream phenomenon generally remains an unpredictable or unprogrammable occurrence. In my opinion, for untrained average people, it is evanescent in duration and meager in substance. In contrast, the Dream Wafer's goal is to modify the dream contents by dreamers' deliberate choices. Therefore, Dream Wafer is an actively programmable process, albeit within the mandates of the dreamer's genomic variables."

Another student, Brian asked, "What is the difference between night terror and nightmare?"

"Generally, nightmare is REM sleep disorder, whereas night terror is non-REM sleep disorder. As you know, in one night we go through 4 or 5 cycles of sleep. Each cycle starts with non-REM sleep stages followed by REM sleep. The first REM sleep of the night with 10 to 15 minutes of duration occurs roughly 90 minutes after we fall asleep. As the sleep cycles progress toward morning, REM sleeps get longer. That's when nightmares with vivid, scary images occur, namely in the latter half of night.

On the other hand, night terror mostly occurs in the first third of night. During that part of night, more of the non-REM sleep occurs than the REM sleep. Typically, the night terror lets the person experience terrifying feelings while having very vague imagery, if any, or no dream at all.

If people have sleep disturbances during non-REM sleep, apart from the night terrors, they may engage in multifaceted behavior, such as sleepwalking, sleep talking, sleep eating, or bed-wetting. It is also known that such non-REM sleep disturbances tend to be genetically loaded. I mean, they tend to occur more often in certain families."

Brian asked again, "Doctor Jupitren, you said earlier that it takes about 90 minutes for the sleeper to have the first REM sleep of the night. Then, how come some nappers dream even during a 20 minute-napping?"

"Very good question. It's generally true that during the 20 minutes short daytime naps, EEG registers mostly light stages of non-REM sleep. However, it is known that during non-REM sleep, we still dream although it may not be as colorful or formative as in REM sleep. According to sleep studies, those nappers who dream during the 20 minute-nap might have had ongoing night time sleep deprivation of varying degrees.

It's generally known that a 20 minute-napping invigorates but longer than 20 minutes of napping causes inertia upon awakening. However, conflicting reports say that if a napper sleeps beyond 90 minutes and completes one full cycle consisting of non-REM and REM sleep, he would feel even better."

"Thank you, doctor." Brian responded.

This time, another student, Michael, who was quiet so far, asked a question. "Do you believe sleep disorders may cause major psychiatric disorders?"

"I don't think so. However, in certain psychiatric disorders, sleep disturbances may manifest as their harbingers. A well-known fact is that at the onset of and during such conditions as depressive disorders, psychoses, and bipolar disorders, people experience various sleep problems. Therefore, symptomatic treatment of their sleep disorders alone would not thwart the progression of those disorders. They require disorder-specific treatments."

"Thank you, doctor." Michael said, "I have another question. Do animals dream?"

"Actually no one knows because they cannot talk about their dreams. We can only speculate based on their REM sleep that some of them might be dreaming.

Cold-blooded reptiles don't have REM sleep. According to the National Sleep Research Project, newborn rats have only REM sleep. In contrast, newborn guinea pigs have no REM sleep at all. Elephants sleep while standing during non-REM sleep but lie down during REM sleep. Ducks in vigil over impending danger, let one-half of their brains sleep while letting the other half remain awake.

Well, I rushed my answer as your assigned class hours are way over. You may want to study on your own about topics like *sleep deprivation* and *sleep hygiene*.

Also, please refer to the National Sleep Research Project report. You will find lots of interesting sleep-related facts."

Dr. Jupitren's lecture had to end right there.

CHAPTER 21
A BUSY DAY WITH SOBIEN MOLTON AND SAM DAYER

Thursday morning's schedule was full for Dr. Jupitren. He had to extend his morning hours to see Dr. Sobien Molton, who had asked for a special unscheduled visit.

Sobien said, "When I was here two months ago, I said my project would go on a few more months. But, I'm almost finished with it. It's lot sooner than I anticipated."

"That sounds good. Then, could you start your work here soon?"

"Yes, but I have a special request before that." As he was saying so, Sobien seemed somewhat uncertain and unsure of himself.

Dr. Jupitren asked, "Please tell me about your special request."

"Well, I could not tell you about it when I was here last time." Sobien became hesitant. "It is that, uh…that I'm very interested…hmm, in trying the Dream Wafer on myself."

"That shouldn't be hard. But would you tell me what made you to think of trying it on you?"

"I can think of a couple of reasons. The first is to get to know more about the Dream Wafers by having a hands-on experience. The second reason is…" Sobien halted there, his expression suddenly distressed, and then he timidly continued his answer. "I have had bad recurrent dreams. In the latest one, I was about to drown in a raging ocean. I was clinging to a log that barely kept me afloat while I was tossed up and down with the fierce waves. But, the log turned into a wounded fish, and a huge shark appeared from nowhere, gnawing at it. Fearing the shark would soon come after me, I let go of the log. I had nothing else to hang on to, and I started to swim. Exhausted, I looked around to see if there was anything else to grab. But I only found more sharks swarming around me. Frightened for my life, I screamed for help but no one heard my wave-muffled scream. The sheer terror woke me up." Sobien seemed almost in tears when he finished his report.

"Just describing your anxiety dream, I see you got quite upset. Would you tell me what has been happening to you lately?"

Sobien described how bleak it had been for him to go through divorce-related stress with ensuing financial difficulties. As he was saying it, his whole persona transformed into sadness itself.

"I'm sorry to hear that you are under such heavy stress. I believe the Dream Wafers would help you to cope better with your difficult situations. Why don't you go through the routine pre-Wafer tests and questionnaire session today?"

"I will. Thank you."

"If you can wait for an extra hour or two after completing the questionnaire, you may have your first Dream Wafers later this afternoon."

"I'll wait for the Wafers."

"Good. Before we end the session, let me say this briefly. I have read some of your research papers about the gene-splicing method, the Chemical Razor. I thought it might be useful in some way for Dream Wafer composition. When I see you next time, I will ask you more about the Chemical Razor method."

"I'll be glad to come back at your convenience."

"I'll need some more time to review your research literature, and maybe you, too, will need some time to see how well the Dream Wafer works for you. So, how about on Thursday afternoon, two weeks from today, at three thirty? Is that a good time?"

"Yes. It works for me. Thank you. I'll be here at that time."

Soon after Sobien Molton went home with his Wafers, Dr. Jupitren retrieved Sobien's baseline data on genome-linked chemical profiles. There were a few red signals indicating the young doctor had some instability of mood and traits of a sociopathic profile. The record of his answers to the questionnaire indicated that his requested choices of intensity on several of the questionnaire items were unusually high, potentiating his Dream Wafers' side-effect probability.

Dr. Jupitren concluded that those findings would require close watch, but any extra tests or evaluations on Sobien did not seem indicated for the time being.

Anticipating the afternoon's visitor Sam Dayer, Dr. Jupitren told Helen, "Let other staff take the incoming calls, and please be ready by one thirty with your recorder and shorthand pads. The Trans-Alpha Jet Air pilot is coming with his lawyer to see me this afternoon."

"Coming with his lawyer?" Helen asked him. "For any legal problems?"

"No, I don't think so. The pilot asked me if I would mind his lawyer's presence, and I said no, as I'm used to having some of my clients come with their advocates, including their lawyers."

"I see. I'll let you know as soon as they arrive."

"By the way, Helen, his lawyer is a woman, Debbie Ascher."

The clock showed it was 1:30. But no visitor was in sight. At 1:45, shortly after Helen's intercom announcement to Dr. Jupitren, a middle-aged woman found her way to his office. With her tousled hair hanging over her flushed cheeks, she appeared distraught.

"I am very sorry, Dr. Jupitren. I'm Debbie Ascher. I presume you were expecting Mr. Dayer, who should have been here fifteen minutes ago. But…"

Dr. Jupitren rose from his chair and motioned for her to take a seat, but she would not sit down.

"Dr. Jupitren, I need your help." She turned her head in the direction of the parking lot a few times and said, "Mr. Dayer is still in the car and refuses to come out despite my urging."

"Did anything happen to him on the way to Acmeon?"

"Contrary to what the recent news said about him, he is not well." She seemed genuinely concerned and said solicitously, "He at times showed a touch of paranoia, and today he seemed worse. He's had some heavy drinking episodes lately. The very reason he asked me to accompany him today was that he knew he was not with it yet. And this afternoon he was out of sorts."

"I am very sorry to hear that. Mrs. Ascher, do you want me to go out with you and say hello to him?"

"Yes, Doctor. Maybe if he sees you, he may change his mind and come in to talk with you."

Feeling some uneasiness, he followed Mrs. Ascher to Sam Dayer's car. They found Sam in his car, covering his face with his hands, mumbling something while sitting in the passenger side seat. Through the half-rolled-down window, they could hear his incoherent verbiage.

Preparing to speak to Sam Dayer, Dr. Jupitren bent his back forward, lowering himself close to the car window, through which he smelled unmistakable alcohol breath. He said calmly, "Hi, Mr. Dayer, I'm Julian Jupitren. How are you today?"

Swaying back and forth with his hands over his face, Sam Dayer would not make any eye contact with anyone and mumbled an incoherent monologue.

"Sam! Can you hear me?" Mrs. Ascher called out somewhat loudly. "Can you look at us?" She tried to open the car door only to find all the doors were locked from inside.

Looking at Dr. Jupitren, she said, "Episodes like this, locking himself inside the car, have happened a few times lately and I carry a spare key." She was about to unlock the driver-side door.

"Just one moment, please." Using hand gestures, Dr. Jupitren asked her not to open the door. "I'll try to see how he is."

Turning to Sam Dayer, Dr. Jupitren asked, "Mr. Dayer, do you want me to call someone else to help you?...Are you not feeling well?...Do you want Mrs. Ascher to drive you back home?"

Suddenly, Sam Dayer yelled out expletives and ranted in so many words, demanding to be left alone, without removing his hands from his face. Then he shouted an obscenity, threatening bodily harm if anyone approached him.

Dr. Jupitren asked Mrs. Ascher, "Was he agitated like this on his way here?"

"No, he was casual, though he was a bit under the influence of the extra beer. He drank it at the kiostrant before we got on the highway. Because he drank, I drove his car from the kiostrant. Soon, he remained dead silent all the way here, and he made me nervous."

"How long ago did he drink the beer?"

"The kiostrant was near exit forty-six on the throughway. So it might have been about thirty minutes ago."

Dr. Jupitren explained that Sam Dayer, in such derailed state, might bolt out on people or injure himself with any additional stimuli. Then he said, "I may have to give him an emergency tranquilizer injection. First, we need to call for police or EMT assistance."

No sooner had he finished saying it than Helen, who was standing behind them, called the police. She also brought the emergency tranq-gun to Dr. Jupitren from his office cabinet.

Sam Dayer did not stop mumbling, and at some moments, he ranted loudly. Noticeably, he was getting more irrational.

Mrs. Ascher unlocked Sam's car door for the police, who'd just arrived, with an ambulance trailing behind. Surrounded by two officers and two

EMTs, Sam quieted himself down considerably. Out of his car, he stood a bit taller and heavier than everyone else. He reeked of alcohol.

In transit from his car to the ambulance, suddenly he lunged violently onto the ambulance driver, who was standing next to the ambulance. Everyone moved in quickly to subdue his random movements. Dr. Jupitren, who was a couple of feet away from Sam, moved quickly close to him and shot the tranq-gun in his thigh, right through his clothing. Sam winced with a grimace, let his hands off the ambulance driver's scruff, and grabbed his own thigh that had taken the injection. They struggled to board him on the ambulance. Inside the vehicle, he yodeled a few more refrains of his ranting only to fall back moments later onto the EMTs' padded tarp bed, to which he was secured with Velcro straps.

The ambulance brought muzzy Sam Dayer to Northwest Hospital ER. Following the ambulance, Mrs. Ascher drove herself to the hospital.

Dr. Jupitren thought one thing did not jibe well with the rest of Sam's overall behavior. He thought it was odd to see his aggressive fuming suddenly subsided when the EMTs arrived. Dr. Jupitren continued wondering. "Was he malingering to begin with? Was he overwhelmed with fear when he saw the EMTs and the police? How much did the alcohol affect his behavior? Was he in the early stage of delirium tremens? Or, Ganser syndrome?"

Later, Dr. Jupitren called the ER doctor, who had just finished the preliminary examination on Sam Dayer and decided to send him to a locked psychiatric observation unit for further evaluation.

He told Dr. Jupitren in a deferring tone, "When the patient sobers up from the alcohol and the tranq-gun effect, the observation-unit doctors will make the final diagnosis. However, until then, we will tag your diagnostic impression on the front page of his ER record: Ganser syndrome; rule out delirium tremens. Is that all right, sir?"

"Yes, thank you very much for the information. While we are on the phone, I'd like to let you know about the tranq-gun dose I used. Despite the large body size of the patient, I gave him a lower than average dose of the tranquilizer because he was already under the influence of alcohol. Therefore, I believe the tranquilizer effect might clear up much sooner than usual."

"Thank you, Dr. Jupitren. I'll take that into consideration when I make further assessment on his mental status."

A short while later, Dr. Jupitren received a call from Mrs. Ascher, who was still at the hospital.

"I'm sorry, Doctor. I didn't expect our meeting would turn out like this."

"I'm sorry, too. I just called the ER doctor, who told me Mr. Dayer would need to be in the observation unit until he gets sober from alcohol and the tranq-gun effect."

"I suppose you would like to reschedule the meeting for another day. But I wonder what you and Mr. Dayer would have discussed if the meeting went as planned."

"The main reason I wanted to see him today was to ask him where he got the counterfeit Dream Wafers. With the information, I hoped to find means to stop the counterfeit Wafer production. Would you be able to give me such information?"

She hesitantly answered, "It would be proper for me to come back with him after he gets released from the hospital and have him tell you everything. Although I have a general idea, the specific details and any relevant documents should come from him. Sorry, I can't help you with that now."

"I understand. I suppose you are not free to divulge any personal information on your clients, anyway."

"Just like you, as a physician, would not divulge information on your patients."

"You're right. However, in this case, unless we stop the mass production of the counterfeit Wafers soon, there will be more incidents like the Trans-Alpha Jet Air."

"I understand. I will do what I can, within reason, without jeopardizing Mr. Dayer's rights."

"Thank you. I'd appreciate any information about where Mr. Dayer got his Wafers."

Later in the afternoon, Dr. Jupitren received a call from Steve. "Hi, I called just to tell you about somebody I saw around lunchtime today."

"Who?"

"Sam Dayer, the pilot."

"Where was it?"

"My sister, Jenny, and I were having sandwiches at the kiostrant near exit forty-six on the Island Throughway."

"And?"

"There, we saw him and a woman...maybe his wife?"

"How did you know he was Sam Dayer?"

"After the Trans-Alpha Jet Air episode, I saw him several times on the news. And today I recognized him right away."

"Aha, so what did you do then?"

"I could have walked up to him, but I didn't, and I just listened to what he was saying to his companion. We were sitting at the very next table."

"Very interesting, Steve. They were supposed to be in my office today. You must have seen them on their way to my office early this afternoon."

"Is that right? Did you get to see them?"

"Not quite. He remained in the Acmeon parking lot. Only the woman, his lawyer, came up to my office and told me why he didn't come in with her. At any rate, did you hear anything from them?"

"Yes, I overheard Sam Dayer say to his lawyer, 'I don't want anybody to know where I got those fake Dream Wafers. You shall not disclose that to anyone, especially to any Acmeon guys. Why did I agree to go to Acmeon Lab today? I shouldn't go any further.' That was the gist of it."

"Did he sound coherent all the while there?"

"Yes, he was. But he was drinking beer and seemed a little high, getting louder. At some point, he was even kidding about the kiostrant workers, and he made his companion chuckle a few times."

After hearing Steve's account, it became clear to Dr. Jupitren that regardless what diagnosis he had, Sam Dayer was very reluctant to tell anyone how and where he'd obtained the counterfeit Wafers.

Dr. Jupitren wondered, "Is he simply embarrassed about how he got the Wafers? Was he involved in any criminal deals? What would be the best way to get the information about where he bought the counterfeits?"

CHAPTER 22
THE UNCLAIMED BAGGAGE

Dr. Jupitren received a call from the psychiatrist at Northwest Hospital's observation unit.

"Hello, Dr. Jupitren, we did an intravenous Amytal interview on Sam Dayer."

"You mean the old truth serum?"

"Yes, for some reason, in the past few years the Amytal interviews have been revitalized and more psychiatrists seem to use them now."

"I've heard about it, too. They said, now a small dose of short acting Benzodiazepine is concurrently used with Amytal. Do you often do the Amytal interview?"

"Well, we use them occasionally in the ER and psych-observation unit for certain cases, such as elective mutism, pathological liars, hysterical aphonias, malingerers, and the like."

"So, how did it go with Sam Dayer?"

"It went well. I agree with your diagnostic impression that he is a Ganser syndrome case. I don't think he is psychotic. During the routine interview, he gave unrealistic, approximate answers, one of which was two plus three being six. But under the Amytal, he became coherent and did not repeat the approximate answers."

"So, under Ganser syndrome, he might have some concealed motivation, probably guarding certain secrets."

"I suspect so."

"Did you hear anything from him about Dream Wafers?"

"Dream Wafers? No, I don't think so. All I heard in his dissociative speech was 'the unclaimed baggage', which he uttered a few times, but I couldn't decipher its significance. He will need more observation on the unit. He is not safe to go home yet."

"I understand. Thank you very much for your call."

Having finished the call, Dr. Jupitren repeated the phrase he'd just heard. "The unclaimed baggage, the unclaimed baggage…This is a kind of riddle."

"Helen, I've a question for you. Let Anne cover the front office and will you come in to my office?"

Helen promptly came to his office feeling curious. Dr. Jupitren said, "When I say a phrase, concentrate on it and tell me the first thing that comes to your mind. OK?"

"Sure."

"The unclaimed baggage." He said it in a robotic monotone.

Helen repeated the phrase a couple of times. Then, without any hesitation, she said, "The airport?"

"The airport!" Dr. Jupitren exclaimed.

"Is that the right answer?" Helen was curious to know.

"Oh, yes, it could be. But I'm not sure yet. Let me think about it."

He told Helen that Sam Dayer, the pilot, had uttered the riddle-like phrase to his doctor at the hospital.

Smiling broadly, Dr. Jupitren said, "After all, come to think of it, your answer could be right." He realized that he had concentrated solely on the figurative psychological meaning of "the unclaimed baggage" of Sam Dayer, relating to his Ganser syndrome. But, Helen sensed it intuitively, and came up with the denoted, concrete object. He briefly explained to Helen what he was thinking about the pilot's bag. Soon after Helen went back to her front office, he called Bill.

"Hi, Bill, how's it going with you? I have a special request today."

"Asking anything about Akandro Oladre?"

"No, not about him. But I assume he is still at the detention center."

"Yes, certainly. We don't have anything new with him yet. What's the special request, Jules?"

"It's about Sam Dayer at the Northwest Hospital."

"How is he doing?"

"Well, reportedly, during the truth-serum interview at the hospital, he said a phrase, 'the unclaimed baggage' repeatedly."

"And? What does that mean?"

"I suspect there might be an unclaimed baggage in Narita International."

"Gee whiz, how did you think of that?"

"Do you remember the news video clips about the Trans-Alpha Jet Air incident? We all watched it several times. We saw the agitated pilot being escorted out of the plane, and from there, he was transported directly to LA General Hospital's maximum-security unit. He remained there until he was transferred back to New York several weeks ago. As you know, when patients are brought into a maximum-security unit, they cannot bring anything from outside unless authorized."

"So what are you getting at?"

"His luggage. If it was not tagged with his name, it must be still in that airport."

"Why wouldn't it be tagged?"

"Because Sam Dayer probably wanted it that way."

"Aha, do you suspect contraband?"

"Precisely. I suspect the bag must have something to do with the counterfeit Wafer."

"Now I get it. So what do you want me to do?"

"Would you talk to Narita Airport people and check if there is any unclaimed bag from that Trans-Alpha Jet Air flight?"

"That shouldn't be hard. But what shall I ask them to do, if they have it there?"

"Please ask them to unlock the bag and describe each item and, if possible, Cyberscope the contents in close-up views. I would like to be there, too, and watch the Cyberscoped images closely. I'm interested in only one thing: the counterfeit Dream Wafers' source."

"Well, Jules. I'll arrange a Cyberscope session and let you know when you need to come to my station. All right?"

"Thank you, Bill. If it's possible, please set the appointment at our off-hours. It will be Japan's main business hours. Although they work 24/7, daytime would be more convenient for them. How about after 6 pm our time. Is that OK with you, Bill?"

"No problem. I'll set it up for around seven in the evening our time tomorrow. It will be eight in the morning the next calendar day there in Tokyo. I'll call Narita now to make the appointment for tomorrow. If the Narita Airport gives me a different time, I'll let you know right away."

"Great. Thank you, Bill. I'll see you tomorrow at seven in the evening."

The next day, the Northwest Hospital doctor told Dr. Jupitren that Sam Dayer was kept in the locked-unit under one-to-one observation, and his mental status did not show much change even after the alcohol and tranq-gun effects cleared up.

Later in the evening, Dr. Jupitren arrived at Bill's office on time. Bill led him to the electronics-packed surveillance room within the precinct. Bill had his cyber-expert officer Morimoto to set up the international Cyberscope and made an easy connection with the unclaimed-baggage department of Narita International Airport.

The Cyberscope operator said, "Hi, Mr. Morimoto, good evening. I'm Suzanna Inoguchi, an administrative assistant to the superintendent. As you see on your Cyberscope monitor, Mr. Takeyama, the superintendent of the airport, is on my right side. On my left side is another assistant, Ms. Kojiro. On your party, are you all set?"

"Yes. We are ready," Officer Morimoto answered on behalf of Bill.

Suzanna said, "Yesterday, we received from you a list of three persons who would be there for this Cyberscope meeting. We need to know who are present on your side. Everyone, please state your full name and title."

After reciprocating all the needed preliminaries and information exchanges between the Narita Airport and Bill's party, Bill asked the Narita staff, "Were you able to identify the owner of the bag?"

"No," Suzanna answered. "We could not find any information on the bag, either outside or inside of it."

"Do you know how the bag arrived at Narita Airport?" Bill asked.

Mr. Takeyama answered, "The only fact we have on our record is that this bag was on board the flight that had to make an emergency landing in the Pacific Islands on its way to Tokyo. It is clear that someone, either the bag owner himself or somebody else, illegally loaded it without the id-tag. Our ground staff found the bag in the cargo compartment of the Trans-Alpha Jet aircraft, and we ended up literally holding the bag. It's a rather rare incident."

"I understand. Please tell us what you found in the bag." Bill asked.

Suzanna stated the following: "After a routine X-ray scanning for any contraband or explosive devices, we snipped its heavy padlock to open it. The bag's entire contents weighed roughly twenty-five pounds."

Suzanna displayed the items in the open bag on the Cyberscope and said, "For your view, we have made a list on the contents."

Four items of clothes including a uniform jacket; 14 pounds;
One bottle of Remy Martin Champagne Cognac; 24 ounces;

"By the way, the listed weights are only approximate measurements; they are just to let you have a general idea of the given item's weight."

Suzanna continued to read the list and identified each item by pointing at it.

One book: A Guide for Travelers going to Capital region of Islet Republic; 1 pound;
Three bottles, separately packaged in 3 boxes; 1000 pieces of round chips per bottle – altogether 3000 pieces -- 6 pounds;
A high power camera in factory-wrapped condition; 2 pounds;
Shaving kit with cream and aftershave lotion; 1 pound; End of the list.

Bill said, "Thank you, Ms. Inoguchi. In the package of those round chips, was there any address, name or telephone number of the manufacturer?"

Suzanna answered, "There was an insert paper in each of those three boxes. However, the insert did not show any addresses or telephone number. It only stated: *'To be applied to skin in the temple area. Limit only one patch a night. Apply seven to eight hours before wake-up time. The manufacturer assumes no responsibility for any side effects or complications arising from the use of these skin patches. The manufacturer categorically declares immunity to any liability.'* That's the end of the statement."

Dr. Jupitren asked Suzanna, "Could you please show the chips in a close-up mode?"

She opened one of the three bottles, took a few chips out, placed them on her palm, and said, "Here they are. Can you see them?"

"Yes, I can. Ms. Inoguchi, could you pick up one chip and read its serial number?"

She took up one chip as requested and said, "It is 64-57-884. Do you need to check anything else?"

"No. Thank you." Dr. Jupitren turned to Bill and said indignantly, "Seven digits! And three thousands of them. Acmeon Wafers should have only six digits. They are definitely counterfeits!"

Bill asked Suzanna, "What would you have done with the bag if we did not call you yesterday and today?"

"According to our policy, we would have sent it to a long-term storage depot if you waited another three days. The long-term storage depot is not within the Narita Airport's premises. It would be kept in a special building under jurisdiction of the Tokyo police. You called us just in time. Now, if you know it, can we have the name of the person to whom this bag belongs?"

Bill had a brief discussion with Dr. Jupitren and then said, "The bag most likely belongs to Mr. Sam Dayer, the pilot of the Trans-Alpha Jet Air flight. However, he might deny that fact. Moreover, it could still belong to someone else unknown to us."

At that moment, Ms. Kojiro, the other assistant, said, "Everybody, excuse me one moment, please." And, she showed Mr. Takeyama the inside of the uniform jacket, which was among the listed items. She pointed at the pocket's inner-flap lining and said, "Mr. Takeyama, we must have overlooked this. Isn't it the name of this jacket's owner?"

Mr. Takeyama confirmed it and said, "Yes, it says, 'Sam Dayer'. Thank you, Ms. Kojiro." Mr. Takeyama turned toward Bill's direction and said, "Mr. Warren, I'm glad we just found the critical information. This bag must belong to Sam Dayer, the pilot."

"That's good. Thank you very much." Bill said.

Dr. Jupitren had a brief exchange of words with Bill and said, "Ms. Kojiro, thank you for spotting it. I have a special request. Would you save the chip that you just read its serial number? Please mail that single chip to Acmeon Lab for a chemical analysis. We will text you our mailing address momentarily."

Then Bill said, "We will notify Mr. Sam Dayer or his personal lawyer to call you about the bag. We will inform them that unless they contact you soon, they may have to find the bag later at the long-term storage depot area. Unfortunately, those three thousand chips you have there are not quite legal materials. If those chips were found here in the USA, they would be confiscated immediately."

Mr. Takeyama asked, "Are you permitted to tell us what those chips are?"

Dr. Jupitren answered, "They are skin patches, which would change one's *yu-meh*, the dream, but what you have there are unsafe, because they are counterfeit items. But they are not narcotics."

Mr. Takeyama said, "Changes one's *yu-meh*? Then, aren't they the Dream Wafers? We heard that the Trans-Alpha Jet Air incident had something to do with the Dream Wafers."

"You are right," Dr. Jupitren said. "I believe the three thousand counterfeit chips in the bag may cause health problems. However, the genuine Dream Wafers promote people's health by therapeutically modifying their dreams and improving sleep as well."

"Thank you for the information." Mr. Takeyama said. "We will classify them as a special medical cachets and handle them accordingly. We will safeguard them until we have final instructions for proper disposal from the Controlled Substance Bureau."

Bill said, "Our officer Morimoto just texted you Acmeon Lab's address and our contact numbers. Please mail the single chip to that address as Dr. Jupitren asked. And as I mentioned, we will notify the owner or his personal lawyer to get in touch with you soon. Please call us for any questions you might have."

"Thank you, we will." Mr. Takeyama answered.

Bill responded, "We thank you and your assistants for your cooperation and extended help. *Arigatou gozaimasu. Sayonara.*"

CHAPTER 23
HELEN'S CAREER OPPORTUNITY

The next day, during the lunch hour, sitting on his office chair, Dr. Jupitren made slow, light finger taps on his desk. That was his habit when he was in the middle of intense concentration or in deep thought. He asked Helen to come in to his office.

Sensing he was in a serious mood, Helen asked him, "Uncle Jules, is everything all right?"

"Yes. Why don't you sit down? I want to tell you something important."

Feeling curious, Helen sat down slowly.

"Lately, I have been thinking about Acmeon Lab's future. As you know, after my afternoon office hours, I usually go to the West Room every day to work for another couple of hours on the *virtual brain*. Soon I'll need to work for longer hours there. So I have been thinking of finding a couple of good doctors and an able business manager who would gradually free me from the routine clinical work and daily administrative matters that I have been taking care of so far.

A few days ago, Jamie asked me about my thoughts for the future of Acmeon Lab and my overall work plan. In an answer to her question, I told her about my thoughts on delegating my routine responsibilities to other dependable people, as I have just told you. Then, Jamie, whose opinion I take seriously, brought up something about you."

Helen became wide-eyed, feeling more curious.

Dr. Jupitren continued, "Actually, Jamie's idea was very similar to what I had been thinking all along. She said that, as an honors student all through your college years, you have shown stable personality and perseverance in your personal and work related matters. Besides, Jamie saw you having very good organizing skills and caring attitude for people, among other laudable personality assets. And she suggested that I might consider gradually delegating the management of Acmeon Lab to you and your future husband. I thought it was a very good idea. If our plan works out well, your presence in the center of Acmeon's administration would make my retirement smooth and easy. How does it all sound to you?"

"I'm overwhelmed by what you just said. I'm wondering if I'll be able to meet such a big challenge."

"You don't have to be the company's start-up CEO. You just need to muster up your interest and pay a little more attention to Acmeon Lab's operation, most of which you're already familiar with anyway. For the next four to five years, gradually you might be able to take full charge of Acmeon's business operations while a couple of new doctors would take over the routine Dream Wafer-related clinical work."

"But, Uncle Jules, if it goes as you just described, I'm afraid I might let Acmeon Lab become stagnant without steady growth."

"Don't you worry! Unlike many popular tech companies that have to introduce new products almost as often as every couple of years to please their customers,

Acmeon Lab does not need to produce new versions of Dream Wafers so often. That much your job will be less complicated to manage. But it does not mean that Acmeon Lab will stop upgrading Dream Wafers toward the next refined versions. We doctors will take care of that. In addition, we will have all the antidotes improved so that we can treat any side effects that might occur due to Dream Wafer use.

If you're concerned about not having the basic skills necessary to lead and manage a business like Acmeon Lab, you can learn and acquire them while you're working here. We don't need to bring in so-called professional CEOs from outside."

Still doubting her own ability, Helen remained quiet.

"Now you have heard me. Please give it some thought, and, one of these days, let me know what you would like to do."

"Thank you for taking me seriously. I also thank Aunt Jamie for having strong trust in me. I will think it over very carefully and will give you my answer soon. Of course, I'll speak to my parents as well."

"Good. If I were you, I would do the same."

Helen thought to herself briefly that it might not be an impossible idea after all.

When she came home, Helen asked her mother in the kitchen, "Mom, did Uncle Jules ever discuss his retirement or Acmeon's future with you?"

"No. But lately Jamie told me a few things about his plan but not about his retirement." Mrs. Humayor stopped what she was doing and asked, "Why, did Jules say anything to you?"

"Yes, at the office this afternoon. It was a complete surprise for me. He said that gradually, in four or five years, I, and my husband, if I'm married, could manage the business part of Acmeon Lab. He said it was Aunt Jamie's suggestion, and he took it as a good idea. I was so surprised I couldn't find the right words to thank him properly."

"Did he say anything about the medical practice part?"

"Yes, he said he will find a couple of good new doctors to help him with the routine Dream Wafer-related work so that he can spend more time doing research on the *virtual brain*."

"Then he was not talking about his immediate retirement."

"No, he was not. He sounded like he wanted to go on and do more research work."

"So, how do you feel about it?"

"I'm kind of excited and scared at the same time. I wondered seriously how my future husband and I could manage such a big and delicate biomedical lab. Without the kind of knowledge Uncle Jules has, how could I or anyone else run the business as well as he has done?"

"Did you tell him about what you were so unsure of?"

"Yes. He sensed it, too, and reassured me." Helen told her mother everything Dr. Jupitren had said to her at the office.

Having listened to Helen, Mrs. Humayor said, "You have always been Aunt Jamie's favorite. She used to say that she wished to have a daughter just like you."

"That's very kind of her."

"By the way, have you seen Steve Spencer lately?"

"Yes, Uncle Jules usually asks him to come to Acmeon when the Wafer program has any security problems."

"Do you like him?"

"A lot."

"Is he a dependable and able person?"

"Yes, and…"

"And what?"

"He is very handsome, too!"

"I remember seeing him. He was charming and good-looking. Do you remember that time I said I would invite him to our home to show our atelier?"

"Yes, you said it to him."

"Have you ever gone out with him?"

"Not really."

"How come?"

"I can't blame Jonathan alone. Maybe because Steve was an Acmeon Lab client? I'm not sure. Uncle Jules used to say that mental-health professionals should have a good enough reason and clear conscience in relating with their clients socially."

"I, too, heard Jules used to say that people in mental-health professions should never take advantage of their clients' predicaments or vulnerabilities in dealing with them either socially or in treatment settings. But, Helen, you are not a mental-health professional. Besides, now Steve is not in active treatment by Julian, either."

"I know that."

"I wish you'd spruce yourself up a little and hold on to your confidence. You're Acmeon's CEO-to-be, remember?"

Helen smiled and remained silent.

"As soon as Dad comes home, we should let him know about what you heard from Uncle Jules today and ask for Dad's thoughts on it."

"Of course, Mom."

Helen helped her mother in the kitchen, setting the supper table for three.

Soon, Helen's father came home and said, "I had a pretty good day. I finished another chapter of my new book before I left my office. How did your days go?"

"Very well. Helen brought home some good news this evening."

"Great. Helen, will you tell me about it while we're having dinner?"

"Sure, it's about my future. An unexpected career opportunity came up, and I want to hear your thoughts on it."

At the dinner table, Helen told him everything that Uncle Jules said to her at the office and what she was thinking about it.

"That's wonderful, Helen. First of all, we all should thank Jules and Jamie for having trusted you so much. I'm very happy for you and feel confident that you could manage it if you put your mind to it."

Mr. Humayor, looking at his wife, continued, "After all, our Helen is very intelligent and capable. She loves to tackle challenging tasks. Don't you agree, Elva?"

"I surely agree with you there. But there is one thing I'm concerned about." This time, Mrs. Humayor looked at Helen and said, "If I may voice it, my concern is that at your age, you ought to spend a good deal of time and energy trying to meet someone and settle down in your own home. By putting too much time and energy into your new career, you might miss that chance."

Mr. Humayor said, "Well, we know balancing between marriage and a career is many modern young women's dilemma. But I'm confident that you would face this career opportunity very well without jeopardizing your personal life."

"I'm very happy that you both have strong confidence in me," Helen responded. "But I still feel overwhelmed by the daunting task ahead. I think I should take business-administration courses this fall before it gets too late for me. I know I have all the credits required to apply for MBA courses. But the next big hurdle will be a financial one, as I'll be working much less hours so that I can study."

"Helen, you should not worry about the extra education expenses. Mom and I have kept a special education account in your name for many years. I believe it will be a sufficient amount to cover the next level of your education."

"Thank you so very much, Mom and Dad."

Mr. Humayor said, "Since we've heard from you about Jules's wish, I'll call Jules and Jamie to thank them tomorrow. Helen, as soon as you feel ready, please let Uncle Julian and Aunt Jamie know that you're willing to meet the challenge, although you're still somewhat overwhelmed. I think Uncle Julian will be pleased to hear that you're thinking of taking business-administration courses."

"By the way," Mrs. Humayor added, "one of these days, let's invite Steve to our home. Dad will be glad to meet him, too."

"Having heard so much about him from both of you, I feel Steve must be a nice, intelligent young man. Of course I'd love to meet him."

"Thank you, Dad. I'll ask him to visit us. When is a good time for both of you?"

Mr. Humayor answered, "Maybe any Saturday, around lunchtime? Since I usually can come home from my office by noontime on Saturdays. Is it OK with you, Elva?"

"Of course. How about you, Helen?"

"It's good for me. I'll talk to Steve and will let you know which Saturday it will be."

The next day at his office, Dr. Jupitren asked Helen cheerfully, "Good morning, Helen. Did you consult your pillow on what I told you yesterday?"

"Yes, I have thought of it carefully and told my parents all about it. They encouraged me and promised to give me their full support."

"I'm very glad to hear that."

"I don't know how to thank you enough. I'm too inexperienced in managing a business. But from here on, I will learn about Acmeon's business with the special goal in mind—I mean the goal you let me have. I'll work very hard at it!"

"I'm very glad that you decided to embrace the opportunity and learn the business."

"My parents were very happy for me and grateful to you. They said they will call you soon."

CHAPTER 24
SOBIEN MOLTON

Later, while sorting things in the office, Helen asked Dr. Jupitren, "Do you have any doctor or doctors in mind who will be working with you?"

"Yes, I have several hopefuls on my new roster. But I will need just one or two doctors to train for a few years. Actually, at 3:30 this afternoon, I'll be meeting with Dr. Sobien Molton."

"I remember him. He had his first Dream Wafers a few weeks ago. Isn't he one of our new clients?"

"Not a client. Initially he came to see me, asking if he could work here and learn about Dream Wafers. When he was here last time, he said he wanted to try Dream Wafers for himself so that he could have a hands-on experience to start with. He is a promising young doctor who is very interested in learning about Dream Wafers."

"Well, then, I should be on good terms with him."

At 3:25 pm a stout man with a moustache strode in showing an assured manner.

"*Guten tag,* I am Dr. Molton. I'm here to see Dr. Jupitren."

"Good afternoon, Dr. Molton. Please take a seat. Dr. Jupitren is with a patient now."

"Well, Helen, you just said it exactly as you did when I first came here."

"Did I?"

"By the way, you had the same purple barrette in your hair on that day, too."

"You're very perceptive."

"That's my nature. When it comes to visual novelties, I remember them well."

Helen didn't repartee but thought to herself, "Is he trying to say I'm a visual novelty?"

Helen said, "Should I pull out your file for Dr. Jupitren? Are you here today for the Wafer follow-up?"

"No, probably I'll just speak with him today. But if he recommends it, I'll go through the tests and questionnaire session. So, about my file? You may pull it out just in case Dr. Jupitren wants to review it. For that matter, I don't care if you read my records. If you decide to read it, you will get to know me that much faster."

"Really? Thank you for entrusting me with your records." Helen meant to make her statement sound a bit cynical, but it came off sincere instead. Dr. Molton wishfully assumed there was no irony in her tone. He decided to feel flattered by what Helen said.

He consulted his Thumputer time display. Getting up from his seat, he announced, "Well, it's time to see the boss." He seemed a little pompous as he stepped toward Dr. Jupitren's office door.

"Doctor Molton, please wait for him." Helen beckoned him to halt his steps. "He must be finishing up the session soon. In a minute, I'll let him know you are here."

"Yes. Ma'am!" He sat back, rechecking the time on his Thumputer and started to scan recent messages on it.

Feeling curious, Helen pulled out his file and peeked in. She found Dr. Jupitren's summary on Dr. Molton's background:

Born of a Portuguese sea captain and a Germanic chemist mother. In good health. 38 years old. High achiever; overly ambitious and anxious. No siblings. Studied genetics after obtaining MD degree. After four years of marriage, he and his wife Brigit divorced two years ago; Brigit did not get along with his mother. She felt neglected by her research-driven husband; she became unhappy with him and distanced herself. He betrayed her by having a brief affair with another woman; this precipitated the breakup of his marriage.

Reported financial difficulty, sought psychotherapy but got minimal help from it; remains anxious. Had nightmares many nights. Became interested in Dream Wafers to ease his anxiety dreams, which involved drowning and menacing sharks.

Having read about Dr. Molton, Helen felt a bit sorry for him. At the same time, she chided herself quietly, "Even if he said I could read it, I should not have done it. I shouldn't peek into others' records for selfish motivations."

Right after a patient came out of Dr. Jupitren's office, Dr. Molton went in.

"Good afternoon, here I am. How are you, Dr. Jupitren?"

"I'm fine, thank you. How did you do with your Dream Wafers?"

"So far my Wafers are working pretty well for me. I have had no more of the anxiety dreams. I no longer dreamt about drowning in the ocean or being attacked by the sharks.

The only questionable thing about my Wafers was that I could not wake up on time in the morning. But once I was awake, I felt I was speeding a little, and then, about two hours later, the revved-up feelings would go away. I wonder if you would recommend that I order new Dream Wafers today. If so, I'll go through my questionnaire anew from scratch."

"I think making the new Wafers would be a better idea rather than continuing the old ones. By the way, I enjoyed the discussion with the SUNY med students you sent to me last month. What topics have you been teaching them lately?"

"The theoretical basis of the Chemical Razors that I have been using in rodent experiments for some time."

"Actually, as I said last time, I wanted to know more about your Chemical Razors, especially in connection with the twelfth module of the Dream Wafer program."

"Are you planning to make changes to the twelfth module only?"

"Yes, for now. There are many genes involved in the twelfth module's operation. I need to modify at least four specific genes, leaving the remaining genes untouched. For those four, I would like to apply your Chemical Razor methods. But once the change is made, the entire 135-item-related genes and chemicals need to go through obligatory permutations to create the final common pathway for the Wafers."

Dr. Molton asked, "With the twelfth module changed, which diagnostic entities will you be treating?"

"Mostly PTSDs."

"I see. With the modified twelfth module, how will it work in the PTSD treatment?"

Using an electronic slide projector, Dr. Jupitren showed a brain in three-dimensional sections and gave an answer to Dr. Molton:

"As we know from the PET and functional MRI research findings, a PTSD person, in anticipation of emotional stirring, will show increased neuronal activation in the *island of Reil*—I mean the *insular* area. This medial structure deals with control of mood, besides other functions. In contrast, the outer part, that is, the dorsolateral area of prefrontal cortex, deals with executive cognitive function. Normally, that part and this *insula* should be in optimal balance.

However, under anticipated stressful action or emotion, the PTSD person's sensitized *insula* will overpower the prefrontal cognitive cortices, and he or she will become dramatically dysfunctional, manifesting the various affective symptoms and anxiety of PTSD.

To reiterate it, when triggered by recalled traumatic events, the PTSD patients will re-experience their emotion taking over their cognition, making them dysfunctional. My way of helping them is to restore optimal balance between the mood area and the cognitive area. The four chemicals in the twelfth module, when genetically modified, may restore the balance better."

Dr. Molton asked, "What would those four chemicals actually do?"

"They will help the PTSD patients by letting them forget the otherwise unforgettable traumatic memories through gene-expression control. It is a *selective chemico-genetic erasure* on the unrelenting emotional memory complex that was formed by trauma."

He turned the projector off and continued, "With the Chemical Razor, as I have read in your research paper, you chemically shear hydrogen bonds between the selected thymine and adenine nucleobases. My question is, wouldn't it result in irreversible gene splicing?"

"Yes, in most instances. But in a few cases, they were reversible. In fact, I'm working on how to get more of the razor's reversible shearing."

Dr. Jupitren said, "The changes to the epigenome made by the Chemical Razor eventually would trickle down to the structure of chromatin. Of course, that would cause certain changes in the function of the genome eventually. In other words, I understand that any modification on the twelfth module with your Razor method may result in a permanent change in the corresponding gene structure. Isn't that what you were saying?"

"Yes, in most cases."

Dr. Jupitren firmly responded, "Then, I have to postpone your Chemical Razor treatment method."

"Only because it may induce permanent gene changes?"

"Yes, I don't want my patients having irreversibly altered genes. I don't have enough information about how those few altered genes will affect the rest of the individual's overall chemical and hormonal equilibrium in the long run. Besides, in effect, the Chemical Razor may trigger mutation of oncogenes, and eventually those genes may randomly induce cancerous cell overgrowth. I cannot justify its use now."

Dr. Molton responded somewhat indignantly to Dr. Jupitren. "If I were in your shoes, I would inform the clients about the potential risks and go ahead with the Chemical Razor application anyway. Of course, before they get the Chemical Razor treatment, I would have them sign a disclaimer about the possible irreversible change."

Expressing his disagreement, Dr. Jupitren said, "PTSD patients will latch on to the Chemical Razor treatment out of desperation, only to regret it soon afterward. I think the unknown risk outweighs the benefit of the Razor treatment and we should consider different treatment methods."

Dr. Molton disappointedly said, "I'm sorry you disagree with me. But I suppose you want to be very sure about the safety of your patients. You seem to be extra careful about this."

"Yes, I am. I'll think of an alternative method in lieu of your Chemical Razor treatment proposal."

During the interview, Molton's cell phone vibrated several times in his pocket, but he did not answer the calls. He grew increasingly distracted from the interview, wondering if the calls came from the same agent, whom he knew only as A.H. The agent had enticed him into a risky deal and handed him big cash bundles about ten days previously.

It all started during a recent upswing of Sobien's mood, when he had an expansive idea of starting his own genetic engineering company without any capital. However, at the same time he realized his financial status was quite embarrassing. So, he began searching for large sums of money. Eventually his path crossed with A.H., the agent from an unstable dictator regime of a Eurasian country.

A.H.'s mission was to get a copy of Acmeon Lab's Dream Wafer program. As soon as A.H. learned that Sobien Molton was being interviewed for a position at Acmeon Lab, he latched on to Sobien and bought him over with big sums of money. Sobien's unsound ambition to start his own business on impulse blinded him. He did not realize what a treacherous bog he was about to fall into by contracting with A.H. Without exercising sufficient circumspection, Sobien bit A.H.'s evil lure with a hidden hook, and he soon realized he could not get back out.

Dr. Jupitren discussed some other research issues with him. Dr. Jupitren was impressed by Dr. Molton's strong interest in the Dream Wafer science. However, he felt somewhat uneasy about the young doctor's excessive enthusiasm not being curbed by desirable ethical and professional restraint. Dr. Jupitren only hoped that he would find such restraint from the young doctor in the near future.

Despite the odds, because of Dr. Molton's exceptional knowledge and interest in Dream Wafers, Dr. Jupitren decided to accept his request to work in Acmeon Lab. He would work under Dr. Jupitren's supervision on a part-time schedule.

Soon after the interview was over, Sobien went outside and checked his cellphone for voice mails. As he guessed, the calls came from Agent A.H., who left unpleasant messages:

"We gave you enough C-notes last week, but no action yet? You'd better hurry. Get it before your promised days are up. Or else, we'll come and take our money back from you. We know where you live. Give us your answer now about when you are going to get it."

After some hesitation, Sobien left a short message for the agent:

"A.H., I need a little more time. Only today, I got hired as a part-timer at Acmeon Lab. I'll get on with your request as soon as I can."

Throughout his questionnaire-135 session, Sobien was very upset about the nasty message. Nevertheless, he managed to finish the questionnaire and an hour later received his second batch of Dream Wafers.

As he left Acmeon Lab's office, he waved his hand to Helen in a made-up jolly manner, but there was a strained, sad tone in his singsongy voice. "I'll be seeing you soon again. So long!"

CHAPTER 25
SAM DAYER AT THE HOSPITAL

After two very busy days at his office since the Cyberscope session, Dr. Jupitren asked Bill to come along with him and see Sam Dayer at the hospital. Bill came in civilian clothes, not wanting to alarm Sam.

Some stable patients were allowed to see their visitors in their rooms without staff's direct supervision. However, most of the other patients needed to be supervised by staff in the open Day Room during the visiting hours. The Day Room was quite noisy despite its large space. Families and friends of the patients had much to talk. There were some crying, yelling, and rare laughter. Sam was by himself in the Day Room corner.

Before walking to Sam in the corner, Bill said to Dr. Jupitren, "Jules, today I'll keep quiet while you talk with Sam. If I have anything to say, I'll wait till you're done talking with him."

"Any particular reason for your silence, Bill?"

"Well, not knowing how his mental state is, I thought my silence might spare him from unnecessary distraction."

"I'm OK with that."

Sam Dayer seemed to have added a few pounds in his middle since Dr. Jupitren saw him last time in Acmeon Lab's parking lot. Disheveled and unshaven, he appeared disinterested in his surroundings, and his gaze seemed distant.

A previous meal's remnant?—dried-up ketchup stains on his beige shirt seemed from mindless swiping of his fingers in parallel streaks. He moved about rather sluggishly. He sat down heavily on a chair.

Dr. Jupitren introduced himself to Sam. "Hello, Mr. Dayer, how are you doing today? I'm Dr. Jupitren. Do you remember seeing me at the Acmeon Lab's parking lot, not too long ago?" Dr. Jupitren extended his open right hand.

Looking at him askance, Sam shook hands hesitantly without saying anything.

"This is my friend Bill Warren."

Bill shook hands with Sam, who was still on his chair. Bill greeted him. "How do you do?"

Sam Dayer still remained quiet. It was apparent to Dr. Jupitren that the hospital had given him moderate sedation, possibly for agitation. Dr. Jupitren thought Sam's apathy was probably from the effects of his medications.

"Are you having a good day?" Dr. Jupitren asked.

"No, I'm not happy here. I don't even know the names of the drugs they are giving me. I don't know when I'll be discharged, either."

"Do you have any family visiting you here?"

"No, only my lawyer comes to see me once in a while."

"Mrs. Debbie Ascher?" Dr. Jupitren asked.

"Yes, but how did you know her name?"

"Well, I met her on the day you came to Acmeon Lab with her. Don't you remember?"

"Oh, yes, you were there. Now I remember. I was beside myself then."

"Do you have any family living here in New York?"

"My wife lives with our daughter in South Hampton."

"Do they know you're here?"

"Yes."

"Didn't they come to see you since you got here?"

"No."

"Why not?"

"I told them not to. I'm ashamed of myself. I'm embarrassed to see them here."

"Why such embarrassment?"

"It's a long story."

After a pause, Dr. Jupitren asked him, "Do you mind telling me some of the story?"

Sam picked up his head, peering into Dr. Jupitren's face carefully, and answered, "My job was bad for my sleep. I had bad dreams because of my stressful job schedule. Then I saw the ads on the Dream Wafers from a chemical company in the Islet Republic. I bought a bunch of them and used one almost every night. I thought it worked for my dreams, but my sleep got worse. I could not wake up on time, even after nine or ten hours of sleep. Actually, I got confused many times, even on my job."

Right at that point, Dr. Jupitren could have asked Sam what the chemical company's name was but decided to wait for a better moment and said instead,

"Sorry to hear that, Mr. Dayer. So what did you do finally?"

"Unfortunately, before I realized the Wafers were no good, I bought a bulk of the Wafers from the same chemical company. I thought I would make some money by selling them to the brokers I knew in Tokyo. I then carried three thousands of them on board without telling anyone. I know it's not legal. I regret badly for what I did."

After a brief pause he continued. "I vaguely remember the episode on board Trans-Alpha Jet Air. I applied the Wafer to myself only about six hours before the flight, not thinking clearly. From all the news, you must have learned about the scenes I created in the cockpit. I get chills even now when I see the news video clips again. How stupid I was!"

Regretting his past misjudgment, Sam Dayer visibly became anxious. In turn, his anxiety seemed to have made him a bit more alert. As his conversation with Dr. Jupitren went on, he became a little more focused.

Dr. Jupitren asked, "What are you going to do with those three thousand Dream Wafers?"

"I've got to find them first."

"Do you mean you haven't heard from Mrs. Ascher about your bag yet?"

"No." Sam Dayer looked puzzled. Dr. Jupitren explained to Sam how he learned from the Narita Airport staff about the bag and the wafers. He added, "Right away we informed Mrs. Ascher about your bag. I guess she is still in the process of getting your bag. It might take some time since it's an international matter."

Sam seemed very surprised but relieved and was eager to talk to Dr. Jupitren.

Dr. Jupitren finally asked. "What's the name of the chemical company in the Islet Republic?"

"My lawyer told me not to divulge any information unless she was with me. But if I'm open with you, I hope you will help me. I'll tell you everything you want to know." Sam briefly hesitated but said, "The name is Lyon Albert and Company…What will you do to them? And to me now?"

"I only want to write to them or call them and ask them to stop selling the Wafers. They should stop manufacturing the Wafers altogether. Those Wafers were made on defective software and are harmful."

"Then, can I sue them?"

"You may discuss it with Mrs. Ascher, but I'm afraid it will be an uphill battle for you."

"Why?"

"On the Cyberscope, I saw and heard the Narita Airport people read the manufacturer's disclaimer. They found it in the Wafer package insert in your bag."

"Really? What did the disclaimer say?"

"It said the manufacturer assumed no responsibility at all and declared immunity to any liability."

"Do you think the Wafers are still in Narita airport?"

"Yes, I think so."

"What do you think will happen to my Wafers?"

"Except the single chip that they took out for my chemical analysis, I believe the remainder is still in the original package. But the Wafers will be classified here in the States as illegal chemicals, because they are harmful counterfeits and will be confiscated if you have them brought to the States."

"Damn it!" Sam exclaimed, thwacking his own lap with his palm.

"May I ask you how much you paid Lyon Albert and Company for those Wafers?"

"Nine dollars apiece, totaling twenty-seven grands. Now they're all wasted for nothing!"

"Just in case you didn't know it, my Acmeon lab makes the genuine Dream Wafers based on individual's health and genetic information. Without those information, they can produce only unlawful counterfeit Wafers, which can be very harmful. The Lyon Albert and Company's Wafers should be destroyed. Are you willing to discard them?"

Sam Dayer reluctantly said, "I'm mad at myself for my stupidity. Now I suppose I should listen to you, but I'll speak to my lawyer before I decide to throw them out."

Bill Warren finally stepped in and said, "Mr. Dayer, I work for the police department. But I'm not here to question you; I just came along with Dr. Jupitren as his friend.

Let me add this for your information. Three days ago, I have informed your lawyer, Mrs. Ascher about your bag right after Dr. Jupitren and I had the Cyberscope interview with Narita Airport staff. Your bag must be still at Narita. If the Narita staff or the Tokyo police send the bag to you, you should first report it to the New York State Health Department and then dispose them if permitted to handle them. I don't believe you will be able to keep them, although you paid for them, because they are categorized as a class-five controlled substance by the Federal Drug Administration."

Sam was sad but felt relieved and said, "Thank you both. I would rather give up the twenty-seven thousand dollars than lose my job."

Dr. Jupitren and Bill thanked him for his honesty and left him.

Requested by Dr. Jupitren, Bill immediately contacted Lyon Albert & Company, inquiring about Sam Dayer's account. Bill found the company's key persons, to whom Dr. Jupitren communicated regarding the nature of their counterfeit production.

With a clearance given by the Islet Republic Security Intelligence Service, Bill requested trade records for Lyon Albert & Company from the country's Foreign Affairs & International Trade Department. After waiting for two full days, Bill received reports from them indicating that Lyon Albert & Company produced thousands of Dream Wafer copies using generic gene templates. Then and there, they sold those Wafers to European and US markets. Sam Dayer was among the ill-informed naïve buyers of such products.

Using the information that Bill secured, Dr. Jupitren sent an official e-gram to Lyon Albert & Company urging them to stop the production of counterfeit Wafer copies immediately.

Much later that day, an e-reply from Lyon Albert & Company came to Dr. Jupitren. The message said that they had already stopped manufacturing the faulty Wafer copies. However, prior to stopping the Wafer production, unaware of the potential ill-health effect of those Wafers, they had sold the bulk of their products to a government in Eurasia. Dr. Jupitren surmised that it could be the same Eurasian government that had used the extracts of the counterfeit Wafers in riot control.

Later, Dr. Jupitren received the single piece of counterfeit Wafer from Narita Airport. His analysis of it confirmed that it lacked the proper wake-up program in the twelfth module.

Feeling very uneasy about the widespread counterfeit Wafers, Dr. Jupitren realized that he should devise a new objective test. It would measure the degree of mental impairment as well as the countdown time required to recover from such impairment among counterfeit Dream Wafer users. He would name the test 'Waferlyzer'. Logically with the new test, he would be able to individualize the effective treatment dosages of Antisom for somnambular patients.

CHAPTER 26
ACMEON STAFF MEETING AT LA CORNUCOPIA

Selecting a venue near Acmeon Lab, Dr. Jupitren arranged a staff dinner meeting at Restaurant La Cornucopia. He announced that after the dinner, there would be a discussion on a new project.

Unaware of Acmeon Lab's dinner meeting, Steve and his sister, Jenny, were also there at the same restaurant, celebrating her new invention the *Optical Wall thermometer*. Steve and Jenny were on their second course of dinner when Helen and Dr. Jupitren arrived. At that moment, Jenny received a phone call. She excused herself and stepped away from the table.

Steve got up from his seat, greeting them. "What a surprise to see you here! Good evening, Dr. Jupitren. Hi, Helen."

Dr. Jupitren said, "Hello, Steve, please don't get up. We are having a staff dinner meeting here this evening. Good to see you."

Having found Steve with a pretty woman, Helen suddenly felt uneasy and took a good look at the woman who was slowly walking to the far corner of the restaurant hall, talking on her wrist phone.

Helen asked Steve, "Are you enjoying your dinner?"

"Yeah, we came out to celebrate her new product. She is—"

Before Steve could finish his words, Dr. Molton, Zenon, and Yaru arrived all at the same time and their loud greetings drew Helen's attention away. Helen didn't hear what Steve said about the woman he was with.

After the usual exchange of greetings, everyone sat down except Jenny, who was still standing near the corner of the hall, talking on her phone.

The Acmeon Lab people took the restaurant's conference suite, which was separated from the rest of the restaurant by four glass walls and had a perfect acoustic buffer. The suite being in the center of the main dining hall, other restaurant guests could see the Acmeon staff in it but could not hear anything they were saying. Likewise, Acmeon Lab people did not hear any clamor or loud conversation from the restaurant patrons in the main hall.

Through the whole course of dinner, Helen felt vague jealous tension each time she glanced at the woman with Steve. They were sitting several tables away from Helen, but they were beyond the glass walls. She thought of walking over to Steve's table and introducing herself to the woman but thought better of it, deciding that it was not her place to do so. Suddenly, Helen felt Steve was very far away.

Sitting with Steve at the table outside the glass-walled conference room, Jenny asked, "Who is the young man over there next to Dr. Jupitren?"

"He must be the new assistant to Dr. Jupitren. I heard his name is Dr. Sobien Molton. I haven't seen him before, but Dr. Jupitren told me about him a few times."

"What kind of doctor is he?"

"A specialist in genetics and chemistry, I heard."

"He is a good-looking man. Is he married?"

"I don't know."

"I wonder if the brunette sitting in front of him is his wife."

"No, she is Dr. Jupitren's niece Helen, Acmeon Lab's office manager. She is a very lovely person. I'll be going steady with her."

"Really? She is pretty. Did you meet her lately?"

"No, it was over a year ago. I first met her when I went to Acmeon Lab. It's a long story. I'll tell you more some other time."

"All right."

Jenny asked, "Shouldn't we go over to their table now and introduce ourselves?"

"Maybe in a while. We can't hear what they are saying. But look at them! From the way they are reading their printed materials, they seem quite busy with their agenda."

Steve changed the subject. "By the way, are your customers sending in their purchase orders for your new invention? I mean the Optical Wall thermometers."

Jenny answered with a big smile, "It has already been started, and I've received lots of orders to install them. I'll be riding my air-scooter like a flying witch all over the tri-state area."

"It's wonderful. You're going to be rich and famous."

"Granted that's true, now I need to find a nice, attractive man to fall in love with."

Meanwhile, in the restaurant's conference suite, Dr. Jupitren presented his ideas about the new testing device. He announced that the device would be called 'Waferlyzer'. He said that it would be a useful tool as long as there are counterfeit Dream Wafer users with wake up problems.

Dr. Molton asked, "What will be the Waferlyzer's actual size?'

"The breath analyzer itself is about one cubic foot. But other attachments, such as the laser printer, GPS, wireless transmitter unit, and lithium-solar hybrid batteries are packed together over two pairs of casters, it will be easily two cubic feet. I have drawn the Waferlyzer's design in detail. What I will need from all of you is…"

Dr. Jupitren handed his planning sheets along with assignments to each attendant and said, "I will go through every step of the manufacturing process with each of you when you are actually hands on at your assigned work. I will ask Helen and her staff to keep daily progress logs on each subproject.

Dr. Jupitren made a general remark. "If everything goes as planned, the estimated completion date of the Waferlyzer will be within thirty days from now. Just for your information, the state Health Department and two major funding firms that you all know of fixed the due date. It was not our own choice."

Much Q & A's went on at the Acmeon staff's table.

In the meantime, having finished their dinner, Jenny and Steve were waiting to find an appropriate moment to introduce themselves to the Acmeon people and then go home.

Jenny said, "Maybe we should take a French leave. I don't want to disturb them. Besides, my air-scooter's scheduled time is running out. If it runs out, I have to reset it. It's kind of a hassle."

"Is it that complicated to reset the scooter's schedule?"

"It takes a bit of time because I have to call the master travel-point setters and ask them to reschedule it. If they are busy with others' requests, I have to talk to a robot instead, which usually means a bit longer to reschedule because the robot has to confirm my identity by asking more questions than the real person does."

"So how much longer can you stay here, Jenny?"

"Only two to three more minutes. I have to be back in my air-scooter seat in twelve minutes."

"OK. Then we'll leave now."

Steve left with Jenny. He saw her off on her air-scooter. Then he hurried back to La Cornucopia, hoping to see Helen. However, everyone had just left.

He called Helen, but her phone declined to answer because it was programmed to lock out after a certain time at night. Steve remembered what Helen had told him days earlier. She would keep her phone programmed to lockout through her workday evenings. She wanted to economize her time and use the saved time for study-related tasks as well as for sleep and rest. She called it a *selective time-shielding*.

On the following day, Thursday, Acmeon Lab was at full throttle with the new project.

CHAPTER 27
HELEN IN WASHINGTON, DC

Acmeon's staff started a six-days-a-week work schedule on the Waferlyzer project. It would last for a whole month until they reach the target date.

Because of Helen's *selective time-shielding*, Steve could not find any right time to call her, as she was constantly tied up with her work. She said a few times, "In my schedule, there is literally no crack to break through."

Steve used to tease her by saying, "With no chink in your armor, to which battlefield are you marching today?" However, Steve thought it was very unlike Helen not to call him at all for a whole week. He missed her very much and wanted to see her. He himself was extremely busy at Perihelion Energy Company, as the US Defense Department had recently commissioned his company to manufacture tons of solar transformers for new helicopters' surveillance instruments.

Steve finally decided to go over to Acmeon Lab, hoping to talk to Helen in person. Although he expected that his calls would be blocked again, he tried to call her anyway. Somehow, this time, much to his surprise, he was able to leave a voice message on her phone. In his message, he said he was on his way to Acmeon Lab and wanted to see her there.

While driving to Acmeon Lab, Steve received a text message. "How strange, Helen is texting me from Washington, DC!" He pulled over his car and read it:

"Hi, Steve, it's me, Helen. Am at Smithsonian Business Institute, Wash, DC. In the middle of class. Can't speak w U now. Will call U later at 7:30 pm."

Steve thought, "Make a U-turn? Or go on to Acmeon Lab and ask Dr. Jupitren about what Helen is doing in DC?"

Steve would need another fifteen minutes to reach Acmeon Lab. Without much hesitation, he restarted his car and headed to Acmeon Lab. As he was passing by K Street, he was sweaty and felt very thirsty. He went into the diner Allegory for a cold drink.

It was dinner time, and the place was getting crowded. He bought a tall glass of iced Moca-Mola and sat down on a barstool. Swiveling his seat a little, he could watch the *Cyber Tribune* news panel on the wall. After a financial review, it featured science news. He heard "Acmeon Lab" being mentioned. It drew his immediate attention.

The news said: "*Dr. Jupitren, the inventor of Dream Wafer announced yesterday that there would be a new tester called Waferlyzer… It will test the degree of mental impairment of a person due to Counterfeit Wafer effect and the countdown time required to recover from…It takes less than five minutes to complete the test. The Waferlyzer will be available to hospitals, police forces, and other public domains in two months.*"

Steve imagined Acmeon's staff working hard day and night on the Waferlyzer. Then he thought of Helen. "She was probably on some urgent mission to Washington for Acmeon. But why all the way there? And not telling me about it?"

As he was tilting his glass' bottom up to finish his Moca-Mola, Steve's gaze rested at a table on the mezzanine floor. There he saw the side profile of his sister's face. Jenny was sitting at a table with Dr. Molton. Steve waved his raised hand at them, but they were busy talking and did not see him. He glanced at his Thumputer time display. It was 6:45. He did not wish to disturb his sister's dinner date. Besides, the traffic was building up by the minute. Dr. Jupitren might leave his office for the West Room in fifteen minutes. Steve decided not to go up to the mezzanine and just left Allegory.

At Acmeon Lab, Steve saw Dr. Jupitren still in his lab coat along with Zenon and Yaru, who were checking their work materials. Steve went to the work area and said, "Hello, everybody. Good evening."

Zenon and Yaru quietly waved their hands to say Hi to Steve and then continued their work. Dr. Jupitren paused what he was doing when he saw Steve walk in.

"How're you, Steve?"

"I'm all right, thank you. I hoped I would see Helen here. But I have received her text message from Washington, DC a little while ago. I wonder what she's doing in DC."

"She is taking some courses there."

"Courses! That's what she said, too. Do you know what kind of courses?"

"She said the subjects are genetic informatics and industrial organization. She is taking a mini-course on business administration."

"That sounds like lots of extra work for her. But why all of a sudden?"

"She said she would take the course now because it's available only once this time of each year."

"That's surprising. Will she be there for long?"

"No, she has already been there over a week and will be back in a few days."

"Really? That's still a long time. How's she doing? I haven't spoken to her for so long."

"Yesterday she called me from DC and said she was doing well with the course she is taking."

"That's nice to hear. By the way, on my way here, I heard the *Cyber Tribune* news about your Waferlyzer. It must be a very useful testing tool."

"It certainly will be. We are working on it six days a week."

Wishing not to disturb Dr. Jupitren's work any further, Steve bid good-bye and left Acmeon Lab.

At 7:30 pm a call from Helen hit Steve's wrist-phone. He quickly pulled his car over.

"Hi, Steve, how are you? Finally we got connected. Were you very busy?"

"Yes, but how about you? What are you doing there in DC?"

"I'm taking a mini-course."

"Dr. Jupitren told me about it. But why take the course now?"

"I wanted to take the course for some time and found that it is given now. But it would not be given again till this time next year. So, I took it."

"I see. How are you doing there?"

"I'm doing pretty well. I'm learning lots of new stuff. Three more days to go… By the way, how is it going with you and the lady friend?" Helen sounded somewhat standoffish.

"What lady friend?"

"The blonde I saw with you at La Cornucopia when Acmeon had the meeting."

"Oh, I saw her again today."

"You did!" Her voice sank.

"Yeah, she was having a dinner with Dr. Molton today."

"What did you say?"

"They were together at Allegory this evening, seemingly having a good time. I saw them from a distance, but I didn't have time to talk with them."

"I don't understand what you're saying. Didn't you mind she was with someone else? Are you not going out with her anymore?"

"Going out with her? With Jenny, my sister?"

"Did you say Jenny, your sister?"

"Yes, didn't you know that?"

"No, I didn't."

"That evening at La Cornucopia we were celebrating her new invention. I told you then she was my sister, Jenny."

"I see it now. I must have missed what you said because it was quite noisy. Afterward, before our meeting was over, you left with her. Since then, all this time, I was kind of glum, thinking about you and her."

"I'm sorry, Helen. Were you upset with me?"

Helen didn't say anything except, "Um…"

"Right after the meeting, why didn't you call me and ask who she was?"

"I almost did, but I didn't want to be so forward. Besides, I was busy with many different things to take care of, and within a couple of days, I had to come down to DC."

"I called you several times after my work hours, but every time, your phone was locked out for your selective time-shielding management, as you explained it to everyone."

"Sorry, I should have kept the phone open for you."

"Thank you, Helen. I'm glad we've cleared up our misunderstanding. So what are you learning at the Smithsonian?"

"I'm learning new stuff about business management, cybersecurity, and genetic-information processing."

"They all sound quite new to me."

"I'll tell you more about them when I return to New York."

"Good! When are you returning?"

"Thursday morning at 6:30."

"Which airline?"

"American Air Shuttle to JFK."

"Do you want me to pick you up from the airport?"

"No, thank you. My Mom said she will."

"Then, I'll see you after you return from DC. Well, take care, Helen. I missed you."

"Me, too. I'll talk to you soon. Bye, Steve."

Steve thought, "She is usually assertive about her work matters, yet she seems so shy when it comes to expressing her personal feelings."

Days later, early Thursday morning at JFK Airport, Steve saw Helen's mother at Helen's arrival gate.

"Good morning, Mrs. Humayor."

"How are you, Steve?"

"I'm very well. Thank you."

"It's nice of you to come out to see her. She asked me to pick her up and go straight to Acmeon Lab for the Thursday morning meeting."

"That's Helen all right, going straight to work from the airport. How about her breakfast? Will Helen and you have any time for a light snack before she goes to her office?"

"Yes, I was thinking about stopping for a quick bite at a diner on our way to Acmeon Lab. How about you?"

"If you don't mind, I'd like to join you and Helen."

"Certainly, please come with us. Helen will be very happy to have breakfast with you."

"Thank you. I will."

Air Shuttle commuters were briskly filing out of the gate. Steve and Mrs. Humayor fixed their gazes on the arrival gate.

Steve said, "Helen doesn't know I'm here."

"I'm sure she'll be very happy to see you. Now, over there, I see she is coming out."

Mrs. Humayor stretched her arm up, waving at Helen. "Over here, Helen!"

Helen saw her in the crowd and raised her waving hand with a smile, which grew to a happy beam as she spotted Steve standing next to her mother. Helen's pace got brisk. She gave her mother a good-morning hug.

As Steve took Helen's heavy carry-on from her hand, she gave him a hug and said, "I'm very happy to see you, Steve."

"I'm very happy to see you, too, Helen."

After Helen retrieved her luggage, Steve suggested they all go to Allegory and have a quick breakfast together.

While eating at the diner, Helen was eager to give them a quick review about some of the subjects she'd taken in her two weeks at the Smithsonian Business

Institute. She also said what her cybersecurity instructor quoted during the class about the latest news. It was about a wide sweep hacking attempt by a dictator regime in a Eurasian country that aimed several US industries and one of the targets was Acmeon Lab. However, the hackers didn't get what they were looking for.

Steve said, "I'm glad Acmeon did not lose anything to the hackers. I'm pretty sure Dr. Jupitren already knows about it, and Acmeon's IT team must have been alerted."

"I think so, too. The cybersecurity course I took made me think of a few specific questions on Acmeon's security status. I'll ask Uncle Jules about them later."

"Well, Helen," Steve said, "you seem to have learned something new about cybersecurity."

"I believe so. Next time, if you and Uncle Jules talk about the Wafer program's security, I would follow your conversation a little more closely."

"That's nice, Helen. I'm proud of you."

Mrs. Humayor said, "You both seem very much into your work. Steve, will you be going to Perihelion this morning?"

"Yes, soon after we finish our breakfast here."

While Mrs. Humayor and Steve were talking about the recent hacking incidents, Helen gave her plate a clean finish and sipped her coffee.

Smiling at Helen, Steve said, "Helen, it looks like our great city, DC, didn't feed you well."

The breakfast was light and quick, as Helen and Steve had to get to their offices on time. Steve motioned to the waiter for the tab. Paying for the three breakfasts, he said, "This breakfast is my treat for you ladies."

Mrs. Humayor and Helen thanked him in unison.

Pressured for time, Steve bid good-bye to them and headed to his office.

In the car on their way to Acmeon Lab, Mrs. Humayor asked Helen, "So, how are you feeling?"

"I'm fine. Everything is good."

Days later, Steve received a call from his sister during his lunch break.

"What's happening, Jenny? I couldn't believe my eyes when I saw you with Dr. Molton at the Allegory mezzanine."

"Did you see us there? Why didn't you come up and say 'Hi' to us then?"

"I waved my hand, hoping you would see me. But you didn't. I thought both of you were quite enthralled with each other and I decided not to bud in your tryst. Besides, I had to rush to get to Acmeon Lab."

"You're right, Steve. We hit it off nicely. It was a fun evening. Actually, he is a very interesting, spunky guy. I like him. He's a charmer!"

"How did you two meet?"

"You know that I saw him for the first time at La Cornucopia, but we couldn't talk with each other there. I think the La Cornucopia people told him who I was. The next day, he sent a long text message to my Luxen Tech office. Guess what he wrote. It was funny. I'll read it to you now, if you have time."

"OK, Jenny. Go ahead."

"His text message was like this: *Hi, I am Sobien Molton from Acmeon Lab. I saw you yesterday at La Cornucopia, but unfortunately, I only saw you through the glass wall and you were sitting many feet away. But whenever I looked at you from my seat, to which I was tied down with an invisible seat belt throughout the evening, your radiant beauty let my heart race against my genius brain. Your clutch on me was so strong that I could not give full attention to the flow of the meeting I was in.*

I asked the restaurant's manager who the man at your table was. To my great relief, I was told he's your brother. Now I'm inviting you to share your time with me at a dinner in the very near future. I hope you will say yes and rescue me from my love-smitten lugubriousness.…And he left his phone number."

"Jenny, are you making that up?"

"No, Steve. That's exactly how he texted it."

"You must have been flattered by his eccentric message."

"I couldn't help but re-read his message, and naturally, I replied yes to his invitation."

"Great, Jenny. I'm glad for you. I guess you're going to see him again."

"Of course. He and I found that we had much in common. When I told him about my Optical Walls, he was genuinely fascinated about the topic, and he impressed me with all his educated questions. By the way, Steve, what's with you and Helen? Anything's happening?"

"Oh, well, we are not like your express train. There are no scintillating sparks, but we feel a steady glow between us. Guess what? Couple of weeks ago when you and I had dinner at La Cornucopia, Helen saw us and she thought you were my new date, and she was quite upset."

"Poor thing. She must have been miserable. Maybe I should give her a call and make a lunch date with her one of these days. Maybe I can meet you and Helen at the Village Bistro at Glen Street Plaza, since distance-wise it's convenient for all three of us."

"That would be nice. Thank you, Jenny. Let's meet. She will be happy to get to know you, too. Anyway, Helen and I are doing OK."

"Great. I'm glad to hear that…well, I've gotten distracted so far off and almost forgot why I called you today. I soon need to check some research data from your Perihelion Energy's physics archives."

"Are you having any new problems with your Optical Walls?"

"Actually, the Optical Walls' thermal control system needs some minor adjustments in coupling with the geothermal pump in some new buildings. And, I need specific technical information from your company's archives. If you can spare some free time at your Perihelion, just like the last time, you could help me to navigate through the archives. I'll manage it within an hour. Is that OK?"

"Sure, Jenny. After five in the afternoon, any weekday is good."

CHAPTER 28
DR. JUPITREN'S THREE CLIENTS

Monday morning, Dr. Jupitren started his work in his office as usual. The first client was Mr. Cervantes, a chemist, who came in for his initial interview. At one point in the interview, he asked, "How can I retain my dreams better and longer?"

"Would you tell me why you want to retain them longer?"

"Well, once in a while in my dreams, I would try to decipher the molecular structure of new chemicals that I was working on. Upon awakening in the morning, by recalling my dreams, I would come very close to solving the challenging questions. Yet the dream-revealed solutions would slip away within a short time after I wake up."

"I see. The Dream Wafer might be able to do something for your request. But apart from what the Dream Wafer can do for you, when you wake up, before you do anything else, why don't you immediately write down the new dream contents?"

"I'll try to do that. That sounds like a very good idea."

Mr. Cervantes had another issue, "About three years ago, I had a number of my work-related thoughts but now, I cannot find my notes or drawings despite my meticulous record-keeping habits. I wish I could dream and return to my life three years back and recover those important creative thoughts I had then."

To complicate the issues of his memory, Mr. Cervantes reported that he was seriously exposed to a carbon-monoxide leak in his house about three years ago. The gas leak was from the tobacco brands, on which he was running chemical experiments in his basement. On that day his wife was away for a few hours to attend a church meeting, escaping exposure to the same gas. When she returned home, she found him semi-comatose with a flushed face. She brought him to the ER, where he was given oxygen treatment and headache pills. Around that time, he had a patchy lapse in his memory.

Mr. Cervantes asked, "Do you think the Dream Wafers could possibly help me recover my thoughts from that far back?"

"Probably, yes. I can say you might try the Dream Wafers, but there could be some limitations because of the carbon monoxide poisoning history.

Our memories are stored in special forms of protein throughout the brain, mostly in the area called hippocampus. Therefore, they are susceptible to metabolic changes. If your memories from three years ago, despite the carbon monoxide exposure, did not go through such metabolic decay but were embedded in your long-term memory centers, there would be a fair chance to recover the embedded facts by dreaming about them. You might well be able to recapture them with the Dream Wafers' long-term memory-retrieval function, especially if they were very important thoughts or were charged with strong emotions."

Wide-eyed, Mr. Cervantes asked, "Doctor, is it really possible that I could dream about what I thought three years ago?"

"Well, haven't you ever dreamt vividly about some of your forgotten childhood experiences? Furthermore, not just in our dreams but in a wakeful state, some of our childhood experiences that we recall can be vivid and detailed. It all means that our memories on those childhood days must have been stored in our long-term memory. Likewise, our memories on our thoughts and actions from three years ago must be still there, too.

"That's exciting. I shall certainly put my memory-recall requests on the questionnaire."

"Your desire to remember your work-related information from dreams reminds me of the German chemist Friedrich August Kekule von Stradonitz, who discovered the structure of the benzene ring, known as the Kekule's hexagon formula as he was coming out of one of his dreams."

"Yes, yes, I know his benzene hexagonal ring, with alternate single and double bonds between the adjacent six carbon atoms. I wish I had Kekule's luck in my work!"

"As you go through the questionnaire," Dr. Jupitren said, "later in the Annex library, I will help you to make appropriate choices of intensity on certain questions' sub-items. Please wait for me in the library, if you can."

The next client was Mrs. Dalton. It was one of her follow-up visits. She had many questions about understanding the meanings of her dreams. Among her questions, the dream symbols were her main concern. She said her Dream Wafers had been working well for her and she no longer got lost in strange places. Nevertheless, she was puzzled by what each element in her dreams represented. She gave some examples, such as falling off cliffs, watching fires, flying like a bird, and so on.

She pulled three different books out of her book bag, saying, "I've been reading these books on dream symbols but found these books sometimes contradicted in interpreting certain symbols. Could you help me to decide which book is the right one to read?"

"I see you're reading about universal dream symbols. Just like the dream dictionaries, I think those books are neither wrong nor correct. May I give you a suggestion? When you think of a certain part of your dream, the very first thought that comes to your mind will be the important one that is worthy of paying your attention to. The universal symbols in those books might disagree with what you fetch through your own free-floating thinking or free association with your dream elements. However, you should stick to your own thoughts that your free association let you have, rather than changing the meaning according to the book's universal-symbol information. You are the owner and author of your dreams!"

"Would you explain why the first thought that comes to my mind is that important?"

"We have various thoughts in a given moment. It is generally believed that more urgent or more important thoughts have higher charges of energy than less urgent or less important thoughts have. Therefore, while competing for expression, the thoughts that have higher energy charges reach our conscious mind sooner than the other thoughts with less energy charges.

Of course, you can have the second or third thoughts, and so on. Then it would get complicated, and you would need extra time to deal with those new thoughts. At the end, despite all your diverse effort, you may remain undecided on the final meaning of your dream. That's because even though you are dealing with one dream, the ultimate answer to your search for its meaning might come to you in more than one slant or hue. I should say finding more than one meaning from one dream is not necessarily wrong.

So, as far as understanding the meaning of dream symbols is concerned, we should not be contented with having a universal meaning from reference books alone. Those books will provide only a general guideline. We should look for our dream's symbolic meaning that is uniquely applicable to us within the context of where we are in our lives. Mostly, those contexts would include four relationship areas: first, my relationship with myself and second, my association with other people. The third is my link with the nature around me and, finally, my relationship with God."

"Thank you, Doctor for your explanation. I'll pay more attention to my own free floating ideas when I search for the meanings of my dream."

She took the pre-Wafer tests and went to the Annex Library for her questionnaire session.

The next client, Mr. Effelbaum, who was erudite in Judaic literature on dreams, reported that he was doing well with his Dream Wafer application but had certain questions. He asked, "I often brood over dreams' self-prophesying power. Do you believe in such concept?"

"Well, let me say this to answer you. Many psychologists believe that dreams are a vicarious wish fulfillment. A person, prompted by intense wishes or anxiety, may go one step further and award a self-prophetic potential to wish-fulfilling dreams. Therefore, after dreaming about X, Y, or Z, the dreamer might believe that X, Y, or Z is going to happen in reality. To reiterate it, our anxiety and strong wishes seem to generate a belief in dreams' prophetic potential.

To perpetuate people's belief in the prophetic nature of dreams, sometimes people actually experience or witness certain parts of their dreams come true in reality. For instance, one might actually see a person on the very day or within a few days after dreaming about that person. Then it is up to the dreamer to take it either as a coincidence or as a fulfilled prophecy. Which one to take seems being influenced by certain personal wishes or anxiety beside the person's many unique circumstances."

"Thank you, Doctor. Do you think people's thoughts on dreams' prophetic meanings have changed over the years of human history?"

"It seems that in ancient times, more people believed dreams were divine foretelling. Furthermore, those believers tried to fulfill the prophetic meanings by living in ways to actualize or become a part of such dreams. In the old days, people usually acted intuitively as far as accepting the prophetic meanings of dreams were concerned. Therefore, if their dream was perceived as a scary or dangerous one, they would consult a soothsayer in order to find a way to annul or counteract against it. To comply with the soothsayer's instruction, sometimes they would go beyond the limit of common sense and ignore others' safety, acting out atrocities prompted by their blind zeal to protect themselves from prophesied dangers.

Similarly, even some modern men, under anxiety, seek mediums' direction, listening to palmists reading their fate, and heed astrologers' soothsaying, albeit less often than in the ancient times. Most people in modern times seem to let their dreams be a general reference rather than a spiritual mandate or prophecy on their lives. Yet some people are still prone to cling to the earlier ways of believing in dreams' prophetic meanings.

Since there are so many different attitudes regarding the prophetic nature of dreams, even for experienced psychiatrists, sometimes it is difficult to differentiate if a person's perceived prophetic meaning of a dream is a delusion or a genuine religious belief."

Mr. Effelbaum questioned, "Does that mean people should not believe in dreams' role as a conduit for divine messages?"

"I don't think it's a matter of either/or. Not every dream, but some dreams would strike people harder than other dreams, subjecting them to turn to God for guidance. However, ultimately, it would be the person's choice influenced by the dreamer's religious belief.

Certain canonical dreams were taken as divine prophetic messages and they were interpreted by the dreamers themselves or by others. The well-known prophetic dreams of Joseph, Daniel, King Nebuchadnezzar, and the three Magi are good examples.

Whereas, in the book of Job, there are verses that say, 'I look for relief from my pain. But *You* terrify me with dreams; *You* send me visions and nightmares...' Unlike in the instances of other biblical dreams, Job who was struck with extreme calamities, nevertheless did not seem to have labored to decipher the prophetic meanings of his dreams. He knew that what's happening to him was in God's will and he seems to have accepted the whole messages without elaborate interpretation.

Mr. Effelbaum, I hope what I have said so far serves as a partial answer to your question on dreams' prophetic meanings."

"Thank you very much, Dr. Jupitren. I will ponder over what you've said today."

All day long, more clients came seriatim to have their questions answered and requests fulfilled besides their Dream Wafer renewals.

CHAPTER 29
AKANDRO OLADRE'S CONFESSION

Bill contacted the Laurence Harbor master, who said that right after the previous year's hurricane, the Port Authority Police rescue team found an unidentified man's body near the harbor shoreline. The dead man did not have his ID's on him. Therefore, they brought the body to the Middlesex County medical examiner's office in North Brunswick, New Jersey, where they kept detailed forensic examination records on the person.

After much paper work and e-communication with the Middlesex County offices, Bill was able to get a copy of the dead person's facial photo from their records.

Bill showed the photo to Akandro at the detention center. Akandro immediately recognized Alfonso Ramos in the picture. So, Bill contacted the Middlesex County medical examiner's office again and gave them additional information about the dead person's identity and Akandro's possible criminal involvement with him. Soon, in response to Bill's request, the medical examiner's office released to him a full copy of their forensic pathologist's report on Alfonso.

Bill brought the report to Dr. Gupta, a woman medical examiner, who was on duty at the forensic department of the detention center.

Bill explained the Akandro's case to her and asked her to review the medical examiner's report on Alfonso. Also, he requested her to attend his questioning session on Akandro in a week or two. He said he would ask for her medical opinion during that session. The video recording of the session would be sent to the DA's office afterwards.

Two days later, Bill received a call from Dr. Gupta, who said, "I've read The County Medical examiner's report on Mr. Alfonso carefully and I asked our detention Center's lab to do DNA test on the detainee Mr. Akandro Oladre's hair. I'll try to have the test result by the time you have your questioning session. The result will be available in a week."

Bill thanked her and said he would schedule the questioning session accordingly.

After a week, Bill arranged a meeting with Akandro and his public defender, and officially invited Dr. Gupta for a medical examination on Akandro.

Meantime Bill called Dr. Jupitren and gave him a detailed interim report regarding the progress of his investigation on Akandro.

Following the schedule, Dr. Gupta and Bill arrived at the detention center for the questioning session. Akandro's lawyer, Mr. Shen was there at the portal area waiting for them. He said that he had secured a room with video-recording capability within the visiting area. Then, he called Akandro's unit to have him brought to the room.

Mr. Shen verified everyone's identity and said to Akandro, "Mr. Akandro Oladre, I have told you earlier why we are having this meeting with you. Do you have any questions about the purpose of this meeting?"

"No, sir."

Mr. Shen turned to Bill and asked him to commence his questioning.

"Thank you, Mr. Shen." Bill then faced Akandro and said, "We know that you had been with Alfonso Ramos shortly before his disappearance. The other day I showed you a facial photo of a dead person, and you recognized him as Alfonso Ramos right away. The police department now has detailed information about the condition of his body. I want you to answer honestly to all our questions."

Bill asked Mr. Shen if Dr. Gupta could examine Akandro. Mr. Shen answered it would be all right for a licensed physician to examine him.

Then Bill asked Akandro, "I see that you're wearing your beret again. Will you take it off so that the doctor can check your face and head?"

Akandro slowly removed his hat. Bill asked Dr. Gupta to examine Akandro.

Examining Akandro, she said to him, "I see quite big scars in your left ear. Please tell us what happened to your ear."

"Oh, that was from a bike accident. I couldn't brake on a downslope and ditched it, hitting a tree. That's how I got hurt on the left side of my head."

"How old were you at that time?" Dr. Gupta asked.

"I was a teenager, fourteen or fifteen?"

"What about this area behind the left ear? You don't have any hair here."

"It was from the same accident. I fell off the bike. I got a cut on the head and lost a bunch of hair. And my head was bloody."

"What about this scar on your left wrist and hand?"

"It was from another accident that happened a few months ago."

Dr. Gupta indicated to everyone that her part of the examination was finished.

Bill resumed his questioning. "Last time you said you just took Alfonso's watch off his wrist and left him there. But didn't he try to stop you from taking his watch?"

"He tried, but I managed to take the watch and ran off."

"You managed. What do you mean? What did you do at that moment?"

"He pushed me, and I hit him hard in the face and took the watch off his wrist."

Bill asked, "What happened to him when you hit him?"

"He fell down."

"And what happened next?"

"Because the storm got bad, I left the deck."

"You left him lying there on the deck, in the storm?"

"Yes."

With disbelieving stare, Bill continued his questioning. "Didn't you know that he was dead before you left him?"

"No, I didn't know."

"All right then, are you sure you didn't take anything else from Alfonso that day?"

"Yes, I'm sure. I only took his watch."

"If you didn't know he was dead, how could you occupy his house immediately after the accident? Since then, you practically have been living in the dead man's house. Didn't you take his wallet?"

"No, I didn't."

"What about your left-ear injury and the loss of hair behind it?"

"They were from the bike accident, as I told the doctor already."

Bill requested Dr. Gupta to list the pertinent medical findings with her opinion for the record. She referred to the Middlesex county medical examiner's report and the current detention center's physical examination record.

"First of all, the medical examiner's report says there was no evident salt water in Alfonso Ramos' lungs. This usually means the cause of death is not by drowning in the ocean. It's probable that he was dead and then was submerged into the ocean afterward."

Dr. Gupta continued to go over the report and said, "Next, the medical examiner's report has an X-ray study, which revealed fractures of the C-5 and C-6 spines and spinal-cord compression at that level."

"What's the significance of the spinal cord compression?" Bill asked.

"It could be from the hurricane-related injury or it could be due to violent attacks resulting in this degree of injury. An ordinary punch in the face would be unlikely to cause such a fatal neck fracture. It's more likely that the neck injury was due to a blow from a heavy object."

"From the medical view point, can the cord compression be the possible cause of his death?"

"Yes, I think it is possible."

She continued her review. "The report confirmed there was no sign of strangulation. But the examiner reported that the bruise on the left side of the neck can't be missed.

There is a 1 x 1 inch wide alopecia, behind left ear, surrounded by thick curly hair. The part of the left ear's helix (edge of the earlobe) is missing with scars.

The next finding the report describes is a trace amount of curly human hair in his mouth and stomach. The medical examiner had done a DNA test on those hairs. They were not the dead person's own hair but someone else's."

"Dr. Gupta, you said you would have the DNA test result on Mr. Oladre's hair. Right?"

"Yes, the test results confirmed that the hairs in the dead person's mouth and stomach proved to be identical with Mr. Oladre's hair."

Bill thanked Dr. Gupta and resumed his questioning Akandro. "How did your hair get into Alfonso's mouth?"

Akandro didn't say anything.

Bill said. "Alfonso bit your left ear, and his bite took your hair, too. Isn't that what happened?"

Akandro remained silent.

Bill asked Dr. Gupta, "Any other medical opinion, Doctor?"

"Yes, just one more finding. Judging from the scars' color and texture, Mr. Oladre's scalp and ear scars do not appear to be many years old. They seem to be few years old."

At that point, everyone threw a sharp look at Akandro. Bill resolutely said, "Now, this is your last chance to tell the truth, Akandro."

Mr. Shen added, "Mr. Oladre, please tell us what you remember. If the statement you make now later proves to be false, you will bear additional charges for having made such false statement. Please state just the true fact that you remember."

Finally, after some more hesitation, Akandro said, "I lied about the bike accident." There was a long pause.

Mr. Shen asked Bill to resume the questioning.

Bill prompted Akandro, "So, what really happened?"

"That day, I needed money badly. I went to his work deck. It was a stormy afternoon and was getting dark. I said that if he didn't give me the money, I'd snitch on him for his connection with an illegal-immigrant smuggling ring…He pushed me and yelled at me, saying he didn't care. So I said I'd take his watch instead and tried to pull it off his wrist. Then he pushed me again, yelling, 'Get lost!' So I got him in a headlock with my left arm and tried to take his watch. Then he turned his head and bit my ear and my head. It hurt me a lot, and I let him off the headlock grip, but when I felt blood dripping down over my neck, I got mad and I grabbed a metal pipe that was nearby and hit him in his neck with it …

I swear I didn't mean to kill him. But he went down right after I hit him. It was already dark, and in the stormy wind, I couldn't tell whether he was breathing or not. I got scared, thinking he could be dead. And then I took his wallet and wristwatch before I ran off." Akandro now dropped his head down and said no more.

Then Mr. Shen asked Dr. Gupta and Bill if they had any other questions.

Bill asked Akandro, "What was the name of the ship?"

"It was *Jubilee Queen*."

"Where is the watch now?"

"I don't have it."

"What happened to it?"

"I was mugged and lost it."

"Where did the mugging take place?"

"The City Library parking lot."

"Is that right?" Bill then said, "I don't have any more questions. Do you, Dr. Gupta?"

"No, I don't, either."

Mr. Shen asked the guards to escort Akandro back to his detention unit.

As they were leaving the correctional center, Bill told Dr. Gupta and Mr. Shen that according to his own research on government records, the *Jubilee Queen* was among the ill-fated ships that were wrecked and sank during the hurricane.

Bill said, "After all, then it's possible that Akandro left the dead man on the deck and it was the raging hurricane that swept him down to the ocean with the wrecked ship. According to the marine patrol's record, Alfonso's body was found in the morning after the hurricane subsided."

Soon Bill told Dr. Jupitren how Akandro's case ended. Dr. Jupitren said he felt relieved that Akandro would not cause any direct harm to Acmeon Lab any time soon. He also thanked Bill, complimenting him on his persistent work and praised Dr. Gupta for her professional handling of the case.

CHAPTER 30
PLANNING WAFERLYZER-II

One morning, Dr. Jupitren had been interviewed by the *Cyber Tribune reporter*. The interview was about the second version of Waferlyzer. The ending remark by Dr. Jupitren was, "Sometime early next year, there will be *the Waferlyzer-II*, which will be essentially the same as *the Waferlyzer-I*, except that its testing covers more than the Dream Wafer-related chemicals. It will detect blood concentration of carbon monoxide, cannabis, alcohol, morphine derivatives, and a host of other abuse prone chemicals. It will also compute the tested person's countdown time to recover from the detrimental effects of the detected substances."

The interviewer's concluding comment was, "It seems the Waferlyzer-II will be a very useful addition to the existing medico-legal assessment tools. Thank you, Dr. Jupitren."

Dr. Jupitren returned to his office in a good mood. Sobien Molton walked up to him and said, "The staff and I watched the TV news on Cyber Tribune's interview with you about the Waferlyzer-II. You did a great job answering the interviewer. Congratulations!"

Helen and a few others joined and complimented him likewise.

Sobien asked. "So, I was wondering when you might want to call for another ad hoc planning meeting for the Waferlyzer-II." With a smirk, Sobien looked at the others around him, saying to Dr. Jupitren, "And I thought we all would appreciate a special bonus for what we have gone through past few months with the Waferlyzer-I."

Dr. Jupitren approvingly smiled and replied, "I'd like to thank everyone for your extra effort. Because of your hard work, we were able to finish our Waferlyzer-I project on time. Helen already has the bonus checks for everybody. She also has the new work-assignment list for everyone, and we will have another dinner meeting at La Cornucopia this coming Friday evening. Of course, the meeting's main agenda will be about planning for the Waferlyzer-II. At that time, before ending the meeting, Helen will distribute your bonus envelopes."

Zenon and Yaru returned to their work areas, quietly hooraying in gesture and whistling.

"Yaru, do you know something? Now we can forget about our LXG stun guns and CRs." Zenon seemed sure of it.

"What do you mean?"

"Bill Warren said Akandro will be in prison for a long time."

Yaru, not quite convinced, asked, "That's good but what about Akandro's two lackeys, Tick and Tack? They can still bother us anytime."

"No, they won't. They act only if Akandro gives them money and tells them what to do. And, Bill said that lately they haven't even answered Akandro's phone calls. I suppose they figured out Akandro was locked up."

Yaru, with a sigh of relief, said, "That's good news. I'll not bother with the stun guns now. But we still have to be careful, because although he is locked up, Akandro still can manipulate Tick and Tack."

As they were talking, Helen came by and handed the work-assignment sheets to them. "Yaru, your team has an extra page because it has a list of a dozen gentronics companies you will be dealing with." Turning to Zenon, Helen said, "This is for your team. The algorithm on page six is only a suggestion. The next three pages are for both of your teams. Those pages illustrate the technical names and drawings of the Waferlyzer-II's new parts, which Dr. Jupitren designed. He said please feel free to ask him any questions about the Waferlyzer-II plan."

"Did you draft this algorithm?" Zenon asked Helen.

"Yes, why?"

"You can write this kind of algorithm only if you had substantial knowledge of gene informatics and administrative experience. I'm very impressed."

Helen just smiled and thanked him for his compliment and did not say anything else. She recalled the fresh information that she had recently amassed from the Smithsonian Business Institute course. She was glad about having taken the course because it had already given her new confidence.

She added, "Please review your assignment sheets carefully and finalize them by the Friday meeting. I'm sure both of you will come up with plenty of good ideas."

After Helen left them, Zenon said to Yaru, "Look at this algorithm. This is a super job."

Reading it carefully, Yaru shrugged his shoulders and said, "Maybe she was pulling your leg. I don't think she drafted this. Someone else must have done it for her."

Zenon, tilting his head, said, "I don't think she would lie about this. We'll see more of her wits this Friday."

Helen went to Sobien Molton's office and handed his new work-assignment sheets to him. Rather than paying full attention to the sheets, he kept on writing something in his e-pad and said without looking at her, "Considering what I did for the first Waferlyzer construction, I'm expecting nothing but the lion's share of the bonus. I trust that you proportioned the bonus accordingly."

Pretending she did not mind his rudeness, Helen said plainly, "I'm sure Dr. Jupitren is well aware of your contribution. On the eleventh page, here, in the upper half of the page, you see those numbers in a table format. Please try to calculate those formulas by this Friday's meeting. Dr. Jupitren is counting on you."

Sobien did not pay attention to the page that Helen was showing but raised another awkward question instead. "Was it Dr. Jupitren or you who decided how much everyone's bonus should be?"

Helen felt like saying some sharp words of annoyance to him for being off-key but again said nicely, "Well, Dr. Jupitren has been fair with everyone, and of course it was he who apportioned everyone's bonus amount, and he will do it next time, too. Please do the best on your next assignment again, and you will be rewarded handsomely."

Only then, did he thumb through the assignment sheets and said loudly, "Wait a minute! This is a two-man job. I don't think I can finish it all by myself before this Friday. I'll be trailing behind everyone by a long shot. For crying out loud, I may slow down everybody else's pace."

Helen felt an urge to walk out on him but kept her composure and said matter-of-factly, "Even if you can't finish the calculations by Friday, it will be all right. Dr. Jupitren will understand. About the genetic-probability table, I can search the references for you so that you can spare some extra time and concentrate on your computations only."

"What are you saying?" Looking at Helen, he asked, "Did you say you'll retrieve the references on the probability table?"

Helen nodded yes and said, "Sorry, when I drafted the assignment sheet, I should have spent a little more time to include the references for you. If you wish, by 4:30 this afternoon, I'll get the full copy of the references from the archives of our library."

"You're full of surprises. Are you sure you know where to locate the specific references?"

"Yes, I think so. It should be in the *Genetic Informatics*, and the authors should be Eisenberg and McElroy from Miami University."

Sobien got up from his seat, looking straight into Helen's eyes. "Now, since you have given me the exact site to look up—thank you—I'll do it myself. You can stay out of it!"

Helen, still keeping her cool, said, "I'm sorry if I offended you, but I only wanted to help you save time for the assignment."

As she was leaving him, Helen felt grateful to Dr. Jupitren for his encouragement, which had led her to take the Smithsonian Business Institute's mini-course and she became quite knowledgeable about the subject matter at hand. She felt she was getting self-confident with her newly acquired knowledge.

She thought, "If a two-week course gives me this much knowledge and confidence, how will it be after the two-year MBA course?" She caught herself smiling while walking back to Dr. Jupitren's office.

"Uncle Jules, I have distributed most of the assignment sheets. I've got only few more to go."

"Very good. By the way, you said last week you were thinking about taking a two-year MBA course in DC. But have you given a second thought to taking similar courses in New York instead?"

"Yes, but the Smithsonian Business Institute course seemed more appropriate for me than those I'd found on my search in the New York area so far."

"But why don't you search for them again here in New York? I'm saying this partly because of my own concern for Acmeon Lab and partly for your own growth as a businessperson. While taking the course in New York, you can bring what you learn from the classes and apply it right here in Acmeon. Think about it. Doing so, you can finish every working day by applying your newly acquired theories into practice right here in Acmeon. You might make some mistakes along the way, but Acmeon will absorb them for you. You may work on one-third of your current schedule, and Anne will fill the remaining two-thirds. You can train her as you go.

As you grow in your business-management skills, a couple of years later, you will just have a changed job title and continue to work here. If you're away in DC, during your absence, we will need someone else to replace you. Anne alone will not be able to fill your post completely without much more training and extra help."

"I'm sorry, I hadn't thought of all that."

"Besides, if you are away to DC for two years, you will have to uproot many of the ties you have developed in New York. Last but not least, I wonder what will happen to you and Steve if suddenly there is a two-hundred-fifty-mile separation between you two for that long two-year gap."

Helen very sincerely said, "Thank you. You have figured it all out for me. I'll rethink about my September plan."

CHAPTER 31
THE FROZEN GATE RAIL

At home, around nine thirty in the evening, Dr. Jupitren realized that he should go back to his office because he had overlooked a time-sensitive matter: he forgot to set the tsetse-fly incubator timer on. Unless it was turned on before ten, the chromosome experiment he had been running for a long time would be wasted. He told his wife, Jamie, that he would be back in an hour, and he headed to his Acmeon Lab office in a hurry.

As his car approached Acmeon Lab's parking lot, he saw the security gate rail was up, which meant a car left the parking lot short moments ago or just pulled into the lot. He drove around the entire Acmeon premises but saw no car.

He wondered, "Who could have possibly come in and gone at this hour?" Feeling eerie, he rushed into the building. The hallway lights were on. He tiptoed to the elevator, intensely concentrating to pick up any sound or noise. Yet only heavy silence prevailed except the clicks of his footsteps. He then realized the building's entire CCTV camera system was down for repair that day.

He got off the elevator and walked toward his office. Near his suite entrance door, he found a crumpled gas-station receipt lying on the hallway floor. He picked it up with his left hand and started to press the door's key code with his right hand. Before he could complete the four-digit code, the door slid ajar because of his finger pressure on the code pad.

Feeling very uneasy, he quickly turned the waiting room lights on and walked farther to his own office in a super-alert state. This time, he tried to unlock his office door by putting his key code, but the same thing happened—the door slid ajar before he completed the code input! Feeling puzzled and suspicious, he entered his room and turned the light on. There was no apparent disturbance in the office but he called Bill right away before he did anything else.

"Bill, sorry to call you at this late hour."

"No problem. I'm still at my precinct. What's happening?"

"I'm in my office. I think someone was up here this evening after I left around five."

"Anything's missing?"

"No."

"Did you find anything unusual?"

The Frozen Gate Rail

"Yes. The gate rail was up in the open position as I drove in. But there were no cars in the parking lot. Inside the building, I found a gas-pump receipt on the hallway floor at the bottom of my suite entrance door. The unnerving thing is that not only the office suite entrance door but also my own office door was left unlocked. I always lock those doors when I leave for the day. And now those door locks don't respond to my codes and I cannot lock them."

"That's puzzling. Which gas station receipt was it?"

"Mohawk on M Street."

"What time was it stamped?"

"7:15 tonight."

"It's now 9:45. So the receipt was made two and a half hours ago. Jules, don't stay there. Someone could be still hiding in your lab area. Quickly get out, and please come over to Mohawk Gas Station. I'll meet you there. Let's check Mohawk's CCTV camera images together. Jules, how come you went back to your office at this late hour?"

"I forgot to set the incubator timer on and came back just to take care of it."

"I see. John and I will leave for Mohawk now. We'll meet you there."

"I'll leave my office right after I turn on the incubator timer, which is at another room in this suite."

"Please don't linger on too long. Come right out of there. If you need to take care of anything else there, John and I will come back with you to your office later."

"Thank you, Bill."

Dr. Jupitren quickly went to the incubator room. Scarily, he found the incubator room door was also left unlocked. As soon as he turned the incubator timer switch on, he went to check Helen's office door, which was left unlocked, too! But there was no sign of disturbance in those rooms.

A surge of adrenaline made him tense. He felt his heart racing and hands getting clammy with cold sweat. He rushed out to his car. He felt as if some hidden eyes were watching him from somewhere.

Soon he sat in his car feeling a little secure. He drove slowly in the direction of the exit, looking out for any clue. How strange! The security gate rail was still up. Frozen? Or someone just drove out? He stopped his car next to the gate and looked at the rail very closely. Surprisingly, he saw a wooden wedge that had been shoved into its hinge. It was the wedge that held the rail up!

Feeling violated by the not-yet-identified intruder, he drove to M Street in a hurry. He pulled in at Mohawk Gas Station, where Bill and John were recharging their tri-hybrid police van.

Dr. Jupitren said, "Thank you for helping me. Besides what I've told you about my office doors, there were a couple of other things I found very strange."

"What were they?"

"Not only the two doors but also the incubator room and Helen's office doors were left unlocked, which never happened before. And the second thing was the parking-lot security rail. It was propped up in the raised position with a hard wooden wedge shoved into its hinge. It looked like a door stop, I thought."

Bill responded, "We should take a look at it when we go up to Acmeon's parking lot. But now let's check the gas station's CCTV camera records."

Helped by the manager of Mohawk Gas Station, they reviewed the gas station's CCTV camera images, starting from 7:00 pm on.

Bill said, "Look here, Jules! Do you see who this is? The 7:14 pm image? He is fueling his car from a gas pump."

Dr. Jupitren said, "I see him clearly, but I can't recognize who he is. And, why did he come all the way to my office area, dropping the gas-pump receipt? Who could he be?" Dr. Jupitren was very puzzled.

The three of them drove to Acmeon Lab's parking lot. The security gate rail was still up in the raised position. Bill asked Dr. Jupitren, "I know everyone in Acmeon carries an electronic rail opener, but are there any other offices that share the rail opener for the Acmeon parking lot?"

"No. Only the Acmeon employees can enter the lot by using their own rail opener."

"Jules, is there anyone who works late at night in Acmeon?"

"Only Helen usually works longer hours than everyone else. But today she went home early."

Bill checked the wooden wedge and asked John to bring a roped nail gun out of their van. Bill shot the nail with attached rope into the wooden wedge and John pulled it out of the hinge. The rail came down to the closed position. Bill secured the wedge in a special container and brought it to Dr. Jupitren's office. Bill and John checked the locks and handle knobs of Dr. Jupitren's office door and the locks of other rooms.

Meanwhile, Dr. Jupitren closely examined the wedge in the container. He found faint letters and some numbers printed on one flat side of the wedge. It appeared like a trace of a rubber-stamped name. He asked Bill and John to join him in identifying what the fading words on the wedge were.

Bill used a special lamp and deciphered that it was a lumberyard's name and address: Giovanni & Sons Lumber in Smithtown, Long Island, New York.

Bill said, "Wait a minute…I remember the lumberyard's name." He opened his e-note and scrolled through his note lines and said, "Here it is! The address in my e-note is the same as the wedge's address. So, is it possible that somebody brought the wood piece from the lumberyard to Acmeon Lab's premises?"

"How did you happen to have that address?" Dr. Jupitren asked Bill.

"When I interrogated Akandro Oladre at the precinct before his transfer to the detention center, I made him place a phone call to his ilk Tick on speaker phone mode. So, I could listen to their conversation. At that time, my GPS registered Tick's location and it was this very lumberyard in Smithtown. I can go to the lumberyard in the morning and ask the owner if he knows who the figure in the Mohawk's CCTV camera image is."

Then Dr. Jupitren's phone rang. It was from Jamie. "It's eleven o'clock, hon. Did anything happen at the lab?"

"Yes, but everything is under control. Don't worry. I'll be home in about half an hour."

The three of them continued searching for further clues at Acmeon Lab. Bill said he and John did not find anything suspicious from the locks of those three rooms. Dr. Jupitren then asked them to take a close look at the shoe prints inside his office and the other rooms.

Bill asked, "Do the maintenance crew clean the floor every day?"

"Yes, every day but the waxing is only on Mondays." Looking down at the floor, Dr. Jupitren said, "Since it's Monday today, I see they did the waxing in this east wing—mine, Helen's office, and the other rooms, too."

"That's good. Then what we may see on the floors now could be pretty reliable clues." Using special police lamps, Bill and John examined the footprints very carefully.

Bill cross-checked those shoe prints against a detective's e-manual on shoes. He said, besides his own and John's shoe prints, he identified four different well-known brands of shoes. One of them was quickly identified as Dr. Jupitren's own shoe print. According to the e-manual, the remaining three brands were Olympia walking shoes, size seven; Nike sneakers, size nine; and MacSprint running sneakers, size ten. Offhand, Dr. Jupitren had no idea who among the Acmeon workers wore those sneakers. Dr. Jupitren thanked Bill and said he would do some more of his own amateur detective work in the morning.

Bill said, "I'll bring the Mohawk's CCTV camera images to the lumberyard in the morning and will try to find out if Tick is the one in the image. If the lumberyard people can't identify who it is, I'll show it to Akandro at the detention center and have him tell me who it is."

At 11:30, feeling tired from the tension and excitement, everyone went home.

CHAPTER 32
TYPE O, RH-NEGATIVE BLOOD

In the following morning, Dr. Jupitren came to his office very early. Under the daylight, he saw a semicircular, very faint pinkish smudge on four doors of his office area. —doors of the suite entrance, his office, Helen's and the incubation room's. The smudge was around the base of the door handle's stem, which he must have overlooked the night before. The smudge was so faint that even Bill and John did not spot them under the night light.

From each door, he took a scraping sample off the smudge to identify what it was. As he suspected it, they proved to be blood. On further tests, those four doors' samples were all O, Rh-negative.

He called Bill, who was on his way to the lumberyard in Smithtown.

"Good morning, Bill. Did you get some sleep last night?"

"Yes, I slept very well. Anything new?"

"Yes. This morning, I found very faint blood marks on those four doors around the bottom of their knobs."

"Is that right? We must have overlooked them last night. Or the intruder might have come back to your office area after we left. We'll figure it out. At any rate, have you checked the blood type?"

"Yes, I have."

"That information will be useful at some point. I'm halfway to the lumberyard. I'll let you know what I would find out there."

"Thank you, Bill. I'll talk to you soon."

As soon as Helen walked in the office saying 'Good morning' to Dr. Jupitren, he asked her to do a computer search for Acmeon employees with blood type O, Rh-negative.

After several minutes, Helen came up with a list of few employees with the said blood type. Dr. Jupitren saw the list and stopped at two names: Sobien Molton and Zenon Zelinski! He briefly thought of something, then shook his head and said, "No, it's unlikely!"

Helen asked, "Anything's wrong?"

"Well, I'll explain it to you later. By the way, Helen, you know that I also have the O, Rh-negative blood type. Don't you?"

"Yes, I do. Some time ago, Aunt Jamie told me about it. She said you needed blood transfusions while your battalion was stationed in the Kabul area. And because your blood was uncommon O, Rh-negative type, the army's blood-program doctors had to make special arrangements to get the right type of blood for you."

"You're right. O, Rh-negative occurs in less than 5 percent of general population. Thank God, I'm well now…Let's see who else here has O, Rh-negative."

Dr. Jupitren kept on reading the list and asked, "Helen, I see here Narnia Bojore. Isn't she working in our maintenance department?"

"Yes, she is."

"How old is she?"

"About in her mid-fifties. Is anything wrong with her?"

"I don't know yet. I want to speak to her in person. Could you have her come up to my office now?"

Helen made a few interoffice calls and reported to Dr. Jupitren. "A short while ago, her son came in to pick her up to take her to an orthopedic doctor."

"Did they tell you what her problems were?"

"They said it's her hand injury."

"Well, when she returns, we'll talk to her."

Helen went back to her desk to check her e-messages from the previous night.

Soon afterward, Bill called Dr. Jupitren. "Jules, I showed the Mohawk Gas Station's CCTV camera image to the lumberyard foreman."

"What did you find?"

"The foreman recognized the image right away and said it was Tom Bojore's face. He said Tom has been working at the lumberyard for over two years. He also said Tom was a good worker and was quite dependable. It seems unlikely that Tom is Akandro's lackey Tick."

Dr. Jupitren asked, "Anything else about him?"

"I asked the foreman if I could speak to Tom. But he told me that Tom was not in this morning because he was attending to some family errands."

"I see. Bill, while you were out there, I got a list of a few Acmeon employees who had the same blood type as the trace blood from the door handles. And guess what? Among them, I have found a woman worker whose name is Narnia Bojore. I think she is Tom Bojore's mother."

"Very interesting. Did you speak to her?"

"Not yet. Her son came to Acmeon this morning and took her to an orthopedic doctor."

"Well, well, they must be the ones who came up to your office last night. I wonder whether Tom Bojore could be Tick, who spoke with Akandro on the speakerphone in my precinct's watch-house. Anyway, I'm on my way to the correctional center. I'll show the CCTV camera picture of Tom Bojore to Akandro and see if he recognizes him."

"Very good move, Bill."

Having finished talking with Bill, Dr. Jupitren went right back to the sessions with his morning patients. Soon after a patient left Dr. Jupitren's office, Helen hurriedly came in asking him to read a page of a message. It was a printout of an e-mail message from Narnia Bojore, written late in the previous night.

The message was as follows:

Hi, Helen,
I hope you read this e-mail first thing in the morning when you come into your office. I did not call you at your home because it was very late. Now it is one o'clock in the morning.

This morning, I will go to work by 7:30 at the maintenance department. But soon I will need to go to a doctor's office for my hand injury.

This morning, you might have found the main gate's security rail was raised up and not working. Also, you might have found the main door of Dr. Jupitren's suite, and all the inside offices were left unlocked. When I return to Acmeon Lab, I'll explain everything to you. If you need to call me, my number is 098-765-4321. Thank you. - Narnia Bojore

Having finished reading the message, Dr. Jupitren asked Helen again to have Narnia Bojore see him as soon as she returned.

Meanwhile, at the detention center, Bill pressured Akandro to reveal the identity of the person in the gas station's CCTV camera image. Akandro swore he did not know who it was.

Near noontime, Helen had Narnia Bojore come up to see Dr. Jupitren. Narnia's right hand was in heavy wrapping, which held a splint for the injured finger.

"Hi, Mrs. Bojore, how did you get hurt in your hand?"

"Last night, I had a tough time with some offices in the east wing of this floor, because the electronic lock system in the whole area malfunctioned.

At 6:45 the cleaning staff reported to me about the lock problem. I came up to this East Wing trying to fix the problem but I couldn't solve it. So, I called the lock system's technical-support line, and the person told me he would call me back in half an hour. In the meantime, by 7:30 pm my son, Tom, was to bring me four boxes of cables for the new storage bins in the shipping department.

Because he does not have an Acmeon parking lot gate opener on his car and lately lost his cell phone, I went to the gate ahead of him and raised the rail with my opener. With an idea at the spur of the moment, I put a wooden wedge into the rail hinge. I thought Tom would be able to drive through without my being there at the gate, as it was likely that I would be tied up on the telephone with the technical-support person. And in that rushed moment, as I put the wedge in the rail's hinge, my right hand was caught in there, and my finger was hurt. Then I rushed back to this third-floor office area."

"I see. I'm sorry you got hurt. What did the orthopedic doctor say about your finger?"

"He said my finger joint was sprained and the skin around it was torn."

"I hope you will recover quickly."

"Thank you."

"By the way, was the wood piece yours?"

"Yes, Tom gave it to me some time ago. I use it to hold doors when I work on locks and keys because I work in the maintenance department."

"I see. I understand Tom tried to help you here last night."

"Yes, after Tom unloaded the cables at the shipping department, he came up to the third floor to help me. Meanwhile, the Island Lock-Masters called me and said the earliest they could send their technicians would be at one thirty this afternoon. So, we left around eight o'clock last night."

"I see. What was the problem with the locks?"

"Opening the doors was not the problem, but some of them couldn't be locked. So, I had to leave those offices unlocked. In fact, this office door was one of them. I hope it didn't cause much inconvenience to you or anybody."

"That's all right. Don't worry about it. Then did you leave the gate rail up as you left the parking lot?"

"Yes. I needed to rush home to put an ice pack on my hand, and I thought no one would bother with Acmeon's offices for the night."

"I see. By the way, did your son have any nicknames?"

"We used to call him Tommy."

"That's it? No other names?"

"No. Why? Doctor, is he in any trouble?"

"No, not at all. You shouldn't worry. Mrs. Bojore, in fact, last night we had not just the lock problems but some other unusual things and I'm trying to gather as much information as possible from all sources. So, please bear with me because I have a few more questions and they are not directly related to your work."

"I understand, Doctor, I'll answer your questions without worrying."

"Thank you. Did you say your son did not have his cell phone?"

"Well, he used to have one, but a while ago he said he couldn't find it. But his cell-phone contract will be up soon, and he said he would buy a new one anyway if he cannot find the misplaced one."

"Did Tom tell you about anybody he worked with at the lumberyard?"

"I didn't hear much about any workers there, but once he told me he had an argument with a man who worked there per diem."

"Do you remember what they argued about?"

"Yes, but not the details of it; Tom said it was about his, I mean Tom's cell phone. Tom asked the man if he took Tom's cell phone, and it led to an argument. Other than that, I don't know the details."

"Could you give me Tom's lost cell-phone number?"

"Yes, sure." Mrs. Bojore gave him the number, which Dr. Jupitren wrote down in his note pad.

"Did your son tell you the man's name?"

"It sounded like Teeco. I don't know the exact spelling."

"Do you know if that person, Teeco, still works at the lumberyard?"

"Tom told me that for some reason the owner fired him a few weeks ago."

"I see."

Dr. Jupitren thought Teeco could be Tick, Tihko Piroiz. He also wondered if the lumberyard owner would know where Teeco lived.

Dr. Jupitren still had unanswered questions: out of the shoe prints on his office floor, owners of the three pairs were not identified yet.

He asked, "Now, Mrs. Bojore, I have to ask you a rather odd question. Do you mind telling me the brand names of Tom's and your sneakers you wore last night?"

Surprised and curious, she almost snickered nervously but kept her composure and said, "Well, the pair I was wearing is Olympia."

"The size?"

"Seven. And Tom always wears only one kind of sneakers, Nike, size nine."

"Thank you very much for being patient and answering all my questions. Now, why don't you go home and take it easy with your hand today? By the way, if you keep your injured hand raised above your heart level, it'll hurt less because in that position there will be less congestion in the hand. We'll ask your assistants to meet with the technicians from Island Lock-Masters this afternoon."

"Thank you, Doctor." Mrs. Bojore left.

He went over the time of events from the previous night again:

06:00 pm Dr. Jupitren went to the West Room at the Plant. No one at East Wing

06:45 pm Office-cleaning staff reported to Narnia Bojore re the lock problems.

07:15 pm Tom Bojore fueled his car at Mohawk Gas Station.

07:20 pm Narnia Bojore put the wooden wedge at the gate rail, hurting her hand.

07:30 pm Tom came through the open gate to deliver cables.

08:00 pm Tom and Narnia left Acmeon. Dr. Jupitren went home from the Plant.

08:00 pm - 09:45 pm No one at Acmeon?

09:45 pm Dr. Jupitren arrived at Acmeon to turn on the tsetse-fly incubator timer.

10:00 pm Dr. Jupitren left Acmeon to meet Bill and John at Mohawk Gas Station.

10:00 pm - 10:45 pm No one at Acmeon?

10:45 pm Dr. Jupitren, Bill, and John came to Dr. Jupitren's office.

11:30 pm Everyone left Acmeon.

Having reviewed the list, Dr. Jupitren thought of doing something else. He got up from his seat and examined his floor carefully. In one of the four corners, he discovered that a MacSprint shoe print was on top of the Olympia and Nike prints. It was obvious that the MacSprint wearer came in after Narnia Bojore and her son left at 8:00 pm. With further examination, he found another clue: his own shoe prints, as well as John's and Bill's, were on top of the MacSprint print.

He thought, "Then the MacSprint wearer came in either during 08:00 pm - 09:45 pm or possibly 10:00 pm -10:45 pm. Who was he?"

Later, Bill telephoned Dr. Jupitren and said, "I showed Akandro the Mohawk's CCTV camera image of Tom Bojore. But Akandro did not recognize who it was. So, Tom is not Tick."

Dr. Jupitren asked Bill, "Please check the cell-phone number that Tick used when he answered Akandro's call from the precinct in your presence."

"Well, I have to check my e-note, but offhand I remember the last four digits. They were 7227."

"That's it!" Dr. Jupitren exclaimed. "Tom Bojore's mother told me that at the lumberyard, there was a per diem worker whose name sounded like Teeco. And that person stole Tom's cell phone. She gave me Tom's lost cell-phone number, which ends with 7227. In fact, Tom and the other one, who I'm sure now is Tihko Piroiz, had argued about Tom's missing cell phone."

Bill responded, "Now the picture is clearing up. So when I made Akandro speak to Tick on the speakerphone right after Akandro's arrest, Tick was actually using the phone he stole from Tom Bojore. But we don't know Tick's whereabouts yet. The lumberyard owner may or may not know it. I'll ask him about it soon."

Dr. Jupitren said, "According to Tom's mother, that worker Teeco was fired a few weeks ago. I hope we find Tick's whereabouts soon. By the way, out of the three unknown shoe prints, I have identified two owners. Tom's mother wore Olympia size-seven walking shoes, and her son, Tom, wore Nike sneakers, size nine. We still have the MacSprint, size ten, unidentified."

"Jules, you're turning into a shoe-print detective. You'll be our consultant for our next difficult cases involving shoes and shoe prints!"

"No kidding! Bill, I'll see my next patient now. We'll talk again soon."

After finishing his interviews with a few Dream Wafer candidates, Dr. Jupitren reexamined his office floor very carefully. He checked the floor where he kept his computer towers. He found a distinct MacSprint size-10 shoe prints on the floor. He thought, "It is quite possible that the MacSprint wearer came close to my office computer last night. Did he know that our CCTV system was down for repair yesterday?"

He scraped dust samples off the MacSprint sneaker print on the floor and examined them under a special microscope. Then, through a few chemical tests, he separated the following three elements: boron, phosphates, and a trace of silicon.

He compared the dust samples with several other floor-dust samples within Acmeon Lab. However, those chemical elements were not found among them.

He telephoned Bill and explained what he had found from the MacSprint sneaker-print dust. "Bill, we now know the MacSprint sneakers have been someplace where boron, phosphates, and silicon were on the floor. What do you think of it?"

"Well, well, Jules, as you know, silicon is used in many different industries, from semiconductors, rubber manufacturers, solar panels, batteries, construction materials, paints, and sealants…there are so many of them I can't single out any one product in particular. Do you have any thoughts on it?"

"I agree with you. It's quite confusing. But the silicon trace that I got from the MacSprint sneaker prints was a rather pure kind. I can't be sure but it may point to some solar-energy-related industries. Besides, there were phosphorus and boron traces as well. Boron and phosphorus being electron-imbalance inducers, they are used in converting silicon into a semiconductor. So I suspect the MacSprint wearer treaded somewhere solar-energy products and semiconductors are manufactured."

"You're right, Jules."

"So, around Acmeon Lab, do you know any companies that deal with such products?"

Bill answered thoughtfully, "The famous solar-energy company in Elizabeth, New Jersey is at a far distance. Maybe, the Luxen Tech and Perihelion Energy Company? They're within twenty five miles from Acmeon."

"It's an odd coincidence!" Dr. Jupitren said, "Steve's sister, Jenny works at Luxen Tech and Steve works at Perihelion Energy Company. Can you think of any other companies?"

"No, not really, Jules. Do you want me to check on the work area floors of those two companies? I can go there under any pretense if I need to."

"Oh, no, thank you, Bill. You don't need to. I'll figure it out some other way."

"All right, Jules. I have another important piece of information. I'll be quick. I went back to the Giovanni lumberyard and asked the owner about the per-diem worker. The owner said he had to fire the worker few weeks ago because there were too many petty cash irregularities with him. Unfortunately, the owner did not have any contact information on the man because all the information he submitted on the per-diem job application was false with phony telephone numbers and wrong addresses."

"Every bit of it points the man is Tihco Piroiz. Bill, thank you for the information."

He had to end the telephone call with Bill as his Dream Wafer clients were waiting to see him.

Having seen his last patient of the day, Dr. Jupitren checked the days' e-messages. Among a dozen of them he spotted the billing statement from the Island Lock-Masters. Along with the service charges for the repair, it included the following information:

Problem area: Acmeon Lab, East Wing electronic lock system at units E1-4
Onset Time of malfunction: 6:15 pm Monday, June 12.
Cause of malfunction: Probable tampering on E 1-4 by illegal wire snipping.

Dr. Jupitren realized that someone tampered the office lock at 6:15. He questioned, "Did the same intruder return, leaving MacSprint shoe prints near my computer?"

CHAPTER 33
TELL ME SOMETHING

Following Dr. Jupitren's advice, Helen gave up on her original idea of studying in Washington, DC. Instead, she applied to a *Work-and-Study* MBA course at Metropolitan University in New York.

Several days before the application deadline, Helen managed to send the required papers to the university's admissions office. Among those papers, she was particularly proud of her essay on her work experience and strong GMAT scores. Subsequently, after lengthy formal interviews by three faculty members, she received the acceptance letter to the course. The letter indicated that beside the main course, which would start in September, she was eligible for an optional Head Start program in early July. She readily registered for the July program.

Anticipating busy school and work schedules ahead, Helen announced that she would be working on a half-time schedule at Acmeon Lab.

In the middle of the day, Steve was able to speak to Helen on the phone. "Helen, since you told me about your graduate school idea, lately you're becoming practically invisible."

"I'm afraid you're right. It'll have to go on like that for a good while. If I'm lucky, it'll be for two years. If not, three years."

"Is something forcing you to do it?"

"My ambition is."

"Your ambition? Such as having your own business someday?"

"Not quite like that. Are you worried about me, Steve?"

"I'm more surprised than worried…So, what kind of courses do you have to take?"

"Do you really want to know?"

"Yes."

"Why?"

"Because I may want to take similar courses."

"You must be kidding me. What's making you want to take those courses?"

Steve echoed Helen's earlier answer and said, "My ambition is."

"You can't be serious."

Steve didn't reply. He could not explain his thoughts in any other way at the moment and kept himself quiet.

Rushed for time, Helen said, "OK, I'm pressured for time now. So I'll just tell you quickly what courses I'll be taking. They are Marketing Management, Statistical Analysis for Business Decision-Making, and Basic Financial Accounting & Ethics. Also, I'll need to take Behavioral Approach to Business Management and Fundamentals in International Business. Lastly, I'll be taking Computer Essentials, like advanced PowerPoint and Excel proficiency and so on. That's only for the first year…"

"I believe you can handle them pretty well. I see what we learned at New York Polytech Academy overlaps with some of them. But I still don't know what really motivated you so strongly."

Helen teasingly said, "Only if you tell me something, will I tell you more about it."

"I tell you something? Like what?"

Helen coyly but clearly answered, "You have to figure that out for us, I mean for me."

Steve could not understand what she meant. He paused again. Helen wasn't sure if Steve understood what she meant. She asked, "Are you there, Steve?"

"Yes…"

"Please say something." Helen asked.

"I'm thinking about what you just said—that I have to tell you something—but I don't know what you mean."

"Oh, that! If I were you, I wouldn't worry about it."

Steve wanted a clearer answer. "I wish you were more direct and clear about it."

Helen wanted to change the subject. "That's all right. Please don't think too much about it. Now I have some urgent dictation to do for Dr. Jupitren. I'll talk to you soon. Bye, Mr. Smart."

Days later, at home, burning the midnight oil, Helen read a sociology article, which was one of the reading assignments given by her Head Start program of Metropolitan University. It said that the highest rate of unmarried females per unit of population in the United States were found in the West Coast and northeastern cities. The article had some interesting points:

> *More career-aspiring women converge in those megacities because of their rich professional ambience. Having pursued their careers one-track mindedly, those women may succeed in their chosen professional fields, but many of them belatedly realize that they missed the opportune time for marriage.*
>
> *By the time they are financially and emotionally ready for marriage, they find the available male counterparts are lower in career status, younger, and reluctant to commit themselves to marital bonds yet. The women then decide to remain single, relishing their hard-earned livelihoods, and go on living in their familiar cities.*
>
> *Because of their avant-garde cultural, financial, and sociopolitical resources, are those cities turning into human greenhouses for Amazonian women? Well, the population of singles is increasing worldwide anyway. Besides, singleness, childless families, and egocentric rejection of family centered lifestyles seem to have increased in number in the more developed and urbanized regions.*

Helen's perception of this ubiquitous world phenomena made her think that the whole world seemed to be ailing from its regional urban disorders of some kind, but she could not give any specific name to them. Then she felt a thread of uneasiness as she envisioned herself bustling through the city streets among those live statistics and missing her love life. She thought to herself, "Am I going to be one of the stats? Well, I should try to be an exception to that."

One afternoon, Steve called his sister. "Hi, Jenny. Have you got a few minutes for me?"

"Sure, what's up?"

"I want to talk about a few things and get your advice. Maybe I should come over to your Luxen Tech office after I'm done here at Perihelion."

"I'm not busy this afternoon. I can fly on my air-scooter to your Perihelion Energy office. It doesn't take too long for me to get to your office."

"Thanks, Jenny. I'll be done by five today. Please come to my office by then. You know my building has two air-scooter landing pads, *A* and *B*, on its rooftop."

"Yeah, I know. From the *B* pad, I can walk down to your office in less than a minute. I know your suite number, uh, 2624?"

"Right, I'll see you soon. Thank you, Jenny."

By five thirty, Jenny walked into Steve's office still wearing her air-scooter rider's helmet. As she took her helmet off, Steve asked, "Other than being a protective headgear, what else does the helmet do for you?"

"It lets me hear the air-scooter control tower's automated communication on my radio frequency. It tells me how far I have traveled and how much more to go, et cetera."

"I see. Now, I want to ask your opinion about Helen and me."

"Aha, I had a hunch about you bringing it up. Tell me about it."

"Helen said she will be busy working and studying for two to three years and sounded like she had no time for me. She has enrolled for an MBA course already."

"So?"

"I asked her why she was so eager to study now."

"What did she say to that?"

"She said it was because of her ambition. So, I asked her to tell me the real reason. At that point, she said I had to tell her something first. Only then would she tell me more about why she is becoming a student now."

"What do you think you have to tell her?"

"I don't know what she is asking of me. That's why I'm begging you to figure it out for me."

"I should figure it out for you?" Jenny broadly smiled, shrugging her shoulders.

"Yes. I thought you as a woman probably would know it better than I would. What's your take on Helen's wish that I have to tell her something?"

Jenny thought only for a few seconds and questioned Steve, "Do you love her?"

"You know I do. My heart reminds me about that every minute of the day."

"Have you ever said, 'I love you' to her?"

"No, not exactly in those very words, because my whole being and mere presence say it to her all the time."

"What do you mean? You never said you loved her?"

"Correct. I never did."

"Then I feel I know what Helen is asking."

"What's that?"

"I think she wants a sure sign that you love her. I believe she is asking you to let her know that you love her, by actually saying it to her. You should say you're in love with her, you're crazy about her, can't live without her, and other convincing words like that!"

Amazed at Jenny's quick rhetoric, Steve suddenly felt as if a bright light was turned on in his head. "Aha, that's it! How blind of me! I was in the dark all these months. For so long, I simply took it for granted that what she saw in me should be good enough for her and for us. But you're saying she needs my spoken declaration!"

Jenny laughed and remarked, "You've got it. Steve, my dear brother, you talk like a young boy. Where have you been all these languid years?"

"You know I've been concentrating on work, dabbling with all the electronic stuff!"

"Well, we live in the middle of the twenty-first century, but a woman's heart still yearns for the spoken voucher of her man's love for her. It's because the effect of such a voucher invigorates a woman's raison d'être. Verbally expressed love will make her ascend to another level of being. This subtle rite between a loving man and a woman will not change as long as mankind dwells on this planet Earth. No enamored mind can survive silence forever."

"All right, all right, Jenny, if you say any more about the subject, I'm afraid the message of your solemn lesson on love will get obscured. I'm just managing to engrave your profound message in my tabula rasa!"

Jenny, still smiling, said, "I'm glad you've experienced a sudden enlightenment! Come to think of it, as we grew up together through our teens and twenties, on birthdays or on any other special occasions I seldom heard you say 'I love you' to anyone. For that matter, I've heard you say the magic three words to Mom and Dad only once or twice so far. I suppose your outward word routine was different from your inner feeling state through those years. You were a very feeling and loving person with very little verbal show of it."

"Thank you for being generous and understanding me so well. As a big sister, you have been a great example for me in many ways. I can say now I love you, Jenny, and thank you for being such a wonderful sister to me."

"You're very welcome. Now, you've got to tell Helen about your special feelings for her. Spoken words! That's what she is asking from you. I'm pretty sure. I think there is just no getting around the power of spoken words of love, unless you both were born with an unusual knack of telepathy."

"Thanks a lot, Jenny for your good advice. Well, before you came to my office, I'd made a reservation at the Village Bistro for two. And it's about the right time for us to get there. You can tell me at the dinner how it's going with you and Dr. Molton lately. Can we leave now?"

"Yes. Thank you, Steve. Let's go."

CHAPTER 34
AN AFTERNOON WITH MORE DREAMERS

At the Acmeon Lab, the afternoon's first patient Mr. Zukowski, a plumber, came in to renew his Dream Wafers.

"How have you been, Mr. Zukowski?" Dr. Jupitren greeted gently as usual.

"Pretty well, thank you. When I was here first time two weeks ago, I told you that in my repeating dreams, this big amphibian monster used to chase me, threatening to devour me. Right next to me, it would tear up other living things with those saber-sharp teeth and would gobble them up. Scary as it was, whenever it approached me with blood dripping open jaws and saber teeth, I would scream bloody murder and wake up in cold sweat. You said it's my anxiety that caused my scary dreams to recur. So you prescribed the Dream Wafers for me."

"How did the Wafers work for you?"

"It certainly made a difference. Last night I had a similar dream but with a different ending. In the dream, I was working with my favorite iron pliers on underground pipelines when the monster popped up from the wet ground, snapping its saber teeth. Rather than cowering away from it, this time I decided to fight it out. But I had no tools or weapons to fight with, except the pliers in my hand. So, I threw the pliers hard at it. To my surprise, its saber teeth snapped the darting metal pliers, and it started to swallow them. Its gyrating head and grinding jaws made scary noises and movements, but once it finished swallowing, it became instantly quiet. Then it walked away from me! And I woke up, strangely feeling calm. The ending of the recurring dream was quite different from other times.

The only regrettable thing that happened in the dream was losing my favorite iron pliers, because they were an expensive kind. Actually, the pliers were RIDGID Company's press tool. Without them, I can't be a good plumber."

"I see. As you answered the questionnaire last time for your Dream Wafers, did you actually request to see the monster again in your dreams?"

"In a way, yes. I had requested that I would fight and overcome the monster in one way or another."

"I'm glad you got the result as requested. I wonder what the fight with it means to you."

"Well, it's some sort of struggle."

"Struggle? What comes to your mind when you say struggle?"

"The idea of tax came to my mind."

"Tax?"

"Yes, right after I woke up, I thought of the pliers that the monster swallowed. It meant that I lost something valuable. Soon, I made a connection between the pliers and the tax money! I often consider tax as some sort of personal loss rather than dues that I'm supposed to pay. I know I should change my wrong ideas about the taxes. I recently heard from my relatives in Poland that their tax-rate-per-income range is almost four times the rate we are paying in the United States. So, I shouldn't complain."

"I see. Then about the amphibian monster, what does it seem to represent?"

"Naturally, all the tax collectors and different forms of taxes. There are so many kinds of taxes with different names, and I cannot list them all, but you know what I mean."

"Well, why an amphibian?"

"It means the monster is everywhere, on land and in water; likewise, wherever I go and whatever I do, the tax collectors are there. Aren't they?"

"Yes, I can understand that."

"Dr. Jupitren, can you upgrade my next Wafers so that I'll have a peaceful dream next time?"

"I believe it can be done."

"Then in the next dreams, I would ride the tamed monster rather than fighting it."

"Well, I hope so. But do you still want to see the monster in your dream again?"

"Nooo! I'd rather not."

"Then, Mr. Zukowski, please indicate that when you answer the questionnaire today."

"Sure, I will."

The next client was Mr. Cervantes, the chemist. As he entered Dr. Jupitren's office, he seemed quite happy.

"Good afternoon, Mr. Cervantes. How have you been?"

"Very well. Thank you. I'm sure you remember what I wished to accomplish with my Dream Wafers."

"Certainly I do. You wished to retrieve your thoughts and memories from three years ago."

"That's right!" Mr. Cervantes was beaming and continued his report with excitement. "After several applications of my Dream Wafers, something happened in my dreams. It wasn't anything scary or bad but plainly strange. It was a kind of repeated riddle with numerology."

"Numerology?"

"Yes. Since my early years, I've been fascinated by mnemonics built on numerology. Maybe that's why I dreamt those strange dreams that I'm about to tell you. Years ago, when I worked in a chemical firm in the DC area, I used to go to the technology section, subclass TP (Chemical Engineering) of Library of Congress. There, I spent hours in the TP section to get technical information for my chemical engineering work.

Two weeks ago, while I was on my Dream Wafers, I had recurrent dreams for two nights in a row, with almost identical scenes. In those dreams, every time I went to the Library of Congress, the main-entrance door of the library remained locked without a clear explanation. However, each time in the dream, I saw a big bulletin posted on the locked door displaying these numbers: 7-5-13. Naturally, I tried to figure out what they meant. Could you guess what they were?"

"No, I can't. All I can think of is July 5th, 2013."

"Initially, that's what I thought, too. But my wife suggested that the dreamt numbers on the Library door could be related to my numerology. Then I deciphered it immediately and told her that 7-5-13 stands for *G-E-M* according to the ordinal numbering of alphabet letters; *G* being the seventh, *E* the fifth, and *M* the thirteenth letter. Only then, I recalled that I had written the word 'GEM' with a magic marker on top of a box. Almost at the same time, I remembered that I stuffed the box with my important papers as we were getting ready to move to the current house. It was around the time of my carbon monoxide poisoning three years ago.

As soon as I remembered that, I ran downstairs to the basement. There, among the several unopened big boxes that were stacked up in the corner, I found the very box marked 'GEM'. It was at the bottom of several stacked boxes. When I opened it, I screamed for joy, because all the chemistry questions and answers on the project that I had worked around that time for many months were there in my own handwriting! Those work records were real stuff, not dreams, that I wrote down then."

"That sounds wonderful."

"Well, some of the information in the box was what my chemical company still needed, and I gladly presented it to my chief engineer early this week. The chief brought the written information to the company's president right away, and they were very happy to have it. They said, because of the unexpected information that I brought to their attention, they would be able to expedite a certain chemical project that had been in slow progress until recently. They said I'll get some form of credit for the information."

"That is a very fortunate turnout for you, Mr. Cervantes. Probably that carbon-monoxide episode caused your patchy memory loss and made you forget about the GEM box for so long."

"But the Dream Wafers made me dream about it in riddles! I'm glad the Dream Wafers helped me to go back to the time when I marked the box."

"Well, after all, dreams are riddles anyway. I'm very happy for your recovery of your gems."

"I'm very happy, too. By the way, I followed your suggestion and I wrote down about my dreams as soon as I woke up in the mornings and I remembered them much better. Also, I think the Dream Wafer is helping me to remember my dreams better, too."

With another refill of his Dream Wafers, Mr. Cervantes thanked Dr. Jupitren and returned home with boosted gusto for more work.

Dr. Jupitren's next client, Mr. Wong, came in and reported, "My Dream Wafers have worked well for me. Every night, as I requested, I was in my old hometown seeing my parents and all my brothers and sisters. Outside my old home, I was among my boyhood friends. Most of them are deceased now but in my dream everyone was there as the good old days. The Wafers were very good remedy for my nostalgia. I have three more doses left. If I stop the Wafers now, would it be OK?"

"Certainly, you can stop if you don't need them any longer. You can restart them anytime in the near future."

"Good. I'll order more Wafers today and may use them a couple of months later."

"I'm afraid that is not the most ideal way to order your Wafers. The best time should be as close as to the time when you actually need them."

"Why is that so?"

"The Wafers are made based on your present physiological state, which constantly changes over time. That's why the pre-Wafer testing is needed to check your current physiological state just before you renew your Wafers. So, if we make your Wafers now and you use them two months later, they may not work the best."

"I see. Then I'll come back when I need them."

"That's the best way."

After interviewing several more clients, Dr. Jupitren felt he needed a brief respite. He came out of his office and told Helen, "I don't have any more clients to see this afternoon. I'll sit in my chair for about twenty minutes to rest. If I don't come out after thirty minutes, please knock at my door."

He closed his eyes and soon slipped into light dozing and had a dream. He saw Steve's sister, Jenny, on her air-scooter, flying toward a tower. There was another uncouth, wild man on the ground, waving at Jenny on the air-scooter, but she ignored his brisk hand semaphore.

Getting angry for being ignored, the wild man on the ground took off one of his sneakers and irately threw it at her air-scooter. The thrown sneaker transformed itself into a giant lump of lead, hitting the air-scooter. Its heavy impact on the scooter forced Jenny to crash-land behind the tower. Then the wild man vanished, wearing his sneaker only on one foot.

The airborne lead lump transformed back to a sneaker and fell into the hands of the spectating dreamer, Dr. Jupitren. It was a MacSprint running sneaker! Dr. Jupitren happened to be there on the ground and saw the whole thing from the beginning.

The air-scooter's crash-landing noise changed to a door knock, which woke Dr. Jupitren up and he heard Helen's voice. "It's past thirty minutes now. Are you OK?"

"Yes, I'm fine. Helen, please come in."

Helen noticed Dr. Jupitren in his chair looking a bit haggard and tired. "Do you feel a little better?"

"Yes, I do, thank you. I must have dozed off. Actually, I meant to ask you about your MBA course registration."

"It's already done. In fact, I've enrolled for a Head Start program, a two-credit course that started already last week right after the Independence Day and it will continue through October. But in September, I'll start the main courses, all in New York."

"That's nice. I'm glad that you'll stay in New York. By the way, as you know, Acmeon had an intruder lately. It was on the day when our CCTV camera was down for repair."

"Do you know who it was?"

"Not quite. We ruled out Tom Bojore and his mother. They're good people. They happened to be in Acmeon buildings that night just to do some extra work, as you know. Someone else was here that same night. But there was no severe damage. Have you noticed anything unusual around Acmeon lately?"

"Yes, as you've brought it up, I just remembered one thing that I forgot to tell you. It didn't sit right with me. It was at lunchtime last Friday. My office was very quiet. There was no one in the waiting area, and the overhead music was not on. You weren't in your office. My office door was ajar, and I could hear Dr. Molton, who was standing in the hallway not too far from my office. He was talking on his cell phone to Steve's sister, Jenny, and it was on speakerphone mode. It seemed that he didn't mind the speakerphone mode being on, or else he was unaware of his phone being on that mode. He usually speaks loudly anyway, and I could hear everything they were saying. I did not like what I heard. They were disagreeing about something."

"What did they say?"

"He said something about his new business. Then Jenny disagreed with him, and suddenly he raised his voice. He said she was talking just like you, not agreeing with his ideas. He said he was determined to do it his way because it will bring in more money. He angrily said, 'If you don't want to pay for the pipers, I'll do all the juggling and tooting by myself!' and abruptly ended the call."

Releasing his clenched jaws, Dr. Jupitren sighed and said quietly, "I thought he had learned a lesson from his divorce experience, but apparently he did not. His ambition and greed are pulling him from under."

Dr. Jupitren then recalled the initial pre-Wafer test results on Sobien that raised a diagnostic warning. He thought to himself, "I should've taken it more seriously and have done closer follow-up on Sobien with a few more tests."

After Helen stepped out of Dr. Jupitren's office, suddenly he recalled what he had dreamt before she knocked at the door. When his dream recall came to the scene in which he caught the MacSprint sneaker that bounced off Jenny's troubled air-scooter, he had an association that pointed to Sobien Molton. He could not help but suspect that it was Sobien who tampered with the door locks of his office area and snooped around his computer that night.

Through his office intercom, Dr. Jupitren said, "Helen, please come back to my office. I've another important matter." Helen stopped what she was working with Anne Brown and returned to his office.

Dr. Jupitren said, "Please do a couple of things for me when you can. One way or another, tactfully find out the brand name and size of Dr. Molton's sneakers. And, find out if he recently visited Jenny Spencer at her Luxen Tech work areas. Strange as it may sound to you, it's quite important for many of us."

"It'll take some time for me, but I'll try my best."

Unaware of how meticulously Dr. Jupitren had been tracking the trace of the recent intruder, Sobien Molton was busy communicating with the agent A.H., now known as Ajnin Hsilomed, who had left another scary message on his cell phone:

"Because you screwed it up, my government had to hire a team of hackers. But they didn't get it. Since then, we found Acmeon already filed with the FBI Internet Crime Complaint Center, and Acmeon's IT guys are blocking my government's second hacking effort. If you don't produce it soon, my government's secret service will eliminate you."

Feeling frightened, Sobien left a voice message for the agent:

"I tried to copy the program a few days ago but did not get very far. I have a different plan now. I need another guy for the kind of job you are asking me to do. When he is ready to do the hacking from outside, I have to be inside and tell him exactly when to do it, because now I know Acmeon Lab's operating schedule. I know which

anti-hacking programs I should disable before the outside guy starts hacking. But to hire him, I need more C-notes from you."

Later, the agent left his answer:

"According to the order I got from my government, you have to produce it by the end of this month, or else my government's secret-service cleaning squad will come to deal with you. They will replace me, too…I'll leave three hundred C-notes with Jungle Cat at the Midtown Club by noon tomorrow. When you get the C-notes from him, make sure you count the money before you leave him; lately Jungle Cat put his sticky paws on some of the secret money. If he misbehaves again, he will lose his paws."

Frightened for his life, Sobien emptied his whiskey bottle. He fell asleep while thinking of whom to contact for the outsider job.

CHAPTER 35
MACSPRINT SNEAKERS SIZE TEN

Midmorning at Acmeon Lab, Dr. Molton walked into Helen's office holding a cup of coffee. While stirring his coffee with a teaspoon somewhat carelessly, he complained, "The gate is not responding to my gate-rail opener again. Will you have the maintenance people fix my gate opener or the gate itself? It's the second time the darned thing happened! Here's my gate opener."

"Yes, I'll take care of it right away." Saying it complaisantly, Helen looked down at his shoes. They were not sneakers but a pair of well-polished, regular walking shoes. She did not know what to do to learn about his sneakers. At that moment, his teaspoon slipped out of his hand and fell down on the floor right next to his shoes. Instantly, she got out of her seat and reached for the spoon and said, "Nice and clean shoes! Who does the shoe polishing for you?"

"My shoe-polishing machine does. Without the machine, I don't think I can keep all the five pairs of them shiny like this. I've another, different polishing machine for my sneakers as well."

"Really? What brand of sneakers do you have that you let your machine do the polishing?"

"Durawalker, MacSprint, and Johnny Liner."

"Do you own them all?"

"Of course."

"Are they all the same sizes?"

Finishing his last sip of coffee, he looked at her and asked, "What's the matter, Helen? Are you interested in my shoes or in me?"

Helen felt she'd been caught red-handed and shrugged her shoulders with a grin and said, "I was just carried away. Sorry."

"Don't be sorry…Ah, the sneaker size? That's no secret! Squarely size ten, all of them, same size."

With a wad of tissue, she wiped the spoon dry and handed it back to him.

He said, "Thanks. Did I answer your questions?"

"Yes, you did. You're very funny."

"Call me when the gate opener is fixed."

He swaggered out of Helen's office, whistling an old tune from the early 2030's.

Helen thought, "What else did Uncle Jules ask me to find out about Dr. Molton? Oh, yes, has he been to Luxen Tech's work area recently? How am I going to ask Jenny about his visits there?" Instead, Helen called Steve at his office. "Hi, it's me."

Steve stopped what he was doing and said, "The sun must have risen from the western horizon today, as I'm getting a morning call from you! How're you?"

"I'm good. Thanks. I need your help."

"Whatever help you need, I'll do my best. You know that."

"Yes, Steve, I know you will. Would you ask Jenny about the recent visitors at Luxen Tech, especially at the work area?"

"You mean how many of them, who, when, why, et cetera?"

"In a way, yes. But I'm interested in only one person."

"Who?"

"Dr. Sobien Molton."

Feeling curious, Steve said, "Jenny told me he lately came to visit her there at Luxen Tech very often. But why do you need to know that?"

"Yesterday, Uncle Jules asked me to find out if Dr. Molton had been to Luxen Tech recently."

"Why can't you ask him directly?"

"Uncle Jules told me to check it without asking him. I don't know why."

"Well, I hope it's not a serious matter. Is that all you need to know, Helen?"

"Yes, that's the whole answer I needed. Thank you, Steve."

"Nothing at all. It was great to hear from you. Have a lovely day."

"You, too. I'll tell you more if I learn what Uncle Jules is up to."

Back to her work routine, Helen checked the incoming office e-mail messages. Among them, there were several e-mails and voice messages from Dr. Molton's clients. They said in gist, *"Dr. Molton, you informed us that if we accepted your new treatment method, we would come and see you only once or twice a year rather than several times in order to get the new Dream Wafers. However, you said your new method might produce 'significant changes' in our dreams. What specific health effects will your new method have on us? Overall, are we going to pay a lesser fee for your new treatment method than for the old method?"*

Helen brought those e-messages to Dr. Jupitren. He just read the inquiries from Dr. Molton's clients and said very little about it. Then he asked Helen, "Were you able to get any information about what I asked you yesterday?"

"Yes. Dr. Molton has been to Luxen Tech's work area rather frequently of late to see Jenny Spencer, and his sneakers are all ten in size. He has three brands of sneakers: Dura Walker, MacSprint, and Johnny Liner."

"Excellent, Helen. I don't know how you managed to get that information in such a short time."

"I was just lucky. But, may I ask why you don't want to ask him directly about those things?"

"It's a bit involved. I thought it would be better to handle the matter this way for the time being."

Helen returned to her front office.

While he was by himself, Dr. Jupitren sank into deep thoughts. "It seems certain that Sobien Molton was at my office computer area that night. Why? What was he looking for? At some appropriate time, I should ask him about it.

In addition, what about those inquiries from his clients? Sobien must have been feeding his clients with tantalizing and premature information about his new treatment method. He said there will be 'significant changes' in his clients' dreams. He was probably alluding to the permanent gene-alteration idea, which I have clearly disapproved a number of times."

While waiting for the technical information on Waferlyzer-II to be printed, Dr. Jupitren found brief free moments and called Bill Warren. He explained to

Bill about all the clues pointing to Sobien Molton, who had made an unpleasant visit to his office during that night.

Dr. Jupitren told Bill that the silica dusts that were detected from the MacSprint sneaker prints on his office floor gave him the final clue to identify the sneaker owner.

Bill complimented Dr. Jupitren's amateur detective work and said, "I'll keep an eye on Sobien Molton. Also, I'll check Akandro's conversation with his underlings, Tick and Tack. For now, Jules, relax and just do your Dream Wafer-related work. If you need me, I'm one click away."

CHAPTER 36
STEVE AND HELEN

Once again, after a dinner at La Cornucopia, the Acmeon Lab engineers and techs scrutinized the blueprint of the Waferlyzer-II in the glass-walled conference room of the restaurant.

Following an hour of Q & A's on the Waferlyzer's technical information, assignments were made regarding the actual assembling of parts and writing the user's manual.

Dr. Jupitren said, "In order to determine the new tester's accuracy, we will follow the usual *standard-controlled, comparison-study* design. Each testee with a known genome will give two consecutive breaths; one breath for the control, that is existing chemical-analyzer machine and the second breath for the new Waferlyzer-II. Then the results between the two breath-samples from the same testee will be compared to see if both machines yield the same data. If not, we will know with what margin of error the new machine will perform.

Next, we need to decide the test-run size. According to the latest FDA bulletin, it should be minimum three hundred for the kind of apparatus as Waferlyzer-II."

At that point, Sobien Molton made an unexpected remark. "Based on Eisenberg and McElroy's genetic probability table, which nowadays is a genetics gold standard, my calculation indicates that the test-runs require a lot more than three hundred samples, maybe a thousand or more…This will delay the launching date of Waferlyzer-II by several more weeks."

Everyone seemed baffled. A short while later, to everyone's surprise, Helen took a few sheets of paper out of her document binder and said, "Dr. Molton's calculation is correct, when it is based on Eisenberg and McElroy's genetic-expression probability table that was published two years ago. However, I was able to retrieve the revised table, which was published three months ago in *Genetic Informatics* by the same geneticists of Miami University. According to the revised table, three hundred test-run samples should be sufficient. I'm glad this number coincides with the number Dr. Jupitren mentioned earlier. Please see the revised table copies and my calculation here." She circulated her calculation sheets along with the revised table reprints and the correlating references. Everyone was very surprised at her input.

After an intense scrutiny of her calculation, everyone agreed with Helen's opinion. Dr. Molton complimented her, albeit feeling a bit embarrassed, and said, "A great job, Helen. You're a bundle of constant surprises. I concede to your research result without reservation." Saying so, he got up from his seat, gesturing a knightly salute toward her. Everyone seemed amused. Some of them applauded, making it more dramatic.

Dr. Jupitren remarked, "I'm glad we agreed on the number of required test-runs. It looks like we'll be able to launch the new version on time. I thank you both, Sobien and Helen, for clarifying the needed test-run sample size."

Helen remained quiet but thought to herself, "Many thanks to you, Uncle Jules for encouraging me to take the Smithsonian Business Institute mini-course. I did not anticipate I would use the very probability table that I learned from the course so soon!"

At the closure of the meeting's main agenda, Helen quietly distributed the pre-announced bonus envelopes to each attendant staff. They seemed happy with what they found in the envelopes except Sobien, who unabashedly muttered words of dissatisfaction.

As everyone was getting up to leave the restaurant, the manager of La Cornucopia came to the meeting room, thanked everyone for having enjoyed a full-course dinner at his restaurant again, and shook hands with some of Acmeon's staff.

As Sobien Molton walked up to the manager to shake hands with him, Dr. Jupitren saw the MacSprint logo on Sobien Molton's sneakers. He stared at them, silently saying, "Must be size ten!" He felt his buoyant mood slide down one notch, grounding him with uneasy vigilance.

As they were coming out to the parking lot, Helen whispered to Dr. Jupitren, "Did you see Dr. Molton's sneakers?"

"Yes."

"Did you confirm anything after you saw his sneakers?"

"Yes."

"Is Dr. Molton going to be all right?"

"I hope so."

"Uncle Jules, after the good dinner meeting we just had, you sound not so happy."

"I'm fine, Helen. The meeting was good. You were superb…but his sneakers are still bothering me." He felt a twinge of anger toward Molton. However, soon he toned down his strong judgment and reminded himself again that Sobien must be struggling with a serious psychiatric illness and emotional pain that others were not aware of.

Driving homeward, Helen reviewed her day. All day she had asserted herself with work-related matters and yet tried not to offend anybody. By calmly tolerating Sobien's repeated rudeness, finally she'd received a knightly salute from him. The engineers did not grudge their admiration for her intelligent presentation. The planning meeting had ended placing Helen's credit on the far plus side. Uncle Jules also seemed satisfied with how the meeting went. Yet, somehow, she felt tired and wistful. Suddenly she felt a certain inner void. She felt she was ready for a second wind, maybe an expression of special recognition or reward. Or a show of affectionate adoration from someone dear to her.

As she passed by the hospital area, her feelings sank into an elegiac tone, and she reminisced on Jonathan in a flash. Oddly, almost at the same moment, her wrist-phone buzzed, and she connected the call to her car phone. It was from Steve.

"Are you still at the dinner meeting?"

"No. The meeting's done, and I'm on my way home. I'm so glad to hear from you, Steve."

"So am I. How did the meeting go?"

"Very well. But it's unlike you. You seldom called me at this time of the day."

"True. But I called you because I want to see you. Did you drive past L Street already?"

"No, not yet. I'm near the hospital."

"Good, I'm near the kiostrant Amor Patriae on the Lovers' Lane right now. How soon can you get to Amor Patriae?"

"In less than ten minutes."

"Great, I'm about the same distance away from the kiostrant. But I'll try to get there ahead of you and wait for you."

"By the way, I had dinner already at La Cornucopia before the meeting. Didn't you have your supper yet?"

"Yes, I did, too. But I just want to see you there. OK?"

"Yes, it's fine, Steve."

Unlike many other times, she detected some excitement in Steve's voice. Feeling relieved, as if she was lifted from a difficult swamp, she sped with renewed energy and felt her heart racing. As she pulled into Amor Patriae's parking lot, she saw Steve getting out of his parked car.

He, too, saw her car pulling in. He walked close to her car and helped her park in a narrow spot between two parked cars. Stepping out of her car, she saw Steve walking toward her with his arms stretched open to her.

Under the not so dim light, she could read from his expression how happy he was to see her. Suddenly, she felt as if her whole body was drawn to a strong magnet and slid into his embracing arms. She felt his hands' tender clasping touch through her summery clothes. They felt intense surge of happiness from the embraced closeness with each other. Reciprocating his passionate hold, stroking his hair, Helen wanted to whisper her heightened affection into his ears. But she felt a trifle breathless and took in a sweet, deep breath, readying herself to whisper it to him. At that very moment, both Steve and Helen whispered to each other at the same time, "I love you!"

Unlocking the embrace, they looked at each other without words, only to embrace again, and Steve said, "I've waited all this time to tell you this. I couldn't wait any longer. I love you, Helen."

"I love you, too, Steve."

Blissful time slipped them into "lovers' oblivion," and their ensuing passionate kisses halted their sense of time. Finally, they regained their awareness with the proverbial questions, "Where are we? What time is it?" Then they realized the parked cars on either side of hers had pulled out and gone already. Steve and Helen found they were standing at the edge of the Lovers' Lane, under a festoon-like red maple branch, a short distance away from her car. Hand in hand, they looked up at the summer's starry sky. Inhaling the fresh breeze, they felt intoxicated by Cupid's touch. Drenched with a sudden shower of love, Helen's spirit soared, and she felt a bit faint and needed to lean on Steve's shoulder as she walked back to her car.

Helen drove home savoring the unexpected exciting moments she'd shared with Steve.

After reliving the excitement all over again by telling her mother what had happened not too long ago, Helen fell asleep wishing to reenact the evening's bliss. She thought, "If I was on the Dream Wafers, would I see Steve at the Lovers' Lane again in my dreams?"

CHAPTER 37
JENNY'S CALL TO HELEN

Next day, near the end of her lunch hour, Helen received call from Jenny Spencer.

"What a surprise to get a call from you, Jenny. How are you?"

"So-so, this is a personal call, Helen. Since I saw you and Steve at the Village Bistro, a few things happened to me, and I have some questions for you. To be exact, I've at least three things in mind. I know you're very busy, but I thought you would help me."

"Anything you say, Jenny, I'm all ears. Please tell me."

"OK, then, the first thing is about getting the Dream Wafers for myself."

"That's an easy one. I can set up an appointment with Dr. Jupitren for you. Do you have any particular day in mind?"

"Yes, I do. But let me ask you the other questions first."

"OK. Please tell me. I'll see if I can answer them on the phone now or later."

"Well, I wanted to know how it's going with you and my brother."

"It's going very well, thank you. I've a lot to tell you about it. The remainder of my lunch hour will not be long enough for us to go over it on the phone. You still have the third question, you said."

"Yes, I'm wondering how Sobien Molton is with Acmeon Lab's people. I mean, with Dr. Jupitren, with you, and with other people there. I want to know what you think of his character."

"Well, Jenny, to answer your questions will take some time…" Helen thought briefly and said, "Maybe we could meet after five o'clock this afternoon. I finish my work by then. But if you need the Dream Wafers urgently, I can help you make an appointment with Dr. Jupitren now. Do you want me to start it?"

"No, thank you. Please tell me about the Dream Wafers later when we meet."

"Sure."

"Helen, since I'm the one who called you, the treat will be on me this evening at any restaurant of your choice."

"Oh, no, thank you, Jenny. Every day I drive by your Luxen Tech office as I go home from Acmeon. I can easily stop by at your office by five thirty or five forty. There's no need to go to a restaurant, where it could be rather distracting. Let's just meet at your office over a cup of tea. Shall we?"

"All right, if you insist."

"No problem, Jenny."

"OK, then. I'll see you around five thirty at my Luxen Tech office."

Meantime, Dr. Jupitren at his office, received a call from a junior physician in family practice, Dr. Joel Stein. He said, "The reason I called you is that this afternoon I have seen one of my outpatients, a fifty year old male who had a cardiac bypass two months ago. He is also being treated for schizophrenia at the Bleuler Psychiatric Clinic. His post-op cardiac condition is stabilizing, but his psychotic status took a sudden turn for the worse after he tried a Dream Wafer. His name is Mikelo Lenkos. Is this patient known to Acmeon Lab?"

"I remember a female patient by the same family name, Lenkos. She is one of my patients, but I don't think I've treated Mr. Mikelo Lenkos. Let me check if your patient is related to Mrs. Lenkos. It will take me less than a minute."

While his e-record was retrieving Mrs. Lenkos' family history, Dr. Jupitren asked Dr. Stein, "Which symptoms did flare up?"

"Mostly auditory hallucination and unclear thinking. On the contrary, his mood was a little better, and his affect seemed less flat than before."

"I see. Here, I've Mrs. Lenkos' record. Her husband's name is Mikelo. I've not treated him personally. Most likely, his wife let him try her Wafer. As you know, despite our warnings, some patients share their medicines with others, often with their family members. If your patient Mr. Lenkos used his wife's Dream Wafers, he might have had negative responses."

"Thank you for the possible explanation. I'm going to check with Mr. Lenkos to see if that's what actually happened. If so, I'll tell him to stop using his wife's Dream Wafers and refer him back to his psychiatrist at the Bleuler Clinic."

"I agree with your plan. I'll call my patient Mrs. Lenkos and advise her not to share her Wafers with her husband. While we're on the subject, let me say one thing briefly. The Dream Wafers are not necessarily contraindicated for patients with schizophrenic disorders or certain subtypes of bipolar-spectrum disorders as long as they apply the Wafers made through cross matching with their own genome. However, serious problems could occur if one uses someone else's Wafers, intentionally or by mistake."

"I see. Were there any psychiatric patients who could not use their Dream Wafers because of their psychiatric status?"

"Yes. If the Wafer program detects any *acute psychotic state*, in the middle of the initial *polygene analysis* the Wafer program signals such diagnostic probability. And if their genome cannot accommodate their dream request, the Wafer composition will stop. If that happens, those patients should rely on antipsychotic medications. They should not use the Wafers during the *acute phase* of their illness."

"I understand. Thank you for the information."

In the front office, Helen made a copy of the e-message from the Special Review Committee of the FDA that was addressed to Acmeon Lab. It was about the questionable methodology of Dr. Sobien Molton's new Dream Wafer idea. Helen brought the copy to Dr. Jupitren.

"You seem to be in a good mood today, Helen."

"I feel great. Things are going well for me."

"That's nice. I'm glad to hear that."

Dr. Jupitren saw the e-message from FDA and gave the copy back to Helen and said, "Although the letter came to our address, they sent it to Dr. Molton's attention. Please give it to him. I hope he would come to me for my response to this FDA letter."

Sensing the delicate nature of the matter, Helen refrained from questioning about the letter and quietly went back to her office.

At her desk, she took the liberty of browsing the open letter in her hand and understood that the FDA's Special Review Committee turned down Dr. Molton's research proposal. The message underlined that Dr. Molton failed to demonstrate his new method having a sufficiently high benefit-to-risk ratio.

After a while, Dr. Molton walked in, and Helen handed the e-message print-out to him. He impetuously flipped the pages to get to the bottom line. Realizing what it said, he made a ferocious facial expression and uttered audible profanities, crumpling the papers with his both hands. Helen wished she could be somewhere else at that moment. She feared for a split second that she might become the target of a messenger killer's rage.

She did not say anything to him. Everyone else within earshot remained quiet. She went on with her work-related matters, softly talking to others in the adjacent offices. She hoped Dr. Molton would ask her if he could see Dr. Jupitren at that moment so that he could discuss the FDA's rejection letter, but he just walked away.

However, almost at the end of the afternoon office hours, he returned to Helen's office and asked her, "Is Dr. Jupitren in?"

"Yes, should I give him a buzz?"

"Yes, I have to ask him to renew my Dream Wafers."

Helen was disappointed that he did not mention anything about the FDA letter. She hoped he would bring it up with Dr. Jupitren and have a good talk to resolve the smoldering tension between the two.

Before Helen could call Dr. Jupitren, he came out of his office with his last patient of the day. When he saw Dr. Molton standing there in the waiting area, he bid good-bye to his patient and said, "Hello, Sobien, do you want to see me?"

"Yes, I wanted to ask you to renew my Dream Wafers, but it seems to be getting late for the day. Should I come back at another time?"

"No, we can go over your Dream Wafers now. Come on in."

They sat down in Dr. Jupitren's office. "Are you thinking of any new dream themes this time?"

"Yes. I'd like to change it from a dingy routine to an explosive, dynamic one. I imagine in the new dream I would like to go through unchartered wilderness, getting lost a few times and then, finally, finding my way back."

"Well, that's quite a different theme for a change. After another breath analysis for the dioxides and gene reassessment, why don't you complete the questionnaire this afternoon in the Annex Library? Please keep the answers to the questionnaire on a draft mode. Tomorrow, I'd like to go over certain parts of the draft with you, if you don't mind. I want to make sure you get the best-suited Wafers for your needs. Once we streamline the overall choices, you'll get your Wafers sometime in the afternoon tomorrow. Is there anything else?"

"Yes, I wanted to let you know about something that I've been doing on my own. But, it'll take a bit of time to explain. Maybe tomorrow, if you have some time, can I see you in your office?"

"Yes, someone just cancelled her eleven o'clock appointment tomorrow. We could meet at that time. In fact, I also wanted to ask you about a few things of importance."

"Thank you. I'll see you tomorrow morning at eleven."

As Dr. Molton walked toward the exit door, Dr. Jupitren's eyes caught the unmistakable logo of MacSprint on his sneakers once again.

Meanwhile, Helen did not want to be late for Jenny. She quickly finished the pre-Wafer tests for Dr. Molton and hurriedly left for Jenny's Luxen Tech office.

Dr. Jupitren, too, left his office early because he had promised Jamie that he would accompany her to a store in the evening to get a birthday present for Helen.

In the Annex Library, Sobien started to key in his answers to the 135-point questionnaire for his Dream Wafer order. He left his answers on the draft mode.

Having finished the questionnaire in an hour, he checked his watch. Then he decided to take a walk outside the building. For some reason, he repeatedly looked at the fire-escape ladders of Acmeon buildings.

In the meantime, without telling Helen, Steve took a chance and came to Acmeon Lab hoping to surprise her, as she usually worked beyond five o'clock. However, he could not spot her car in the parking lot. He wondered, "Did she leave for the day already?"

Steve went up to Helen's office on the third floor only to find both Helen and Dr. Jupitren had left for the day. He called Helen on her phone but heard an outgoing announcement: "The person you called is driving. Please record your message after the beep."

As he was heading to his parked car, he noticed a lone person walking around near the Plant building. He squinted at the figure against the westerly sunset's glare. "Isn't that Dr. Molton?"

Unaware of being watched by Steve, Sobien Molton went around the Plant building, checking doors. He found every door of the Plant building was locked and would not open for him. Still sauntering outside the Plant, Sobien took out a pen and jotted down something in his pad. He then looked up at the roofs of the building and stopped near the fire-escape ladder, jotting down some more notes.

Steve decided to leave the area without letting Sobien know that he was there. Steve was about to start his car when a flame-red open convertible pulled in and dashed to the point where Sobien was standing. A silhouette of a capped young woman with flowing hair stepped out of the car. Steve could not abandon the surprise scene in progress.

CHAPTER 38
JENNY'S LOSS

As the young woman walked briskly toward Sobien Molton, he hastily tucked his writing pad into his pocket and greeted her with a long embrace. Steve rolled down his car window a couple of inches, hoping to hear them, but they were beyond earshot. He only watched them.

For a moment, Steve thought, "Is she possibly Jenny? No, she can't be. Jenny doesn't drive a convertible. She only flies on her air-scooter."

While Steve was wondering, they hopped in the convertible and zipped out of the parking lot. Right away, he called Jenny, who was in her Luxen Tech office waiting for Helen's arrival any minute.

"What's up, Steve?"

"That's what I should ask you, Jenny. What's up with you and Sobien Molton?"

Jenny quickly told Steve that lately Sobien had distanced himself from her, acting erratic, at times being unreasonably furious over trivial matters. She would let him have his way in most of their arguments. But there was one thing they couldn't agree on, her money! The money matter was about to break their fast-developed relationship.

Jenny said sadly, "A few days ago, Sobien talked about breaking off from Dr. Jupitren for basic theoretical differences in gene modification. Besides, Sobien said he was planning to start his own genetic-engineering company and asked me for a big loan to build his own business from scratch."

"How big a loan?"

"You wouldn't believe it. The amount he asked for is more than enough to buy all of Acmeon Lab buildings."

"Are you going to lend him the money?"

"No way! I've invested most of my funds in Luxen Tech shares. As people say it, I'm paper rich but cash poor. If it were a much smaller amount, I would just have given him the money without making a loan out of it."

"Jen, how do you feel about him?"

"Lately, I'm in great doubt. Something has dropped out of our relationship and I can't seem to find how to recover it."

"So, what are you going to do next?"

"I asked Helen to give me some ideas about how Sobien was doing at Acmeon Lab."

"What did she say?"

"Helen said she and I could meet here at my office today because my questions are so involved and will take some time. In fact, I'm waiting for her now. She will be here any minute. She is such a nice and smart girl. How is it going with you and Helen?"

"Very well. I have to thank you, Jenny, for what you told me the other day. I took your advice seriously and told Helen how I felt about her and said I loved her. She was very happy. I feel very good that I'd said that to her finally."

"I'm happy for both of you."

"Thank you, Jenny. So, what time is Helen coming there?"

"Around by 5:30. But you didn't tell me why you called me."

"I'm sorry, Jen. I don't know if this will help you in some way or only aggravate you. But I've to tell you anyway. Several minutes ago, I saw Sobien meeting with a young woman. For a short moment, I thought that woman was you. I couldn't recognize her face because of the distance. She drove in and picked him up from the Acmeon Lab parking lot, where I'm right now."

"By any chance, was she driving a red convertible?" Jenny asked knowingly.

"Yes, do you know her?"

"Unfortunately, yes. She's five years older than Sobien. She's a divorcée without child. An heiress. Her grandfather is the founder of Lancaster Steel and Alloy Company. I knew Sobien was often seeing her lately. He said he was meeting with her only to get the loan, but my hunch tells me otherwise."

"I'm sorry, Jen. I wasn't much help to you. But is there anything I can do for you?"

"Well, in time, I'll let you know. Thank you, Steve…I hear the front gate buzzing. Helen must have arrived."

"All right, Jenny. Hope you have a good talk with her. Say a special hello to her for me."

Steve drove out of Acmeon's parking lot. He kept on thinking about what Jenny told him about Sobien's selfish ambition involving another woman. "Poor Jenny!" Steve felt sorry for his sister.

Meanwhile, at Jenny's Luxen Tech office, Helen sat down and opened a small bag of cookies she'd brought in, and Jenny made some green tea.

Jenny asked, "How are things with you and my brother?"

"Wonderful."

"I know my brother pretty well. He is usually outspoken, but he's so, so shy with women. I just heard from him that lately he told you he loved you. Did he?"

Helen, glowing with happy smiles, answered clearly, "Yes."

"He did? When?"

"It was yesterday."

"See? What did I say! It took more than a year for him to say it to you."

Helen had a brief abstracted moment and said, "Probably it was I who caused him to take so long a time…"

"You? Why?"

"I believe it was because of Jonathan, my late boyfriend. According to my therapist, I grieved Jonathan's cancer death for an unusually long time. More than a few times, I told Jonathan that I would not let myself fall in love with anyone else. Then, in his last weeks, he said that he prayed to God asking Him to let me find someone just like him but in better health. He cried quietly as he said it. What a beautiful heart he had! I didn't allow myself to open up to anybody for so long, thinking about him."

"I see. Such a beautiful story you're telling me! He must've been an exceptional person. Finally, you and Steve both have found each other. That's wonderful. I'm sure Jonathan would not blame you. I'm very happy for you and Steve."

Then Jenny, in a sad tone, asked Helen what Acmeon's people had been saying about Sobien Molton's personality. "Do they like him there at Acmeon Lab?"

"Yes and no…I'm not sure whether I can tell you everything openly. After all, he is your sweetheart and…"

"Yes, Helen. But I want the real facts as they are, as honestly as possible, please!"

"OK. Let me say this. He is smart and often funny, but he shows poor temper at times. He covertly expressed his objection to Dr. Jupitren's opinion. A few times, I heard him speaking ill of Dr. Jupitren behind his back. Sometimes, being presumptuous and unpredictable, he's made other workers uncomfortable with his sharp talk and cutting remarks. Often he can be imposing with his words or just with his presence, and then, for no apparent reason, he gets morose and quiet. Some people at Acmeon said his mood was rather changeable and unstable."

Jenny said, "I'm afraid I felt that way about him, too. Did he ever curse in the office when angry?"

"Yes, I've heard him swear a few times. But he never targeted any particular person with his profanity. I guess he just ventilated his frustration."

"Did you or anyone at Acmeon ever feel scared of him?"

"I don't know about other people, but lately a couple of times I've felt frightened for split seconds. How about you, Jenny? Do you ever get scared of him?"

Jenny, filtering her emotion, answered in a low tone, "I've felt it several times. He can be quite overbearing. Last time, he yelled at me and said if he were forced to choose his career ambition or me, he would rather choose his career over me. I felt so hurt, and his yelling frightened me."

Drying her tears with tissues, Jenny ruefully continued. "I think he is now in hot pursuit with this heiress to get a huge loan from her. It all started after I told him I could not give him that kind of money. The amount he was asking was humongous. I think the woman is seeing him not just for the loan. I feel she enticed him for other reasons, which pushed me out of my tie with him. I was crazy about him. But I'm getting disillusioned badly. Now I feel I'm relegated to mop up the spilt milk." Jenny reached for more tissues.

Helen felt a bit awkward for having unreservedly voiced her own happy mood a short while ago. She felt her own happy feelings toning down as she thought of Jenny's loss and sadness. Helen said, "How could he ask such an unreasonable loan from you? It's terribly unfair of him."

Jenny also told Helen that Sobien Molton was thinking of splitting from Acmeon Lab and starting his own genetic-engineering company, but he would need not just that huge sum of money but also most of Dr. Jupitren's Dream Wafer software.

That sounded ominous to Helen, as she feared if Uncle Jules disallows Sobien any easy access to the Dream Wafer programs, Sobien might act out his hostile impulses against him. Helen felt she could guess why Uncle Jules was having such a tense relationship with Dr. Molton lately. Helen felt a twinge of resentment toward Dr. Molton on Uncle Jules's behalf.

Wishing to boost Jenny's mood, Helen recounted all of her inventions and extraordinary achievements with abundant praise. Yet, Jenny felt sad, realizing that her hurtful emotion gripped her beyond what Helen's well-meaning consolation could undo.

Jenny thanked Helen for her openness and encouraging words. After Helen left Jenny's office, Jenny called Steve and told him that she had confirmed her fear that she would be losing Sobien Molton. Steve tried to comfort her and at the same time felt strong indignation and crossness against Sobien.

CHAPTER 39
SOBIEN MOLTON'S MIDDLEMAN

The next day, having already seen a new candidate and some revisit patients, Dr. Jupitren checked the rest of his morning schedule:

10:00—keep it open; Bill might call
10:20—a new candidate for Dream Wafers
11:00—Dr. Sobien Molton
11:30—Esclepio Pharmaceutical Company chemist, manufacturer of Antisom
12:00—Deputy Commissioner for Science and Public Health of the FDA

A few minutes after ten, Dr. Jupitren received a call from Bill.
"Jules, I have pressing news for you. Are you free to talk now?"
"Certainly. I kept the ten o'clock spot open for twenty minutes, as you said you might call me."
"Good. It's a bit involved. Richard Hunt called me a while ago. Guess what? Sobien Molton approached him!"
"Really? Why?"
"Sobien Molton, not knowing about Richard's connection with us, sent a middleman to Richard asking him to hack your main Dream Wafer program and copy it for a huge fee. Because Molton used an alias and hid behind the middleman, Richard never met Molton. However, the middleman met with Richard yesterday and asked him to destroy the original Dream Wafer program after copying it. Richard told me that he recorded his conversation with the middleman. Recording any conversation is Richard's job routine. Of course, Richard turned their request down and called me. In fact, Richard already gave me a copy of that conversation."
"How disgusting! It's too creepy for words! But how did Richard know that the man behind the middleman was Molton?"
"Well, Richard initially showed a pretended hesitation and said to the middleman that the job was too risky and he wouldn't do it. Then, the middleman left him a money order for three thousand dollars saying, 'Mister, this is just for you listening to me. I hope you change your mind and call me back.' Richard

contacted the money order-issuing bank and confirmed that it was Molton who bought the money order. Molton most likely didn't intend to give the money order directly to Richard. Molton just gave it to the middleman, who decided on his own to use it as the seed money to tempt Richard."

"Thank God! Richard is on our side. Now, Bill, what would you do with Molton if you were in my shoes?"

"Well, I would reinforce the security of the Wafer programs, because Molton will try to get other hackers to do the job. Maybe Richard can help you reinforce your anti-hacking program, or Steve Spencer can, too. I'll follow up on Molton closely and stop him from causing any damage to your lab. I may arrest him on the spot."

"Bill, I'll be seeing him in less than an hour. Today I was going to tell him to quit working here, because he and I have irreconcilable differences in our Dream Wafer composition methods."

"But, Jules, may I suggest that you hold it off for a while and don't fire him yet? I'm going to have my guys from the industrial espionage unit watch his attempts and get more definite evidence to convict him. It's a matter of time. We may arrest the middleman, too."

"All right. I'll take your advice. Thank you, Bill. You're always there looking out for me."

"Not a problem. I'll call you again." Bill ended his call there.

Immediately, Dr. Jupitren called Steve to ask him to install additional protection on the Wafer program soon and explained why. He told Steve what Bill said about Sobien Molton and his middleman.

Steve said to Dr. Jupitren, "It reminds me of what I saw yesterday in the afternoon…" Having told Dr. Jupitren in detail about Sobien's behavior around the Acmeon Lab building's fire-escape ladders, Steve added, "Somehow, I didn't feel right about how Dr. Molton has been behaving lately. My sister Jenny told me she was very disappointed with him, too. Did you ever suspect he might be doing something devious?"

"Yes. I suspected he was after our Dream Wafer program. What Bill told me today confirmed it. That's why I called you right away. Will you reinforce the Wafer program as soon as you can?"

"Yes, I will. But why wouldn't Bill stop Sobien now from doing any damage to Acmeon?"

"Bill said he has plans to do it at a more appropriate time."

"I see. I'll start adding the extra security to your programs this evening, right after I'm done at Perihelion."

"That's great. Thank you, Steve. Offhand, do you have any particular anti-hacking program in mind?"

"Yes. It's called Mr. PHELPS, a software-locking program. Once Mr. PHELPS locks a program, no hacking is possible. However, if you need to unlock it, you just put in your own six-digit security keys. A Stony Brook University engineering student, William Berry, invented Mr. PHELPS a long time ago. What I have is the most recently updated version of it. If any hacker ever goes through the Mr. PHELPS-protected program, which has never happened so far, it will interrupt the copying process by deleting every tenth program line of the copy. At the same time, it will retrieve the hacker's cyber-identity information."

"Sounds good. What time will you be here?"

"About six thirty this evening and I'll start installing the lock on each of the twelve modules at the Plant. Then, if I still have time, I'll install the same Mr. PHELPS on the questionnaire program, too. Otherwise, I'll finish it by tomorrow afternoon."

"That's great. Is there anything you may need from my office?"

"Oh, yes. I'll need new security codes before I start the lock installation. Would you create the twelve new codes, one for each of the twelve modules, and four more for the questionnaire program? I'll need them as I install Mr. PHELPS. Each code should have no less than six alphanumeric characters but case sensitive."

"I certainly will make those codes up and give you the list before six thirty this evening. Thank you very much, Steve."

"You're very welcome. It's my pleasure."

At 11:10 am, Dr. Molton showed up for his eleven o'clock appointment, looking strangely distraught. With a carelessly tucked-in shirt that was ballooning out of his belt, tousled hair, and muddy shoes, he appeared as if he had been to some rough places.

"Good morning, Dr. Jupitren."

"Good morning. You look tired. Is everything all right?"

"So-so. Lately, I'm distracted by a number of personal matters."

"Well, was that why you wanted to order dreams with the new theme?"

"That's right. In fact, the dream theme is just like how I'm feeling lately."

"Is that so? Yesterday, you also said you wanted to tell me about something that you've been doing on your own."

"Yes, it's a science project, but it's only a rough plan for doing something with genes."

"During this session, I thought we would go over your pre-Wafer baseline draft that you made yesterday. But, first can I hear about your science project instead?"

"Yes, that's fine with me. As you know, out of twenty-three thousand genes that are implicated with various diseases, about thirty-five hundreds of them are already confirmed. I'm thinking about starting a business by using those confirmed genes. I can sell the test results to the tested individuals by giving them the gene based prediction on certain diseases they are susceptible to develop."

"In fact, we know that there are already a number of such gene-based businesses. What kind of predictions will your new business be making? Can you give me some examples?"

"It will be something like this: [Your genome based test indicates that the probability of you developing type II diabetes before age 45 is 65%] or [You have Alzheimer gene APOE-3 and the probability of you developing Alzheimer type dementia by age 65 is 75%]."

"What will the individuals do with such scary information?"

"It'll be up to them. They may consult specialists or take preventive measures, if such measures are known."

"But what if there are no known preventive methods? The individuals will be doomed with fear for the rest of their lives. Furthermore, the health-insurance and life-insurance industries might take advantage of such information by charging them high extra premiums or not insuring them at all."

Shaking his head in disagreement, Sobien said, "But just like the people who pay the fortune-tellers to get a glimpse into their future, I'm sure lots of people will buy my genomic prediction despite the uncertainty about what to do with the information."

"I cannot go along with that." This time, Dr. Jupitren shook his head in disapproval. He continued, "I know nowadays, despite the FDA's strong warnings, many genetics-based quasi-medical businesses with similar ideas as yours are thriving, mainly for profit. However, I'm afraid they are causing more harm than good to those who are being tested."

Making light of what Dr. Jupitren just said, Sobien made another remark. "In fact, I was thinking of forming support groups or Internet groups with individuals who had been given genome-based predictions on the same diagnoses. Depending on how I set up the Internet groups, I can collect additional fees from them."

"I'm afraid you are running ahead of yourself. According to the revised clauses of *Life Science Ethics* guidelines, you should not promote those genetics-based tests unless there are sufficient preventive medical measures available against the predicted diseases. Only then, we might use such tests proactively for the tested persons. At any rate, I think it's not the right time yet for the kind of business you're describing."

"I anticipated you would say what you just said. But I'll not give it up."

"Is there anything else you were thinking of doing?"

"Yes, I'm thinking of using recombinant genes to replace the existing neuronal genes of patients with anxiety so that they will eradicate their anxiety above a certain level of it altogether."

"Here we go again. Manifest anxiety depends on many genes' expressions, which are affected by a continuum of environmental variations. People's responses to those variations are built-in parts of necessary human affect. I strongly believe you cannot and should not control the feeling tone of a given person aiming that his anxiety will remain below a certain fixed level permanently. They'll act like zombies! You'd call it an anxiety-free state, and you want to profit from it."

"But I'm sure there are many people who will want it my way."

"That's because they are desperate, just like a drowning man trying to grab even a straw. In their current affective agony with anxiety, they would grab anything that might relieve them from such agony for the moment. But they will regret it. As you must know it well, anxiety is one of many other associated symptoms of dozens of disorders. They need comprehensive treatment, not necessarily just the genetically engineered anxiolytic methods. You're proposing an irreversible gene-alteration methods while there are other established methods of easing people's anxiety without the kind of risk your recombinant gene method has. I cannot endorse your treatment plan."

Sobien Molton did not agree with what Dr. Jupitren just said and brought up other related issues. "I'm going to have my own genetic-engineering research lab someday. I need to use data like your Dream Wafer program and other researchers' theories. I will try to get the necessary computer programs from other inventors and researchers."

Saying so, Sobien realized that he needed to get hold of Acmeon's Dream Wafer program not just for his business ambition but also in a much worse way to appease the life-threatening agent Ajnin Hsilomed.

Dr. Jupitren said, "You seem to consider those research results are plain sheets of papers or mere data chips. But every research result is like a new edifice that belongs to those who did all the painstaking work to build it. Accordingly, we may enter the new edifice with due deference, in order to acquire the essence of it regardless of its size. We should not think of *just getting* those programs without proper gratitude and substantial recompense for the authors."

"Are you saying then you cannot let others use your Dream Wafer program?"

"Not quite as you said it. My Wafer program is presently open to anyone who is willing to use or improve it within the ethical limits that I follow strictly but not to those who are primarily interested in taking advantage of it and, at the end, might hurt others."

"So you're implying that I'll hurt others at the end."

"I'm afraid I cannot rule out that possibility completely."

"You are disagreeing with everything I've said. Are my ideas so risky? I think my thoughts are way ahead of most of you, the older generation with rigid mind."

"Sobien, you're entitled to have any opinion of me or anyone else, but let me say this for you. You seem to believe that your zeal for your own achievement justifies your hasty action, often disregarding the needs of others and bypassing the very process you need to go through as a scholar and a moral scientist. You may think I'm conceited but I hope you preserve your professional discernment and don't betray your Hippocratic Oath!"

Sobien Molton muttered, "I don't think our talk is going anywhere…I don't think you would believe me if I told you anything else about my Chemical Razor technique."

Sobien did not wait for Dr. Jupitren's rejoinder and kept on saying, "By lowering the polymorphism expression of norepinephrine transporter genes, my Chemical Razor technique's risk should be reduced significantly. I can demonstrate it if I can get enough number of volunteers among Acmeon Lab's clients! The only problem is that I don't know the specific procedure yet, with which I can lower the risk of my Chemical Razor method at this time."

At that very moment, Dr. Jupitren felt tempted to tell him about all the improper behavior Sobien had been showing since he came to Acmeon Lab, including his recent furtive attempt to copy the Dream Wafer program and then destroy the original. Sobien's MacSprint sneaker marks on his office floor flashed in his mind.

However, Dr. Jupitren recalled Bill's advice not to let go of him yet. Therefore, Dr. Jupitren stopped himself from taking his next step, which was to tell him to resign from Acmeon Lab right there and then.

Sobien Molton got up from his seat, saying, "I feel exhausted. No one understands me. I want to put off my Dream Wafer composition for another day. Excuse me." Sobien hurriedly left the room.

Looking at Sobien's dejected stance as he walked out of his office, Dr. Jupitren felt sorry for Sobien. Dr. Jupitren also sensed that Sobien was clinically depressed with reactive grandiose ideas and was in need of treatment. However, Dr. Jupitren desisted from telling him about it at the moment, lest Sobien would change any well-meaning advice into a reason for new arguments and then berate himself or blame others for his predicament.

Dr. Jupitren immediately reviewed Sobien's baseline data off the draft mode that Sobien recorded on the previous day. There were the familiar red signals that Dr. Jupitren had seen and worried about weeks earlier. Those signals indicated the young doctor had signs of mood instability and a touch of sociopathic trends. This time, unfortunately, the mood instability was much more prominent than before.

In the late afternoon, while waiting for Steve to arrive, Dr. Jupitren received another call from Bill Warren.

"Hi, it's me again. How's your day going?"

"Pretty full, as usual."

"Jules, I thought I should let you in on this one without delay. It's about Sobien Molton again."

"More on him?"

"Yes. I told you this morning that Richard had sent me a copy of his recorded conversation with Molton's middleman. I found something else from it."

"What's that?"

"I replayed the message a few more times because the middleman's voice sounded familiar to me. After a good deal of searching in my mind, I decided it's the voice of Akandro's lackey Tick, Tihko Piroiz, who lately did not show much loyalty to Akandro. Detached from locked-up Akandro, Tick recently freelanced around on his own. Then he was picked up by Sobien Molton this time. Can you believe it?"

"How did you make that connection?"

"As I told you some time ago, when I cross-examined Akandro at my precinct, I had him speak to Tick on the speakerphone and I heard their conversation. That's when I heard Tick's voice for the first time. So, to be sure, today I went to the state detention center to let Akandro listen to the recorded conversation between the middleman and Richard Hunt. Akandro immediately recognized the middleman's voice and said, 'That's Tick's voice!' Right there, I asked Akandro if he recognized the other voice in the recorded conversation. He said he could not identify whose voice it was. Naturally, Akandro had not known Richard at all. Then, I asked him if he knew what Tick was doing lately.

Akandro said that he heard Tick was working for a doctor whose name was Sobien Molton!"

Dr. Jupitren said, "So it's obvious that Sobien hired Tick as a middleman. But, how did Tick find a way to contact Richard to begin with?"

"To some cybercriminals around here, Richard is known mistakenly just as the 'super-hacker'. Richard told me that because of his misunderstood identity, he sometimes solves difficult cases sooner than his FBI coworkers might anticipate. The reason is that many criminals approach him for a hacking job and divulge their illicit plans, thinking Richard is one of them."

"Now I see the picture more clearly. By the way, is Tick still at large?"

"Yes, he is. But, Jules, that's not the end of my report today. There is another important piece to it. I asked Akandro if he knew Sobien Molton. He said yes. Akandro said he had worked for Sobien previously. Do you remember the episode when two thugs put the bug behind Po Kim's picture? Those two thugs were sent by Akandro. And it was Sobien Molton who hired Akandro then. They were trying to steal the main Wafer program on that day. So, if I may say it again and bore you with the obvious details, Sobien Molton hired Akandro, and then Akandro hired Tick and Tack. Now, Tick, on his own, is trying to hire Richard!"

"Really! Not knowing who was behind that bug episode has been bothering me all this time. But now, knowing Molton was behind it bothers me even more. It's hard to believe Molton has been after Acmeon's Wafer program for that long. At any rate, thank you very much, Bill for your persistent detective work, protecting me and Acmeon."

"No need to thank me, Jules. My middle name should be 'Detective'. Well, did you say Steve will reinforce your Wafer program's security?"

"Yes. He is very familiar with the programs by now. He will be here soon this evening to install software locks on all Acmeon's programs."

"That sounds good and right on time. Tomorrow my precinct will prepare affidavits for arrest warrants on Molton and Tick."

Unaware his freedom would soon be clipped, Sobien Molton was thinking of other plans to steal Acmeon's program files. He mumbled to himself, "If I get the files this time, Ajnin Hsilomed will leave me alone. Besides, I can demand the cash balance from him."

Sobien went to the place where Ajnin asked him to come out. It was a noisy café in the middle of New York City. Sobien tried to convince Ajnin that next time, he would get the Wafer program for sure. Ajnin, hiding behind his dark purple eyeglasses, threateningly said to Sobien, "During the last week's riot, my government ran out of the Islet Republic's Wafers. I will not go into all the details of the riot, but one thing is clear. If you don't produce it soon, my government will send silent bullets to you and me both. Do you hear me? You and I both will be dead!" Ajnin was very desperate and seemed scared for his own life as well.

Sobien gulped a few more big swigs of whiskey as he explained his new plan to Ajnin.

CHAPTER 40
SOBIEN MOLTON'S OUTBURST

"Have you gone mad? Stop it!" Jenny loudly hollered, covering her face with her half-folded arms against the aimless flailing of drunken Sobien Molton, who'd just come from his meeting with Ajnin Hsilomed.

Jenny felt helplessly cornered in her own office.

Molton staggered. He muttered in a disjointed drawl, reeking with alcohol. "I've tried so hard all these years…to get somewhere, be somebody but I'm nobody. No one wants me!…no one understands me…I hate you all…my vengeance is killing me…"

"How could you say such horrible things?"

Jenny took cautious backward steps away from him, moving toward the door that would open to the hallway. He became more boisterous, loud, and irrational. He stepped forward and started to push her roughly and ranted, "You refused to give me the lousy loan. You wrecked my life!"

From the top of Jenny's desk, foolhardily he picked up a weighty metal picture frame with jagged edges and held it up high over his head. He tried to throw it at her, but it was let out of his shaky hand at a misjudged moment and it was tossed straight up instead as high as the ceiling and fell heavily down on his own head, just like a vertically falling shrapnel. The picture frame slid off his head and fell on the floor with cracking noises, its glass pane breaking into many pieces.

Instantly, with his palm he pressed on his head, where the picture frame fell. A streak of fresh blood streamed down on his face and neck. He barely controlled his stance. He tried to sit down on a nearby hard chair only to flip it down with his off-aimed weight, and plopped down on the floor covered with broken glass pieces. Then he started sobbing.

Jenny called the Luxen Tech security guards. They rushed in, picked him up from the floor, and gave a quick look at the cuts in his head and palms. Ignoring his drunken ranting and struggling, they decided to take him to the Northwest Hospital ER. At that very moment, Jenny could not leave her office to accompany him to the ER. She asked the Luxen Tech guards to request the ER staff to call her later about his condition.

After seeing him off to the hospital, back in her office, Jenny felt helpless, sad, and angry. She wished she could vent her surging upset feelings to someone but could not think of anyone except Steve or Helen. However, she thought, "They must be busy wrapping up for the day. I'll call them a little later."

Wiping her tears with still-shaky hands, she cleared the broken glass pieces and mopped Sobien's blood off the floor. Then, wanting to wash her hands, she was about to step out of her office.

At the threshold, as she usually does whenever she leaves her room, she turned her head back to scan the condition of her office. Under her desk, she spotted Sobien's shoulder bag. Its main zipper was half-open, and she could see an unfamiliar plastic piece sticking out of it. She went over to examine it. To her astonishment, out of the bag she found an incendiary kit with an igniter. For her, it was nothing but an object of horror.

"What in the world was he going to do with this? This is crazy! Now, what do I do with this? Hide it from him and everyone else, too? Or throw it away and pretend I didn't see it? Or just call the police? No, I don't want to do any of them now."

She called Steve. As usual, his pleasant, reassuring voice answered her,

"Hi, Jenny, what's up?"

"Are you still at work?"

"Yes, but I'm not at Perihelion Energy. Now, I'm at Acmeon Lab doing some computer work for Dr. Jupitren."

"Do you have a few minutes to talk?"

"Sure."

She told him what had happened in her office a short while ago and what she found in Sobien's bag. Having listened to her in silence, Steve asked, "Are you OK, Jenny?"

"Yes, I'm a little better now as I'm talking to you. I feel sorry for Sobien. He really needs some help. He cracked himself up with his own ambition and self-pity."

"I'll be done in about thirty minutes. I'll swing by your office, and we'll go and see him at the hospital ER. Not too long ago, I heard Dr. Jupitren say that Sobien seemed in need of treatment for his depression."

"I see. I thought of that, too."

"Jenny, about the fire-setting kit, why don't you lock it up in your office for the time being? At the moment, Sobien won't be thinking clearly anyway. We'll ask him about what to do with it much later, when he is sober. Don't you think it would be better that way?"

"Yes, I agree with you. I'll keep his bag in my office. Now, I'll stay here because they might call me from the hospital. I'll see you soon."

A little while later, a call came from the hospital.

"Hello, this is Dr. Roy Blau from Northwest Hospital ER. I have called this number just to inform you about Mr. Molton's condition. Are you Mr. Molton's family member?"

"No, I'm a friend of his."

"Is any of his family members there?"

"No, I'm the only one here, and I don't have any contact information on his family."

"Then let me just tell you that his scalp wound and palm lacerations were stitched up. His head X ray showed no deep injury."

"That's good news. Is he sobering up, Doctor?"

"Not really, if he drove a car within the past few hours without a major auto accident, it's a miracle. His current blood alcohol level is over two times of the legal limit."

"Then should I come to pick him up a little later?"

"No, I don't think you should. The ER nurse reported that he was heavily intoxicated and in his slurred speech, he revealed some dangerous thoughts, and we are waiting for a psychiatric consultant, who will be here within an hour."

"Could you tell me what dangerous thoughts he had?"

"Well, I can inform you only this much: beside certain self-destructive thoughts, he talked about fire setting. He needs further evaluation."

"Thank you, Doctor. Please let me know about your final decision on him."

"Yes, I will."

By then Steve had arrived with some snacks for Jenny. Steve and Jenny exchanged thoughts on Sobien Molton. Steve told her everything about Molton that he'd heard from Dr. Jupitren. Then Jenny told Steve what she'd just heard about Sobien from the ER doctor.

Jenny asked, "Do you think he really approached Dr. Jupitren and Acmeon Lab with a bad intention from the beginning?"

"It all seems to point to that. I'm sorry you got involved with him in the midstream. So, what will happen to you and him?"

"It doesn't look good. There is no one else to blame but Sobien himself for his predicament." Jenny answered sadly, thinking that her budding affection for him had been ruthlessly crushed.

Steve asked, "Do you know much about the woman he started seeing?"

"Her name is Kerbera Wilson. Other things about her—I've already told you before."

"What a name for a girl! Kerbera sounds awful. Do you know what Kerbera means?"

"No, I don't. But the only thing I heard from Sobien about her name was that her grandfather picked the name for her even before she was born."

Reading Jenny's sad mood, Steve tried to draw her out of it by telling her something he knew about the name Kerbera. "I know there is a program from MIT called Kerberos that has almost the same spelling as her name. It's a network-authentication protocol that includes antiviral programs. I think the Kerberos programmers picked that name for the same reason as her grandfather did."

Jenny quietly listened to Steve. "As far as I know, Kerberos is a ferocious three-headed dog in Greco-Roman mythology. The dog is to guard and protect King Hades. I remember reading that during my mythology course. Hades was in charge of the dead and the riches of the underworld and was powerful. But despite his power, Hades still needed protection by Kerberos. So it seems her grandfather, who you said was the founder of Lancaster Steel and Alloy Company, mercilessly gave her that name, only changing the ending '-os' to '-a.' I'm sure he hoped Kerbera would protect his company as fiercely as Kerberos protected King Hades. Is Kerbera Wilson a vicious woman like the king's Kerberos?"

"I don't know." Jenny did not seem amused by Steve's distracting attempt.

Another phone call came in from the hospital. "This is Northwest Hospital ER, Dr. Roy Blau speaking. Is Ms. Kerbera Wilson there?"

Jenny answered, "Hi, Dr. Blau, is this about the patient, Dr. Sobien Molton?"

"Did you say Doctor Sobien Molton? Is he a physician?" Dr. Blau asked.

"Yes, he is."

"Thank you, I didn't realize that. Are you Ms. Wilson?"

"No, I'm not, but I'm his friend Jenny. Ms. Wilson is not here."

"Well, our patient Mr., I mean Dr. Molton insists that I should speak to Ms. Wilson only. I'll go back to him and ask if he wants to speak to you. May I have your full name, please?"

"I'm Jenny Spencer."

"Jenny Spencer! By any chance, aren't you the inventress of the Optical Walls?"

"Yes, I am."

"What a surprise that I'm speaking to you. I've always admired you and your work, Optical Walls of Luxen Tech! And, many times…I wish I had a little more time to talk with you about…but, going back to Dr. Molton's request, I'll ask him if he would like to speak with you. Please hang on."

While Jenny was waiting for the doctor's return, Steve asked, "What did the doctor say?"

"He said he recognized me because he knew about the Optical Walls of Luxen Tech."

"Why wouldn't he? The Optical Walls made you lose your anonymity a long time ago. You should be proud of yourself."

Dr. Blau's voice returned to resume the call. "Sorry, Ms. Spencer, Dr. Molton is adamant about with whom he wants to speak, and it's only with Ms. Wilson. He did not want to speak with anyone else. Do you happen to have Ms. Wilson's telephone number?"

"I'm sorry, I don't. I'm sure Dr. Molton will remember it if he gets sober."

"You're right, Ms. Spencer. I'll ask him later."

"As a friend of Dr. Molton, may I ask you if he is being discharged from the ER today?"

"I'm sorry, Ms. Spencer. He is being two-PC'ed to the psych ward today."

"What is two-PC?"

"It stands for *two-physicians' certificate*. When a patient needs a psychiatric hospital-based observation or treatment and yet refuses to enter the hospital, the state can request any two physicians, often two psychiatrists, to reexamine the patient. If the two doctors concur with the original psychiatrist who made the recommendation for in-hospital treatment, they can override the patient's objection, and the person should accept the admission recommendation. So, two-PC is almost synonymous with involuntary admission to a psychiatric hospital."

"I see. But what happens if the person still believes he does not need to be in a psychiatric hospital?"

"Well, he can request in writing to be discharged from the hospital. Since the hospital legally has seventy-two hours or three days to respond to his written discharge request, the unwilling patient's written request has been called *a three-day letter.*"

"I see."

"In some instances, patients become calmer and better in three days and get discharged. However, as it is most of the time, if the patient's mental status does not change much in the three-day period, the patient's discharge request will be reviewed in a mental-health court, where a judge hears the patient, the treating psychiatrist, and both sides' lawyers to make the final decision. The outcome could be either the patient's release or certification for intensive treatment for an additional fourteen days."

"Thank you, Dr. Blau, for your explanation. Would it be all right if I saw him in the ER area this evening?"

"I think your presence might agitate him. It would be better if you could see him when he is sober, maybe tomorrow?"

"Thank you, Doctor. I'll take your advice."

Feeling exhausted, Jenny ended the telephone call. As she sat at her desk, face-to-face with Steve, they heard a vocal duet flowing out of her audio instrument on the wall that made her teary. Steve murmured, "Oh, that's Franz Lehar's *Lippen Schweigen.* What a lovely song!"

Steve urged her to have some snack before leaving her office. He opened the snack pack that he had brought for her and took out ham sandwiches and iced tea. Nibbling on the sandwich, Jenny appeared near tears at times and murmured, "Poor Sobien! I didn't realize how unstable his mood was."

"Are you OK, Jenny?" Steve was solicitous.

"Yeah, I'll be all right."

By the time she finished the sandwich, Steve had tidied up her office by putting things in their right places. Steve and Jenny locked up Sobien's shoulder bag in her office cabinet.

"Jenny, do you want me to drive you to your officetel?"

"No, don't worry about me. I'll be fine. I'll ride my air-scooter."

"Are you sure?"

"Yes."

Steve escorted her to Luxen Tech's air-scooter parking area. As she got on her air-scooter, Steve said, "It could have been much worse."

"You're right. Well, I'll be at my officetel in twelve minutes."

"Drive it carefully."

"I will. Thank you, Steve, for coming over."

"Not at all! Take care."

Next day Steve called Helen and told her what happened to Sobien Molton.

Soon Helen called Jenny, "I've heard from Steve about what happened yesterday in your office before Dr. Molton went to the ER. It must have been rough on you…If there is anything I could do for you, Jenny, whatever it is, please call me anytime…I'm available."

"Thank you, Helen. I was afraid something like that might happen but not so soon. It's comforting to know that I can depend and lean on you and Steve."

With Bill Warren's police affidavit against Sobien Molton and Tick, the state judge had issued an arrest warrant on them.

Meanwhile at Northwest Hospital, feeling unhappy about the psychiatric unit's rigid rules, Kerbera Wilson hired a lawyer for Molton and made requests to the hospital and mental-health court for Molton's early discharge. However, in view of the arrest warrant, the court gave authorization to have him transferred to Silver Lake psychiatric hospital in Connecticut. Reportedly, Kerbera Wilson visited him at the Connecticut hospital every day. Sobien Molton never called Jenny back.

Jenny felt sad as she realized that her relationship with him was quickly withering away. As time passed by, she felt compelled to let go of her faint hope of winning him back. Eventually, she decided to stay away from Sobien.

Since then, for Jenny, fretful nights with bad dreams ensued. Her daily routine suffered from a lame pace. Luxen Tech people began to notice her usual personality losing luster and energy. Eventually, Jenny spoke to Helen and made an appointment with Dr. Jupitren at Acmeon Lab.

In the session, after carefully listening to her personal history, Dr. Jupitren reassured her that the Dream Wafer would work for her. He asked, "So, do you have any particular kind of dreams in mind?"

"Yes, I want to revisit the Mediterranean beaches all by myself, in this hot summer weather. Most of all, even if it will be only in my dreams, I wish to feel free from my upset feelings and anxiety."

"Those themes are quite popular. I see you have already finished the breath analysis and genome test. Please answer the questionnaire-135 carefully in the Annex Library, and the Wafers will be ready within one or two hours. Usually the Dream Wafers start to work within the first week of application."

"I understand. I can't wait to see the result. Thank you."

Jenny carefully completed the questionnaire in the Annex Library. Two hours later, Helen came into the library with Jenny's Dream Wafers.

"It's good that you have your Dream Wafers now. They will help you feel better soon. The *Wafer User's* instruction manual is in this folder. If you have any questions, call me anytime."

"Thank you so much, Helen."

"You're very welcome. Good luck with your Dream Wafers."

CHAPTER 41
STOP NOW AND THEN

After seeing the last patient for the morning, Dr. Jupitren projected his vision far into the future. He thought of developing much more refined dream inducing programs with simplified Wafer manufacturing processes.

As Dr. Jupitren contemplated all the possible future developments, he thought that Sobien Molton, who fell into his own trap, was a real letdown for everyone. If Sobien maintained a different professional outlook and right commitment, he with his vast knowledge in neurogenetics, would have made a significant contribution to genetic dreamology through the future R & D of Acmeon Lab.

Helen realized that some of Sobien's Waferlyzer-II related workload went to Dr. Jupitren, who had been extremely busy even without the extra burden. Around noontime, inside Dr. Jupitren's office, Helen asked, "Uncle Jules, will you be all right with all the added work without Dr. Molton's assistance?"

"Thank you, Helen, for asking me about it. Since Sobien went to the hospital, I have been quite busy, and I have been recruiting new doctors for some time. As you know, I have already interviewed a number of candidates. And as of yesterday, I have chosen three new doctors who will be starting to work here very soon."

"I'm very glad that you have already found those new doctors. I'm sure they would be wonderful people."

Helen came back to her desk and thought to herself, "Well, I'm glad. Those new doctors will also lessen my Waferlyzer-II related workload while helping Uncle Jules. But I still have to work part time and spend extra time training Anne Brown. On top of it, I have the Head Start program assignments. Will I have any time left to see Steve? How am I going to manage it all?"

Thinking about her work schedule, Helen tried to organize her office papers but felt tired and heavy eyed. Somehow, she reminisced about the picture images of the Sandman from her childhood fairy-tale book. She started mumbling to the Sandman, "You are trying to make me sleepy, but I'm going to make a special concoction to keep you off. I'll mix Spartan sweat, the Far East Asian elixir-of-education frenzy, and a tincture of academic-skills-programs galore. They will make the first concoction. But, that's not enough…I should add the elixir of super-mnemonics that I will get from Mnemosyne, the goddess of memory and *selective time-shielding*. And mix all those in a tall glass, and I will drink the daily concoction for two years. Will I survive the ordeal?"

Suddenly, she started to run as she was fiercely castigated by long-bearded Khronos, the god of time. Very soon, she came to a blind alley, where she was about to be buried alive under the crushing pressure of thousands of clocks and watches piling up on her. She yelled out, "Help! Anyone's out there?"

Helen felt someone gently shaking her shoulder and heard a familiar but distant voice. "Helen, are you all right?"

It was Dr. Jupitren, who saw Helen slumped over piles of her work papers. In her brief dozing, she moaned and seemed distressed by something in her dream. So, he came by to awaken her from her restless midday slumber.

Straightening herself up, Helen realized what happened and instantly felt mortified. "Gosh! I fell asleep over these papers. I'm so embarrassed." Saying so, she threw a light chastising look at Anne in the same office for not waking her up sooner. Resuming her usual self, Helen said, "Doctor Jupitren, were you waiting for me a long time?"

"No, don't worry. You came out of my office less than half an hour ago."

"I see. But this has never happened to me before. I'm so sorry. Did you want to dictate any letters? I see you're holding some papers and return envelopes."

"Yes, but not now. Why don't you get some fresh air or sip a cold drink and come into my office. I want to hear more about your scheduled trip to Washington, DC."

After brief moments, Helen in Dr. Jupitren's office, said, "I thought I had a recipe for a special drink."

"What did you say?"

Helen told him about her concoction dream she just had and asked him, "I wonder if I should try a Dream Wafer."

"Why?"

"Because I have been feeling very anxious and worried about how I'm going to take care of all the things I'm supposed to. Lately, I've had restless, broken sleep with bad dreams. I just dreamt of being crushed as tons of clocks and watches fell over me."

"We tend to dream even during a twenty minute-nap if we had poor sleep in the preceding nights. You must have been sleeping poorly."

"Yes, lately I couldn't sleep well at night. During the day, I get tired easily and I'm feeling badly rushed."

"Do you mean you have more things than you can handle within the given time and you feel you are rushing?"

"Yes. In fact, I feel I'm rushing a lot, not seeing details of things."

"Do you want to see the details of things a little better?"

"Yes, I do. How can I do it?"

"My experience with the subject matter taught me a certain method. But it demands your special attention."

"Really? Uncle Jules, would you tell me about your method?"

"Well, take a seat and I'll explain it to you. Imagine you are an archer. There would be three different levels of difficulty when you want to make the bull's-eye. If both you and the target randomly move at the same time, it would be very hard for you to hit the target. But if you were standing still while the target was moving, or if the target was standing still but you were on the move, it would be a little easier. However, the third setting with the least difficulty would be when you and the target are both standing still. This ideal third setting in real life is rather rare. So, if you want to see the moving things a little better, wouldn't you rather stop moving yourself?

Therefore, when you are rushed, you just *stop now and then*. That's all. Most people do it without knowing they are doing it. But many people don't do it enough. If you consciously and purposefully stop, then you will see a whole lot of new things in detail that you have missed when you were rushed. When you stop, you will discover the hidden solutions as well.

So, if I were you, for now, I'll try more of the *stop now and then* rather than the Dream Wafer."

"But, would you explain a little more about what it means to stop?"

"Well, I meant literally to stop or pause what I am doing and *let myself intensely observe* my own thoughts, acts, and surroundings. At the stopped moments, I question, 'Where am I in relation to what is going on now, why am I doing what I'm doing, how am I affecting others around me, what's there that I must do now, what realistically needs to be done next?' and so on. It takes only a few minutes or a few seconds, depending on the subject matter. I remember David Roper, a Christian writer, once wrote '…life should be less hurrying and more noticing.' I think he said it for us to appreciate certain spiritual insight, yet I think his words struck a chord with what *the stop* was meant to be. If you come up with too many things to pay attention to, while in *the stop* mode, you may make a list or better yet a checklist for your follow-up."

"I see. But I hear some people, on the contrary, try not to think of anything at all and call it TM or transcendental meditation. I wonder what the difference is between *stop now and then* and TM."

"In transcendental meditation, people concentrate either on a certain mantra or on silent counting of their own breaths in order to block off all other thoughts. I mean, by engaging in meditation, you're dispelling your distracting thoughts, but it is usually in preparation for subsequent self-observation, which demands much focused, concentrated thinking. So, in contrast to the TM, by practicing the *stop now and then*, you are intensely and intentionally accentuating your self-observation right there and then. That is, just like the archer, you bring yourself to a stand-still state in order to aim at the immediate task at hand. If you first train yourself in meditation, *stopping now and then* will become much easier to do.

When you're driving a car, even if you know your way to your destination very well, don't you still question yourself *now and then* about where you're and therefore in what direction you ought to steer? During the few seconds, in which you raise that question and have the correct answer to it, you stop thinking about the driving act per se but your car would continue to run well because you're an experienced driver. Eventually you will be able to reach your intended destination.

However, consider the opposite situation, where you *did not stop to think* about your destination *now and then* and your car veered away from the right direction. The result would be that despite your intense concentration on the driving act itself, sooner or later you would find yourself in a wrong destination. So, we can say your driving skill per se was excellent but you brought yourself to a wrong place because you did not do the necessary *stopping now and then* during your driving. This is just one simple example of *stop now and then* in our daily routine. Everybody does it without thinking about it as such, but we can practice it more consciously or intentionally. We can apply it practically to everything we do."

Helen genuinely nodded, affirming what she just understood. She said, "I kind of understand what you mean by *stop now and then*. Thank you, but I've never intentionally tried it or TM so far. Do you practice both methods yourself?"

"Yes, quite often. It is either/or. But more often than not, I try both of them. I have to remind myself to practice them more diligently, or else I tend to forget to do them altogether. And beside those two methods, there is something else."

"What do you mean? Is there a third method beside those two?"

"Yes, but I wouldn't call the third one a method. I would rather say it is *the Way*."

"What is that, *the Way*?"

He smiled and answered, "It is very much more than a method. And it is something you practice every day, as so many others in the world do."

"I don't understand what you mean."

"You know it well. People call it prayer, and I believe it is the most profound of all the known ways to see through ourselves. Also, it is the very way by which people reach the Utmost Being, whom most people refer to as God. In our mundane lives, I believe prayer is a unique pathway enabling us not just to see what we have missed but also to transcend the frail human limit, which is bound to loom up to anyone. Regardless which religion, or even for those who claim they are without religion, prayer is a universal outcry, reaching for the Supreme Power. It is like our breathing, which no living person can do without."

After a while, Helen asked him again, "Often I have felt I'm not the only one rushing through. Many people I know rush through many things worse than I do. Don't you think so?"

"Yes, I'm afraid we all are rushing. It's modern man's problem. Most of us are overloaded with information and things to do. It seems the introduction of computers in our lives made the information-overload more prominent and apparent. When you think of everyone in the world being a potential cyber-information generator, aren't you scared of drowning in the sea of information? It seems to me that before we could start building the modern-day Noah's ark, the torrential information rain had already started. As the flood level rises, people have little choice but to rush through the massive information just to stay afloat, missing much of it at the end.

It is not only impossible but also unnecessary to meet all the information challenges or things to do. That's why we need to *stop now and then* to look at ourselves realistically so that we can deflect those irrelevant waves of information and non-essential things. It means that we have to prioritize our choices at all times based on our needs and reality. Such prioritizing can be done well when we stop or pause the very thing we are engaged in. By doing so, we will save time and be able to pay attention to more pertinent and essential matters. By stopping, we could be selective and have time to achieve something unique and meaningful.

So, I believe stopping now and then will help us gain new insight and let us steer ourselves in the right direction in everything we do. In that sense, *stopping is a gateway to eureka moments in many things we do every day*. After all, it may sound paradoxical, but we have to stop so that we can go further in the right direction."

"Thank you very much for your special lesson, Uncle Jules."

"You're very welcome. Now, will you tell me about your fieldwork in DC?"

"Yes, as I told you other day, starting tomorrow I'll be taking off for a whole week. It is for the new Head Start program's fieldwork assignment. It is in Washington, DC. I have to attend the weeklong federal committee meetings there as an auditor. So, before I leave this evening, I'll review again with Anne Brown about what she needs to do in the office while I'm away."

"Well, don't try to do too much, too soon in DC. It is your birthday today. Happy birthday, Helen! Jamie asked me to tell you that she brought your birthday present to your home early this afternoon."

"Thank you, Uncle Jules and Aunt Jamie, for being so good to me. I'll remember to practice your lesson whenever I can."

In the afternoon, Dr. Jeffrey Ellenberg, a colleague and a psychiatrist from Silver Lake Hospital in Connecticut called. "Hi, Jules, I called you today to let you know something about my patient Sobien Molton. I understand he had been working as your assistant at your Acmeon Lab before he became ill. Am I right?"

"Yes, you are."

"More than once during my routine interviews, he revealed his detailed plan to set fire on Acmeon Plant. However, as of today, he is denying his intent to do it. Probably by downplaying it, he is hoping to be discharged from the hospital. Have you been aware of his threats?"

"Yes, but not about his specific fire-setting plan. Did he say why he would do such a thing?"

"Well, from what I gather, he tends to act out according to his immature motto, which says, 'If I can't have it, I will squash it.' Apparently, he was not happy at Acmeon Lab because he couldn't have his way on certain matters. But, basically he is prone to go through wide mood swings. When his mood shifts downward he becomes very irritable, and on upswing phases he would become grandiose and recklessly intrusive."

"I concur with your observation, Jeff. Unfortunately, he and I disagreed on certain treatment methodology. It made him very unhappy, and he was annoyed with me."

"I see. Our forensic unit staffs are now fully aware of his fire-setting idea as well as his history of criminal activity that led to his recent indictment. In his hospital chart, we have the legal papers on him from the DA's office."

"The legal status aside, do you think he is improving clinically?"

"At the present, we're giving him two antidepressants, to which he has shown only a mediocre response so far."

"How soon will you be discharging him?"

"Well, last week we replaced one of his two antidepressants with a newer one, which will take two to three weeks before we could see its effect. So, I would say he will be discharged one to two weeks from now. But, even if he gets discharged from Silver Lake, he would have to go to the NY State hospital's long-term forensic program for the duration set by the court.

The discharge question brings me to another point, which is about his visitor. He has only one visitor, a woman whose name is Kerbera Wilson. She is talking about having him discharged into her custody soon so that she can move with him to a place in the West Coast. She avows that she could manage on her own if he was discharged now. But I know, because of his mental and legal status, he can't leave the hospital at the present time."

"I understand. Anyway, thank you, Jeff, for informing me about his fire-setting idea. I only hope his mood disorder will respond to your treatment."

"I hope so, too, Jules. Oh, another thing. Soon after he was assigned to me, I called NY State's program, *The Committee for Physicians' Health* to register him as part of our admission routine, because he is licensed in New York. I'm sure you have heard of the program."

"Yes, I have. I understand it's run by the Medical Society of the State of New York to help physicians with mental-health problems."

"Right, Jules. I wanted to give you a heads up just in case the committee calls you about him one of these days."

"Thank you very much, Jeff. I myself should have called the state program before he went to your hospital."

"Don't worry about it. It didn't take much time to refer him to the committee."

CHAPTER 42
STEVE TO THE WASHINGTON, DC MEETING

On the first day of August, Thursday morning, Steve thought, "Today is Helen's birthday. I'll give her this surprise present later in the evening."

However, just before the lunch hour, Steve was called to see his company's president, Mr. Goettenberg in his office. The president said, "I have something very important to tell you. This morning at our company's special board meeting, the board members recommended you to attend a meeting in Washington, DC, that starts tomorrow, Friday, and it will last about a week."

"Tomorrow, sir?"

"Yes."

"What kind of meeting is it?"

"The Defense Department has formed a liaison committee with the Energy Department's National Solar Energy Commission. And our company was invited to present the technical data about our products at the committee meetings."

"Is anyone else from our company attending the meetings?"

"Yes. I'll be attending. I will join you in most of the sessions when you have your presentations. I'll be bringing actual samples and miniaturized models of our company's machines to demonstrate to the engineers and the involved committee members."

"I see. Would you tell me on which specific products I should prepare for the meetings?"

"First of all, I'm sorry to give you such a short notice to prepare yourself. We received their invitation very recently to begin with, and on top of it, our board members did not convene until this morning, and finally we chose you at this morning's meeting. Well, regarding what to prepare, I think among other things, they will ask you technical questions about the solar-powered Dronette and its capability to fire the LXG stun guns through remote control. So I hope you can collate basic technical information on Dronette as well as other data, especially on our company's solar-energy transformer systems."

"I understand."

"Our first presentation will be at three o'clock tomorrow afternoon. I'm sure you'll be able to prepare for it until then."

"Well, the time is rather tight, but I'll do my best to have the technical information at my fingertips by then. I'll regroup the data on the first-version Dronette as well as the latest Dronette-6.12 from our Perihelion's technical archives."

"Sounds good. If it goes well throughout the weeklong meetings, our company most likely will strike up contracts with the feds. You now realize how important your presentation will be for our company. I want you to know that all the board members of Perihelion Energy unanimously recommended you to represent our company. They all said you will manage it very well even with such a short notice."

"Thank you, sir."

"Oh, another thing. Please pick up the itinerary with the hotel reservation and the air tickets from Nancy at the general-management office. She will give you the meeting schedule outline, too. I'll leave for DC this evening, and will see you tomorrow at the three o'clock presentation. But it would be better for us to compare our notes before the presentation. So let's get there by 2:15. Is that all right with you?"

"Yes. I'll see you at that time."

As soon as Steve reviewed his itinerary, he called Helen. "Hi, Happy birthday to you, Helen."

"Thank you."

"Where are you now?"

"I'm at Acmeon's office, making a packing list."

"Packing list? What for?"

"This evening I'm going to DC for a fieldwork assignment of my Head Start course."

"What a coincidence! I, too, have to leave for DC tomorrow morning."

"Really? What's the occasion?"

"My Company is sending me to attend a federal committee meeting in DC, which will last a whole week starting tomorrow."

"By any chance, will you be attending the newly formed liaison committee meeting between the Defense Department and the Energy Department's National Solar Energy Commission?"

"Yes, I will be, but how in the world did you know that?"

"My course assignment is to attend that very liaison committee meeting, as an auditor, at least three hours daily for six days, except Sunday August 4. Of course, at the end, I have to submit an extensive report for the course credit."

"Wow, I'm so glad. I'll be seeing you there the whole week. And possibly we'll be able to celebrate your birthday on Sunday, that's three days after your birthday."

"Thank you, Steve. Are you coming with other people from your company?"

"Just another person, the company's president, Mr. Goettenberg. How about you?"

"I'm in a group of four women students. Four of us will share two rooms at Beacon Hotel and Corporate Quarters on Rhode Island Avenue."

"Great, I'll be staying at the hotel where the liaison committee meetings are held. It's at JW Marriott Washington on Pennsylvania Avenue. Are you driving to the airport?"

"No, my Mom will."

"Well, then. I'll see you in DC soon. My first presentation will be at three o'clock tomorrow afternoon in the Grand Ballroom Theatre. Maybe you could see me at that meeting. It'll be a terrific experience for both of us."

"Yeah, I agree. I'm looking forward to the whole thing, especially to seeing you very often. Most likely, I'll be attending your afternoon session tomorrow. I'm so happy."

"Me, too, Helen. I love you."

"I love you, too. I'll see you in DC!"

Steve realized that he would need to wait a few more days before he could give the surprise present to Helen.

At Acmeon Lab, Dr. Jupitren took over the Waferlyzer-II related work that was originally assigned to Sobien, who was still in the hospital. In addition, Dr. Jupitren had to see Dream Wafer candidates and clients as before.

The US Department of Veterans Affairs and the Department of Health and Human Services in particular steadily referred veterans with PTSD to Dr. Jupitren for Dream Wafer treatment. Among them, there were a number of war veterans with a chronic form of PTSD, who had been in Afghanistan and were now in their late forties and fifties. Many of their anxiety dreams and recurrent night terrors abated with Dream Wafer applications. As time went on, it became apparent to all concerned that when their psychosocial therapy was combined with Dream Wafer applications, they responded much better than when they received the psychosocial therapy only. Those veteran patients alone kept Dr. Jupitren very busy.

Meanwhile, at the two federal departments' joint meeting in DC, Steve gave a presentation, elaborating on a number of strong points about his company's products and manufacturing methods. As Steve expected, the main interest expressed by the committee was about the company's solar-energy transformer systems, LXG stun guns, and Dronette-6.12. As the presentation went on, Mr. Goettenberg, using the theater's huge screen, demonstrated the samples and models of the items that Steve presented, and he and Steve proficiently answered many related administrative and technical questions.

In the auditors' section, among many attendees, Steve spotted Helen, who remained keen-eyed and alert, jotting down information in her notes.

After the presentation, several VIPs complimented Steve. Mr. Goettenberg, too, personally recognized Steve's professional competence and technical knowledge. "Steve, your presentation was excellent. I'm reassured you'll deliver the requested information very well at the next week's meetings, too."

"Thank you, sir."

Out of many surrounding faces, Helen's smiling face came into Steve's sight. Addressing to Mr. Goettenberg, Steve gladly introduced her. "This is my dear friend Helen Humayor from Acmeon Lab." Then Steve turned to Helen and said, "He is Perihelion Energy Company's president, Mr. Goettenberg."

"How do you do, Mr. Goettenberg?"

"Hi, nice to meet you, Ms. Humayor."

Steve said, "She is here with her graduate-school friends. They are from New York and are auditors to this meeting."

"I see. How did you like our presentation?"

"It was excellent. I thought you both made many strong points about Perihelion's manufacturing methods. I'm sure the audience got your messages clearly that your company's methods would cost much less than other manufacturers' methods while keeping it all pro green. I have learned a lot about your company's fascinating products."

"Thank you. That proves Steve did a great job."

"Thank you, Mr. Goettenberg. But each time you demonstrated the samples on the screen, I could sense the committee people being quite convinced about our products. You made the convincing final punch every time you explained."

Mr. Goettenberg got busy trading a number of additional Q & A's with inquisitive engineers while he put the samples back into the original containers. At the same time, Steve, too was busy answering other inquirers' extra questions.

Helen went to join her class friends in the hotel's atrium.

A while later, Mr. Goettenberg came back to Steve, who was with a circle of reporters from the Washington area. "Steve, sorry to interrupt your conversation.

Excuse me, folks, I have to borrow him and tell him something very important right now!"

"Tomorrow, Saturday, there will be a full day's official meeting starting at eleven, as you see in the schedule, and you will be busy. By the way, tomorrow's meeting will be at the Senate Meeting Room without any auditors. It will be quite intense. So, in order to plan our presentation for tomorrow and for next week as well, I'd like to see you at ten tomorrow morning and again on Sunday at the same time."

Then Mr. Goettenberg discreetly steered Steve out of the reporters' circle and continued in a hushed voice. "At the next meetings, some of them will ask you certain leading questions aiming at our company's secret formulas. Please handle their questions tactfully so that your answers would make them feel satisfied, but you have to be very careful not to give away Perihelion's essential technical secrets. The inquirers are known for their sharp questions that put many previous presenters into inescapable crucibles."

"I understand." Steve nodded his head.

"Steve, I will tell you more in detail tomorrow and Sunday about the likely topics they will ask you at the meetings. It will take about an hour for me to go over those topics with you. Please come to this hotel's Penn Avenue Terrace Balcony at ten in the morning with your presentation papers."

"Certainly. I will be there."

"Are you well prepared for tomorrow's presentation?"

"Almost, yes. I'll use my remaining evening hours to organize technical information on the Dronette's remote functions, about which they said they would ask me more tomorrow."

With a thumbs-up, Mr. Goettenberg said, "That sounds good, Steve. I'll see you in the morning." Mr. Goettenberg left the area.

By then the news reporters were busy talking to other crowds. Steve saw Helen sitting in the lobby. He walked over and sat down on a chair next to her. "Helen, how are you doing so far?"

"Very well. Today I've learned many things about DC and the fed departments' agenda. But most of all, it was so nice to see you at the podium."

"Thank you, Helen. Did you pick up some new information from my presentation?"

"Yes, lots of it. You did a great job. You were confident and very convincing."

"Thank you. Were your friend students there, too?"

"Yes, they all said your presentation was excellent. I haven't told them yet who you are. So you got unbiased compliments from them."

"That's nice. Are they still here?"

"No, they just went back to the hotel ahead of me. I'll meet with them at dinner in our hotel's restaurant by six thirty, and we will discuss what we learned today."

"It's almost six thirty. How are you getting back to your hotel?"

"I'll take a cab. It's only about a mile and half away from here. Steve, do you want to join us at our dinner discussion by any chance?"

"No, thanks. I'll be busy preparing for tomorrow's presentation. My schedule starts at eleven tomorrow. It will be at the Senate Meeting Room without any auditors. I'll see Mr. Goettenberg at ten tomorrow morning before the scheduled meeting starts. On Sunday morning, I'll see him again at ten for about an hour to prepare for next week's presentation. Then I'm free after that. What about your schedule tomorrow and Sunday?"

"Tomorrow, four of us will be attending as auditors at two different workshop sessions of the liaison committees. It will be most of the day. On Sunday, at four o'clock, we'll meet with a professor at Washington University. It will take a few hours, and then the four of us will get together again at dinner, discussing our audit report."

"I guess you don't want to miss the evening discussion with your friends."

"Right. So, can we meet around noontime on Sunday?"

"Great, that's just what I was thinking, too. I'll meet you then at Beacon Hotel's main lobby on Sunday. Is the hotel address 1615 Rhode Island Avenue?"

"Yes. Its full name is Beacon Hotel and Corporate Quarters."

"I've got it. When is your written report due?"

"Within seventy-two hours after the joint fed meeting ends next Friday. So, my report is due the following Monday afternoon."

"That's an awfully tight schedule with no slack at all. So you need to keep good notes every day. By the way, which day are you returning to New York?"

"Friday. It's a morning flight. All four of us have the same schedule. How about you?"

"I have a Friday morning presentation and my return flight is late in the afternoon."

"Then, I'll miss your Friday's presentation. I'm sure you will ace it, too."

Helen hailed a cabby in front of the hotel taxi line. Hearing the cab's engine start, they walked hand in hand to the cab. Stopping next to the cab, Steve threw his arms around her and kissed her tenderly. Steve, holding the cab door for her, gently said, "Don't work too hard. Good night, Helen."

"Good night, Steve. I'll see you on Sunday at noon. Sweet dreams!"

CHAPTER 43
HELEN'S SURPRISE

Sunday at noontime, Steve came to Beacon Hotel & Corporate Quarters. The hotel lobby was bright but cool, defying the outside hot August temperature of Washington, DC.

Dressed in a light, summery business outfit, Helen stepped out of the elevator to the main floor with genteel steps and smiled at Steve, who was waiting for her in the main lobby. Steve walked toward her and greeted with a happy smile. The lobby was busy with hotel guests. In the midst of them, Steve and Helen found two sofa seats.

"Hi, how did your meeting with Mr. Goettenberg go this morning?"

"Very well. Did you have a good night's sleep?"

"Yes, as usual. And early this morning, I drafted a part of my course report. In the remaining time, I was able to speak to Uncle Jules briefly. He seemed busy from early morning"

"Are they short-handed at Acmeon?"

"Yes, for now because of the Waferlyzer-II project. But it won't be too long. Uncle Jules hired three new doctors, and they have just started their work. They will pitch in by doing a number of things. For now, they are to help Uncle Jules and will be doing much of my share of the new Waferlyzer-II related work as well."

"That's good news for everyone. You must feel relieved."

"Yes, very much. Uncle Jules found those doctors rather quickly. I'm so glad about it."

"Do you know anything about them?"

"Yes, a little. Uncle Jules told me about those doctors on the phone. I know their names and some of their professional backgrounds. Actually I jotted down this information while I listened to Uncle Jules this morning."

Helen looked at her memo pad and said, "Dr. Arnold Anderson is a medical doctor who studied human genetics and information engineering on genetics during his postgraduate years."

"He must be very knowledgeable in genetics."

"I think so, too. The other doctor is Brice Burbridge, an MD and PhD, a graduate of NYU School of Medicine and is a neuroanatomist with special study in genetics and neurophysiology. Uncle Jules said this doctor has many scientific research ideas and uncle is going to have him speak about his theses at the next Acmeon Lab's monthly professional staff conferences over number of months."

"Another doctor with strong professional background!"

"Right. The third doctor is a woman, Carmen Chanteur, MD, an experienced neurologist. A graduate of Sorbonne University. She is a statistician with human-genetics research experience." Helen put her memo pad back into her bag.

"A nice job! Helen, an excellent reporter, you are. By now, Dr. Jupitren must be very happy to have them on board."

"I'm sure he must be."

"Now, Helen, you haven't had breakfast yet, I guess."

"No, not yet. How about you?"

"I had a cup of coffee with a piece of Danish a few hours ago when I met with Mr. Goettenberg, and I'm ready for a hearty meal. Now, the outside temp is above ninety degrees. Let's just stay indoors and try the hotel's restaurant."

"That's a good idea. I think it is the hotel's brunch hour at this time anyway. I heard that this hotel has the Washington, DC area's number one Sunday brunch."

"That's great. Let's give it a try."

Sitting face-to-face at a table, swaddled with the posh interior of the hotel restaurant, Helen and Steve relished the lavish brunch buffet choices.

"Three days belatedly, I'd like to say again, 'Happy birthday!' to you, Helen."

"Thank you, Steve."

"Did you make another birthday card for your mother this year?"

"Yes. Before I left New York, I hand delivered it to Mom at the airport."

"I'm sure she was very pleased with your card."

"Yes, she was."

After a while, Steve brought up a question. "Today is Sunday. I know your family is Presbyterian. Are your parents regular churchgoers?"

"Yes, they are."

"What about you, Helen?"

"Whenever I can, I attend the Sunday liturgical services. How are your Sundays?"

"My Sundays?" Steve put down his fork and knife. He thought of something briefly and said, "Let me start with my parents. My father, a third-generation Unitarian, has gone through many changes over the years. My mother came from a Methodist family. She stood by her belief in Trinity doctrine and Jesus-centered soteriology, which my father was slow to accept."

"What is soteriology?"

"I'm sorry, Helen, I should have explained it to you before I said the word. It means studying salvation doctrine. It is an unfamiliar term for many people. Theologians often use it."

"I see. Then does your father not believe in salvation through Christ?"

"Not initially, but, yes, later. At the beginning of their marriage, my parents had different doctrines, although they were both Christians. Do you know that only ten to fifteen percent of Unitarians are doctrinal Christians, while the rest of them are liberal freethinkers without formal creed? And, some of them verge on cults and are atheistic, self-worshipping philosophers. Many of them are involved with politics and are liberal extremists.

Having started with basic belief in one almighty God, my father gradually moved from his own father's and grandfather's Unitarianism and began to practice the Methodists' way of Christian life that my mother stood by.

Unitarianism has a long, complex history. It will take many hours to review the history of Unitarian churches and how their doctrinal code changed along with the history of Europe and North America. But, offhand, I can tell you that some well-known people were Unitarians."

"Who were they?"

"Isaac Newton and John Milton in England; in America, Thomas Jefferson, John Adams, and Benjamin Franklin; and a not so well-known Spanish doctor and reformer, Michael Servetus, who was executed at age forty-two for having written his books on non-Trinitarian theory. The historians say John Calvin and his followers, the founders of Presbyterian churches, condemned Servetus as a heretic for not believing in the Trinity and pressed for his execution by slow burning."

Then Steve caught himself and said, "Sorry, Helen, I got carried away. I realize it's not a good topic at a dinner table. Shouldn't we rather talk about something lighter?"

"Oh, no, I don't mind it. Let me hear you a little more. So, was your father one of the Unitarian Christians, who you said were ten to fifteen percent of all Unitarians?"

"Yes. He was a Unitarian Christian all right. But now he is more of a Methodist in his belief and way of life."

"Just like you?"

"Yes." Steve continued, "I didn't want to bore you with Unitarianism's history. But let me finish it by telling you just one interesting tangential story about them. I heard it from my grandfather. There is a town in Cape Cod with the name Cotuit, which was dubbed as "Little Harvard." In the summer months, the Bostonian Unitarian churches would close—I mean the churches would go into summer recess. And the Bostonian churchgoers, many of them being affiliates of Harvard, would flock into that town, Cotuit, during the summer, either in their summer houses or rented places. They congregated on Sundays, making the 'Summer Cape Church' of Cotuit. Naturally, that church became a status symbol for high achievers and the elite. My grandparents never went to the Cape Church but remained in Lowell all year-round. Cotuit is well-known for its oysters, but people don't hear much about the 'Little Harvard' tale."

"Very interesting. So on this Sunday, you're in Washington, DC. What do you do as an evangelist with a Unitarian pedigree?"

"Just like you said about what you do on Sundays, whenever I have time and opportunity, I still try to attend Sunday worship services. But the reason why I brought up the subject of religion was only to ask you if your parents might make any issues with my father's family background being Unitarian."

"Oh, I'm sure they will not question your character or personality, based on what your father's or your religion is. They began to like you after what I told them about you. I truly believe your parents' religion is not an issue for my parents."

"Thanks a lot for giving them good reports on me. That's reassuring. It brings me to the next point of what I wish to say. I wanted to make today a special landmark day for you and me. I think it will be more than your birthday celebration, since I have prepared something for you."

Helen was getting curious about what he just said. Steve readjusted his jacket lapels with his hands. With curled fingers he smoothed his hair above his ears a couple of times. Then he got up from his seat, moved closer to Helen's side, gingerly assumed a Tebow position, kneeling on the floor, and took out of his jacket pocket a small, lidded box. Finally, he looked up to her in all seriousness.

Helen got up from her seat, blushing and smiling.

People at the nearby tables looked at Steve on his Tebow kneeling and then at Helen. Many of them froze their ambrosial fork and knife maneuvers and looked at both of them alternatingly with a quiet show of admiration.

Steve, still in Tebow position, looked up to her again, extended his hand, and gave her the box, saying, "Helen, I want to make this a token of my lasting love for you, and I ask you to accept this and my solemn vow that I will be your lifetime loving companion."

Feeling a surge of surprise and happy feelings, she opened the box. A twinkling diamond ring was sitting in it. Helen looked at the ring blissfully with a happy smile. With her free hand she reached for his hand and urged him to stand up. When he sprang up on his feet, she kissed him sweetly and said,

"Thank you, Steve. I love you. I'm happily accepting this ring, engraving your vow in my heart."

Steve took the ring out of the box. Gently putting the ring on her finger, he felt a surge of joy and affection for her. He kissed her tenderly and said his vows of love for her again, oblivious of the people watching them from nearby tables.

CHAPTER 44
UNCLE JULIAN'S ADVICE LIST

Back in New York, Helen felt happy and relieved once again to hear from Dr. Jupitren about the three new doctors, who had been busy working since their first day. They were young and energetic. She welcomed them wholeheartedly.

In the subsequent general staff meeting, Dr. Jupitren introduced the new doctors to all the Acmeon employees, who extended their friendly, welcoming greetings to the newcomers. Dr. Jupitren announced that the new doctors' role in Acmeon would be doing research in addition to the routine Dream Wafer-related work. They would take over Dr. Molton's unfinished work and assume some of Helen's administrative roles.

As Helen's main *work-and-study course* was to start soon in September, she realized that she needed a major change in her work schedule.

She went to Dr. Jupitren in his office and said, "I thought I would split my hours half and half between Acmeon office work and my school work."

"Any problems with that?"

"Yes, I was very wrong in my estimate. Would you allow me to work only one-third of my time for Acmeon and devote the other two-thirds to do my course work?"

"I hope the two-thirds of your time will be sufficient for all your course-related work."

"I think it will be."

"Whatever hours of work you can give to Acmeon Lab are fine with me because now we have three new doctors beside Anne Brown. It will be easier for you to take time off. However, I'll let you decide flexibly about your work schedule under one condition."

"One condition?"

"Yes. While working here on a part-time basis, I want you to bring to Acmeon much of what you will be learning from your courses. I mean, you should apply your newly acquired knowledge to the daily business operation of Acmeon Lab. That's the condition."

"Thank you so very much. I'll do my best to go by what you're saying. After all, my program is a work-and-study MBA course. For me, it will be a study-and-apply program."

"I'm glad to hear that. And I know you will not misuse your time. In the future, whenever it becomes necessary, you should take an educational leave for a week or two at a time. You'll most likely need those leaves before your finals."

Dr. Jupitren continued his suggestion for Helen. "Please don't forget your long-term goals. Someday, you'll be in charge of the entire Acmeon Lab operation. I want you to have that new self-definition and remind yourself of your new role at all times. Once you decide to accept your new identity, you'll be surprised that you would begin to see things that you've overlooked before. From now on, keep your eyes open and learn everything that goes on around here at Acmeon whenever you can."

"Yes, I will remember that."

"Well, there are certain areas that I want you to pay more attention to than before." Saying so, he took a sheet of paper out of his desk drawer. In a more relaxed, calm voice he added, "About those areas, rather than giving you my advice only once verbally, I have made a written list for you so that you can go over it again from time to time."

As Helen received the sheet, he said, "Whenever you read the list, please remind yourself of who you are and who you will be. By the way, what you are holding is only the part-I of the list. A couple of years later, I'll give you the part-II."

Helen began to read the list silently while he waited for her to finish reading it. The list had the following advice:

** Try to be fully aware of and be part of every step of *client-centered humane treatment* given to all Acmeon Lab patients. Try the same approach with the staff. That is, the *staff-centered working relationship* with every Acmeon staff member. It means seeing things from *their* perspective.

** Do care for all your Acmeon staff to the extent of knowing their names, family ties, wishes, and financial statuses.

- ** Maintain your own physical, mental, and spiritual health.
- ** Monitor Acmeon's financial strength by making your own diligent assessment of it. That is, with or without the report from the finance department.
- ** Give proper rewards to others and yourself for a job well done.
- ** For every item listed above, develop your own concrete plans, checklists, and feedback systems from you to others and vice versa.

Still holding the paper in her hand, Helen said, "Thank you so very much. This list is already making me see myself in a different light."

Dr. Jupitren smiled and said, "Let your humility and empathy be the guiding principles whenever you interact with others. Learn about others' needs from their perspectives, no matter how trivial such needs might appear to be. Once they know you're on their side, they will start to listen to you earnestly. You also need to *stop now and then* in order to see things that are worthy or need to be seen."

After a brief pause, Dr. Jupitren asked Helen, "Is Anne there in the front office now?"

"Yes."

"I would like to talk to her, too."

"Shall I ask her to come in now?"

"Yes. Please come back with her."

Anne Brown and Helen came in.

Dr. Jupitren asked them to sit down and said, "Anne, as you may know, soon Helen will be working fewer hours, either half or sometimes only one-third of her usual hours because of her new school schedule. During her absence, I want you, Anne, to pick up Helen's usual office-related responsibilities. Of course, Acmeon Lab will compensate you for your extra work. So, will you be able to increase your work hours? If your answer is yes, I will communicate with the personnel and finance department about the change right away."

Anne cautiously said. "Yes, I think I will be able to. But I'm not sure how soon I'll be as efficient and knowledgeable as Helen is."

"I know you will do fine." Helen said. "I've seen you learn very quickly whenever there were new things in the office. Besides, I'll be here on a part-time schedule."

Dr. Jupitren added, "Anne, I believe you'll manage it well."

"Thank you. I hope I will meet both of your expectations."

"Anne, if it gets to be too much for you, just let me or Helen know. I'll get some extra help for you as we go."

"Thank you very much for your reassurance." Anne said. Helen, too, thanked him, and they returned to their desks.

Days later, Helen called Steve during her lunch hour.

"Hi, Steve. Guess what I got on my fieldwork assignment paper."

"You mean the grade?"

"Yes."

"Did you get an A?"

"No."

"Then B?"

"No"

"C?"

"No!"

"Don't tell me you got a D!"

"Of course, not. I got an A-plus!"

"Naturally! How could you get less than that after you checked with me so many times and had so many questions?"

"Are you trying to claim a part of the credit?"

"Well, didn't I share a lot of good information with you? So don't you think you should share with me the good feelings that the Alpha-plus brought you?... Are you begrudging me?"

"Oh, no, I can only say a big thank-you. Actually, I called you now to tell you about a special note that I received from Uncle Jules. It's a list of his advice."

"Advice?"

"Yes. The other day, he gave me a list of things that I have to be extra mindful of around Acmeon Lab. I put a title to it, 'Uncle Julian's advice list.' I'll show you the list someday soon. There is something special about it, because in some indirect way, you are in it, too."

"Do you mean his advice to you has something to do with me?"

"Yes. That's right."

"That's strange. I'm very curious. I sure want to find out what it is. By the way, can you guess what happened to me after my presentation at the DC fed meetings?"

"No. I hope it's something good."

"Yes, it is. Mr. Goettenberg said our company received a few contract proposals from those fed departments, and he promised me a big raise, too."

"That's wonderful. I'm very glad. You deserve it."

"Thank you. So, when will you show me the 'Uncle's advice list?"

"Maybe on Saturday, next week, at my parents' home?"

"At your parents' home! Thank you for the invitation. At what time?"

"At lunchtime, around noon?"

"That's a good time for me. Great! I'll be glad to come and see you and your parents. In fact, I have something quite important that I wanted to tell you at an appropriate time. I have been thinking about it for a while. It's something to do with my personal plans."

"Is it another good news, I hope?"

"Yes, it is. But depending on how you look at it, it could be a mixed blessing. I'll explain it in detail next Saturday at your parents'."

"Now, I'm the one getting curious. Can you tell me about it now?"

"Well, not now on the phone. But may I tell you in person when I come to your parents'?"

"All right, I'll wait, as you say."

"I'll be seeing you soon at your parents'."

Later in the afternoon, Steve called his sister at her office. "Hi, Jenny, I want to ask you about a few things."

"OK, Steve. Actually, I was about to call you and ask if you could come here to my office and go to Northwest Hospital ER with me either today or tomorrow."

"Why, Jenny? Are you not feeling well?"

"It's not my health problem. The hospital called me about Sobien Molton."

"Isn't he now at another hospital?"

"Yes, he is. When he was transferred to the other hospital, the Northwest ER people did not send his jacket along with him."

"His jacket?"

"Yeah. I don't know why it took so long for them to call me now. They said I should come there to the ER supervisor's office and pick up the check I wrote to Sobien, which they found in his jacket pocket. I remember that he came to my office a couple of days before his head injury. At that time, he asked me to lend him one hundred fifty dollars for his car's gas because that day he did not have his credit cards with him and his gas tank was almost empty. So I wrote him a check for the amount."

"But why can't they simply mail it to you?"

"The hospital administrator said there was another matter. They also found a receipt for a recent gun purchase in his jacket pocket, and they wanted to ask me some questions about him and me."

"What a strange coincidence! Did the hospital say you must come with someone else?"

"No, they didn't say that. I just wanted to ask you to come with me because they said that I could come with a friend or my lawyer if I wanted to."

"I see. I'll come to your office tomorrow evening, and we'll go to the hospital together. Jenny, I'll be at your office by five thirty tomorrow, OK?"

"Thank you, Steve. I'll see you tomorrow. But didn't you say you wanted to ask me about a few things?"

"Oh, yes. It's about my Perihelion Energy job and other matters. I want to have your advice on them. I may need a big help from you, too. Can you spare some time after the visit to the hospital tomorrow?"

"Sure, Steve, anytime."

CHAPTER 45
DR. ROY BLAU AND JENNY

The following day, Steve and Jenny went to the ER of Northwest Hospital after their work hours. The ER receptionist led them to the evening administrator's office.

There, a nursing staff met them, "Hello, I'm Nancy Feinstein, the ER's evening supervisor. I presume you are Ms. Jenny Spencer and you, sir?"

"I'm Steve Spencer, Jenny's brother."

"How do you do? Please take a seat."

Then she pointed at the jacket that was on the clothes tree next to her desk and said, "Mr. Molton wore this jacket when he was brought to this ER. Do you recognize it?"

"Yes, it is his." Jenny answered.

Ms. Feinstein said, "After Mr. Molton was treated for his scalp and hand lacerations in the ER, he was transferred to our psych unit for observation. Soon afterward, he was transferred out to Silver Lake Psychiatric Hospital in Connecticut. Somehow, our ER staff overlooked the jacket, and later they locked it up as an owner-un-identified item. A few days ago, the ER staff went through their scheduled periodic clearing of the locker and found the jacket. Since the owner did not come forward within a reasonable waiting period, this time they searched its pockets and found a check you wrote to him and a recent gun-purchase receipt that had his name on.

Our hospital did not have any record on his family. So, we called you. We didn't contact him at Silver Lake hospital yet because his mental status is still unstable according to the treating psychiatrist at Silver Lake."

"So you have some questions about the check I wrote, I assume."

"Yes, our hospital administrator wanted to make sure that your check had nothing to do with his gun purchase. The administrator already contacted the gun dealer and confirmed that Mr. Molton paid in full for the gun at the time he purchased it. However, our hospital lawyer asked me to question you whether the check was your partial payment for the gun, which he might have bought for you."

"What a farfetched theory!" Jenny said. "I absolutely had no idea that he ever had bought any firearm."

"However, for the record, would you tell me about your check? The key question here is how he happened to have it in his pocket."

"Well, he often came to my office just to visit with me. We were close friends. A few days before his head injury that brought him here, he asked me to lend him one hundred fifty dollars for his car's gas because that day he did not have his credit cards with him and his gas tank was almost empty. So I wrote him a check for that amount."

"Now I understand it. Lastly, I have to ask you…do you know where he kept his gun?"

"No, I don't. Neither can I guess!"

By then, Ms. Feinstein's computer printed a page of a document, which she handed to Jenny, saying, "Thank you, Ms. Spencer, for your patience. Here, my computer's voice-recognition program transcribed what we have just said. Would you read it over and sign it if it's a correct transcript?"

While Jenny was reading it, Ms. Feinstein said to her, "I will give you a copy of that paper."

"Thank you."

Having finished reading it carefully, Jenny signed it. Then, this time, Ms. Feinstein asked Steve to serve as a witness and sign at the bottom of the paper.

He read the preprinted entry on the witness line and signed it.

Giving the signed paper back to her, Steve asked, "Ms. Feinstein, what will you do with the check? Could Jenny take it back?"

"Yes, first I will make a photocopy of the check with a notation on it. Ms. Spencer, please sign below this notation, which simply states you took the check back."

"Thank you. I will."

After signing the copy, Jenny took the check and then asked, "Ms. Feinstein, what will become of his jacket?"

"Well, our hospital will contact Silver Lake Psychiatric Hospital and will discuss with them about what to do with it. Besides the forensic test results on the jacket's bloodstain is going through the last clearance step by the police. We presume it is his own bloodstain, but the police and hospital's lawyers wanted to make sure it is not someone else's. The whole thing got complicated because of the gun-purchase receipt in his jacket. The police are still searching for Mr. Molton's gun. I don't think they have found it yet."

At that moment, someone knocked at the office door. A good-looking young man wearing a white lab coat walked in to speak to the supervisor. Seeing Steve and Jenny in the room, he said, "Excuse me, folks, I'll take just one quick moment to tell the supervisor something important."

Then he spoke to Ms. Feinstein. "Nancy, the patient on bed number seven needs a blood transfusion this evening, and the blood bank needs your countersignature. Please take care of it as soon as you can. By the way, your phone must be off the hook. I heard only busy signals. So I came in."

As he turned around and hurriedly walked to the door, Ms. Feinstein said, "Yes, Dr. Blau. I'll take care of the signature right away after this. Actually, we are almost done."

Then Ms. Feinstein checked her telephone. She realized that the bottom hem of the jacket on the clothes tree, very near the desk, had pushed the telephone mouthpiece aside off the hook. She moved the jacket up to a hook one notch higher on the clothes tree, clearing the space over the telephone, and repositioned its mouthpiece. Steve and Jenny quietly observed what she did with the telephone.

As the three of them were coming out of the office, Jenny thought the name Dr. Blau was familiar and asked Ms. Feinstein, "Was that Dr. Roy Blau?"

"Yes, do you know him?"

"Not really. On the day when Dr. Molton was treated in the ER, I spoke to Dr. Blau on the phone about the patient. At that time, the doctor said he knew who I was."

"That's interesting. You must be a famous person."

"Not really."

"Maybe he is one of your fans. What is your profession?"

"I work on solar-energy equipments."

"I see. You're an engineer. That's wonderful."

Steve asked, "Has Dr. Blau been working here for a long time?"

"Well, he came to our hospital ER right after he got his board certification in emergency medicine three years ago. He is very kind to his patients. He is really a nice, dependable doctor."

A short while later, as Jenny and Steve walked toward their car, their paths crossed with a doctor in a white gown who was coming toward the hospital building. It was the same doctor they'd seen a short while ago in the supervisor's office.

When he was about to go past them, he said, "Hello."

Steve responded, "Hi, I presume you're Dr. Blau."

Dr. Blau stopped to say to Steve, "Didn't I see you and your wife just a while ago in Ms. Feinstein's office?"

"Yes, you did. But Jenny is not my wife; she is my sister."

Jenny, looking at Dr. Blau, said, "How are you, Doctor? I'm Jenny Spencer."

Roy Blau smiled at her and said, "I'm very glad to have met you in person finally. Since I spoke to you about Dr. Molton last time, I thought of you and your Optical Walls, hoping to meet you someday, and this is it!"

After having a friendly conversation with them, he said, "For me, today has been a good day, as I've met you both. I wish I could talk with you a little more, but I have to return to the ER now. I hope I can visit you someday, Ms. Spencer, at your Luxen Tech office."

"Sure. Please come by and see how my company manufactures the Optical Walls. I'll give you a tour of the Plant. It's nice to have met you, Dr. Blau. Good evening."

"Thank you for your invitation. Good-bye, Ms. and Mr. Spencer."

Jenny was impressed by his jaunty, genuine manners and handsome looks.

Steve said, "He seems to be a nice man."

"I think so, too."

Later, on their way back to Jenny's office, while driving his car, Steve said, "I think it was Sobien Molton's jacket that let you meet Dr. Blau today."

"What are you talking about?…Oh, you mean the phone being off the hook! Is that some kind of good omen?"

"I hope so! We'll see." Then Steve asked, "Did you have any hint that Sobien had a gun?"

"Never! Not a clue."

"When you told me about the gun-purchase receipt in his jacket pocket, I immediately thought of his shoulder bag with the fire-setting device that he left in your office. Bill Warren found out, as I have told you, that sometime before Sobien came to Acmeon to work there, he hired Akandro Oladre to copy Acmeon Lab's Dream Wafer program and then to destroy the original. Sobien Molton is a dangerous character. I'm glad you broke up with him. Well, after all, Kerbera Wilson helped you by coming between you and him."

Jenny became pensive and silent. Steve did not say anything further while they were driving back to her office building.

Only after they sat down back in her office did Jenny ask Steve, "Yesterday you said on the phone that you were going to ask me about something. So, what was it?"

"I was thinking of getting a few more years of schooling and getting a higher degree. It means I may have to reduce my work hours or quit the Perihelion job altogether if needed. My question is how I'm going to manage my time, working and studying and worse yet, how to cope with the high cost of schooling at this stage of my life."

"Are you talking about your tuition?"

"Yes."

"How much?"

"I don't know the exact amount yet. Four days ago, I had the last of three interviews with the postgraduate-program directors at New Century University. So when I get the answer from the university, I'll know the exact amount. I only know the ballpark figure. It is for two years. Will you be able to give me a loan for my tuition? I don't have enough time to go through the student-loan application now."

"I'll be happy to. It's not a big problem for me. After I send some money every month to Mom and Dad, I still have lots of money left over. Sometimes I say to myself, 'What am I going to do with all this cash in the pantry bins and buckets?'…Well, I'm just kidding. But seriously, I can help you with your two-year tuition."

"Thanks a lot, Jenny…Projecting into a few years ahead, I think I'll be able to pay you back the whole loan, within three to four years after my graduation. When I pay you back the loan, I will top it off with interest, which should be a couple of percent above the prevailing student-loan rate then."

"That sounds very reassuring. But if you do very well in your courses, I would rather not charge you any interest."

"Really?"

"Yes, I mean it."

"Wow, I can't thank you enough, Jenny. It sounds like I have no choice but do well in my courses."

"That's a positive outlook all right. By the way, what will happen between you and Helen with all the school plans you both have?"

"You mean our marriage?"

"Yes, when are you going to get married?"

"I did not tell Helen about my school plan yet. I'm going to surprise her by telling her that, God willing, we'll marry soon after we both finish our master's courses. Next Saturday, I'll be visiting Helen at her parents'. I'll tell her and her parents about it then."

"It sounds great. You have synchronized your school plans; and then will get married on top of your new degrees. I envy you."

"But, Jenny, I have this uncanny feeling that you'll be married way before me and Helen."

"How nice and encouraging! I'll take your words and may use them as a mantra in my self-hypnotizing meditation sessions."

"I second it. Make it a more elaborate fantasy—Helen will be in your bridal party, and I'll be one of the groomsmen or the best man at your wedding—all of that before our own wedding!"

"I say amen to it. Thank you, Steve."

"All right, Jenny, you are very welcome."

"Have you told Mom and Dad about your school plan?"

"Yes, I told them on the phone, not too long ago. They were very happy to hear about my plan."

"Did you tell them everything?"

"Of course, besides the school plan, I told them about Helen, my job, how much money I'll be short of, and that I would ask you for a loan on my tuition, et cetera."

"What did they say about Helen?"

"Dad said when he and Mom first met Helen two months ago, they knew she would be the right person for me. Dad said I had a good eye to see people's character. Both Mom and Dad said they liked her a lot and wanted to see her again. Mom also said she wished you and I would come out to New Jersey to see them more often."

"Well, the last time you and I were at Fort Lee home was around Easter. So it was already four months ago. Maybe you and I should go out to Fort Lee one of these days."

CHAPTER 46
MEGA-MEMORY WAFER

Dr. Jupitren was quite surprised by the *Cyber Tribune's* science-section news. It was about a Dream Wafer variant that was recently devised by a Far East Asian scientist, Dr. K and his group.

In search of memory-boosting drugs, prompted by the education frenzy of that country's culture at large, Dr. K and his group had reverse engineered Dr. Jupitren's original Dream Wafer mechanism. They altered the expression of genes that were responsible for the metabolism of memory-related chemicals such as acetylcholinesterase, dopamine, and norepinephrine. And, they named it Mega-Memory Wafer or MMW.

The country's news media had reported a number of high school students who displayed newly acquired photographic memories after they applied MMW. One of the students memorized a two-hundred-page book, cover to cover, after reading it in three days. Another student mastered one semester's social studies reading material in one week.

Their Nationwide TV news aired a featured program on Thai, a fourteen-year-old student among Dr. K's MMW research subjects. It was a replay of the interview that was recorded in a public TV studio. First, the TV show-director announced to the studio-full guests, about one hundred of them, "As you can see, in this transparent jar, I have forty folded cards. Each card bears a number, ranging from one to forty. Now, I will ask forty volunteers to come forward one by one and pick a card from this jar. As you unfold the card, please loudly call out the number you picked, then say your last and first names, birth date, and birth year. Afterward, when I call out a random number from one to forty, Thai will repeat the called out person's information from his memory."

Following the directions, each of the forty volunteers in the TV studio did what he or she was asked to do. While listening to them, Thai asked some of them to spell out their names for him.

Afterward, the TV show-director engaged Thai in other instant memory stunts for several minutes. He then said to Thai, "Now, as I explained it to you earlier, I will call out a random number from one to forty. The studio guest who was assigned to that number will stand up and Thai, you will give us that person's information."

"Well, that shouldn't be hard." Thai said.

The show-director called about twenty random numbers, one at a time. Thai identified everyone correctly by his or her name, birth date and year. The audience went wild with applause.

The show-director said, "It's obvious that I can go on asking the remaining twenty people to stand up to my call of their assigned number and Thai would give us the right answers."

However, one skeptic person asked the show-director, "Excuse me. Can I call out a few more numbers that you did not use yet and see if he can give us correct answers?"

"Sure, we still have good ten more minutes of show time left," the show-director said. "So, please use any number I have not used yet. But do you know which of the numbers ranging between one and forty, I've used or not used so far?"

"Yes, I do."

"You do? Then you, too, must have an extraordinary memory."

"No, no, I don't have that kind of memory. I did not memorize which numbers you called out. I mean, I could not remember all those random numbers even if I tried to. So, as you called out those random numbers, I simply checked them off the list in my note pad." He held up his note pad for everyone to see. "Can I call out from the remaining numbers now?"

"Yes, go ahead. I'm sure Thai is ready at any time."

To every random number that the skeptic called out from his notes, the corresponding persons stood up seriatim and Thai gave out correct answers every time. After calling about seven people and getting the right answers from Thai, the skeptic finally said, "Now I believe Thai is real." Everyone gave roaring applause to Thai and the skeptic person.

The news said that Mega-Memory Wafer manufacturing was extremely expensive and it would take some time before the public would be able to afford it.

One news editorial from Thai's country commented:

"As the MMW becomes affordable for many people, the entire nation's education system will need an overhaul in order to accommodate the massive new breed of genius students with photographic memories."

Since the MMW news broke out, Dr. Jupitren had spent a few very busy weeks. During that time, in addition to his routine work of seeing his clients, he did extensive literature review on the subject of increased memory. He also retrieved and reviewed the records of his own past experiments on memory function. Additionally, he allotted much of his time to communicating with Dr. K.

At Acmeon Lab's monthly professional staff meeting, more than the usual number of staff showed up. Welcoming the new three doctors was the first on the meeting's agenda. After other routine agenda were taken care of, they discussed about MMW.

A young chemist from the Acmeon's clinical lab department stood up to summarize what he learned from the late news media. He ended his remarks by asking a question to Dr. Jupitren. "Do you have any additional technical information or any known facts on MMW?"

Dr. Jupitren answered, "Adding to what you have just summarized nicely, let me share with you certain things I have learned about MMW so far. During the past couple of weeks, I was able to communicate with Dr. K, the innovator of Mega-Memory Wafer.

As I anticipated, he informed me that his group altered the genes that metabolize chemicals involved in memory function. They used very similar methods as those, with which we make the Dream Wafers. The main difference was that they used lot more of the new advanced technique to process DNA than we did. Therefore, they succeeded in much shorter time in inventing the MMW.

Since I dealt with the memory-related chemicals in my past experiments about ten years ago, I retrieved my project notes from that time. The outcome of one of my experiments pointed to an abnormally enhanced memory, hypermnesia, among some of the experimental subjects.

At that time, early in the experiment, I found that the unexpected hypermnesia was due to my experiment's design error rather than my original intention. The error was found in the subjects, whose memory-related genes' expression was *jacked up* above the normal limits. The abnormally increased memory function was not what I wanted to create. So, I immediately excluded those subjects from the experiment, and I followed them up separately for a year until their brain functions returned to normal.

With the unexpected findings, I consulted a then prominent Canadian geneticist. He informed me that he had similar results as mine, and yet he went one-step further with his experimental subjects by keeping them on the heightened level of memory. This, he said, was a big mistake on his part, because a few of them later developed a form of progeria, which is premature aging and shortened life span. The same geneticist later found that the jacked-up expression of memory genes precipitated mutation in the longevity genes, which caused progeria with marked drop in growth-hormone levels.

I believe that Dr. K's group duplicated a similar method in manufacturing MMW without being aware of MMW's serious effects on other genes. Subsequently, I e-mailed all the alarming facts to Dr. K's group. He replied right away, thanking me for the warning. He said he would stop the MMW experiment immediately."

Dr. Anderson asked, "According to the Canadian geneticist, how soon did the persons with increased memory develop longevity-gene mutation?"

"The mutation was observed after 10 to 12 months of being on the heightened level of memory. It was not observed among those who were maintained on the hypermnesia for 6 to 9 months."

Dr. Burbridge asked, "If the photographic memory was due to involved genes' excessive expression, can we make it less excessive and apply the weaker version of Mega-Memory Wafers to individuals with other conditions, such as learning disorders?"

"That is an excellent question." Dr. Jupitren answered. "I think it would be possible someday. Once we learn the specific methodology that Dr. K's group adopted to create their MMW, we will know in which direction our next research should go. Furthermore, with Dr. K's agreement, we might consider a joint research to discover such milder version of safe Mega-Memory Wafers."

At that point, Dr. Chanteur, the neurologist commented, "Apropos of Dr. Burbridge's question, in addition to learning disorders, I think, theoretically a milder version of MMW could be used someday to treat other conditions, such as convalescent phase of brain trauma and certain cognitive developmental disorders.

Moreover, its other possible indication would be for treatment of mild to moderate dementia. Of course, it will be an addition to the existing anti-dementia medicines rather than replacing them."

"Excellent points, Dr. Chanteur."

Then Dr. Jupitren said, "Regardless the choice of a mild versus strong version of it, MMW is forcing the brain to work at a very active pace even during the person's sleep. However, the human brain needs rest. If not rested, it may lead to an organic brain syndrome or a psychotic state. We need extra-caution when it comes to altering memory function. All those ideas are calling us for tons of research work, of course."

Then another staff asked, "Were there any Acmeon's Dream Wafer clients who showed the progeria signs or the biomarkers of altered longevity genes?"

Dr. Jupitren answered, "So far, there were none. I believe it is because when our clients made their requests on the multi-item questionnaire, the requested intensity on each item was rigorously tempered down by our Dream Wafer program and was kept below the upper normal limits. As a result, we were able to keep the Dream Wafer safe, whereas in the case of the Mega-Memory Wafer, Dr. K's group exceeded the upper limits by their intended teleological design."

CHAPTER 47
JENNY'S QUESTIONS ON DREAM WAFERS

As Jenny hoped, her Dream Wafers let her sun bask at the Mediterranean beaches. The bright sunlight she saw in her dreams lingered on pleasantly after she woke up. Strangely she felt her dejected feelings melting away within a week of the Wafer application.

When she saw Dr. Jupitren for her next batch of Dream Wafers, she reported the positive effect of her Wafers and asked some questions. "Lately, I have been dreaming that I was at the Amalfi Coast in Italy and at the beach in Nice, France, basking in the Mediterranean sunlight. I'm having very good mornings. I understand that the sunlight promotes certain neurotransmitters, which in turn would maintain our mood. Likewise, insufficient sunlight would induce less of those neurotransmitters, and this might precipitate even depression. Am I right about it?"

"Yes, you are."

"Then, I have a question. Could the Mediterranean sunlight in my dreams help my mood in the similar way as the real sunlight would?"

"That's a very interesting question. In fact, no one ever questioned me about that yet. The bright sunlight that you see in your dreams cannot have the same kind of mood-lifting effect as the real sunlight would."

"Thank you. I expected it to be so. It's obvious that the solar energy is the real thing. Granted, is there any harm in exposing ourselves to too much sunlight during the daytime while being on the Dream Wafer at night?"

"I don't think so. But, too much sunlight has been blamed for higher incidence of skin cancer, while appropriate amounts of ultraviolet light B has been credited for vitamin D synthesis in our skin."

"According to some researchers, *arctic hysteria* or *mania* and *imitative hysteria* were reported in arctic areas, and they might be causatively related to unusual arctic light patterns, mostly too much of it. In contrast, some Finnish people, having less sunlight, would suffer often from depression due to decreased neurotransmitter formation. In temperate zones, I don't know of any reported mania cases due to too much sunlight."

"Thank you, Dr. Jupitren for taking extra time to explain it to me." Jenny left Acmeon Lab with her renewed Dream Wafers.

On her way to her office, Jenny thought that her Optical Walls, because of their link with light energy, might have some effects on the emotional state of Optical Wall users. She thought of doing her own reference search about light-related neurotransmitters and hormones. To read up on the subject, she stopped at the Library of Modern Science.

While searching for optics and light-energy-related literature there, she came across hundreds of authors under the index subjects. One of the authors happened to be Roy Blau, MD, PhD and his article's title was "Diagnostic Use of Optical Illusion to Measure Degree of Binocular Visual Maturation." She glanced through the article. She was glad and felt as if she was with him face-to-face and muttered to herself, "Is my glad feeling a kind of illusion?"

A few days later, in her office, Jenny checked messages on her desktop device. To her happy surprise, one of them was Dr. Roy Blau's voice message:

"Hi, this is Roy Blau from Northwest Hospital ER. I was very happy to have met you and your brother the other day. I would like to visit you someday at your Luxen Tech Company office and get a chance to learn about your Optical Walls as well.

Please let me know when I could visit you. Would you give me a call at 516-789-0123 or e-mail me to royblau@penmail.com? I will be looking forward to hearing from you soon. Take care. Good-bye."

The other message was from her local air-scooter dealership:

"Hi, Ms. Spencer, this is New England Air-scooter Sales Manager Tom Hogan. Not too long ago, you asked if we had new air-scooter models that had extra safety features with suspension balloon capability and automated anti-collision mechanism against other drones. We now have three such models, and I'll be more than happy to show them to you at your convenience. I hope to see you in the near future at our M Street dealership. Thank you."

She replied to Dr. Blau via an e-mail:

Dear Dr. Blau,
I am glad that you have called me. If you have a free afternoon on any weekday, please give me a call an hour in advance before you would come over. I will be able to meet you in my office first. Then, we will go to the Optical Wall-manufacturing site, which is only a mile away from my office. I will be happy to give you a tour through the site. Jenny Spencer

Then she thought of trading her air-scooter for a new model that had extra safety features and could suspend itself in midair with helium balloons for emergencies.

CHAPTER 48
STEVE'S VISIT AT HELEN'S

Around noontime Saturday, Steve parked his car in front of Helen's home. He saw rows of coral carpet roses near the brick house walls. In the middle of the grass covered front yard, there stood a pair of red crepe myrtle trees in their full bloom. Near the mailbox, bright pink dianthus and a multitude of candy-stripe cosmos drew Steve's attention. The entire floral front made Helen's home look beautiful. Just looking at the outside of the house, he felt welcomed.

As he walked on the path halfway toward the house, someone inside the house opened the door. It was Helen. She waved at him.

Holding the bouquet of roses in his hand, Steve waved back at her. As he entered the house, Helen kissed him on his cheeks.

"How beautiful your home is!"

"Thank you, Please come in."

Steve handed the rose bouquet to her.

Sniffing the roses with deep breaths, Helen said, "Welcome! You're bringing a special fragrance to our home, just like these roses. I love them. Thank you."

Mrs. Humayor just came out of her kitchen to the front door welcoming Steve.

"Thank you for inviting me, Mrs. Humayor."

"You're quite welcome. Please come in and make yourself at home."

Soon after Steve came in and sat down, Helen's father walked in from outside, still holding his car key, and went over to Steve, who got up from his seat to greet him.

They shook hands.

"Hello, Mr. Humayor, I'm Steve Spencer. How do you do, sir?"

"Hi. Nice to meet you, Mr. Spencer."

"Please call me Steve. Thank you for inviting me."

"You're welcome. Lately, we have been talking about you very often. I'm glad to see you in person at last."

"I'm glad to see you all in your home."

"Please sit down and make yourself comfortable."

"Thank you."

Steve sat down and looked around the living room. There were many books on the bookshelves and on the floor as well, which made the room look like a library.

Seeing what Steve was looking at, Mr. Humayor said, "You probably wander why our living room has so many books. We are renovating our study room to install new computers and a better lighting system. Sorry, we couldn't finish the project before your visit here today. Pardon the living room's look."

"Oh, it looks all right to me. Those books seem to be mostly on American history."

"Yes, you're right. I refer to them frequently for the history class I'm teaching at Adelphi University. Lately, I am going over the American-Mexican War history. At this morning's class, I reviewed the reasons of Texas and New Mexico's different ranks of entry as a state to the Union. I enjoy my work, especially interacting with many young folks at the university. How about you, Steve? Enjoying your work?"

"Yes, most of the time. But there are certain times when I cannot say I'm enjoying my work. That's when I don't have enough time for an important project and yet have to complete it by rushing."

"It's a rather familiar situation for many of us. But when I'm confronted by similar situations, I often think of the odd but true maxim, '*When in a hurry, take a detour rather than a shortcut.*'"

"How true it is, Mr. Humayor. Lately, in my kind of work, taking shortcuts ended in unexpected delays. I'm beginning to see the meaning of the maxim."

Helen joined in the middle of their conversation and said, "Dad, are you giving Steve a history lecture?"

"No, hardly. We are just sharing some facts of life."

"I see. Dad, shall I bring in the new computers and lighting fixture boxes from your car trunk? We'll be having lunch soon."

"Yes, thanks. But, Helen, the stuff might be too heavy for you. I'll bring them in later."

Steve got up and said, "I'll go to the car with Helen."

"Thank you, Steve. Then, I'll go in and get changed to be on time for lunch."

Soon Steve and Helen came back with the items and placed them in the study. "Thanks, Steve." Helen said. "Please relax for a few minutes."

Sitting by himself on the sofa, Steve looked around the interior of the house. He felt some artists' hands must have touched its every nook and corner, as they were as neat and beautiful as outside.

After a short while, as Mrs. Humayor came to the living room, Steve said, "Mrs. Humayor, once you said you would show me your art room."

"Yes, I could let you peek at it now. Helen is in the kitchen fixing something to drink. Come along with me."

As an extension of the living room, just five steps up on the split-level, there was a door with ornate glasswork that opened to the sunny atelier. The room was about fifteen by fifteen feet. It had two easels near the windows and two high chairs with wicker seats and backrests. On the wall shelves, Steve saw oil-paint bottles of different colors, paint thinners, palettes, paintbrushes, and Conté crayons, et cetera. In one of the floor corners, there were open toolboxes with a canvas trimmer, framing vises and small circular saws, and more.

Through a bay window in the northwest wall of the room, Steve could see the distant, hazy terrain of Connecticut beyond the gray-blue horizon of Long Island Sound. The Connecticut shoreline was veiled behind shimmering heat that was rising from the calm summer ocean. From an acoustic wall unit, Mozart's "Turkish March" piano piece was flowing out blithely.

There were some finished and half-finished oil paintings. An oil portrait of a beautiful young woman was among several paintings on the wall. Steve asked Mrs. Humayor, "Is that portrait of you or Helen? I cannot tell."

"That's my Mom's."

"You mean Helen's grandmother?"

"Yes, it was painted when she was in her twenties."

"Ah, three beautiful women over three generations! All three of you look so much alike and radiate glowing beauty…"

"Thank you for your compliment."

Steve took a close look at the room's setup and said, "This room is sunny and cozy. A real handsome workshop!"

"Thank you. Helen and I come up here quite often, painting and listening to music."

"You must be enjoying lots of calm and relaxing time in this room."

Mrs. Humayor, with unexaggerated pride, explained about several finished painting items in the room. Some of them were Helen's work, and the rest were Mrs. Humayor's, but to Steve, they were indistinguishable and all seemed beautiful artwork. Steve felt her modest manner was just like that of Helen.

Helen had just come in with three glasses of lemonade on a tray.

Mrs. Humayor said, "Oh, I have to be back at the kitchen because I left the onion soup on the stove. I'll see you at the dining room shortly. Excuse me, Steve." She took one lemonade glass with her and headed back to the kitchen. Sipping the lemonade, Helen told Steve when and how she started receiving her painting lessons. Mrs. Humayor was her first art teacher followed by several other teachers since she was eleven. Answering Steve's questions, Helen explained about many different drawing media, steps of the drawing lessons she took for the use those media; and about base materials such as canvas, paper, fabric, synthetic boards, variety of walls, and so on. She pointed at the specific objects in the home art room as she talked about them.

They were about to come out of the atelier, when Steve saw an almost-finished charcoal-drawn portrait, about 1x1.5 feet in size that was leaning against a table in the corner. He stopped and looked at it. Surprisingly, it was a portrait of him. In it, he posed in front of a computer in an office setting.

"Did you work on this portrait?"

"Yes. It still needs a little more touch up. How do you like it?"

"It is awesome. An excellent drawing!"

"When it's finished, I'll give it to you."

Suddenly Steve felt special gratitude and closeness to her but could not find the right words to describe his feelings. Instead, he gave her a big hug with surprise kisses, and said, "I'm very touched. Thank you very much, Helen. I love you!"

Soon, they came to the dining room.

During a sumptuous lunch, Steve had a nice, long chat with Helen's parents, who, contrary to his expectation, brought up no issue about his family's religion. Steve found them to be down-to-earth, very caring, intelligent people with modesty that he repeatedly saw in Helen likewise. It was a very heartening experience for Steve to talk with the three of them.

Back in the living room, Mr. Humayor asked Helen to let Steve hear about the *Uncle Julian's advice list.* And, he said, "If you don't mind, Helen, I want to listen to you read Jules's advice list again."

"Of course, Dad, I don't mind. Please stay with us here."

Helen's mother, too, came in and joined them.

Helen read the list aloud. When she finished reading it, Steve asked, "The other day you said somehow I was in that list. But, I didn't hear any of that. The list sounds more like basic principles of good business management. So, did I miss anything?"

Helen answered. "Before Uncle Jules gave me this list, he said that he hoped someday, not just I but also the man I would be married to, could be in charge of managing Acmeon Lab's operation. Uncle Jules said by then he would be retiring."

"I see!" Steve responded. "It sounds like a plan with a good omen. I will take the *'decree'* very seriously."

There was a brief, thought-laden silence in the room. Ending the stillness, Steve said, "Not too long ago, I told you, Helen, that I might be taking postgraduate courses similar to yours."

"I remember that. I thought you were kidding."

"Well, I was quite serious. I've also told my parents and my sister Jenny about my plan that I would take two-year courses toward a degree."

Helen showed happy surprise. "You did?"

"Yes, but I may have to work only on a half-time basis or even less if necessary so that I can concentrate on my course work for the two-year study period. I asked Jenny to give me a loan for my two-year tuition. She yessed it, and not wanting to see me get cold feet on it, Jenny gave me the tuition loan right away. Besides, she said she would not charge any interest if I do well in my study."

"That's wonderful!" Helen interjected.

Steve continued. "Very soon, I'll be speaking to my company's president, Mr. Goettenberg about my school plan. I'll ask him to let me work on a half-time schedule. I hope he will approve of my request even though he wants me to work full time and oversee the new contract work that is about to begin.

Helen, my wish is, we finish our two-year courses first and then get married with the blessings of your parents as well as of my parents!"

Saying so, Steve turned to Mr. and Mrs. Humayor and courteously said, "Would you allow me to ask for Helen's hand in marriage and bless us?"

Mr. Humayor thoughtfully said, "Steve, knowing you and Helen love each other, Elva and I are very happy for both of you. Our approval to your request was there even before you came to our home today. And, your school plan makes me feel very good since Helen will be tied up with her course work at the same time as yours."

In a happy tone, Mr. Humayor said to his wife, "Elva, do you want to add anything else?"

"Well, you said everything I would have said."

Helen and Steve thanked for their wholehearted approval. Helen said she was very happy for their trust in her and Steve. With a happy countenance, Mr. Humayor rose from his seat and went over to the love seat, where Helen and Steve were sitting. Mr. Humayor extended his hand for a handshake with Steve, who politely stood up to respond to him.

Shaking hands with Steve, Mr. Humayor said, "Congratulations! Your plans resonate like music out of two well-tuned musical instruments. I'm very happy for both of you."

"Thank you, sir."

Mrs. Humayor said, "May God bless you!"

"Thank you, Mom and Dad!"

On the following Monday, Steve spoke to his company's president, Mr. Goettenberg about his need to change his work schedule to half time, starting in mid-September.

Mr. Goettenberg was rather disappointed as he was counting on Steve's full-time commitment for the new fed contracts. He tried to have Steve change his mind, even offering a double bonus. However, he realized Steve's resolve was quite firm. Eventually, Mr. Goettenberg agreed to have him on a half-time basis. Then he said, "Steve, I wish you succeed in getting your degree as fast as possible."

Thanking Mr. Goettenberg, Steve mentioned that he would try to incur minimum disturbance to his unit's operation despite his schedule change. To that end, he would recommend an able worker from the company's existing pool of engineers. Then, with the president's approval, he would show the engineer how to manage the new assignments so that the two of them would seamlessly maintain the expected productivity.

Mr. Goettenberg was pleased to hear Steve's suggestion and his concern for the company.

CHAPTER 49
ACMEON LAB THREATENED AGAIN

At the criminal court hearing, Sobien Molton's lawyer made a special plea based on his bipolar disorder history. The resultant court decision spared him from going to the prison. Instead, he was transferred to the state hospital's forensic program for a long-term treatment. Tick was arrested for abetting Sobien Molton's criminal schemes on numerous accounts. Akandro was sent to prison for involuntary manslaughter. Nevertheless, Acmeon Lab was not quite safe from further attacks.

Often hogging the public phone in his prison unit's common area, Akandro made frequent phone contacts with Tack who was still at large. Akandro admitted to Tack that he was locked up in the prison and could not give him any more money. Akandro said if Tack wanted to get some money, he should do jobs for Sobien Molton instead. Akandro gave him Molton's telephone number.

Tack made immediate phone contacts with Sobien Molton, who hired him to pick up the unfinished business—to get the Dream Wafer program! Sobien tried to rationalize that he had to do it because of Ajnin's threat. All along, Bill traced and tapped their conversations, which were filled with illegal, violent ruse against Acmeon Lab.

Dr. Jupitren asked Bill, "How is Molton going to pay Tack to do the evil job?"

"My industrial espionage unit found the source of the money. Sobien Molton finagles large sums of money from this woman Kerbera Wilson, who is in blind wooing with him. Molton then doles it out to Tack. However, Kerbera doesn't seem to care to know what Molton is doing with the money she has been giving him."

Dr. Jupitren sighed, saying, "I wish Sobien Molton was better by now with the treatment he has received at the hospitals. It's taking too long."

"What's wrong with him?" Bill asked.

"I'm afraid he is still unstable in his mood and is psychotic in his thinking. Usually, people call his condition a bipolar disorder, but there are different subtypes of it, and they should be treated accordingly. I think Sobien is bent on vengeance, all prompted by his persecutory delusions that he is being wronged by others. To make it more complicated, such persecutory delusions are mixed with grandiose ideas that he will solve all human anxiety with his invention. He believes he can usurp the Dream Wafer templates for his invention. He must hate me because I'm in his way. Often, a bipolar person's grandiose ideas manifest in daring, rule-breaking behaviors. That's why both bipolar disorder and sociopathy, are often seen in the same person."

"I see. The diagnosis alone doesn't tell what's underneath. Jules, there is another thing I have to mention. When you're on the phone with Steve, John or me, please don't go into any specifics about Acmeon's security matters, because I'm afraid your calls will be wiretapped by the crooks. On my part, I'll increase police surveillance with my men over Acmeon."

"Thank you, I'll be careful with my phone calls."

"Making an exception to the prison ward's rule, we let Tick speak freely on his cell phone with Tack. According to our wiretapping on their conversation, Tack is armed with an LXG stun gun and a CR device. Besides, he carries a Ruger P89, a semiautomatic handgun. He has no permit for any of them."

"Any plan to catch Tack?"

"Yeah, we have a pretty good one. It's a matter of days before we clip his next move and arrest him. Out of the four, Tack is the last one who needs to be locked up."

However, neither Bill nor Dr. Jupitren was aware of Ajnin Hsilomed's dark grip on Sobien. Even the hospital doctors did not know why Sobien's hospital course showed unexplainable ups and downs. They assumed it was his bipolar phases showing the so-called rapid cycling. Only Sobien himself painfully knew why. All along, Ajnin made his demands to Sobien usually during the visiting hours but not much through phone calls, and their conversations eluded Bill's wiretapping surveillance so far.

Sobien fell into anxious, depressed state every time Ajnin visited him. Sobien very much wished he could get out of the quagmire he was in with Ajnin. However, Sobien regretfully realized that he could not back out of the devilish deal he'd made with Ajnin.

With the hospital treatment team's effort, Sobien at times made some improvement in his mood, which eventually let him reclaim mood-congruent clear thinking. This new level of thinking made him regret more intensely about his entanglement with Ajnin, and he would ponder how he could get out of it. However, his improvement lasted only for a short while. Then his recurrent unstable mood would reclaim him, making his judgment falter all over again.

During one such dreaded visit, Ajnin threatened Sobien again. "If you mess it up and the cops find out what you are doing, the scrubbing agents will remove you before you snitch on my government. You know too damn much about what my country is doing!"

Realizing he went too far with Ajnin's pack, Sobien felt he had no choice but go on as coerced by them. Just to appease Ajnin and his mounting threats, Sobien told Ajnin that although he was locked up in the hospital, he would send his computer-savvy lackeys to get Acmeon Lab's main program copy.

Ironically, at nighttime, Sobien felt relatively safe from Ajnin's physical threat, since he was in the security-tight state hospital's locked ward. However, to ward off Ajnin's periodic daytime threats, he thought of asking the hospital authorities to discontinue Ajnin's visitation.

Yet, Sobien was afraid Ajnin would become more violent if his visitation was cancelled. Sobien could not ask his psychiatrist, Dr. Santiago to cancel Ajnin's visits. Sobien had dreamt that he had an inescapable tight leash around his neck, hauled by a vicious behemoth that had Ajnin's face.

Dr. Jupitren told Steve in person everything he'd heard from Bill about Sobien Molton and Tack. He told Steve about Bill's request not to talk about anything regarding Acmeon's security during any telephone conversation.

To safeguard the Dream Wafer software and instrument in the Acmeon Plant, Dr. Jupitren asked Steve to create exact copies of all Dream Wafer programs, and make photographic catalogs on the Plant's essential hardwares with detailed technical specifications. Steve estimated that to complete the project, it would take him a little over one week of his evening hours.

Once again, Steve had to carry his LXG stun gun and CR device on him whenever he came to Acmeon. He didn't feel safe while working alone at Acmeon Lab late in the evenings, although he knew Bill's surveillance team was backing him up.

Steve urged Helen that even during the daytime, she should carry her LXG and CR on her person all the time, although he loathed the very idea. Helen felt she might need to use it someday.

One whole week went by without any new incident at Acmeon Lab.

Sobien Molton, still in the hospital, asked Kerbera Wilson for a sum of money again.

In the hospital courtyard, Sobien Molton first made sure that no one was within earshot. Then, desperate Molton snarled loudly at Tack. Hearing Molton's deafening demands on the phone, even the cold-blooded Tack felt Molton sounded fiendish. Tack could not figure out where Molton's such brutal desperation was coming from.

On his cell phone, Molton yelled at Tack. "This time you must get the copy of Acmeon's Dream Wafer program no matter what! After that, you should destroy the original software and the hardwares. You do whatever you've got to do to get it done. If you have to use your Ruger, you use it! I don't care. Do you hear me?"

Clever as they might have been, Tack and Sobien Molton had no idea that their daily scheming parleys had been wiretapped by Bill Warren's team for weeks.

John Collins said to Bill, "I suspect this Tack will start prowling around Acmeon Lab sooner or later, and will try to find any crack in Acmeon's security. Before Tack ventures himself into Acmeon's premises, most likely he will wiretap Dr. Jupitren's conversations. Don't you think so?"

"Yes, I do, too," Bill thoughtfully answered John. "In fact, this morning, while you were away on your assignment at the Supreme Court in Mineola, Louis on your espionage team told me that he'd picked up the first few signs that Tack wiretapped Dr. Jupitren's office conversations already."

John said, "Then, I have an idea. We will ask Dr. Jupitren and Steve to have telephone conversations and leak out some made-up messages, which Tack will wiretap. The message will let him believe that Acmeon security is not tight. Then, most likely he will start his move. Once we detect his next plan of action, we will zero in and arrest him, most likely somewhere in Acmeon premises."

"That's a pretty good idea." Bill said. "First I have to discuss it with Jules and Steve. Come to think of it, we're fortunate to have this *Omni-Wave Tapper*. As you know, with it we can tap anyone without being detected, and they cannot tap us unless we purposefully let them. Therefore, we can safely monitor the whole show. We will suggest our idea to Jules."

Next day evening, Bill went to the Acmeon Lab in person to explain his plan to Dr. Jupitren and Steve. They liked the idea.

A few days later in the evening, a fabricated message, a trap for Tack, went off from Steve, who was working in Dr. Jupitren's office. Steve called Dr. Jupitren at his home. "Hi, Dr. Jupitren, this is Steve. Finally, I've completed copying the entire Dream Wafer program as of today. In addition, the technical cataloging with photographs and drawings of the main hardware in the Plant was completed also. Knowing that these are very important documents, I don't want to leave them on your desk. Where shall I place the Dream Wafer program copies and the Plant's equipment documents?"

"Why don't you put them in the walk-in safe in my office?"

"I see you have two of them here in your office. Which safe should I put them in?"

"The bigger one with a gray door next to my desk. It's quite tall. Can you see it?"

"Yes, I can."

"As you eyeball it, it's seven feet tall and seven feet wide. The interior is twelve feet deep to the back wall. Once you walk inside, you'll see some chemical bottles on the wall shelves. They need to be kept at a certain cool temperature. So, it's a little chilly in there. At any rate, you can put the copies and documents in that safe. You will see a green box against the back wall all the way inside the safe. Please leave the program copies and photo-catalog papers on top of the box. From now on, I will keep them there, since it's the safest place in Acmeon."

"I understand you clearly. But, don't I need a code to get inside the safe?"

"Oh, yes. There is something I have to tell you about the code. I'll give you one code number now but it is good only for once. Next time, if you want to open the safe again, from outside or from inside, you need a new code number. As you face the safe, in its right upper part, there is an LCD panel showing a four-digit number. But, that is not the code itself. Can you see it?"

"Yes, I see the four-digit number. Do you want me to read it to you now?"

"Yes. To calculate the code itself, I'll need those four digits. What are they?"

"They are 7395."

"Good. To come up with the new code, I start with this 4-digit number and have to follow a mathematical formula. About the formula itself, I'll have to explain it to you later in person, because it's complex. For now, let me calculate the code. I have to use a calculator. Please give me a moment."

"Certainly."

After a short while, Dr. Jupitren said, "Here, I have it. The new code number is 2-22-1732, which happens to be George Washington's birthday, just in case you misplace it. But as I've told you already, this code is good only for once. The code is always a seven-digit number. Of course the 4-digit LCD number also changes each time."

"I've got it. Since I'm all done with what you asked me to do, I will not be in Acmeon starting tomorrow. Today is my last day here for the project. I'll place all the copies that I have made in the larger safe, on top of the green box, which is all the way inside, as you said."

"Well done, Steve. Thank you very much again. I'll speak to you next week in person about compensating you for the work."

All that time, Bill monitored their conversation with *Omni-Wave Tapper*. He went over to Acmeon Lab and spoke to Steve, who was still there by himself, waiting for Bill.

Bill said, "Our *Omni-Wave Tapper* detected that Tack wiretapped your entire telephone conversation with Jules. But Tack doesn't know that we detected his tapping."

"Great, we are on the right track."

From that day on, the *Omni-Wave Tapper* indicated that every call Dr. Jupitren received or sent out was wiretapped by Tack. Dr. Jupitren thought that at an appropriate time in the near future, he should contact the State Hospital administrators, requesting stricter limitation on Sobien's privileges and more individual counseling in view of his continued criminal behavior.

To give Tack another false information, this time Bill made a telephone call to Dr. Jupitren. "Hi, Jules, for the next three or four days, most of my squads have to cover an army-helicopter-manufacturing installation in upstate New York. They have been warned about some terrorist scare, and our team was recruited to do stakeout shifts there. So, you will not see much of us as we will be sixty miles away. I will let you know as soon as we come back to Long Island Precinct. As I said, most of my squads will be gone for three or four days. Only a skeleton crew will remain here, taking care of routine business during that period."

Bill confirmed that his false message to Dr. Jupitren was wiretapped by Tack.

On the same day, Bill wiretapped the conversation between Tack and Molton as well.

Tack said to Molton, "Don't worry. This time for sure, I'm going to get the Wafer program copies and the Acmeon Plant-equipment description in a couple of days. But, I may not have chance to destroy the Plant's hardwares."

Molton said to Tack loudly, "Don't bother with the hardware stuff. Concentrate on the Wafer's software. When you bring me the Wafer program, I'll pay you well."

Dr. Jupitren told Helen about what Bill, Steve, and he had been doing for several days. "Helen, as you heard, the stage is set for Tack and his gang to play out their blunder. I anticipate that on any day, Tack will try to break in. So, you should leave your office by the time everyone else leaves. For a while, especially for next four days, don't stay in the building by yourself in the late afternoon."

"I understand."

Then Dr. Jupitren said to Helen hesitantly, "Helen, wouldn't you feel safe if you carried your LXG and CR device with you for a while?"

"Yes, I would."

"Good. Please keep them on your person all the time. There is just one more thing I should let you know. Bill has set up for us this emergency-signal system, which is wirelessly connected to Bill's precinct through our Thumputers. We will use it just in case anyone breaks in here. In three minutes, we will give it a practice run. I have told Bill that we will send him your practice signal at two o'clock sharp this afternoon. I have done my practice run already this morning. To send the distress signal, you just push the red button on your Thumputer three times quickly. If it goes well, your Thumputer will vibrate for two seconds. It means Bill received your signal all right and his GPS registered your location."

CHAPTER 50
HELEN WITH LXG

For a whole week, before Steve and Bill sent out their false messages to Dr. Jupitren, Tack drove in the city's North Mall parking lot several times just to check on the Acmeon Lab employees' parking pattern. He found all of them left Acmeon Lab by 5:30 pm, except Helen and the doctor who often left the building around 6:15 pm or even later. So, Acmeon's parking lot was quite empty by 5:30 pm. However, the adjacent North Mall's main parking lot had a good number of cars that belonged to the shoppers at the mall. Tack also noticed that the Acmeon's outdoor CR for the CCTV camera, unlike the portable CRs, was powered by regular AC line, not by batteries.

Having wiretapped all of Dr. Jupitren's recent telephone conversations, Tack decided to take advantage of Acmeon Lab's vulnerable situation. Tack thought that all he needed to do was just grab the Dream Wafer program copies and the Plant documents from the bigger safe. There was no need for him to hack or sneak in to make the copies by himself. He thought his chances couldn't be any better.

However, there was one crucial thing that Tack did not have yet— The seven-digit code to open the safe. The George Washington's birthday number that he wiretapped a few days ago would be no good by now.

Assuming that only Dr. Jupitren or Helen must know the secret-code formula, Tack had a wicked plan. He hoisted his LXG stun gun, CR, and Ruger P89 handgun on his waist holster.

With two hired gunmen, he went to Acmeon Lab at 5:15 pm. They parked their getaway car in front of the chocolate store in the North Mall parking lot, close to the Acmeon Lab buildings. By parking there at that hour, they could hide among other cars.

Sitting inside the car, Tack watched Acmeon employees leave for the day. He saw Dr. Jupitren and Helen also leaving by their cars. It was not what he had anticipated. He thought Helen would leave much later than everyone else would. He got very annoyed.

For a moment, Tack thought of breaking in Dr. Jupitren's office anyway, but then he was unsure about how he would open the locked heavy safe door. Finally, he decided to try the break-in at another time when either Dr. Jupitren or Helen would remain in the office, since they were the only ones who seemed to know the code formula.

Tack and his two accomplices were about to drive out of the area when, unexpectedly Helen's car returned to Acmeon parking lot.

Earlier, when Helen hurried out of her office with Dr. Jupitren, she'd forgotten to take with her the final version of her term paper that was due the following morning. She needed to fetch the paper. Helen got out of her car and quickly went inside the building.

Tack thought he was lucky for a change.

Tack first sent out one of his two gunmen. Tack told him to make sure Helen was still in her office. The gunman appeared lanky and quick. Soon, the gunman radioed back to Tack from inside the building. "Yes, she is by herself, talking to someone on the phone in her third-floor office."

Tack confirmed that there was no sign of police in the surrounding area. Then he came out of his car and walked briskly toward the building, dragging his left foot. Another man remained in the car, engine running. With his stun gun, Tack cut the AC power line, disabling CCTV camera and its CR over the Acmeon entrance.

Inside the building, Tack took quick, stealthy steps to the third floor and met with his sentry, the lanky man. The entire third floor was empty, except Helen's office. The two of them tiptoed to her office door and pressed their ears on it, trying to hear the sounds from inside.

They heard she was still talking to someone on the phone. Not knowing how long she would be on the phone, Tack decided to barge in, but her office door was locked from inside.

Hearing the fumbling noise from the door, Helen loudly shouted, "Who's out there?" Then she heard repeated sharp knocking at the door. Every knock gave her a horrible, hair-raising jolt.

Helen shouted again, "Who is it?"

A man's deep voice demanded, with harsh knocking at the door, "Open it!"

"Who are you?"

Helen's nervous hand reached into her bag for her LXG, which lately she carried with her all the time, since both Steve and Dr. Jupitren urged her to.

Steve, at the other end of the phone, said in an alarmed voice, "Whoever it is, Helen, don't open the door. I'll call Bill right now."

Helen rapidly whispered, "I don't like this!" and let go of the telephone, pulling her LXG out of her bag, activating it at the same time.

At that point, the intruder disabled the door lock with his LXG, causing metallic sizzling noise.

Helen with her Thumputer, sent the three emergency signals to Bill, but the intruders were already inside her office. As the two men with their hand-held weapons briskly walked toward her, she managed to hide her LXG quickly in her pants pocket and stood up behind her desk. She decided not to use her LXG, feeling the odds for her to withstand the two-armed men were poor.

Right away, they overpowered her and tied her wrists with a rope behind her back. It all happened in a flash. She felt her pounding heartbeats in her throat, paling her face.

They forced her to walk ahead of them to Dr. Jupitren's office. There, she had to tell them the office door's lock code. Once inside the office, Tack spotted the gray safe, which was bigger than the other one.

As if checking how solid the safe door was, Tack raised his handgun and, without any warning, shot at the middle of the safe door, making Helen stunned and frightened. He demanded in a menacing tone, "What's the safe door's code number?"

Helen's ears were still numb from the deafening noise of the gunshot and the ricocheting bullet off the heavy safe door. Fear stricken and tremulous, she hesitated.

Tack brought the smoldering gun tip close to her cheek and growled through clenched teeth, "Wanna lose your pretty face or the thing in the safe? What's the code?"

Cringing from the gun tip that was still hot, Helen felt her neck stiffening. She tremulously pleaded, "I have to use a calculator to figure out the new code. Because after the safe door is closed, next time it needs a new code."

With her chin, she pointed at a calculator on top of the nearby desk and said, "I need to use that calculator. Will you free my hands?"

Knowing what Helen said about the code was true, Tack ordered his accomplice to untie her wrists. First, she needed to get the four-digit number from the LCD panel on the safe's door and she tried to get closer to the panel. Before she took her second step, Tack shouted, "Stop right there! I'll read it." Obviously he knew what Helen was going to do. He loudly read the four-digit number while pointing his gun at her.

With freed hands, Helen jotted down the four digits and started calculating the code. Tack glared at each of her movements, keeping his handgun pointed at her.

After a long, nervous repeated figuring with the calculator, she said, "You can try one of these two numbers." She held out two numbers on a piece of paper.

"You open it!" Tack yelled at her.

Her hands still trembling, she tried one of the two numbers. It did not work.

"Don't you pull any dirty tricks on me!" Tack stretched his arm, pressing the gunpoint against her back, and screamed at her, "Hurry up!"

Feeling the gunpoint pressing between her shoulder blades, she slowly wiped her sweaty forehead with her hand and dried her palm on the side of her pants, over which she felt the LXG in her pants pocket.

She tried the other code and this time, the heavy safe door was pulled open, much to her relief.

Ordering the lanky man to tie her wrists again, Tack instantly rushed into the far end of the safe to get close to the green box, on top of which he spotted program discs and thick documents. He began to put those items hurriedly into a plastic bag that he brought in with him.

Meanwhile, the lanky man was tying Helen's wrists with the rope. Groaning and wincing from the pain in her tightening wrists, she seemed inching herself away from the man to ease her wrists' pain, moving close to the safe door. Suddenly, she threw her weight on the door, closing it with a dull, locking click.

Stunned by her quick action, the lanky man first turned to the door and attempted to open it by turning and pulling the safe's doorknob a few times, while Tack was screaming from inside the pitch-dark safe, calling the accomplice's name and trying to communicate with him.

Seizing that moment, Helen dashed out to the hallway, the incompletely tied knot dangling from her wrists behind her back. She kept running toward the exit door at the end of the hallway, wriggling her wrists and untying the last loose knots with her fingernails. Once her hands got free, still running, she pulled her LXG out of her pants pocket.

The lanky man gave up on the safe door and came running after her. By then, Helen passed half of the hallway to the Exit sign to downstairs. Behind her, she could hear the lanky man pursuing her and his puffing breaths nearing. She collected herself, turned around and shot her LXG ray at him once. He instantly staggered and slowed down but kept on pressing forward nearing her and almost caught her by her sleeve. Realizing that she had escaped his seizing attempt, this time he pulled out his LXG.

Helen ran faster toward the exit door, pushed it open, and took one step on the flat top-floor-landing of the staircase. She heard his LXG ray hit the side post of the doorframe with a sharp, metallic clang just as she cleared herself behind the door. She kept on running down the stairs.

Near the first-floor level, she almost collided into Bill, who, with John and two other officers, was running up the stairs.

"Helen, are you all right?" Bill asked.

"Yes, I'm…" Helen was out of breath. Saying so, she bent forward, panting, and leaned on her knees with her hands. Then, pointing at the top of the stairs with her hand still holding the LXG, she said to Bill, "Two men are upstairs. One was right behind me. I shot him once with my LXG and saw him slowing down. A couple of seconds later, he took a shot at me with his LXG, but I wasn't hit. Maybe he is armed with a gun, too. Be careful! He is coming down this way. The other one was locked up inside the safe."

Surprised at what Helen just said, Bill asked, while at the same time scanning the top of the stairwell, "Got locked up in the safe?"

"Yes." Helen nodded, catching up on her breaths, and said, "I'll explain it later. Be careful. The one inside the safe has a handgun."

Bill told John, "Call the precinct, and have five more guys rush over here on code red."

Still watching up the stairwell, Bill said to Helen, "John and I will carefully walk upstairs to the third floor by this staircase. Jack and Louis, you take the elevator. But, Helen, can you stay downstairs on this first floor, somewhere safe for the time being? Take this this *collar-clip* and communicate with me. By the way, Steve's call and your distress signal came to us almost at the same time. That's how we knew you were in trouble. Steve said he'll be here soon."

"Good! Are you going to open the safe?" Helen asked Bill.

"Yes."

"Then, I have to come up with you to Dr. Jupitren's office, because I have to calculate the code by using the LCD number on the safe's front panel."

"Oh, no, Helen, please don't come up. Why don't you stay in one of those rooms on the first floor? I will call out the number from the safe panel and you will figure out the new code and call me back through your *collar-clip*. You shouldn't be on the third floor at this time. It's too risky."

"OK, Bill, I'll stay in the Conference Room B. Thank you. Please be careful."

Meanwhile, the elevator brought Jack and Louis to the third floor. Jack told Bill through his *collar-clip*, "Bill, we found a gangly man lying in the hallway near the exit door, semiconscious but still holding his LXG gun. We'll take care of him."

They quickly removed the LXG from his hand and handcuffed him, who was still lying on the floor. Seconds later, Louis heard a tiny voice coming out of the handcuffed man's pocket. Louis motioned to Jack to listen to it.

The voice said, "Tack! I see a police van with five cops pulling in…Three of them are getting out of the van…and they are going to the building now. What are you guys doing? Get the hell out of there! The remaining two cops here are blocking the parking lot exits. You don't have much time. If I don't hear from you in sixty seconds, I'm gone!"

Jack and Louis realized that there must be a getaway car in the nearby parking area. Jack communicated to the code-red team on the ground, "Stop all cars. Block all the exits. I suspect there is a getaway car in the nearby parking lot. Be aware the driver must be armed. We don't have any description of the car yet."

CHAPTER 51
TACK

Locked up in the dark, chilly safe, Tack banged the door with his handgun, screaming useless threats and profanities. While searching for an inside light switch, he knocked a few chemical bottles off the shelves, breaking some of them. He couldn't find the switch, and he floundered in the dark.

Bill and John dashed into Dr. Jupitren's office. Bill spotted the flashing four-digit number on the LCD panel of the safe door. He read it aloud to Helen downstairs. She started to calculate the code number.

By then, Dr. Jupitren and Steve had rushed in. There, not seeing Helen next to Bill, Steve asked, "Is Helen all right? Where is she?"

"She is all right. She's on the first floor, in Conference Room B."

"Steve, why don't you run downstairs," Dr. Jupitren asked, "and see how she is doing, and please stay with her."

"Yes, I will." Steve rushed downstairs to Conference Room B.

Bill said to Dr. Jupitren, "Tack is trapped inside the safe. But he is armed with a handgun, an LXG, and possibly a CR device. How he ended up in there, we will hear from Helen later."

Right at that moment, Dr. Jupitren said, "Just a minute. I smell a toxic fume; it's coming out of the safe. Bill and John, please open all the nearby windows. It smells like decompressed carbonyl fluoride; probably, he broke its container inside the safe. It's a rather lethal gas. We have to open the safe quickly, or else he may die from the toxic fumes."

Steve was relieved to see Helen in Conference Room B on the first floor. He held her close to him and said, "Thank God! You're safe."

Helen, still in heightened tension, was in the middle of calculating the safe's code for Bill.

Three officers on code red walked into Dr. Jupitren's office. Bill quickly briefed them about what was happening.

Bill stood close to the safe and loudly said, "Takis Tantalos, can you hear me?"

A faint but audible voice and coughing sound sifted out through the safe door. "Yeah, I can. Let me out of here! I can't breathe. I can't see anything."

This time, Dr. Jupitren moved closer to the door and loudly said to Tack through the door's hinge area, "Listen carefully. I'll tell you how to turn on the inside light. First, move close to the door till you can touch it. Then, in your left-side floor corner, next to your left foot, there is a floor switch. You step on it with your toes."

"I got the light! I can see now, but I'm choking on the gas!" Tack yelled out, coughing violently.

Dr. Jupitren commanded him again. "Now, move to the right. Get the yellow mask from the top shelf, and hold it over your nose and mouth very tightly with both hands."

Bill and Dr. Jupitren could hear the dull but distinct thud from inside as Tack dropped his handgun onto the floor so that he could hold the mask with his two hands.

By then, Helen called Bill back and gave him the new code she'd calculated. Bill repeated the code to Dr. Jupitren, who started to press the seven-digit number on the door's keypad.

Bill alerted his officers, "Be ready! Just in case the suspect jumps out of the safe and starts wielding his weapons."

At Bill's head-nod signal, Dr. Jupitren pulled open the safe door. Tack staggered out of the gas-filled safe, coughing and gagging.

"Takis Tantalos, you are under arrest!" Bill bellowed.

Almost at the same time, Dr. Jupitren rushed inside the safe, holding his breath, and activated the safe's ventilation system.

Overcome by the toxic fumes, Tack bent forward, still coughing, and did not care to look at the officers who surrounded him in a combat-ready, alert stance. By lowering his hands, he removed the mask from his face.

Jack and Louis swiftly handcuffed him.

Bill asked him, "Where did you park your car?"

"In front of the chocolate store's entrance."

"What kind is it?"

"A brown SUV."

"Who's sitting in there?"

"Krumo Atto."

Bill immediately communicated with the code-red team on the ground about Tack's arrest and alerted them to look out for the brown getaway SUV.

An instant answer came up to Bill. "We've already spotted the brown SUV with its driver inside. We surrounded the car with three of our patrol cars.

The SUV is in front of the chocolate store's entrance in Parking Lot 4, next to Acmeon's lot."

"Great. The driver's name is Krumo Atto. He is armed. Be careful. We are coming down to you guys. Meanwhile, try to disarm him and spare any shooting if possible."

Helen and Steve peeked out of the conference room window. They saw the parked police vehicles' red, white and blue emergency lights flashing, and heard the blaring loudspeaker of the code-red team on the ground:

"Krumo Atto! We are the police. Turn off your engine, and open your car door slowly."

Everybody could hear the car engine stop and saw the car door opening slowly.

"Drop your car keys through the open door!"

Out of the open car door, a bunch of keys fell out.

"Drop all your weapons slowly on the ground!"

A handgun, an LXG, a CR device, and a KA-BAR combat knife were let out through the open door.

"Hold your hands up high, and step out slowly."

Krumo behaved as he was ordered.

Two officers handcuffed him. They picked up the weapons and car keys from the ground.

By then, Bill and the other officers, Dr. Jupitren, Helen, and Steve all came to the site of the ground action. There, everyone heard from Helen about how Tack ended up in the safe just before Bill and his three officers arrived at Acmeon.

Bill said to his crew, "Job well done. People will hear about brave Helen's silver bullet in the news tomorrow! Thank you, everyone." Then, turning to Dr. Jupitren, Bill said, "It worked out all right. No one got hurt, I'm glad."

Dr. Jupitren echoed, "What a surprise Helen was to all of us!" and looked at her with a proud smile. Then he said to Bill and his crew, "Thank you very much, Bill and everyone. I really appreciate what you have done today for Acmeon."

Steve and Helen joined Dr. Jupitren in appreciating Bill and his officers' professional job. Bill's squad took the three criminals away.

Dr. Jupitren said to Bill, who was about to follow his squad, "Bill, I'd like to invite you and everyone on your squad to La Cornucopia for a dinner this evening. Please invite everyone to come there by eight o'clock. OK?"

"Yes, I will. They will be glad to join. Thank you, Jules."

Dr. Jupitren went back to his office with Helen and Steve. The ventilation system prevented the toxic fumes from spreading throughout the building. Dr. Jupitren quickly neutralized the remaining toxic chemical on the floor and secured the broken compressor into a special container.

Then, Dr. Jupitren noticed an unfamiliar plastic bag next to the green box in the safe. In it, he found the fake discs and old scrap papers that he had left on top of the green box. He said, "Tack must have stuffed them into this bag as soon as he came in the safe. Tack's bagging those stuff must have taken him an extra minute, giving you, Helen, the chance to shut the safe door!"

"It was a good thing that you had placed those stuff there on top of the green box!" Helen voiced her relieved feelings.

The safe went back to its normal state.

Dr. Jupitren opened the small safe in his office. In it, he saw the genuine copies of the Wafer program along with the technical drawings and photographs of the Plant equipment that Steve had just completed.

Dr. Jupitren said, "I owe you both a great deal. Especially Helen, I was so impressed by your brave act today. Just like what Steve did with the Chromega watch, Helen, you safeguarded Acmeon Lab's security once again! I just remembered what people used to say about your Mom. They said that Elva is usually modest and gentle but has a gutsy undertone that would show up at the right moment of any emergency. Today, it made me think that you took very much after Elva's courage."

Helen said, still in an excited tone, "In fact, I was surprised at myself today, but believe me, I was very, very scared. Before I triggered my LXG at him, for a split second I thought he might kill me if I didn't use my LXG. And I completely forgot that my CR was not turned on. I'm glad the man's CR wasn't activated, either. Anyway, he didn't get hurt badly."

Steve said, "Helen, I'm just so proud of you! Thank God you didn't get hurt."

Then Dr. Jupitren checked the clock and said, "It's almost eight o'clock. Let's leave for La Cornucopia. I called the restaurant earlier and told the manager a dozen of us are coming for a big meal."

They all had a late dinner at La Cornucopia and felt relaxed, talking about the day's unexpected event.

CHAPTER 52

ROY AND JENNY WITH HER OPTICAL WALL

Dr. Roy Blau came to Luxen Tech Company to see Jenny. After some genial talk with each other, they went to the Luxen Tech Plant, where Jenny's invention, the Optical Wall was constructed de novo.

Jenny gave Dr. Blau a VIP tour of the Plant. He carefully listened to her about the theoretical rationale for every step of the optical wall's construction. Every technician or engineer who was working there greeted Jenny and her guest with courtesy. They answered every question Dr. Blau asked, and explained to him the subject matter by relating to the Optical Wall console manufacturing steps in progress. Dr. Blau was very impressed by the ingenuity of her invention and the Plant's setup. From the outset, her whole person that radiated charm, intelligence, and warmth captivated him.

She then brought him to an auditorium, where they saw several workers doing the routine floor-maintenance check for Optical Wall usage. She told them that she was going to demonstrate the Optical Wall partitioning in the auditorium to an important visitor and asked them to vacate the area for a while.

As they were gladly leaving for the staff lounge in the adjacent building, Jenny jestingly said to them, "It seems today my VIP guest doubled your afternoon break time. To resume your work here, please return in about half an hour. My demonstration on the Optical Wall will be finished by then."

When the auditorium was vacated, Jenny said to Dr. Blau, "I'll show you how this auditorium can be partitioned into four small rooms within matter of minutes. Afterward, if needed, each room could be partitioned into any number of smaller rooms."

With several manual commands on her handheld remote control, by projecting light beams with many different colors and densities, she created four separate rooms out of the entire auditorium.

"As you see, those four rooms were almost instantly created. Now I'll turn them into eight rooms."

Within a few minutes, the auditorium turned into eight smaller rooms. Each room could have the same or a different configuration depending on the need or purpose of the partitioning.

"It's magic!" he exclaimed.

They entered one of the eight rooms. Each room was big enough to accommodate three classroom desks of top size 2 x 3 feet, and several chairs. Each room had a pilot beacon and light switches near the door. Jenny touched a light switch with three levels of brightness. Each touch caused the brightness to increase to the next level, and immediately the room became very bright.

"How is the electric power supply done to each of those rooms?"

"From the solar transformer atop the auditorium."

"What happens on a very cloudy day?"

"Well, the natural-gas generator will take over."

"I see. How about the soundproofing?"

"Please follow me. I'll show you something."

She led him to the very adjacent room and asked him to remain there. She then went back to the original room and raised her voice, calling him loudly several times. Soon after that, she returned to his room and asked, "Did you hear me?"

"Yes, but very faintly. And I couldn't tell what you were saying."

"I called your name loudly a number of times."

"You did? I did not recognize that. What did you actually say?"

"I called out 'Dr. Roy Blau!' a few times, and then I said, 'Hi, dear Roy, can you hear me?' also a few times loudly."

"You're being funny. Anyway, I didn't hear any of that. Well, please call me 'dear Roy' from now on."

"All right, dear Roy, please call me Jenny. If you played a piano at fortissimo, it is about ninety decibels. But, it will be heard like a quiet whisper in the adjacent rooms; I believe the whisper is about fifteen decibels or lower."

"How do you let the optical barrier block those high-decibel sounds?"

"Well, one layer of the Optical Walls digitalizes the ambient analog sound waves, and as it converts the digitalized electronic waves back to analog waves in massively reduced intensity, it produces large-scale sound suppression. With that, people would feel the soundproofing to their comfort level."

"That sounds like a magic within the magic. What about the room temperature?"

"Each room has separate thermostatic capability." Jenny activated the noiseless air-temperature control system, which quickly changed the room temperature to the requested level.

Being impressed again, Roy questioned about the noiselessness of those fans. Jenny answered, "It's because the thermostatic system concurrently utilizes the digitalized sound suppression mechanisms, too."

"Very interesting. Is it easy to reverse those eight rooms back to the original single hall of the auditorium?"

"Yes, it's almost as easy as putting on the reverse gear instead of the forward gear in your car. But the bigger task and a lot more time-consuming part of the reversal is the actual removal of all the furniture items from those rooms. Usually, we remove the furniture after we let the Optical Walls vanish. Now I'll reverse the rooms back to one big hall."

Jenny gave commands on her handheld remote control. Quietly the eight rooms transformed back to one big hall.

"A real magic! The partitioning process seems very user-friendly." Roy couldn't help but express his amazement.

As the workers returned to resume their maintenance check in the auditorium, Jenny and Roy sat down in the auditorium's entrance foyer.

"Well, we have talked enough about my optical walls. Now can we talk about you, Roy? What do you do with your free time when you're not working at the ER?"

"You'll think I'm crazy when you hear my story."

"Really? Please tell me."

"It is a rather unusual story. I collect eyeglasses."

"For an emergency medicine doctor who is interested in optics and ophthalmology, that doesn't sound like an unusual thing to me. I once read your research article. The title was 'Diagnostic Use of Optical Illusion to Measure Degree of Binocular Visual Maturation.' Is your eyeglass collection related to that article?"

"No, it is totally unrelated. Thank you for paying attention to my work…From the beginning, I have collected more than a few thousand pairs of eyeglasses. Most of them being secondhand."

"Thousands? Secondhands? Now that is strange! Why so many? What for?" Jenny almost said, "That's crazy."

"Well, I learned initially at my Sunday school and later during my primary school's social-studies classes that there were many parts of the world where people did not have any basic medical care, let alone the proper eyeglasses. I was so naïve then. Later, my eyeglass-collection idea started right after I began wearing my own eyeglasses. I'm myopic, nearsighted, as you can guess from the eyeglasses

I wear. When I put my first eyeglasses on, to my great surprise, I could see things so clearly that I was very happy. Actually, I was ecstatic. At that very moment, I decided that I should share my experience with those who could not afford the needed eyeglasses."

"Aha, now I understand it. How wonderful. It's not some sort of a weird hobby but a special charity work!"

"Yes, my free time is quite taken up with that. Fortunately, I have two friends. We work together. All three of us share much of our time for it."

"How long have you been doing the charity work?"

"A little over fifteen years, since my high school years."

"That's wonderful. You must have a lot of stories about it."

"Yes. Someday, I may tell you all about it and about my two friends."

"Then, you must have very little time left over."

"I still find some free time. I manage to run average 30 minutes daily, 6 times a week; one or two hours' tennis with my friends, once or twice a week. The rest of time is mostly spent on studying various topics in medicine or attending selected updating courses. To keep up as an emergency medicine specialist, one has to be in good command of old and new medical knowledge, practically in every field of medicine. It takes lots of time. To put it more bluntly, it is 'forever'! Well, once a student, forever a student, you included. "

Even after a good deal of talking in the Luxen Tech Plant, Jenny and Roy felt they still needed a lot more time together. Later that very day, they went out to a fancy restaurant for a cozy dinner, talking about their life stories for a few more hours.

As weeks went by, their overlapping interests hastened mutual friendship and sparked burgeoning affection. Telephone calls between them became more frequent, and they enjoyed each other's company. Soon, they began to partake in each other's social functions, and people often saw them together at various venues.

As time went on, they felt more attracted to each other. Roy felt that Jenny's natural beauty and her caring, exquisite manners let her be a very lovable person. Likewise, Jenny's heart warmed up to his wholesome personality, gentle but decisive deportment, and handsome appeal. Their genuine care and shared affection made a galloping segue into a serious relationship.

In the meantime, since Steve and Helen had started their postgraduate courses, they began to follow unusually tight work schedules. Often they found it very difficult to spare even a short free time to make personal telephone calls to each other.

It made their once-in-a-great-while rendezvous so much more precious and dear. Very often they texted or e-mailed to each other about their course work-related questions and answers. Steve at times inserted his own or quoted-romantic sonnets in his text messages to Helen. More often, they reviewed and critiqued each other's course-related term papers before submitting them to their instructors or professors. They adapted to their austere work and study schedule, forgoing the usual pastime activities they used to have before.

As their semesters accumulated, Helen steadily grew stronger in her managerial competence at Acmeon Lab. Likewise Steve became an indispensable person at his Perihelion Energy Company.

CHAPTER 53

DREAM WAFERS FOR DR. SOBIEN MOLTON

One evening at his home, Dr. Jupitren was having one of his own *stop now and then* moments. Suddenly, he felt something was amiss. He realized that he was remiss in his duty as a psychiatrist and a fellow human being.

One sting of inner compunction seized him: "I detested Sobien for what he did against Acmeon Lab behind my back. But his thoughts and behavior must have been at the mercy of his illness. Rather than abhorring and ignoring him, I should have helped him to recover his health that was lost to the clutch of his illness. What is there that I can do for him now?..."

He did not hear Jamie, who called him a couple of times, asking him to come to the kitchen for a dessert. Finally, she came to him in the living room, where he was sitting on a low sofa with eyes closed, still thinking.

"Hon, are you so tired? Please come to the kitchen and try the apple pie I baked."

Continuing his *stop now and then* moment, he lightly held on to her hand and got up from his low seat. Then, he suddenly remembered the Dream Wafer of Joan Q and John Q. At that moment, he uttered, "Yes, yes. That will do."

Jamie assumed he was happy about her pie idea, but he was actually thinking about how Joan Q's Wafer helped John Q. Dr. Jupitren kept on thinking about how to help Sobien Molton by using Joan Q's Wafer model.

The next morning, Dr. Jupitren called the state hospital to speak with Sobien Molton's psychiatrist, Dr. Santiago. The doctor said his team's treatment result on Sobien was not encouraging. Sobien remained unstable in his mood despite the treatment he received with antidepressants and mood stabilizers. He was often ill tempered and very irritable.

Dr. Santiago said that he was puzzled by Sobien's inexplicable mood changes. Often, being very anxious and moody, he would turn sad for no apparent reason. At other times, he would be euphoric and carefree. Dr. Santiago was quite unaware of the episodic jolts that Sobien took from Ajnin.

To Dr. Santiago's great surprise, Dr. Jupitren said that he wanted to offer his Dream Wafer treatment for Sobien as an adjunct to the current treatment. Dr. Jupitren asked, "Can I visit you and Sobien at the hospital to explain the Dream Wafer treatment plan and obtain Sobien's consent for the treatment?"

"Yes, you can. But the consent I can get from Sobien Molton for you."

"Thank you, Dr. Santiago. Then, to start with, would you speak to the superintendent of the hospital about the Dream Wafer-treatment idea for Sobien, since it's not on the hospital's treatment formulary?"

"Certainly, I will. In order to use a non-formulary treatment method or any off-list medication, according to the hospital's policy, you need to propose such new methods in writing, explaining the rationale and detailed methodology."

"Yes, I anticipated that. So, to the hospital's formulary committee members and the superintendent, I will e-mail Dream Wafer-related references and treatment objectives today. Of course, I'll send you also a complete copy of those informations."

A few days later, Dr. Jupitren received a call from Dr. Santiago, who said, "Knowing Dr. Sobien Molton's current unstable mood state and antisocial traits, I was surprised that he consented readily to your Dream Wafer treatment proposal."

"That's nice. I'm surprised, too."

"Maybe his desperation helped him to dispel his doubts. Besides, he seemed quite moved by the very fact that you initiated the Dream Wafer treatment idea for him despite what he had done to you and your Acmeon lab. He knew that you were aware of everything he did against you."

"I see. He might be struggling with some remorse. By the way, do you think the superintendent reviewed the reference material that I e-mailed to him?"

"Yes. After having reviewed the material, he and the formulary committee people already asked me some questions. Although I had reviewed all the materials you sent to me, I couldn't answer them in full technical detail. Nevertheless, soon after that, the superintendent authorized the Dream Wafer treatment plan for Sobien Molton anyway. So, when you come up to the hospital, please spare half an hour or so for them. They seemed to have some more questions about the Dream Wafer treatment. They are anxious to see Sobien Molton's clinical improvement."

"Thank you very much. I will do that. Within a few days, I'll get ready and call you again."

Dr. Jupitren closely examined the Acmeon's records on genetic profiles and request inputs to the questionnaires made by Joan Q, John Q, and Sobien. After pondering over the involved technical details for a few more days, he decided that in order for him to do the Wafer treatment for Sobien properly, he needed to see him in person at the state hospital. Soon, he told Helen to reschedule his patients for the day of his trip to the state hospital.

At home, he told Jamie about what he was planning to do for Sobien. She said in a somber but pleased tone, "I suppose it was not an easy decision that you've made for him."

"Indeed it was not."

Looking at him with affection and deference, Jamie said, "I knew you were going to do this for him. I will pray that Sobien will accept your goodwill and get better soon. I thank God for letting you overcome your anger directed at Sobien, and offer him your help instead!"

"I, too, thanked God for that."

"I knew you would not lose your good nature and compassion. You yourself said many times that it was his illness that made him act uncontrollably."

"Thank you, Jamie, for understanding me. Well, next Wednesday, I'll drive to the hospital. It will take up most of the day."

On the planned day morning, he went to his office and packed the necessary test materials and equipment for the pre-Wafer tests and the questionnaire program.

He told Helen, "I'll be sending a bunch of data from the state hospital in the midafternoon today. Please relay the data to the Plant staff and ask them to monitor the Wafer composition closely and watch out for any diagnosis-related red signals."

When Helen learned to which state hospital he would be going, she surmised what he was up to. However, to be sure, she asked him, "Uncle Jules, you are doing this for Dr. Molton. Aren't you?"

"Yes. I'm going to try to help him."

"How marvelous! You are repaying your enemy with your kindness."

"I only hope that he will get better. By the way, did you cancel and reschedule all my appointments for today?"

"Yes, I did as you told me last week. Some patients were quite disappointed that they could not see you today. But I gave them the earliest available appointments, and they seemed OK with that. How long will you stay at the hospital?"

"Minimum three hours or so."

"Considering the two and a half hours of one-way driving, you will be away for about eight hours today."

"Yes. Probably I'll drive home directly from the hospital. You can reach me anytime through my Thumputer phone."

At the state hospital, Dr. Santiago and Dr. Jupitren met with the hospital's superintendent and the staff who were involved in Sobien Molton's treatment. They had several key questions regarding Dream Wafer treatment rationale. Dr. Jupitren answered all their questions and explained how the Dream Wafer would help Sobien. By the time the Q & A session was over, everyone seemed optimistic about the proposed adjunct treatment with Dream Wafer.

Later, on the way to Sobien's locked unit, Dr. Jupitren asked Dr. Santiago, "Has Sobien Molton ever been good enough to get a therapeutic pass?"

"No, not yet."

"Did he have any visitors?"

"Yes. As far as I know, there have been two of them."

"Do you know who they are?"

"One of them is Kerbera Wilson, who seems quite involved with him. And the other one is a man whom I have not spoken to personally other than saying "Hello" so far. He used to sign just 'A. H.' in the visitor's log whenever he came to visit Dr. Molton."

"Do you know how he is related to Sobien Molton?"

"He told me very little about A.H. To my insistent questioning, recently Sobien said he owed the man large sums of money and the man had been pressuring him to pay back the money. I felt that each time the man visited Sobien, his condition got worse, despite the extra medications we gave him."

"I see. Do you know the visitor's full name?"

"Yes. His name is Ajnin Hsilomed."

Dr. Jupitren wrote it down in his memo pad and said, "This is a strange name!"

"Yes, it certainly is. I thought the man was strange, too."

"What made you to say so?"

"He never greets people normally. Never smiles. He has piercing eyes. Often he wears sun-glasses, even indoors. He has unusually big nimble hands and short arms, speaking with an unfamiliar foreign accent. Something is strange and odd about him."

Dr. Jupitren looked at the written name carefully and said, "I think this is not a real name. Please read it backward."

Dr. Santiago read it and said, "Demolish ninja! Wow, it's weird."

"Don't you check the forensic patients' visitors closely?"

"Yes, we do. But I think we have missed something here about this visitor. I should ask Sobien about the visitor more carefully in the next treatment sessions."

Dr. Santiago continued. "A few times, after their visiting hours, I had a fleeting hunch that Sobien became sad and anxious because something happened during those visits. Yet, whenever he became sad, we usually assumed it was probably the downward cycling of his bipolar disorder, triggered by the man's pestering over his debt."

By then, they reached the locked unit. Dr. Santiago used his electronic key to open the first door. Once they stepped in, he locked the door behind them. Then they walked about ten feet ahead to the second locked door that would open to the locked unit proper. Those two doors, back to back ten feet apart, were constructed in that way for security reasons. No one could escape through those doors, because always one door was to be kept locked at any given time. The rule was applied for general passage of people, meal carts, patient gurneys, and the like.

From the point of the inner door, two burly attendants escorted Dr. Santiago and Dr. Jupitren to Sobien's room. As they entered his room, Sobien got up from his seat somewhat slowly. He seemed glad to see Dr. Jupitren, but his feeling tone seemed muted, and his usual vigor was missing. Furthermore, unlike him, he became teary as he shook hands with Dr. Jupitren. "It is not Sobien's customary handshake." Dr. Jupitren thought, as he did not feel any bit of Sobien's usual hearty handgrip. Instead, Sobien let it be a mere limp gesture. He seemed depressed.

"How are you doing, Sobien?"

"I'm getting by. I didn't think you would ever come to see me."

"I believe Dr. Santiago has already told you why we are meeting today."

"Yes, he has told me. Thank you." Sobien then looked at Dr. Santiago and said in a subdued voice, "Hello, Dr. Santiago."

"Hi, Did you notice any symptom change since we have tapered down your medication dosage past few days?"

"Um, I feel all right. In fact, I'm less sleepy during the daytime."

"That sounds good. Dr. Jupitren will set up your test items and will help you go through the computer-questionnaire session." Dr. Santiago then turned to Dr. Jupitren and reported to him that for the preceding few days Sobien's medication dosage had been slowly tapered down in preparation for his Dream Wafer application.

Dr. Jupitren thanked Dr. Santiago. Then Dr. Jupitren faced Sobien. "We will start the pre-Wafer tests as soon as every item is set to go. By the way, is Ms. Kerbera Wilson visiting you?"

"Yes, but I'm afraid she is wearing herself out."

"How do you mean?"

"I think she is getting tired of my temper. I'm scared of losing her."

"Well, if you get better, don't you think you'll win her back?"

At that point, Dr. Santiago was paged on his Thumputer for another unit's emergency. He excused himself and said to Dr. Jupitren, "If I don't get to see you again this afternoon, I'll talk to you on your Thumputer phone soon."

"Sure. We'll talk again."

Leaving the room for another unit, Dr. Santiago said to Sobien, "Please keep your hopes up. I feel the Dream Wafer will work wonders for you. I'll see you later."

Sobien, in a sagging voice, said, "Thank you, Dr. Santiago."

Dr. Jupitren asked Sobien, "Dr. Santiago told me that you have another visitor, Mr. Ajnin Hsilomed. How is he related to you?"

"He is…Uh, I owe him some money and he…Uh…" Sobien could not finish his words, and his face became very pale.

"Are you all right, Sobien?"

"Suddenly I feel sick in my stomach." Saying so, Sobien grimaced, pressing his stomach area with his hands, and finished his short answer. "I'll be all right in a minute."

Dr. Jupitren did not ask him again about the visitor, presuming some difficult money matters were involved with a hardhearted usurer, as Dr. Santiago told him earlier. In silence, Dr. Jupitren waited for Sobien until he calmed himself down. A few minutes later Sobien emerged from his mini crisis, and then Dr. Jupitren explained the Dream Wafer treatment plan for him.

Soon, Dr. Jupitren ran the pre-Wafer tests on Sobien, including biometric data collection. He managed to send those data to Acmeon Lab. After that, he sat next to Sobien for over an hour as Sobien answered all the questionnaire-135 items and their sub-items. He made sure that Sobien answered them properly, especially on those items that dealt with antisocial behavior and mood instability. Surprisingly, Sobien was compliant and remained in a fair mood state. The questionnaire session was finished without any complication.

Dr. Jupitren reassured Sobien. "In two days, your Wafers will be here. Please apply them carefully as you did before."

"Yes, I will. Will you be coming back to see me again?"

"Yes, I'll try to visit you again within two weeks, and we will check the Dream Wafers' effects. In the interim, of course, I'll communicate with Dr. Santiago and hear about your progress."

As Dr. Jupitren collected his equipment and packed his computers, preparing for his return trip, he took a sweeping glance at Sobien's room. There were small built-in bookshelves on the wall with some books. One book's title in particular drew his attention: *How to Forgive: A Spiritual Way.*

Dr. Jupitren asked, pointing at the book, "Have you read this book?"

"Yes."

"Whom do you need to forgive?"

Sobien paused briefly before he answered the question. "I thought many people wronged me. My ex-wife Brigit, Jenny, Kerbera, several people at Acmeon, and even you…"

He continued in a deliberate manner, pausing a few times in the middle of what he was saying. "I was angry with you and everyone else…So, hoping to find a way to stop this nagging anger, I started to read the book. But, it made me realize that I was not the one to forgive you and others, but I was the one who badly needed to be forgiven by everyone."

Sobien seemed teary. " The book turned my ideas upside down, and I realized that I was wrong in my thoughts and anger…My premise was wrong. I hope you and the others will forgive me. I have done many reckless, destructive things to you all."

His voice trembled. After a long pause, he said in a pleading tone, "The problem I still have is that I'm often confused in my thoughts, and I'm bent to do wrong things, despite I know they are wrong. When I'm in the wrong side like that, I still struggle with my spiteful feelings. I want to stop feeling that way. Now your visit with the Dream Wafer treatment plan for me is making a world of difference in my dealings with my anger."

There followed a brief silence again.

Dr. Jupitren said, "Sobien, I know you are a good-hearted person by nature. Today, I am convinced of that again. I hope your emotions soon will catch up with your smart intelligence and venturous nature." Saying so, Dr. Jupitren gently offered his hand forward for a handshake and added, "I'm glad I came up here to see you today."

Responding with his two hands, Sobien said, "Thank you very much for what you are doing for me."

"You're welcome. The Dream Wafer will work for you. I'll see you again soon."

Leaving Sobien's room, at the door, Dr. Jupitren looked back to say good-bye to him but closed the door without words, as he saw Sobien turned his face to the wall, drying teary eyes with the back of his hand.

On his way home, while driving, Dr. Jupitren recalled what Jamie had said to him, "…I thank God for letting you overcome your anger directed at Sobien and offer him your help instead!"

Using his car phone, he told Jamie how his visit with Sobien went at the state hospital and said, "Thank you, Jamie, for being on my side with your encouraging words. Now I feel this small but clear sense of triumph over hatred. I owe it to you…I'll be home in an hour."

Dr. Santiago said, "The superintendent of the hospital and Sobien's treatment team are thankfully recognizing the positive effect of the new treatment approach that you initiated. I personally thank you for Sobien. Without any doubt, we know that your forgiveness and the Dream Wafers have made the difference."

Week after week, Dr. Jupitren heard from Dr. Santiago streams of encouraging reports about Sobien's progress. Sobien was maintained on a mood stabilizer and low dose of an antidepressant along with the Dream Wafers.

As Sobien made continued clinical progress, Dr. Santiago petitioned to the court, requesting a therapeutic parole program on his behalf.

One day, Sobien wondered, "Would Ajnin leave me alone if he got all his money back? But, how can I raise such large sums of money now? The only thing I can think of is dare to ask Kerbera. But, if Ajnin finds out she is the source of the money, I'm afraid he might easily change his scheme to racketeering her. I don't want to drag her into a worse dilemma."

Finally, during one of the scheduled treatment sessions, without going into details, Sobien requested Dr. Santiago to bar Ajnin from visiting him.

"Why do you want to stop Ajnin's visits?" Dr. Santiago asked.

Downcast and tense, Sobien answered, "As I have told you previously, I owe him some money and other things. Every time he comes to see me, he harasses me and demands to know how soon I will pay him back. I wish you could just stop him from visiting me for a while."

"According to the hospital's policy on forensic-unit patients' visitation," Dr. Santiago said, "we need to get the forensic-unit administrator's clearance on your request in order to stop Ajnin's visits. The policy applies to every patient on the forensic-unit."

Despite Dr. Santiago's repeated attempts to obtain any additional information on Ajnin, either by asking Sobien or talking to Ajnin himself, no substantial new material came from them. Should Sobien spill the beans to anyone, he knew that not only he but also his close relatives would suffer severely in the hands of Ajnin's rogues.

The forensic-unit administrator heard Dr. Santiago's explanation that because of some matters of debt, Ajnin's visits used to make Sobien's clinical status worse. The administrator and the whole treatment team did not want to see Sobien's improving streak interrupted. Assuming that Sobien was a mere target of Ajnin's loan-sharking, the administrator decided to approve Sobien's request without further questioning.

On the next scheduled visiting day, Dr. Santiago personally told Ajnin in his office, "Mr. Hsilomed, because Mr. Molton's clinical condition has been unstable, his treating team and I decided that there should be no more visitors for Mr. Molton for a while. When he gets a little better, we will restore his visiting privilege, and we will let you know about it."

Instantly, Ajnin surmised that Sobien must have asked the doctor to stop his visitation. Ajnin felt boiling rage and resented Sobien's renege and betrayal. Ajnin bit his tongue to conceal his extreme rage. Saying nothing, he stomped out of the doctor's office.

Afterward, Sobien did not have Ajnin's visits. Instead, during those unstructured hours, he would mingle with other patients. Oftentimes, he would play softball with them, wearing a white baseball cap, in the hospital's courtyard. However, Kerbera was still allowed to visit him.

On some days, there was a person outside the hospital, looking in from some distance. Often using a pair of binoculars, the person watched the patients participating in the outdoors activity therapy program. It was enraged Ajnin, who secretly had been watching Sobien Molton's behavior.

Seeing Kerbera continue her visitation with Sobien, Ajnin was infuriated. Gnashing his teeth, he mumbled a vengeful monologue. "You and your doctors tricked me. No more of your visitors for clinical reasons? Why is your girlfriend still visiting you? After all that money you took from me, you didn't produce anything. Besides, you know too much about me and my government. Before you rattle away about us to the whole world, you shall be eliminated! You think you fooled me. But you wait and see!"

It never occurred to Sobien that he was being watched by Ajnin from outside.

One day, Dr. Jupitren received a call from Dr. Santiago, who reported that Sobien Molton had changed remarkably in his personality. Dr. Santiago said that while talking with Sobien, he often felt he was conversing with a professional colleague, as Sobien was courteous and emotionally stable, proving his possession of vast medical knowledge.

Sobien became quite a different person. He related with others appropriately, and everyone marveled at the transformation of his personality. People could not find any peevish streak in his manners. His sleep pattern normalized. His mood remained stable at euthymic level. He continued his nightly Dream Wafer applications.

Dr. Jupitren kept correspondence with both Sobien and Dr. Santiago. Dr. Jupitren made some adjustments to Sobien's Dream Wafer composition as needed. To make such adjustments, number of times Dr. Jupitren needed to go to the state hospital in person.

CHAPTER 54

ASSASSIN AJNIN

Dr. Jupitren had been running several new experiments on the *virtual brain* model in the West Room. Often he thought it was amusing to see the *virtual brain*'s head move just like a real person's head would. Its movement was seen in response to the routine neurochemical commands given to the neck and shoulder areas.

He remembered the remark made by one of the visiting researchers during the second part of the last symposium: "Your *virtual brain* model has an outer encasing structure that looks like *a real person wearing a white baseball cap.*" Reminiscing on that remark, Dr. Jupitren recalled highlights of the last symposium and thought of doing some new experiments by using the brain model.

Suddenly, he remembered what Sobien Molton said shortly before he was hospitalized:

"By lowering the polymorphism expression of norepinephrine transporter genes, my Chemical Razor technique's risk will be reduced significantly. I can demonstrate it if I can get enough number of volunteers among Acmeon Lab's clients! The only problem is that I don't know at this time the specific procedure yet, with which I can lower the risk of my Chemical Razor method."

Since then, using the *virtual brain* model in the West Room, Dr. Jupitren had done repeated experiments on the Chemical Razor method. He wanted to see whether Sobien's method would show an acceptable level of low risk as he had claimed.

After a spate of pains taking experiments, much to his surprise, Dr. Jupitren found that if one specific intermediary step was modified, Sobien's Chemical Razor method could be applied with much less risk after all!

Dr. Jupitren thought that someday soon he should let Sobien hear about the experiments' result. Specifically, he wanted to let Sobien learn about the very intermediate step that made the difference.

Up in the state hospital, since Ajnin's visitation was discontinued, Sobien almost forgot about his threat. However, Ajnin did not let go of Sobien. Ajnin managed to hear about Sobien's changing clinical and legal status through a recently hired state-hospital mail-room worker, whom they called GG. By using falsified job-application documents, Ajnin wangled to Plant GG there as a new employee, who was his spy. This occurred right after the hospital stopped Ajnin's visitation with Sobien. GG's mail room work assignment was to shred confidential papers and outdated patients' charts as well as functioning as a custodian in the mail room area.

Several months previously, when Ajnin made his very first contact with Sobien Molton, he acted as an agent for his country's despot just to get the Dream Wafer program copy. However, lately, Ajnin had gradually turned into a vengeful ax-grinder, believing Sobien Molton duped him on purpose.

One day, Dr. Jupitren called Sobien Molton at the state hospital. He explained that his recent experiments done on the *virtual brain* proved the Chemical Razor method could be much less risky, if a specific intermediate chemico-genetic step was taken.

In response, Sobien said that he was very glad to hear the news and wished to see the new Chemical Razor procedure that Dr. Jupitren might demonstrate for him on the *virtual brain.* To Dr. Jupitren's surprise, Sobien added, "If you need volunteers but cannot find sufficient number of them for the experiment, I'll be glad to volunteer myself. I'm willing to be the guinea pig for your experiment's replication."

Dr. Jupitren thanked him and said, "However, I don't think you should volunteer for the experiment because at the present time you are still legally the state hospital's patient."

"Oh, you're right. I was so excited that I didn't think of it. Well, then, I'll just ask the hospital administrator for an overnight therapeutic pass. If the hospital grants me the pass, I'll come to Acmeon Lab and observe the modified Chemical Razor procedure on the virtual brain."

The forensic patients' pass application papers routinely went through the hospital's mail room. Excited about his upcoming visit to see Dr. Jupitren at Acmeon Plant soon, Sobien hand-carried his overnight pass application to the mail room. There, as the chief staff of the mail room reviewed his application, Sobien eagerly described that during the pass he would watch Dr. Jupitren's experiment replication on the Chemical Razor. Sobien said the experiment will be in the Acmeon Plant building.

Working in the mail room, GG overheard them as they talked about Sobien's overnight-pass plan.

GG telephoned Ajnin to tell him about Sobien's pending overnight pass.

Ajnin asked,"On his pass, where is he going?"

"Acmeon Lab, Long Island, New York."

"Did you find out at which Acmeon building Molton will be spending most of his time during his pass?"

"I heard him say the Acmeon Plant building."

"Acmeon Plant building! Good. Do you know how he will get there?"

"His girlfriend will drive."

"How did you know that?"

"The pass-request form has lines asking for means of transportation, destination, and who will drive for the patient because the hospital does not allow patients' driving while on psych medications. I just saw his pass request paper in the mail room."

"When is he going?"

"This coming Saturday, 3 pm. They'll be coming back on Sunday afternoon."

"It's good that you're off this weekend. Today, I want you to do something."

"What is it?"

"At your lunch break today, around twelve forty-five, see me at the K9 rifle practice range. I'll give you a special GPS set. You attach it to his girlfriend's car. It has a strong magnet, and it will stick to any metal part of the car, under the bumper or muffler, but put it on any spot that they cannot see. By now, you must know what kind of car his girlfriend drives. Don't you?"

"Yes, I do. Last year's red Ferrari California."

"Good. Which car are we going to drive?"

"The same one that we drove last week to get away from the HB Bank. Is that OK?"

"That'll be good enough. But, make sure to change the license plates."

"I've already replaced them yesterday with the New Jersey plates that we got from the junk yard."

Ajnin said in a hushed voice, "Tomorrow, Thursday I'll drive down to Acmeon Lab area and check out the layout of the Acmeon buildings and the surroundings. So, tomorrow, if there is any change in Molton's pass plan, call me right away."

On Saturday afternoon, Ajnin and GG came near Acmeon Plant a few hours before the arrival of Sobien and Kerbera at Acmeon Lab. Ajnin went with GG to an adjacent self-storage warehouse building, about ninety feet west of the Acmeon Plant. Ajnin had rented a second-floor storage room within the warehouse when he had come to the area by himself on Thursday. In the room, he unloaded his equipment, a pair of binoculars, a brown bag of food, and a long, odd-sized bag.

Following the GPS detector that was tagged to Kerbera's car, GG and Ajnin pinpointed her car's location. With binoculars, they confirmed the Ferrari California. Ajnin watched Molton and Kerbera stepping out of their parked car and walking toward the three-story Acmeon Lab main building.

Ajnin asked, "GG, Didn't you say Molton will be at the Plant building?"

"Yes, I told you so because I overheard him say that."

"But why is he going to the other building? Why not to the Plant?"

"I guess Molton will see the Acmeon's head doctor there in that main building...and maybe see some others who know him, too. Let's wait."

"OK. We'll wait and see. Meantime, let's check our two-way voice transmitter. Go out now and park your car facing south, on R Street behind this building, and call me. Make sure there is no parking meter. I'll be here in this room. Move quickly."

GG did as Ajnin told him to. From the car, he called Ajnin, "Our car is parked exactly where you told me to. There's no parking meter to feed."

"Good. I can hear you well. You can come back here now."

Looking out for anyone watching him, GG snuck up back to Ajnin.

"Did anyone see you coming back here?"

"No."

"How long did it take you to come back up here?"

"About three minutes…I walked. But if I ran, I would make it in half of that time."

"Good.."

A while later, Sobien and several people came out of the main building. Then, in three different cars, they left for somewhere else.

Ajnin and GG followed them in their car. Sobien's group went into a nearby snack bar. Ajnin and GG parked their car on a street spot facing the snack bar's exit door.

Waiting for the Acmeon people to finish their late-afternoon snack, Ajnin and GG waited in their car. GG munched something that he took out of their brown bag and gulped on unnamed drink. Ajnin did not eat or drink anything but made a call to his headquarters and spoke to someone. GG knew whom Ajnin was speaking to.

"I'm about to carry out what I was ordered to do this evening, but I want to make sure, for the last time, whether I must do it or if Molton had another chance."

After silently listening on the phone, Ajnin said, "All right then, I will do it as ordered…most likely it will be around the sunset time since they just went in…You're right, he did not produce any result so far, and he is fooling us by hiding in the hospital. Once it's finished, GG and I will drive to the same hotel where I saw you last time…No, just wait for us there. I'll give the rifle back to you right at the parking lot and you will give me my air ticket…Yes, then GG will drop me off at the JFK Airport, and he will return to his apartment tonight."

Almost at sundown, the Acmeon people came out of the snack bar. Ajnin and GG followed them back to Acmeon Lab area. GG parked his car back on R Street.

This time, Molton, in Dr. Jupitren's car, headed to the Plant building and the others went easterly to the main building.

At the same time, Ajnin and GG quickly went up to their second-floor room of the warehouse building and looked out through a window. Ajnin watched the two doctors. They came out of their car and walked westerly in the direction of the Plant building. The sunset glare made Dr. Jupitren use his hand as a sun visor, but Molton took his white baseball cap out of his satchel and put it on his head.

GG said to Ajnin, "See? Molton is now going to the Plant building."

Ajnin, staring at nothing else but the baseball-capped figure, raised the window sash up just enough to clear his rifle's telescope and tripod and said to GG, "Good. Get me the sniper rifle. Undo the safety pin, and hand it to me."

A few minutes passed. However, for Ajnin and GG it was felt like a very long pause before the Plant room was finally lit up. Standing next to the model brain, Dr. Jupitren gave Sobien a general overview on the *virtual brain*. He discussed with Sobien about when they should put on the *special clean room suit*…Ajnin, unaware of the centerpiece figure being the *virtual brain* head, suddenly felt confused, because there he saw three men, two of them wearing a white baseball cap next to the Acmeon doctor! Besides, they all were veiled behind thin layers of curtains. The curtains seemed to move sidewise, opening or closing, which made his visual judgment very difficult even with the rifle's telescope.

GG asked, "Should I go to the car now? My voice transmitter is on."

"Yes. Go now, and wait there, car running, at R Street, facing south."

"All right. Will do." GG left for R Street.

Ajnin took extra seconds deciding which one was his target. He thought the gray-haired figure without a cap must be Acmeon's doctor, but which one of the other two wearing white baseball caps would be Molton? He thought he should not hesitate too long but should grab the chance quickly. He decided to shoot both of the capped figures.

He pulled the first trigger! He saw the Plant's windowpanes shattering. Almost simultaneously one of the capped figures' head was smashed to many pieces. To his surprise, the torso of the smashed head did not fall down. His trigger finger was ready for the second shot. He aimed at the other baseball cap. At that very moment, Dr. Jupitren saw Sobien was stunned and was still standing next to the remains of blown-up model brain. Dr. Jupitren dashed to him at lightning speed, pushing him away from the center to a sheltered corner of the room. At the same time, Ajnin pulled the next trigger at the capped figure and saw the doctor and capped one both fall down on the floor. Then he heard a loud alarm set off by the broken window, and all the Acmeon buildings' lights lit up brightly. He decided to spare the third shot, or else he would be found. He pulled the sash down quickly, picked up the shell fragments, and bagged the dissembled rifle.

Talking to GG on the transmitter, Ajnin ran down to his getaway car carrying his rifle bag. He and GG sped away unchallenged by anybody.

Responding to the alarm, some people near Acmeon and Bill Warren with John Collin's crew, rushed into the site. There they saw the shattered window and two bloodied men next to the mangled model brain. Molton, with a blood-smeared face, was trying to help Dr. Jupitren, who was lying on the floor, bleeding from the side of his head.

Molton steadied Dr. Jupitren's head with his bare hand and pressed the bleeding points with the other hand, calling Dr. Jupitren's name to check his consciousness. Molton yelled out loudly, "Somebody! Call the ambulance!"

Then he pointed at the window with his head and said to Bill and the surrounding people, "From that direction, someone shot at us twice…Dr. Jupitren pushed me out of the danger spot, and he was hit instead."

While Bill was calling the EMTs, John went back to the police van to bring a portable oxygen tank, as Dr. Jupitren was gasping for air. From Dr. Jupitren's head, blood was gushing out, and people began to doubt if Dr. Jupitren would make it. Molton kept pressing his hand on the bleeding points and watched Dr. Jupitren's vital signs falter.

John's team of officers searched the building area and the streets but found no clue.

Dr. Jupitren bled heavily from one side of his head. He was so exhausted that he could not speak and slipped into an unconscious state.

On board the ambulance bound to Northwest Hospital ER, the EMT crew started the emergency procedures on Dr. Jupitren. As the ambulance came near the hospital, Sobien Molton cautiously let the EMTs take over his manual pressure on the bleeding spots.

Dr. Roy Blau, who was on duty, received communication from the EMT before Dr. Jupitren arrived at the ER. The trauma team's radiologist hurried back to the ER area from another office. From Dr. Jupitren's Thumputer, one of the EMT's on board retrieved the information on Dr. Jupitren's blood type and sent it to the hospital's blood bank. The blood-transfusion preparation went into motion.

However, the blood-bank staff was very concerned because Dr. Jupitren's blood was a rare O, Rh-negative type, and the blood bank happened to have only one pint of the same type blood. Dr. Blau thought the patient would need at least three pints, maybe four. Responding to Dr. Blau's request, they began urgently searching for O, Rh-negative blood throughout the regional blood banks.

At the ER, Dr. Blau made a quick assessment on Dr. Jupitren's head injury. The wounds were: torn right-side temporal muscles, ruptured anterior temporal artery branches, and a probable right temporal bone fracture. He was in a shock state with hypovolemia secondary to sudden blood loss.

While the trauma team performed brisk, life-preserving procedures on him, heavy-hearted people outside the operating room dreaded, with much fear and apprehension, for his life.

Meantime, in another part of the hospital, Sobien was led by an ER nurse into a washing room of the surgical unit, because he was covered with Dr. Jupitren's blood. The nurse offered him a blue hospital gown to wear. Another ER doctor gave an emergency physical examination to Sobien to see if he sustained any serious injury from the fall during the shooting incident. Additionally, for his swollen, painful right elbow and right hip joints, Sobien needed X-ray exams, which ruled out fractures.

Sometime later, Dr. Blau came out of the operating room and returned to the waiting room to give an interim report to those who were anxiously waiting for the news. There were Mrs. Jupitren, several other family members, Helen, Steve, and Kerbera. Bill's team of officers just dropped in after their repeated patrolling.

Dr. Blau said to the roomful people, "The neurovascular surgeon Dr. McCormick and his team concentrated on stopping Dr. Jupitren's bleeding. It was a rather difficult job, as the arterial blood gushed out from more than one spot from right side of his head. The bullet tore the arteries and surrounding muscles. One of Dr. McCormick's assistants replaced me, and I was able to come out of the operating room after seeing that they had begun to repair the torn tissues."

"However, his current blood volume and pressure are still unstable, even after he received a pint of blood that our blood bank had. At this moment, we are infusing artificial plasma intravenously to maintain his blood volume and blood pressure while waiting for the requested pints of blood from other blood banks. A full life-supporting system is standing by. As far as the head bones are concerned, there was an inch-long scratch in the right side of the temporal bone causing a linear fracture of the bone."

Everyone sank in heavy silence, stricken by fear of the unpredictable outcome. An oppressive sense of impending doom seemed to fill the room's air.

Mrs. Jupitren asked, "Dr. Blau, how soon would you get the blood he needs?"

"Well, we have contacted two blood banks that have his type of blood. However, those banks are far away. It will take three or four hours by car to bring the blood here. But the blood-volume restoration must be done right now. So, we are arranging a Medical Emergency air-scooter to hasten the blood transport from those two blood banks, which are in Eastern Pennsylvania. It would still take about an hour."

"Thank you, Dr. Blau."

At that moment, a man who looked like a hospital patient walked in. Hearing what Dr. Blau just said, the man asked, "Dr. Blau, may I ask you what Dr. Jupitren's blood type is?"

Everyone looked at him. Most of them in the room recognized him. He was Dr. Sobien Molton, wearing a hospital patient's gown. His hair was still wet from the shower he'd just taken to wash off the blood.

Dr. Blau answered, "It is O, Rh-negative."

"That's good! Can I donate my blood for Dr. Jupitren? I have the same blood type."

"Certainly. Thank you for your goodwill!" Dr. Blau looked at Sobien for a couple of seconds and asked, "Sir, didn't I see you somewhere in the hospital?"

"Yes, you did, Dr. Blau. You treated me right here in this ER months ago."

"Are you the person who had a scalp laceration?"

"Yes."

"So, you are Dr. Sobien Molton! I remember you now."

"I'm glad you do. Please start the blood-collection protocol on me right away without any further delay!"

"Thank you, Dr. Molton. We will start it right now. Please come along with me."

Mrs. Jamie Jupitren in particular was very moved. With tears on her cheeks, she thanked Sobien in her trembling voice as he passed her by. A glimmer of hope radiated from the heroic man's sure stride as he exited the room with Dr. Blau.

As soon as the two doctors came out of the waiting area, Dr. Molton asked Dr. Blau, "How serious is Dr. Jupitren now?"

"His Glasgow Coma Score is five. Not good. His BP and blood volume are about to drop below the critical level again. If they drop further, as you know it, there's a possibility that he might have irreversible multi-organ failure due to hypovolemic shock."

Sobien anxiously said, "Please hurry! I'm in a good physical condition, and I've no infectious diseases or conditions contraindicating to blood donation. Please do the cross matching as soon as possible, and do the rest of CBC (complete blood count), serology, and other routine tests later!"

The passage of time was very slow for those in the waiting area. Another long anxious hour went by. Dr. Blau came back to the room. Everyone hushed up with heightened expectation.

"During the past hour, with the unexpected blood donated by Dr. Molton, Dr. Jupitren's condition improved from critical to a less serious state with improving vital signs."

"Whew!" someone blurted out loudly.

"Meanwhile, Dr. Molton passed out right after his blood donation that was processed in an unusually rapid succession. Despite the blood-bank staff's great reluctance, he urged them to speed up the two pints of blood collection from him. Just before I came in here, I checked Dr. Molton who was not fully awake, but his vital signs were getting better.

So, now we have two patients: Dr. Jupitren and Dr. Molton. In my opinion, each of them still could use a pint of blood. Therefore, we did not cancel the two pints of blood from the Eastern Pennsylvania blood banks. When we get the airlifted two pints of blood, we will use them to treat the two doctor patients." Having said so, Dr. Blau went back to the recovery-room area.

A long while later, he came back to the roomful people and reported, "As soon as Dr. Jupitren gained his consciousness briefly, he asked me if Dr. Molton was all right. I reassured him and told him that Dr. Molton was not hurt. He was very relieved to hear that.

Later, when I saw Dr. Jupitren again, a few minutes before I came back here, he asked me what happened to his *virtual brain* model in Acmeon Plant. I had to tell him that unfortunately it was destroyed by the assassin's first bullet. Realizing what had really happened to it, he was very disheartened. He became very pensive, and I saw tears in his eyes. I couldn't say anything to him. Soon he fell asleep.

Dr. Molton also regained his consciousness and asked me how Dr. Jupitren was doing. I reassured him that Dr. Jupitren was better because of his blood donation. With a sigh of relief and a faint smile, Dr. Molton, too, slipped into fatigued somnolence."

At that point Helen remembered that there were two Acmeon employees who had O, Rh-negative type blood: Zenon Zelinski and Narnia Bojore. Helen asked Dr. Blau if she should call them and ask for their blood donations.

Dr. Blau thanked her and said, "The airborne ready-to-use blood supply will arrive shortly, and extra donation from those employees may take considerably longer to process; therefore, their blood donation would not be needed at this time."

With continued critical care given by the hospital, which was boosted with the air-lifted blood supply, Dr. Jupitren recovered relatively soon from his pre-shock state, much to everyone's relief. His skull fracture did not result in any serious complication, and there was no evident leakage of cerebrospinal fluid through his nose or ears. However, he was placed on prophylactic antibiotics against any secondary infection in his head wounds.

Dr. Molton, who received one pint of airlifted blood, likewise recovered from his post-blood-donation weakness. He returned to the state hospital after getting two extra days' extension on his pass. He was the only one who knew why the shooting occurred. He had felt profound guilt for his wrong deeds and at the same time felt immense gratitude toward Dr. Jupitren for having saved his life.

Soon after the assassin's rampage, Sobien reported to Dr. Santiago everything about the wrongful involvement he had with Ajnin. Sobien realized that he should accept any future disposition given by the hospital. He felt secure in a way, feeling that staying in the hospital would protect him from Ajnin's future attacks.

A few weeks after the gunshot episode, GG resigned from the mail-room job of the state hospital, and no one knew of his involvement in Ajnin's attempt at Sobien's life.

Sobien complied with his forensic unit's recommendation and decided not to venture out until he would fully serve the time ordered by the court.

CHAPTER 55
THREE YEARS LATER

Acmeon Lab continued to produce Dream Wafers, Waferlyzer-II, and Antisom under Dr. Jupitren's leadership.

The three new doctors, Anderson, Burbridge, and Chanteur, orchestrated their scholarly research and clinical work. In particular, they assisted Dr. Jupitren to move toward his goal, which was to make the Dream Wafers available to more people who could benefit from them through much simpler, easier, and less expensive processes.

Three Years Later

As those three doctors hoped, Dr. Jupitren invited them to join him in his *virtual brain* model restoration. Throughout the few years of the restoration process, they gained vast knowledge of many theories and facts about genes' interplay with myriad brain functions.

Meanwhile, Perihelion Energy Company had manufactured Dronette-8, with multifunctional espionage and defense capabilities, which would be used by peace-keeping UN forces in conflict-ridden regions of the world. Steve was one of the key innovators of Dronette-8.

Bill Warren had been commissioned as a second lieutenant detective, still stationed near Acmeon Lab. His right-hand man, John Collins, was promoted to the level of sergeant.

The state-hospital patient Dr. Sobien Molton, after extensive appeals to the criminal courts, finally obtained a therapeutic parole status. His hope was first to fulfill every requirement set by the parole board and be released from parole status someday so that he would return to research work in genetics.

The assassin Ajnin Hsilomed vanished from upstate New York when his government's dictator was deposed and the new regime forced him to flee in exile. Around that time, North American cybersecurity experts recognized that much of the international hacking activities abruptly dwindled, like distant thunder with occasional faint flare-ups.

Tick, Tack, and Akandro Oladre were still serving time in the state penitentiary. People whose paths had previously crossed with theirs all said the world was better off without their menace.

Zenon Zelinski and Yaru Yanovsky assumed the responsibility of directing Acmeon Lab's computer department.

In the midafternoon on an August day, Steve and his wife Helen with their infant son Justin, came for a visit to the new home of Roy and Jenny Blau.

Jenny was very happy to see Steve's family. "Welcome! How're you guys?"

"Doing very well. Thank you." Helen said. "Your home is beautiful." She handed Jenny a small gift package with multicolor ribbons. "This is for Emily and Timmy. How are the twins doing?"

"They are doing fine. Roy is with them in the backyard…Look at your Justin! Sleeping in Steve's arms."

Steve said, "Justin just turned two months last week and got a few shots of primary immunizations already."

"He did! You two are quickly learning to be good parents."

Roy Blau, wheeling the twins in a double-seat stroller, came around from their backyard, greeting them loudly, "Hi, welcome! How are you doing?"

Steve and Helen said "Hi !" to Roy and fussed over the twins in the carriage.

Then, while Roy stayed with the twins in the backyard, Jenny gave Helen and Steve an interesting mini tour inside the house, except the kitchen. Jenny said she would show the kitchen to them a little while later. After much browsing and lively chatting about the interior of the new house, they came out to the backyard.

They all sat down on the backyard patio chairs, feeling the cool shade of nearby copper beech trees.

Jenny said to Steve, "We hear your Perihelion Energy Company is doing very well."

"Yeah, you bet. Since the fed departments commissioned my company to manufacture energy equipment three years ago, it was the start of sharp upcurve for the company." Still holding Justin in his arms, Steve continued, "Taking the engineering MBA courses, working half time on my job at the same time, getting married, and…, I went through the wringers. But I'm not complaining at all. Looking back, it was actually a happy and rewarding time. In fact, to prove it, I brought you something, Jenny."

Steve let Helen hold Justin, and he took out an envelope from his shirt pocket, which he held with his two hands and passed it to Jenny.

"What's this?" Jenny opened the envelope and found a check bearing a big number.

"That's the two-year-tuition loan you gave me. I was able to add an interest atop it as well. Hope it's an acceptable amount. Thank you so very much, Jenny, for having been there for me."

"I knew you would make good on your words but not so soon!" Jenny gave him a big hug. "I'm so proud of you, Steve…By the way, I want to give the interest amount back to you, as I had promised, because I heard from Helen that you made 3.6 GPA."

"Thank you, Jenny. You really meant it! But Helen and I are doing all right now. So can I ask you to put the interest amount in the twins' piggy banks?"

"Well, Steve, I would rather put it in your Justin's piggy bank."

"Thank you. But Justin is only two months old. And if Justin knew how to talk already, he might say, 'You're very kind, Aunt Jenny, but no banks! I need only stacks of milk bottles."

"All right, Steve, we'll see what to do with the interest…" Jenny turned to Helen, "Are you recovering all right after the baby? Your work schedule must be rough on you."

"I'm almost back to normal, except a couple of pounds more to lose. We've hired a live-in nanny. Without her help, I wouldn't be able to work at all. How about you, Jenny? You have twins to juggle with."

"We, too, have a nanny. Actually, she is one of Roy's aunts. She loves the children and is very reliable."

"That's wonderful."

"But Roy has a rough work schedule. He has an eight-hour shift at the ER. His schedule changes very often—from day to night shift and then back to day shift—each change occurring after only three or four days. Such ER doctors' shift changes are common practice in most hospital ERs. It's hard on us, but we try to adjust to it. We often ride the air-scooter together to run some errands. We try to save as much time as we can."

Roy brought out cold drinks for everybody. Jenny opened the package that Helen brought for the twins. From the package, Jenny found a pair of cute pink and blue baby bibs that would jingle soft music whenever one touched the flowery part of the fabric.

Jenny said, "These are cute. Thank you, Helen and Steve." Putting them on the twins, Jenny said, "The pink is becoming to Emily's rosy cheeks. The blue bib makes Timmy look like a junior sailor! It makes the children look so cute! Thank you, again, Helen…What's the washing instruction?"

"Just remove the tiny solar battery from this end of the windowed Velcro, and you can throw it in the washer. Now, Justin's wearing a blue bib, too. It's the same kind.

Do you know something? Steve designed those bibs to play music on solar battery. Perihelion Energy Company made the initial investment toward its mass production for Steve. His company is happy because they are busy filling bulk orders of those bibs from baby goods stores and the bibs are selling very well."

Jenny said, "Wow, Steve, so you're the inventor of those bibs!"

"Yes, I designed them. I'm glad they are getting popular. In fact, Perihelion bought the patent from me on a one-time deal, and that's what helped me pay the loan back to you sooner than I thought. Without the bibs, I would have probably taken three more years to pay the loan back."

Roy said, "Well, Jenny and Steve, you're one and the same. You both must have the invention genes, which I know I don't have."

They all laughed. Steve said, "Don't you be so sure, Roy. Someday you and Jenny together may come up with some sensational optical instruments. You never know!"

Roy asked Steve and Helen, "Tell us about your work. Was there much change after you both got new job titles?"

"As an assistant administrator," Helen answered, "I'm responsible for various administrative matters in the Dream Wafer Division at Acmeon. I'm learning the ropes on the new job every day. The actual change is that more people are now reporting to me and I have to spend more time listening to them than I did before."

Steve added, "The nature of my work has changed, too. Now, I do less hands-on work than a year ago because I spend much of my work hours delegating detail jobs to dozen different workers. Then, of course, I have to follow up on them. That takes up quite a bit of time, too. Besides, there are more meetings to attend than before. But all that is a lot of fun."

Jenny asked Helen, "How's Dr. Jupitren doing lately?"

"He has not changed much. Still in good health, fully recovered from the gunshot wounds. After he lost the *virtual brain* model, he seemed very, very sad for a while, but he bounced back surprisingly well. He seemed to have regained his energy after the three assistant doctors joined him in restoring the brain model.

When it comes to making any judgments, he is fair and straight as an arrow. He never deviated from his old principle, which is *fairness to all and safety for all his patients.*"

"By the way, what became of the AAPA?" Jenny asked.

"Well, the main criminal instigators within the assembly were arrested. Since then, they stopped bothering Acmeon Lab. But the last thing I heard from Bill Warren was that the assembly finally got dissolved. I think the United League of Astrologers and Palmists, with the help of the police, finally overcame them. AAPA was a very strange crowd to begin with."

While Helen and Jenny were talking, Steve went back to his car and brought in a housewarming gift for Roy and Jenny.

Unwrapping the gift box, Roy said happily, "It's a robotic vacuum cleaner! Thank you very much, Steve and Helen."

"You're very welcome." Said Steve. "I heard from the saleslady that it is the latest model of its kind. It's pretty quiet when it works. It can play music or whistle melodies per your choice. When it gets stuck in some parts of the room or furniture, the music will stop and it will beep, begging you to free it.

And it will announce fifteen minutes in advance when the dust bag needs emptying. Also, when it's done with one room, it will ask, 'Should I vacuum this room again?' and if you say 'No' or remain silent for ten seconds, it will move to the next room to resume its vacuuming work there."

"That's one smart cleaner! Thanks again!"

At that point, everyone heard an unfamiliar chime coming from the dining-room area. Steve asked Jenny, "What's that?"

"Well, it's the call for you to come to the dining room. The dinner is ready to be served. I didn't show you the kitchen before because a famous chef was in the kitchen, busy cooking for all of us, especially for you guys."

"Everyone, please come over to the kitchen first and meet Roy's cousin Douglas. He is the head chef at the restaurant Zuma in midtown Manhattan. We asked him to come out here to prepare a special gourmet dinner for all of us. Today is his day off from the restaurant."

CHAPTER 56
A PARTY FOR DR. JUPITREN

On an early September evening, Helen and Steve organized a party in honor of Dr. Jupitren on the Dream Wafers' tenth anniversary. It was at the Grand Ballroom of *The Metropolitan*, a popular party venue in Nassau County, Long Island, NY.

The invited guests who came to the party were Dr. Jupitren's family and relatives; Steve's and Helen's families and relatives;

Dr. Roy Blau and his wife Jenny; Acmeon Lab staff with their family; Other special guests were Lieutenant Bill Warren and his wife; Sergeant John Collins with his fiancée, and the precinct officers and their families;

Dr. Diego, Chief Scientist and Deputy Commissioner for Science and Public Health from the FDA; an officer from the Special Medical Programs and Ethics

Committee of the FDA; The president and chemists of Esclepio Pharmaceutical Company, manufacturer of Antisom;

Dr. Jupitren's friends, Dr. Santiago from state hospital, some psychiatric faculty members of universities, psychologists with their spouses; and, media crews.

With a round of toasts to the guest of honor from a number of people, a multicourse banquet followed. The party was sprinkled with speeches and words of congratulations praising Dr. Jupitren's iconic invention of Dream Wafer.

In the middle of an unfolding banquet entrée, envoys from the state governor's office and the county executive's office arrived with commendation plaques and huge bouquets of flowers. The party hall was filled with the fragrance from those flowers, and the hall was bursting with well-wishing guests, news camera crews, unexpected envoys, and many busy banquet servers. The overhead festooned glittering streamers stretched from the balcony level blended colorfully with the festive mood of the party.

The envoys' ceremonial statements and the presentation of plaques to Dr. Jupitren made the party full and lively. After much chatting at the round tables, more of off-the-cuff speeches, dancing to potpourri of music, and then the desserts…the mood of the party was merging with a series of slow, soft music.

From the table of guest psychiatrists, Dr. Santiago raised his hand, getting attention of the emcee, Steve Spencer at the dais. Dr. Santiago said he had something to say to the entire guests in the ballroom. Steve asked him to come forward close to the microphone. While Dr. Santiago walked toward the dais, Steve introduced him to the entire guests. Dr. Santiago began to speak:

"Good evening, everybody. As Mr. Spencer just mentioned in his introduction, I am from the state hospital's forensic unit. I would like to say a few words as I express my heartfelt congratulations to Dr. Jupitren on his Dream Wafer work and the Wafer's tenth anniversary.

You all have heard how hard he had worked on the Dream Wafer project from the inception of his original idea. You also know the main concept of Dream Wafer, which is therapeutically modifying dreams by the dreamer's choice. However, most of you may not have known of what I am about to tell you.

Yesterday, Dr. Sobien Molton called me. He regretted that he would be unable to attend this festivity because of the ankle fracture that he sustained two days ago. So, this morning, his wife Kerbera came to my house, hand delivering his letters that were addressed to Dr. Jupitren and to all of you. Dr. Molton asked me to read them to you at this party.

And, Dr. Molton said to me that even though it may cause some shame and embarrassment on him, he hoped his letters would reveal how great Dr. Jupitren has been to him. Dr. Molton also gave me his full permission to speak to you about his psychiatric treatment history.

Almost four years ago, I received Dr. Sobien Molton as my patient at the state hospital's forensic unit for his treatment-resistant bipolar disorder. For many weeks, Dr. Molton responded rather poorly to the treatment given by the hospital treatment team.

Around that time, to my great surprise, Dr. Jupitren called me at the hospital and said that he wanted to help Dr. Molton with Dream Wafers."

Dr. Santiago began to read Dr. Molton's letter aloud:

My dear friends at the party, to my great regret, I have caused so much trouble to Dr. Jupitren and Acmeon Lab. Many times, I attempted to sell the Dream Wafer program illegally to foreign agents. Sometimes, I tried to destroy the program only to bargain with other criminals, just for my warped greed.

Eventually, the legal system apprehended me but my psychiatric condition in its worst point, placed me behind the locked doors of a psychiatric hospital. Yet, I was confused and hopeless. I could not accept that I, a medical genetics specialist, ended up in a psychiatric hospital! Many days I felt I was at the end of my rope. Suicidal ideas frightfully crept into my daily rumination. Despite the intense treatment given by the hospital, my condition would not release me from its cruel grip.

Around that time, despite his full awareness of my wrongdoings against him, Dr. Jupitren unconditionally forgave me, and came to the state hospital number of times, spending 5 hours on the road each time. And offered me a special clinical care with the Dream Wafers.

After I applied the Dream Wafers that Dr. Jupitren custom-made for me, within a few weeks, everyone at the hospital witnessed improvement in my mental status. I had made steady improvement since that time. People said I became a new person.

Then, about three years ago, an unidentified gunman attempted to take my life. But Dr. Jupitren, who happened to be there next to me tried to protect me and was shot in my place. He almost died from the gun-shot wound in his head.

I wish I could undo all the wrongful things I did. Today I wanted to say publically how generous and forgiving Dr. Jupitren has been to me despite all my wayward conduct I perpetrated against him and Acmeon Lab.

I hope all of you, likewise become arbiters of forgiveness, helping and supporting me to go on in the right direction henceforward.

Now, I want to say this to Dr. Jupitren: You pulled me out of my insanity and saved my life! How could I thank you enough for what you have done for me?

You used to say genes are one's destiny. Nevertheless, you and your Dream Wafer changed the direction of my destiny. I thank God for sending you to me and for letting me benefit from your Dream Wafer. You helped me to gain Kerbera Wilson's trust in me, and she and I finally restored our relationship. Now, as a married couple, we are very happy and immeasurably grateful to you for your help and forbearance.

Congratulations on your Dream Wafer's tenth anniversary! If I may count your Dream Wafer's age from the inception of your original ideas about it, I should rephrase it, "Happy twentieth anniversary!"
Gratefully, Sobien Molton

Dr. Santiago put the letter back in the envelope and said, "I would like to add here one thing that Dr. Molton did not mention in his letter. Right after the assailant's gunshot, Dr. Jupitren rapidly fell into a critical state due to heavy blood loss from his head wound. However, the tables were turned around quickly as Dr. Molton eagerly donated his own blood in a timely manner, which spared Dr. Jupitren from slipping into irreversible shock. The two doctors are now literally blood brothers."

Throughout Dr. Santiago's speech and the letter reading, all the guests remained silent, and some of them looked at Dr. Jupitren, who appeared pensive and motionless in his seat.

From his suit pocket, Dr. Santiago took out another envelope and said, "Mrs. Molton gave me this envelope today and asked me to hand deliver it to Dr. Jupitren."

Dr. Santiago, still at the microphone, looked at Dr. Jupitren and said, "However, Dr. Jupitren, may I read this letter as well to all your guests here?"

With a modest smile, Dr. Jupitren nodded his consent.

Then Dr. Santiago unfolded the second letter and resumed reading:

Dear Dr. Jupitren,
In appreciation of your extraordinary devotion to people in need of your ingenious Dream Wafer work, I, Kerbera Wilson, now Mrs. Molton, would like to send you this check to make a donation toward the Acmeon Lab's Research Fund.

I pledge that I will make similar donations every year as long as I can.

I sincerely express my congratulations on your Dream Wafer's tenth anniversary and wish you the best in all you do. Please accept my donation.
With sincere gratitude, Kerbera Molton

In the middle of bursting applause from everyone, Dr. Santiago walked toward Dr. Jupitren and gave him the letters and the check, with a firm handshake, and said, "Congratulations!"

Dr. Jupitren walked to the dais and replied without any shred of bombastic air, "Thank you, Dr. Santiago for your kind words. You shared the clinical work with me in helping Dr. Molton and you spent more hours of direct clinical care than I did for him. You should deserve no less of his appreciation.

Please tell Dr. and Mrs. Molton how you delivered their letters and Kerbera's donation check to me, in the full view of all these friends and well-wishers. I am so honored and happy. I thank Dr. and Mrs. Molton for their goodwill and generosity."

Then, facing the whole audience, Dr. Jupitren thanked everyone for coming and giving him heartwarming recognition for his work.

He also thanked Helen and Steve for organizing the wonderful party. He especially thanked his wife, Jamie, for her unceasing support with patience and love, through many years while he engrossed himself in his own world of research and work.

Turning his attention toward one of the tables, Dr. Jupitren called on Bill Warren and his officers by their names. All the guests could see them. Dr. Jupitren said, "My dear friends from our police precinct, without your special help that my Acmeon Lab and I received over the past decade, we could not have had this celebration tonight. Thank you so very much, gentlemen!"

Responding to Dr. Jupitren's words and the guests' applause, Bill and his officers stood up briefly, waving their hands with broad smiles.

Dr. Jupitren called upon practically everyone in the ballroom by names and thanked each and all. As he spoke, some people could see on the right side of his head and face the subtle signs of sequelae from the gunshot wounds, from which he had recovered valiantly. A slight eyelid drooping of the right eye, hidden behind his eyeglasses, which was noticeable to people who were close to him, was another faint reminder of the gunshot injury.

Finally, assuming his usual humble stance with gravitas, he declared his respect for the dream phenomena and said in an open affirmation that he would go on with his work as before. He continued his address.

"Undoubtedly, people will come up with many new theories on dreams. However, the ultimate truth of dream will be veiled from human search for a very long time. Even when we think we reached the ultimate point, new dreams will beckon us to come forward.

Oblivious to the dream research in progress, people will continue to dream every night, with or without Dream Wafers. The Dream Wafers may help the dreamers feel less anxious and may let them have peaceful feelings in the dreams of their choice. Yet, Dream Wafers cannot completely dictate what many diverse stories people would weave in their dreams, since dream making ultimately depends not only on the mandates of the entire genome but also on the given life circumstances of the dreamers. Billions of people, billions of dreams!

Certain dreams seem to be God sent allegories and riddles posed to searching minds, often repeated throughout people's lifetimes. Many people believe there must be the divine revelation somewhere among all the dreams in the world, just like a well in the vast desert.

Some individuals with evil minds may abuse the fruits of science for which others have worked with lifelong efforts. It may seem for a while that those evil minds prevail and hinder the progress of science. Nevertheless, the truth-seeking world would not stop the forward-spinning wheels of scientific research work. I do hope the Dream Wafers will sit steadfastly on such wheels.

Last night, in my dream, I peeked into a poet's sketch note, where his verses said:

~~*~*   The Pebbles   *~*~*~*~

A Slumber-Land's messenger says,
'Dream Wafers are like the countless Pebbles of a brook.'
The Pebbles craft dazzling Ripples that
whisper endless shibboleth to the sun-lit streams.
While the Pebbles and the Ripples
are unheeded by those who are busy in self-nurture,
The brook will ceaselessly flow through
Immanent God's garden, the Infinite Nature.
Oh, would you ease down your hasty strides
And behold the dazzling ripples' splendor?

I thank you and wish you all, good night and happy dreams!"

~~*~*~* E N D *~*~*~*~*

CHARACTERS AND TERMS

AAPA/Astrologers & Palmists Assembly: Dissenters of orthodox United League of Astrologers and Palmists

Acmeon Lab: The lab, the Dream Shop, Acmeon

Ajnin Hsilomed: International secret agent, coercing Sobien Molton to commit crime

Akandro Oladre: A criminal, hired Tick and Tack, illegally owned a Chromega watch

Alfonso Ramos: Original owner of Chromega watch

Allegory: An old-style diner near Acmeon Lab

Bill Warren: William Warren, a police sergeant, detective, friend of Dr. Jupitren

Brandon Cumlen: Hired Zenon Zelinski for NJ Com-T Park project

Brandon Sweza: One of Dr. Jupitren's clients

Candidate: Someone just starting Dream Wafer

CR device: Counter-ray device, counter-LXG device, works by echoing the LXG ray

Cyberscope: Variant of Skype

Doctor Jupitren: Jules, Julian, MD, inventor of Dream Wafer

Dronette-6.12: Wasp-sized flying robotic spyware with diverse functionality

Elva Humayor: Helen Humayor's mother, younger sister of Dr. Jupitren

Espio-Nano Company: Nano-engineering company dealing with spyware gadgets

Frank Fairmont: Copilot of Sam Dayer

Hank Oswin: Older cousin of Mrs. Elva Humayor

Helen Humayor: Dr. Jupitren's niece, Acmeon's office manager

Islet Republic: Name of an imaginary country

Jamie Jupitren: Wife of Dr. Jupitren

Jenny Spencer: Steve Spencer's older sister, inventress of Optical Wall
John Collins: One of Bill Warren's officers
Jules: Jules Jupitren, Julian Jupitren, Inventor of Dream Wafer
Kerbera Wilson: Heiress, new woman friend of Sobien Molton
Luxen Tech Company: Jenny Spencer's company, Optical Wall manufacturer
LXG stun gun: Laser-X ray-Gauged stun gun, LXG ray gun
Optical Walls: Jenny Spencer's invention
Perihelion Energy Company: An electronics company where Steve Spencer works
Richard Hunt: An IT specialist, a professional hacker
Roy Blau: Medical doctor, Jenny Spencer's suitor
Sam Dayer: Trans-Alpha Jet Air pilot who misused counterfeit Dream Wafers
Sobien Molton: MD, suffers from bipolar disorder, acted against Acmeon Lab
Steve Spencer: Electronic engineer at Perihelion Energy Company, Helen's suitor
Tack: Takis Tantalos, Akandro's hireling/later worked for Sobien Molton
Thumputer: Personal computer worn on a person's left thumb
Tick: Tihko Piroiz, Akandro's hireling
ULAP/United League of Astrologers and Palmists: Orthodox assembly of astrologers and palmists, ULAP disapproved of AAPA's activity
Yaru Yanovsky: One of Dr. Jupitren's assistant engineers
Zenon Zelinski: One of Dr. Jupitren's assistant engineers